THE WANDERING STAR

BOOK 1: THE SHIFTER'S TRANCE SERIES

THE WANDERING STAR

BOOK 1: THE SHIFTER'S TRANCE SERIES

SP MITTSON

NU VOICE
PRESS

NU VOICE PRESS
First published by NU VOICE PRESS 2023
An imprint of Hubhawks Pvt. Ltd
www.nuvoicepress.com

This is a work of fiction and all characters and incidents described in this book are the product of the author's imagination. Any resemblance to actual persons, living or dead, is entirely coincidental.

ISBN: 978-81-966888-4-4

Typeset by Saanvi Graphics, Noida
Printed at Thomson Press
Published by Nu Voice Press

To all those who are searching for an escape,
I hope you find it here.

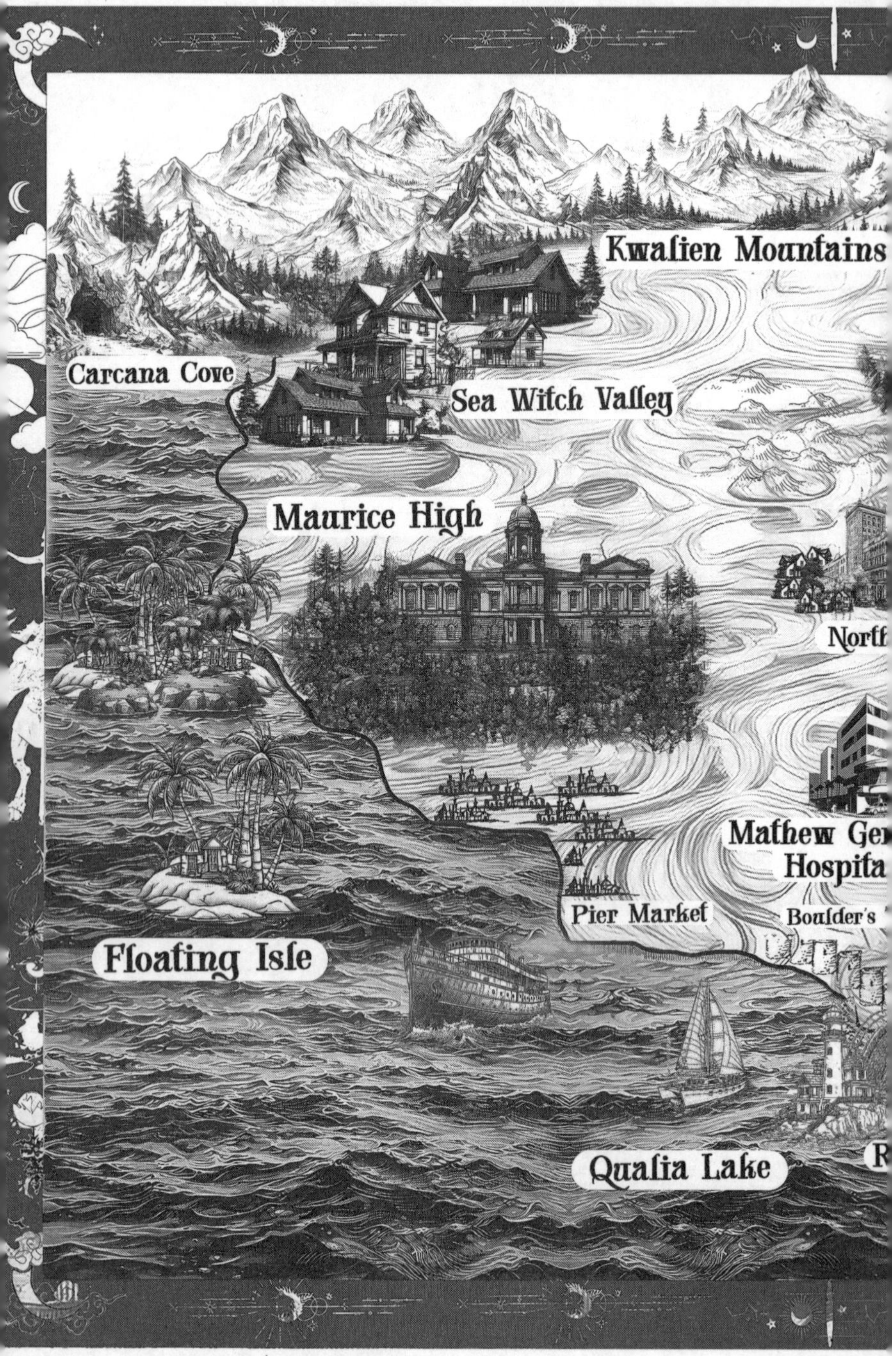
Kwalien Mountains
Carcana Cove
Sea Witch Valley
Maurice High
Pier Market
Boulder's
Floating Isle
Qualia Lake

Old Castle
Deadly Forest
ector Mansion
Red Pearl Glen
Mile O City
Oracle Hot Spring
Cambridge Street
cle
Highway 59
Lumber Mill
Limestone Cave
Waterfall
Murkwood Museum
Swamps
Rill
kety Bridge
Murkwood

Prologue

Six-year-old me,

Finally, I was going downhill. I'd never been downhill before. Honestly, I'd never been outside our mansion. But we, the people of Murkwood, hadn't had any Mayor also. The party was in honour of the first elected Mayor, Phineas Parsons, which I didn't know what exactly it meant, but I heard on the television that the era of Royalty ruling Murkwood had ended with the death of my grappy, Mathew Hector.

Six months earlier, a heart attack took over him when he was overseas, on some political business, and my grandmother, Noni as I call her, had decided to go Democratic Republic.

My mother wasn't happy about any of this. I could tell by the permanent scowl pasted on her face. She had been screaming at me non-stop since I woke up. My caretaker Hannah Scott had been scolded for dressing me up in a witch costume, so she had to change me into the Wonder Woman one, and our house manager, Robin Scott, took the lash about the steak he prepared. Even though it tasted amazing, but mom was convinced that it had gone bad and tasted sour in her mouth.

"It's her tongue that has gone sour," Noni whispered in my ear as I chuckled, but the flash of Mom's eyes made me gutter my laugh. Noni rolled her eyes but didn't dare say anything further and silently watched Mom cut her steak into proportionate pieces. Even Noni was afraid of her daughter.

I arrived at the party smiling ear to ear. The whole ground was decorated like a carnival. The Ferris wheel was going round and round in the air while the carousel spun with so many beautiful horses, lights and colours. There were swings and rides, but most of all, it was crowded. I had never seen so many townspeople at once before. Excitedly, I observed children dressed up in all kinds of costumes gathered together and laughing at the stalls. Some were squirting water with water guns at the ping pong balls resting on the crowns of bottles, while some threw darts at the wall of balloons.

I rolled my eyes as none of them could take the shot. I wanted to show them how it's done when my eyes fell on Peppa Pig. It was a real walking Peppa Pig with a huge pink head and small legs, shaking hands with children and offering them candy. Elated, I let go of my mother's hand and ran towards my favorite TV character.

"ELOISE! Come back here at this instant," Mom screamed, hot on my heels. "We don't have time for this, the Oath-Taking Ceremony is about to start," she called, but I was in my own bliss, enjoying my first party ever.

When Peppa Pig gave me a lollipop shaped like a dinosaur, I impatiently ripped off the wrapper, and before I could even take a lick, Mom caught me by my shoulder and spun me around.

"What are you thinking running around like that?" She bent down to look me in the eyes, her red-painted lips curled into a frown.

"Mommy, I just wanted to meet her. Look, she even gave me a free candy," I showed it to her, smiling, but she held my arms and shook me hard.

"Do you think I care about some stupid fascination?" she demanded. "How many times have I told you to control your emotions?" She narrowed her blue eyes. "I am telling you, Lizzy, no funny business, or it's all on you, and may I remind you of the consequences?" she asked, knitting her brows in anger.

Blood drained off my face as I shook my head hurriedly. Scared.

"Give me that," and with that, she tried to snatch away my candy, but I stepped back.

My eyes widened in shock, not because she had scolded me in front of everyone but because I had stepped into the darkness.

It was daylight a few seconds ago, and suddenly, the pitch-black sky took over. There were a few beads of stars but no moon, and I was standing in the middle of an abandoned carnival without Mom or anyone else. No one was there, not a single soul. It was just me, surrounded by the toxic smell and clouds of ashes.

It wasn't the first time, but it still scared the hell out of me whenever I visited this ghastly place. It was a twisted parody of our own world, the same place but burnt down.

The creaking and moaning sound of old rides covered in algae creeped me out. The green dinosaur candy I held went grey, rotten, and soon it turned into ashes, flowing away with the mist, raising the hair on the nape of my neck.

I screamed and bolted away, brushing my hands clean on my dress while the ashes flowing around itched my throat. My eyes blurred, but I kept running. My primary instinct was to hide, so I sprang towards an outhouse—more of a playhouse. I closed the door with shaking hands.

I was waiting for this to get over when I felt something nearby. I turned to it slowly and learned it was breathing, covered in a robe, and lying over a bean bag. I pulled the robe when suddenly he woke up with a jerk. I fell back, hitting my head on an adjacent wooden wall. A horrifying scream passed my lips as I closed my eyes, covering my ears with my hands, thinking it was a monster, and finally, this nightmare had taken over me.

"Geez! Why are you screaming?" it said.

My scream guttered at the voice. 'It knows how to speak my language,' was my first thought as I opened one eye. He was holding a torch, lighting up the enclosed space.

I glanced at him, blinking rapidly, making out what or who he was, and there he stood—a boy in an Iron Man costume. He was a few inches taller than me but could be of my age.

"Who are you?" he asked in a soft voice, tilting his head. "How did you get in here?"

It was not a monster, but a human, a child, just like me. I had never met anyone before in this unnerving nightmare. Always been alone. Not even my mother could follow me here, but somehow he was here. The warmth of his presence brought me crashing down, I went hysterical, and soon everything started spinning—walls started closing onto me, and it got hard to breathe.

"Hey! Are you alright?" the boy asked in a concerned voice.

But I shook my head. "No, it's scary," I shivered as he offered me his hand, and I grabbed it tightly. He was warm.

"What is scary?" he asked gently, rubbing my hand between his. *That felt good.* "Oh! They are not actual ghosts, just some kids in costume. Did you find them terrifying?"

"No," I shook my head vigorously. "Outside…the darkness," I whispered like somebody would hear me.

"It's dark already?" he hopped towards the door, but I gripped his hand tightly.

"Don't go out. There can be monsters lurking in the shadows," I murmured, my eyes widening in horror. "My mom will come for me."

"Ok, we'll wait for your mom to find you, till then," he sat on the floor, never leaving my hand and pushed his Avengers pail filled with candy towards me. "Go on, have some."

I wiped my tears with the back of my hand, crashing next to him. "How come you have so much candy already?" gawking at his collection.

"I have my charms," he clicked his tongue, as I raised my eyebrow, pursing my lips, restraining my bubble laugh, he nudged me. "Go on, try this. These are my favorites," he passed on a boysenberry-flavoured candy, and I unwrapped it quickly, making a yummy noise as the sweet tangy taste hit my taste buds. "See, I told ya," he must have smiled behind that mask.

"What are you doing here?" I asked him, picking a few more from his collection.

"My brother locked me in," he grumbled. "He is a pain in the ass."

"Hey!" I gasped. "You used a bad word."

"So what," he shrugged.

"Bad words make you a bad guy."

"No, bad work makes you a bad guy," he scoffed. "And don't you like bad boys?"

"Nope, I like good boys," I affirmatively told him. My grappy was a good man, and so is Robin. I didn't like boys like my father. Mom told me they got separated just after I was born, and I haven't seen him since.

"Good for you. Now, let's go outside," he said, crouching to stand up.

"No," I told him, still terrified, pulling him back with his hand.

"Don't worry, I'll protect you from the monsters," he said a little pretentiously. "Or maybe we can fight the monsters together. You know, Iron Man and Wonder Woman."

"You think I can do that?" I asked, blinking at him. "Could I fight monsters?"

"Of course," he said, standing, hauling me up with him. "You don't have to cry. You can just kick their asses like Wonder Woman."

"You make it sound so easy," I shook my head.

"Oh, it is easy. All you got to do is raise your chin high and slash the world around you. You'll be good," he made a swish with the torch pretending it to be a sword. "But not as good as Iron Man," he added as he tapped on the fake arc reactor and pushed open the door.

"Nah, Wonder Woman is better. She has a sword," I argued, walking behind him. Grappy had a huge collection of comics, he always used to read it to me. I miss him sometimes whenever I look at his stash.

"Iron Man has the latest technology," he retorted.

"Artificial technology," I corrected. "But Wonder Woman has primal powers. Iron Man's suits can be stolen, but not her powers." I beamed at him with a little spring in my legs.

"Iron Man can do an insane amount of damage. He'll kill monsters before they even lay hands on his suit," he repeatedly argued. "And he can upgrade his powers, speed and become stronger and faster, but Wonder Woman's abilities are limited."

"Still, he can never match Wonder Woman in terms of strength," I smiled pompously.

And with it, he started laughing, shaking his head. "Aren't you a little stubborn?"

"Aren't all princesses?" I shrugged, but suddenly I felt a vice-like grip around my heart. My face fell, thinking about what my life would have been if I wasn't born this way.

"What happened?" He stared at me for a few seconds. "You don't want to be a princess?" I was astonished as he read me like a book.

I shook my head defeatedly. "I don't like to be locked away in a mansion," I admitted, biting my lower lip.

He hummed. "Don't worry, I'll sneak you out, and we'll travel the world together. Till then, you can enjoy all this candy," with that, he transferred all his candy to my pail.

I gasped, moved by his gesture.

"Really?" I asked excitedly as I sprang to hug him. He stood there like a pole as my hands wrapped around his neck like he didn't know how to embrace me. "Are you my boyfriend now?"

"You want me to be?" he asked, rubbing the back of his neck as I let him go.

It was then I heard my mother shouting my name. Her face had gone blue. I didn't realise I was back in chaos, and soon her eyes fell on me. I knew I would be grounded as I had done it again, and now she'll never forgive me.

"You're in so much trouble, wait till you reach home," she hissed at me, grabbing my hand hastily.

"It's not in my hand, Mom," I tried to free myself, but she tightened her grip till it started hurting. "But this time, there was this boy, he was wearing an Iron Man costume, and he gave me candy too," showing her my pail. She halted, blood drained from her face like she had seen a ghost. Instantly she grabbed it and tossed it aside. All my candy spilt on the ground, breaking my heart.

"Did he see you shifting?" my agitated mother's voice went grave, the one that gives me chills down my spine. She held my mouth between her thumb and finger, pinching me. I grabbed her arm, trying to loosen her grip. "Did he, Eloise?"

I shook my head, terrified of her.

Her blue eyes pierced me. "I am telling you *mija*, nobody should learn about this, or they'll treat you like a lab rat forever. This world will never accept people like you. They'll either use you or kill you," she hissed, making me whimper. "You have to learn how to control this glitch."

Tears rolled down my eyes. "I don't like that eerie place either, I don't want to go there ever again," I snivelled into the sleeves of my free hand. "I hate that I am born with this glitch."

She picked me up and put me in the car, tying the seat belt around. "Then I'll chain you in the vaults till you either learn to control or mask it," she threatened me. My eyes went wide because of the horror she was putting me into. I turned around in search of Iron Man, seeking some comfort, but he was already gone, and the worst part of all was, he never took off his mask, neither I asked him to. I didn't know who he was. Was he a part of a dream of my life or a nightmare of my reality?

Chapter 1

Cobra Queen

"Get your lazy ass up," Mom barged into my room, her Louboutins tapped with each step she took as she ripped open my curtains. I groaned as the sun blinked on my face, covering my plush blanket over my head, pinching my eyes close, and slumbering back into my cocoon.

"Don't make me repeat myself, *mija*," she tugged on my blanket and jerked it away from my body. "Robin has been waiting for you since morning. You were expected by eight thirty in the training room, it is afternoon now." Robin Scott was our house manager, and his wife Hannah was my caretaker. They had been living with my grandparents much before we arrived in Murkwood.

Robin being a He-man, took in his hands to teach me self-defence. My mother had always prioritised my training to prepare me for any danger I might encounter. It's not that I don't enjoy it, fencing is my favorite sport, especially with Sabre, but impalement art was my specialty—knife throwing and archery. Nowadays, we were working with a crossbow. Knowing your strength when you don't know how to deal with your weakness gives some self-assurance.

"MOM, I am already sore," I growled at her, writhing in my bed due to the loss of coziness and warmth. I thrashed and hid my already throbbing head under the pillow, sliding another pillow on my body, searching for some warmth.

"Why are you in your training clothes?" she asked, examining my body.

I remained quiet, not knowing how to answer her question. If I'll tell Mom that today was my crush—Homer's fifth month anniversary, and he's spending a whole day with his current girlfriend—Sophie, and last night she posted a photo with him in her bed, sleeping and naked till torso—I lost it, and for taking out my rage I was in my training room the whole night, punching a sac imagining it as Sophie's face, she's going to whip my ass.

For my mother, emotions aren't part of life. I hadn't seen her smile, not ever. It was like divorcing my father stole her happiness. And all that remained of her was an insatiable workaholic mother whose whole life revolved around Murkwood and protecting me.

And even if, someway, I tell her that I love this guy, she'd snap. 'Love is for weak and makes you do stupid things.' Moreover, she'll make me drop school and confine me in this mansion, like the last time she did when I disobeyed her. Even though it wasn't disobedience, it was something I couldn't control, something I can't control even now, but she'll never understand.

It took me four years, four damn years, to mask myself, to make her believe I got control over my glitch. Somehow, I did, but not completely. And when she was under the impression I was good to go, or I should say, I couldn't be homeschooled anymore, she let me out but only on three conditions—

1. No friends
2. No extracurricular activities
3. No flashy clothes.

In short, I had to stay low-key, hidden away from the world. At that time, I would have agreed to even live with the snakes in the vaults of the old mansion for the rest of my life, as I was dying to go to school and meet other people. To finally start living like the normal girl I wasn't.

"Eloise Hector, I asked you something," she said sternly, crossing her hands over her midsection. I know that voice very well, it was my cue to get up, or the Cobra queen would strike.

I rolled over, blinking open my eyes. "I am up," I grumbled, swinging my legs on the side of my pink canopy bed and rubbing my eyes. She chose the pink colour for my room to make up for not letting me wear any appealing colour. Little did she know, she was rubbing the reality of my life in my face, that I, being the princess of Murkwood, the one everyone wants to be, isn't even allowed to choose her own clothes.

"Did you—?" she asked, not completing her sentence, examining me, her eyes narrowed, a scowl lingered at the corner of her mouth. Her pet tarantula appeared on her arm, somewhere from behind, crawled up her red blouse's sleeves, and rested on her shoulder. I flinched a little, but she didn't. It's like it was the most natural thing in this world to have a tarantula as a pet and to have them hang out with you so casually.

"No, Mom, I didn't shift. I haven't shifted in a long time," the lie rolled out of my mouth naturally, like it does every time she asks me the same question, but my eyes remained locked on her creepy pet. I never liked him. He creeps me out, and trust me, sometimes I think he whispers in her ears.

She stood there, studying my every expression. When her shoulders didn't relax, I quickly turned away, striding towards my table where some books were scattered, trying to pivot. "I was working on a science project all night, and it bored me, so I went looking for some distraction," this was partly true.

Distraction was what I was looking for. I tried to call my best friend Clara, my girl who always listens to my sorrow and comforts me by bitching about Sophie, but she wasn't available on call, as she was abroad, visiting her grandmother, while my other friend, Nathan, slept early. Since he had been interning at Lazer Crazer arcade arena, it tires him out, and these summers, I didn't meet him much. Only a few times, when I escaped out of the window while my mother was on some business trips, I got to catch up with him.

"Fine. Get ready. I am altering your timetable. It's time to take your training up a notch." She turned around, her tone clipped. "I am discussing it with both Hannah and Robin," she placed my blanket aside. "Hannah had cleared a patch in the greenhouse," she kept barking orders. "I am going to the Murkwood Museum, but I want it planted till I return."

"It's Sunday, the museum is closed," restraining my urge to roll my eyes, ignoring her orders about the greenhouse. Even though I love gardening with Hannah, she was natural but I wasn't in the mood today. All I wanted to do was eat Nutella waffles and binge rom-coms on Netflix, crying over my God-forbidden love life.

"I know, but I have a meeting with the manager—Bill, regarding the security breach last Sunday." Her brows furrowed, as her hand immediately reached to grab her charm locket around her neck. It was a cat-eye chatoyant, with a wire-twisted Yggdrasil tree wrapped around it in a gold chain. It's always a comfort to hold it in your palm, it has some qualities to provide you calm, and I know so much about it because I was wearing a twin of it.

But today, she was twisting it in her fingers. Was she nervous about something or scared?

Nah! Nothing can scare the Cobra Queen. I must be reading too much into it.

"But nothing was stolen, right?" I frowned. "You said it could have been some animal." But we don't take anything casually when it comes to Murkwood. It's our duty as Hectors to provide for the townies and safeguard them from any possible danger. My ancestors built this town, they protected it with their lives, and that's what has been expected of us.

She was lost in her thoughts when she hummed, her eyes locked somewhere else on the wall. Her bright red lips parted as if she was remembering something. "Yeah, it was an animal indeed," she cleared her throat, leaving her necklace, to scratch the nape of her neck, and then stood tall, removing the crease of her Moschino white pencil skirt. "But I still want to see the recordings."

Apart from the lumber mill she runs, she held an imperial position in the town council since she was running WEC—Women Empowerment Club, where she helps all the women that reach out to her with their problems, whether personal, social, or financial. And thank God it kept her busy, or she would have driven me nuts.

"You don't have to worry about it," she pressed her lips into a thin line. "All you got to do is train and leave everything else on me, I'll protect you at any cost."

And with that, she started telling me what changes she was making with my schedule, as if discussing a merger with some client, so professional, so cold. Blood drained my face.

She has got to be kidding! It was an advance level combat training schedule. Does she not remember I am just seventeen-years-old?

I groaned internally, not showing my displease to the Cobra Queen. Robin would be pleased with this new regime. He was a ruthless mentor when it came to training me. He doesn't listen or show affection, even for my tears. He keeps making the workouts hard, forcing me to push my limits, and granting me a chance to explore my capabilities.

"Let's go, Vic," she told her tarantula. "And hurry up *mija*! I don't like to wait," she sauntered out of my room gracefully, tossing her copper inverted straight bob hair, leaving me fuming in her wake. I could never be as graceful as she was. She was the most beautiful and terrifying woman, and possessed all the qualities one held to be a Queen.

"And I don't like to be told. Period." I grunted when she was far enough to hear. I tossed my pillow at the door, which she left ajar. It hit the door and fell back limply, like all my hopes of freedom. "Argh!" I screamed as I angrily tossed my water bottle outside the window, which went flying from between the tree branches over the fence and crashed on the road.

I wasn't afraid of hitting someone because Hill Road is the least used road. I sank on my windowsill, admiring the greenery outside the mansion.

When I was a kid, I was thrilled to have a mansion a two miles hike from the town. It's a 15-acre estate with the accommodation predominantly arranged over three floors with the benefit of a substantial, self-contained staff lodge. The mansion's main feature was its luxurious entrance hall leading to the formal sitting room, tea room, aqua room and dining room that overlooked our magnificent grounds adjoining the kitchen in the east wing. The west wing was allotted to two suites, taken over by Noni and the Scotts, and a library, music room, art studio, workshop, and service room surrounded by a chess garden. The first floor had seven suites with ensuite bathrooms, an amphitheater and an arcade room, while the top floor was solely provided to me for a gymnasium, training room, spa and solarium for panoramic view of gardens. The basement holds the oval office—Noni's office, but she always keeps it locked. Only Robin and Hannah are allowed in that room.

The rest was the old mansion, larger than the current one, more like an old castle but was now locked and stood decaying behind the formal lawns, swimming pools, ponds and woodland. They said it caught fire during the reign of Maurice Hector, my great-granddad, so my grappy made this new mansion hiding the older one from everyone's vision.

And when I asked him why we couldn't live anywhere else, like in the city, he told me—a Hector should always be there in Murkwood.

So here I was, Eloise Hector, princess of Murkwood, and my life wasn't a fairytale like what they show us in movies or books—the happy endings. Life gives us lemons, and mine was full of them, making the lemonade sour and undrinkable.

"Eloise! Don't make me drag you down." My mother screamed from downstairs.

"Argh! Why the hell can't you leave me alone?" I tossed my head back, livid, clenching my fists on the sides, stomping my foot hard.

The next time I saw Mom, she was covered in a black bag as she had 3rd-degree burns and was hard to identify, so they didn't show us her face through those fluorescent walls. All they could retrieve was her white Maserati and purse.

Chapter 2

The Devil of Murkwood

When you are born with a glitch, it doesn't go well while you're in an extreme state of shock.

It was noon, I was still sitting in the Mathew General Hospital, leaning on Nathan's shoulder. He was already here when I arrived with Noni and hadn't left my side since then. He had an arm around me, his head rested on mine while he brushed my arm and held the other as if trying to gather my broken self. His warmth was so welcoming on these icy-cold steel chairs.

He was my second friend when I started middle school, I was homeschooled till then. This guy was huge and constantly bullied, our fellow students used to make him do their homework, and sometimes they even stole and copied his projects, and he couldn't stand for himself. I wanted to kick all those guys' asses for that, but I couldn't attract attention, so let's say, some guys found their lockers filled with moths and bees, and Nathan and I became best friends. He gives the best hugs, and right now, he was by my side when I needed him the most.

"Thank you, Huggy-bear, I needed this so much," I snivelled looking up at him. His moss-green eyes behind spectacles were as warm as his hugs. He gave me a hand hug while his mouth lifted into a sad smile. He didn't know about my glitch, he didn't know how much I was glitching when Noni broke the news to me. I had to hide in the washroom to control it as no one except mom had any faintest idea about my powers, or I should say, my curse.

"C'mon, Gummy-bear, I live for this shit." He wiped off a freshly fallen tear on my cheek with the pad of his finger. He calls me that because I had a sweet tooth, and whenever he's sad, I bring him candy like my Iron Man did for me once.

"Did Clara reply?" I asked, checking my phone, but he snatched it from me. People were tagging me in the posts, sending me videos of my mother getting into an accident, the whole night.

All of Murkwood knew about her accident before I woke up today.

As if I magically summoned it, some nurse switched on the television—

"*Footage of the aftermath posted on Twitter shows a white Maserati car crash into the Murkwood Museum after the vehicle went airborne when it got hit by a jackknifed transport truck. The car seems lodged into the Museum, immediately caught fire following the blast and spread rapidly through the museum due to the wooden divider—*"

She clicked, changing the channel.

"That's weird. How quickly the museum caught fire, don't you think?" Nathan cocked his head at the television, frowning his brows. Goosebumps started trailing my arms as I shivered, watching her die. Fresh tears rolled down my eyes.

"Two teams were sent to rescue Ms. Julia Hector from the white Maserati. It was said that earlier, she had a meeting with Mr. Bill Muller, the manager of the Murkwood Museum. She dined with his family and was returning home when she met with an accident."

"Turn this off right now," I flinched as somebody roared from my left. I immediately looked up to find Phineas Parsons, Clara's father and Mayor of our town, fuming. The frightened nurse quickly did as told while Noni reached out to place her small hand on his large biceps.

He was too fit and well-groomed for a man in his mid-forties, with a big buffy body, around 6'2" tall and looked charming even in the night suit, his chocolate brown hair with a bit of grey in the undercut seemed all greasy like he had brushed them a thousand times with his fingers. His amber eyes were filled with remorse when they flicked from me to Noni back. He had never talked to me directly, nor was I allowed to talk in my mother's presence. She didn't even know I was friends with his daughter.

"You shouldn't have come, I'll meet you at the mansion after completing all the legalities," he held Noni's hand with motherly affection. She had a patch of rotten skin already appearing at the edge of her fingers.

"I am fine, I have to see her." Noni shook her head, her winter grey eyes jaded. She looked as pale as a ghost, her rosy-blonde hair was all disarray, the wrinkled skin of her cheeks dangled a bit more, and her under-eyes turned blue. She was in her mid-seventies, but right now, she looked like she had aged a decade in a single day. Noni had a rare skin disorder due to pollution, her entire body gets masked with black burnt patches, but right now, she didn't care. All she wanted to see was her dead daughter.

He nodded when the doctors arrived. Nathan shifted slightly as his parents, Meghan and Ethan Royce, joined them. Their eyes were filled with sympathy as Meghan side-hugged Noni.

"What are they doing here?" Nathan whispered in my ear. *'Duh! They are doctors here,'* I was about to answer when I found him looking elsewhere. I followed his streak of vision to find the reason for the glint in his eyes.

Neil Datye and Crew Rai Denali, members of our school's basketball team, stood near the reception in some deep discussion with the team captain, the Devil of Murkwood—Kayden Parsons.

Every town has this perfect guy who excels at studies and sports, loves competition and has a chivalrous aura that makes everyone go crazy about him. He has a huge fan following, not just girls but teachers and parents, because he knows how to manage his schedule, loves to bake, cook, clean, and does everything that every parent wants from their child and to us, it was Kayden Parsons, Clara's twin brother.

He was tall, around 6'2", with muscular shoulders, a thin waist and strong thighs. Since he was fourteen, he's been hitting the gym, turning his body fat into muscles. And now, at the age of eighteen, he had an incredible muscular body, not buff but lean and perfect. His hair was not so long that it fell in his eyes, not too short that you couldn't hold onto them, but perfect, silky brown. He had the ideal movie star jawline that made every girl drool all over him, kissing his full lips. They threw their panties at him just to have him once. Mother nature was too generous with him, with all the Parsons, but being a devil, he misuses it, or I should say—use it to manipulate people.

Right now, he was draped in an icy blue Balmain T-shirt with jet-black denim, pairing it with Jordans. The veins in his arm flexed as he brushed his hands through his hair.

Was he tensed?

As if feeling my gaze, he turned his head towards me, his hazel eyes found mine, and I felt a zing of heat prickling my skin. A gaze, so cruel, so violent that if it were a dagger, it would have pierced right through me. I hate him to see me like this, all shaken and broken, at my lowest. I didn't like to appear weak in front of him because he was a judgmental asshole who had comments about everything I did at school or pictures I posted on social media like I could never do anything good.

He narrowed his eyes, but they were cold, and for one second, I think they passed from where I was pressed against Nathan, then back to me. He scowled, but within a blink, it was gone. No feelings, nothing was shown on his face. He knew how to mask his emotions very well, and right now, all I could see was a shell of a person with a hollow soul. Cold, icy, and savage.

"God! Breathe, Lizzy, you're making me uneasy with all this sexual tension," Nathan nudged into my shoulder, jerking me awake. At the same time, Neil stepped between us, shaking his head as if stopping his friend from doing something rash, like leaping at me with a hand wrapped around my throat. *I know he wants to destroy me, and the notion is reciprocated. Let's see, who'll win this one? Who's going to survive in the end?*

"Sexual?" I turned my head to him, scoffing. "I wouldn't fuck him even if he were the last guy on the Earth and we were to populate the world. I'd rather light the match and burn the world with my own hands before having him touch me." I ground out.

"Really? I rather have him touch me anywhere he wants. He's so hot, if he'd be gay, I'd definitely let him—" but his words were cut off as cops entered the hospital. Mike Cooper, the deputy chief, had a manila folder in his hands as he made his way towards Noni and Mayor, looking all grim as if he had some bad news.

But my eyes were on his son, who was playing with his lip piercing, brushing his hair tied on the nape of his neck. As soon as his eyes found me, I sucked in a deep breath looking at those tar-black eyes.

"Homer," I murmured, swallowing a newly risen sob. All I desired was to run into his arm and feel his warmth around me. I wanted him to tell me that everything would be fine, that he'll hold me through these dark times, but before any of it could happen, Kayden leapt at him and before a second glance, his hand was holding the front of Homer's red hoodie, dragging him away. Neil and Crew followed him, and what shocked me the most was that none of the nurses or doctors said anything to him.

I turned to elders, but they, too, were busy discussing the case that Cooper didn't realise his son was being bullied.

"God!" Nathan wheezed. "What did he do this time?" He rubbed his forehead.

"He didn't do anything wrong, he never does," I snapped at Nathan, shooting up on my feet, defending Homer. Even though I know Homer was a prankster and played funny tricks like gluing people to desks, throwing water balloons at strangers, writing dickhead on paper, and pinning it to people's backs. He did that to gain people's attention, but he wasn't stupid to prank Mayor's son, who thinks of himself as the King of Murkwood.

Though I wanted someone to prank Kayden, to show him his right place but Homer would never do that.

"Kayden hates me, and that's why he's playing dirty." I hissed, not in the mood to mask my anger anymore. It was so easy to lose myself, to indulge in this war, to bend him down on his knees, show him my true strength.

I always hid behind a mask, trying to portray a feeble princess, keeping people at bay, like my mother wanted, and I had all intentions of doing so, but Homer changed it. He was the first guy I ever became friends with.

When I started school, he hovered around me even though I tried to stay low, but soon Halloween came, and he wore the same Iron Man costume. My eyes were glued to him, and when I asked him whether he was the one who was at the outhouse.

"Yes, will you be my friend, now?" he asked, his hope-filled eyes were cute, and when I nodded my head, the smile formed on his face was breathtaking. I never forgot about my Iron Man and was glad he didn't, either.

And today, he needed me.

I pulled my sleeves up, ready to throw some punches, feeling the weight of my penknife in my pocket, if needed, I knew very well how to use it. I wish—I wish when I had a moment, I hadn't saved Kayden. I wish I had let him die, then I didn't have to endure this control-freak.

I was thirteen and hanging out at Clara's place, as mom was out of town for some business meeting. We were playing wedding pretend play near the pool, and Kayden threw my Valentino rock-studded sneakers in the water, leaving me outraged. So, Clara pushed him into the pool, taking him off-guard. He fell with a splash, and we laughed.

But I noticed he didn't come up, and the water wasn't that deep. I immediately fathomed something was wrong, so I jumped in after him. Before Clara could figure, I was dragging him out. The water wasn't deep, so he had hit his head hard on the concrete.

"Oh Kiddie, Oh, my God, Kiddie." Soon Clara started screaming, holding her head. My heart was already in my mouth.

"Stop shouting and help me—pull him up," I scolded her, beyond terrified.

We pulled him out. "Oh no, oh no," she backed a few steps. "I killed Kayden, I killed my brother." She wailed before running back inside her house, holding her head like she was the one having a headache.

"No, he is not," I called, but she was gone. FUCK! But my concern was Kayden, who wasn't opening his eyes. So, I pinched his nose and blew in his mouth.

Soon I was giving him mouth-to-mouth, which Robin had taught me a few days back. Thanks to my mentor, I knew how to perform CPR.

Soon he gurgled out water as I pushed him to his side, rubbing his back.

"Geez, thank God—Oh my God—Kayden—are you okay?" I felt relief spread through my body, breathing heavily. His hazel eyes were beyond frightened, and shock flashed through his face. As soon as he saw me, he fell backwards, repelled me as if I gave him cooties.

I grind my teeth, waiting for him to thank me for saving his life or something, but he didn't. He just stood up and walked away, brooding. "What a jerk," I whispered after his arrogant departure.

The next moment I ran after him and begged both Parsons not to tell anyone about this. Clara was totally cool with it, saving her ass, but Kayden frowned and crossed his hands over his chest, asking for the reason. My insides groaned, but I gave him my casual shrug, and a warm smile, hiding my panic attack.

"Because we are friends," and it wasn't a big deal, at least for them. Their parent won't chain them in the cell for breaking the rule—attracting attention.

But the next thing he said always stayed with me.

"I don't want to be your friend," *he cringed his nose, insulting me. WTF?*

Clara swatted his arm, and for the first time, I acted in a non-princess way by flipping my middle finger at him, calling him an asshole because that's what he was. I just saved his life, and instead of showing gratitude, he showed me attitude.

I ran away from his place, blocking him from my life.

Somehow, this always-winning asshole with a twisted mind felt I won that day, and since then, we have been at each other's throats.

"*Mija*! Come here," Noni extended her hand for me to hold it.

I turned back to look where Kayden had taken Homer, back to Noni, worrying my lips, wanting to help Homer, but she also needed me.

Sighing, I stepped towards her. She held me as they discussed the truck driver. They found a high dosage of drugs in his blood when he hit my mother's car. Cooper had photographs of the incident that he took out from the camera and the current status of the car, which they held in their custody.

We were taken to a nearby room while they discussed further steps and spread pictures over the table. I felt a little out of space as Cooper kept glancing at me like I was a kid and didn't belong here in this discussion, but Noni was holding my hand like I was the only thing grounding her.

The door opened behind me, and I felt a light zing, but I ignored it because my focus was on one picture, one particular blurred picture where my mother or the lady in the red blouse had a hand in front of her face, shielding herself.

"But it was a right-hand drive," I spoke, raising my head. "And she's sitting on the left side."

Silenced fell over. Time froze with my words, and every eye was fixed on me.

I gulped down hard, ignoring how attention freaks me out. "She wasn't driving that day. There has to be someone else behind the wheels," I told Cooper, handing that picture.

I knew that car was a gift from a business colleague from the UK, and I had ridden so many times on the racetrack whenever my mom took some other car.

Noni raised her eyebrows at me. Meghan gasped as Ethan quickly ducked to scrutinise the pictures, but my eyes were fixed on Mayor, who stood with a taut jaw. His eyes fixed on someone else behind me.

I turned to look, finding Kayden in an eye contest with his father, with a smirk on his face, his shoulders rolled out with hands in his pockets, standing like he was challenging his dad into something, something he knew he'd already won.

What was that about?

Chapter 3
The Glitch

Was my mother murdered?

That was the first thing that struck my mind, what else could be the explanation for the person trying to get this case closed ASAP. He hadn't come further, and there was only one body they retrieved from the fire. Cooper ordered to recheck the grounds, whether someone else had died or some undiscovered body that could be found. God! They were discussing her funeral when I stepped in and made my statement.

But why would someone kill her? The Queen of the Murkwood, what would they gain from it? Was someone trying to rob her? Because she wouldn't give her car to someone else, she never trusted people easily. There were so many questions flooding my mind. I rubbed my temple, trying to grasp all the information.

"Elmo," Homer jerked my shoulder to gain my attention, but I hissed.

"Just because I have red hair, that doesn't make me Elmo," I told him through gritted teeth.

"It's not because of your hair, but because of your nose," he chuckled, booping it. *Don't kick him, don't kick him*, I had to chant not to get violent with him.

I felt heat pricking at the back of my neck like someone was shooting daggers at me, I turned to look at Kayden, whose eyes were narrowed down to where Homer was holding me. I snuggled more into Homer as his eyes shot to mine. The glare was thick and dangerous, something that made me want to run far away.

"What was that about, what did that jerk want from you?" I turned to Homer, who was playing with his lip piercing. I had always wondered how it would feel to kiss him with that metal, would it hurt him?

I ignored how Mayor ordered Kayden to take me home after my scandalous remark on my mother's case. Which I outright denied, telling them I could take an Uber, but somehow Noni wasn't in a state to send me with some stranger. Like Kayden was better than some stranger.

But for her peace of mind, I was about to accept, when Homer scooped in and offered he'll drop me, and I gladly accepted the offer. There was no way I was getting into Kayden's truck alone, even for him, I was the last person he wanted to be close to, I know he was physically repulsed by me like I was a walking disease that would infect him anytime.

I wish one day I do, I want to infect him, to rub my body over him, but the thought of rubbing took me somewhere else, somewhere I never want to go, something which he had already given to hundreds of girls. Heat rushed through my cheeks, remembering how he makes out in every corner of our school, how the girls hump him anywhere, any body part of him, and he gregariously welcomes them.

Homer shrugged. "He was asking about my hoodie."

"This hoodie?" I pointed at his chest while walking through the corridors while Nathan went to the restrooms. "Why?"

"Do you think I'm privy to the motivations of Gigantor?" he snorts.

I carefully examined his red hoodie, which had a flaming skull printed on it, it was his band hoodie. He was a very good guitarist with a great voice, I was totally jealous when he created a group and started hanging out with these people, calling themselves *Blaze*. It's where he met Sophie. My blood started boiling as a picture of him in Sophie's bed flashed before me. I was physically repulsed by him, it was too painful to have him by my side while he belonged to someone else. I let his hand fall, but he didn't notice it as he opened the hospital doors.

Sirens fell on my ear. Flashes, people buzzing, reporters asking questions—it was something I had never experienced before, something my mom had always kept me away from—attention. And now I realise why, I wasn't too fond of it. I hate being asked questions—*How do I feel? What were my insights? What will I do? Was it expected? Was she drunk? Was she high? Was she depressed?*

I halted, raising up my hood, hiding behind Homer.

"Guys, guys! She's not in a state to answer any of your questions," Homer took a step further, trying to seek attention, but out of nowhere, a bald muscular man over six feet blocked me. Robin was draped in all black as he tried to protect me from all those flashes. I was about to bolt, but I froze to the ground. My blood turned icy cold when my eyes fell on my father and his wife with their two boys walking towards me.

A smile spread on his face as our gaze met. A wicked smile. "Hello, daughter, it's time for you to return home."

And that was the last thing I remembered that day. Everything started blurring as beads of sweat dripped off my forehead, my palms became damp, and my body went numb.

Strong hands got me before I could fall, and then everything went black. All I could sniff was *oceans*.

"Hide her," was the last thing I heard from Noni.

IT WAS DARK when I woke up. I found myself standing on the topmost stair of a room with a bit of red light coming from down. I followed the light stealthily, my heart beating fast.

I peeped into an exorbitant room full of books, portraits, and paintings. There was a round table in the middle with a crystal ball on it, but that wasn't a crystal ball. It was more of an orb with mystical purple smoke flowing inside it. I tried to touch it, but I heard whispers. In front of me was a large, crowned mirror with baroque angels and weird symbols. The symbols emitted red light, making the room burn in red colour.

Suddenly, I flinched when a girl ran past me. She was merely around ten or eleven years old. Even though I knew about her existence because I always see her in my anxiety-ridden dreams, seeing her still made my heart beat faster.

The red light was getting absorbed in her straight Mocha-brown hair, which was falling on her shoulders. She always wore the same black-ribbed top with a denim skirt, unicorn shoes, and pink socks.

This girl haunted me every time.

She took the purple orb from the table, holding it in both hands like a handball as she whispered to someone not visible to me. I walked to her and asked. "Hey! Who are you?"

She didn't turn around. Instead, she murmured with exhilaration in her voice. "Here, now take me to my mom. I want to meet her." Her face wasn't visible. I felt she was talking to herself in the mirror.

I stepped further, extending my hand to touch her. Suddenly, creepy shadowy hands emerged from the mirror, caressing the orb.

My eyes went wide, my heart stopped, and without thinking, I sprang towards the girl before the shadow could grasp her wrist. I pulled her back from her shoulders as she screamed a heart-piercing wail, the orb fell to the ground with a clink.

I hastily tried to open my eyes. My heart was pounding against my chest so loudly that I could hear it in my ears. I was drenched in sweat and realised that it was a dream that had haunted me since I was eleven and still sent chills down my spine.

"She's back," I heard Noni's anxious voice. It was when I felt strong hands cradling me again.

"Shhhh…" Somebody whispered in my ears, wiping the sweat from my face. I wanted to open my eyes, but it was difficult as I felt arms around me tighten, securing me as I leaned into them, sniffed oceans, and again, I was out.

Suddenly it was all mist, ashes and darkness, and all I could do was run.

I have been running away from this darkness since I was a child, but this parallel universe sucks me in. It's not in my control to visit this place. It calls to me. Like somebody wanted me there, but I never found even a single soul hanging in like me. So, I never figured out why I was being sucked into this ghastly realm.

What is this place? Why me?

I was in turmoil to find the answers, to stop this torture by my mother, but there was no one to answer, to help me with this worthless glitch. I had tried to tame it many times by meditation with Dr. Dorcas. When it didn't work, Mom chained me to vaults, but still, it didn't stop.

When I was ten, she again chained me in the old mansion for being unable to control my glitch, and with my poor luck, I *poofed* and sucked in again. It was rotten, covered in ashes and mist, purgatory smell hurt my throat, but I was unchained, so I ran. Instead of going out, I ran inside and hid under a bed, where I shifted back to our realm. When I opened my eyes, I found myself in a room which belonged to Leticia. She was the first Queen of Murkwood, my ancestor. She was said to be a great and powerful lady, and my great-great-granddad Hector loved her. They said he fought the Gods to protect her.

But my eyes were fixed on the diary that was tossed under the bed. I picked it up and wiped off the soot before reading the name—*Shadowland*—a handwritten journal by someone called *J.P.P.* A gift from *Umbra-Mae*, but it was struck out with a red pen, twice.

Even though I was just ten years old, I still knew that it had the answer to my question.

I flipped through the old yellowing pages. Most of the pages were torn, and my first thought when I opened it was that the handwriting was exquisite. There was an old pic of twin girls, hardly seven-years-old, one with red hair and the other black holding a dog, used as a bookmark. I crawled out under the bed, near the windows, in the light.

There are fourteen worlds in this universe, seven realms of heaven and seven realms of hell. One of the realms of hell is Sutala, aka Shadowland. It is a shadowy resemblance of a former self, a twisted mirror version of our world, filled with dilapidated and distorted reflections of regular buildings, decayed into sinister subways and abandoned hospitals. Minor changes can even extend to the layout of the city or area, but the geography will turn malevolent if somehow changes transform into huge gaping holes created by unnatural havoc, making the Sunlit realm and the Shadowland collide, allowing the inhabitants to crossover, causing destruction.

These inhabitants are similarly warped monsters or unfathomable spirits outright—shadowfiends, wraiths, and many other unnamed creatures thirsty for blood and flesh. Shadowland is known to be the home of a multidimensional demonic entity—Yamendo, *the Shadow Queen, dark, all black. She is an embodiment of suffering, inhabiting people's nightmares. She becomes powerful by feeding upon people's dreams and has the power to alter them. She traps them into illusions, ultimately making them lose their minds, never waking up, never returning to reality. That's why they call it—the land of hallucinations.*

She breeds in that land, creating her monsters with no minds, no needs, just hunger.

An elite group named the Shadow Walkers can visit the Shadowland and cull these sinister beings. These Shadow Walkers can cross the thin line between the realms without creating any collision, without devising a void. They are the mediators suitable to visit both domains. Their work is to get rid of these monsters, to protect the sunlit realm.

The mirror world and spirit world overlap Shadowland at times. Some people confuse it by calling it Naraka or Hell though the Shadowland shares some qualities with them but is a distinct form. Some even think it is time travel or another dimension, but it's not. If you travel from your hometown to an atrocious future where it's in ruins, that's time travel. If you travel from your hometown to a fantasy forest, that's another dimension. But if you travel from your hometown to a dark, twisted parody of your hometown filled with monsters... then congratulations, and enjoy your stay in the Shadowland.

My heart ratcheted into thunderous beats because the explanation matched the place where I used to visit. The journal was about the kind of monsters you could find there, things Shadow Walkers use against them, rituals, contents, spells, and many more. But I was only interested in this *Yamendo*. I started turning pages quickly to learn more about her. My hands were shaking as I wiped my clammy palms over my dress.

Yamendo *was the princess of* Yamakool. *She was the daughter of* King Damaelus *and* Queen Yamela. *Damaelus was a warlock who had bestowed upon Yamendo the talent of being able to distance herself from her own shadow whenever she wanted. She was a witch that could live in shadow form.*

*One day, she met a voyager—*Maverick, *the heir of the Sun, a Cosmic. He loved going to the places and kept on roaming. They both fell in love, so by using their powers, they created a new world called the Shadowland. He fashioned it for Yamendo, his lover, but she got greedy and wanted more realms to become the Queen of the Universe. Her darkness started spreading, and their children became monsters. She trained them to take over the world when Maverick fathomed her darkness. He tried to burn Shadowland with her in it, but she left her body, took over her shadow form, captured Maverick, and locked him in Shadowland. She made him a prisoner of his nightmares, which he couldn't break, dooming Shadowland in a lifetime of nightfall.*

Many years passed. She used to torture humans, trying to take over the Sunlit realm. When Livana, *the moon of Shadowland, watched Maverick getting tormented every day, every single night, she wept tears of blood. She formed a plan with Maverick's brother, another heir of the Sun, and together, they created an army of High warriors and sent them to fight these dark spirits lurking in the shadows and mist. She descended to Earth to fight and was able to rescue Maverick and trap Yamendo into Shadowland.*

Livana being a powerful Cosmic, seized Yamendo, snatched her powers and locked them into the Wandering Star, *a vessel that can hold an inestimable amount of energy, trapping her in the Shadowland. She was said to be the ice blazing with fire. Her headstrong and passionate nature made the heir of the Sun kneel in front of her. She was the embodiment of love.*

But deceitfully, Yamendo killed her, and with her dying breath, she named Yamendo Forsaken and cursed her

'You bled the Moon on your land, you cursed yourself to seek,
the moonlight for a lifetime…but you won't be able to reach,
A fallen Moon so at rise will cry bloody tears,
You'll try to chase me, but I'll be hiding in your peers,
the day will come when you'll think—you might reign,

We'll re-meet for sure, and your destruction will begin.'

And then she turned to Maverick. 'Take me and raise me as your moonchild,' *she commanded, and with that, she went inside him—her soul, her powers entered him. He picked what was left of hers and escaped the Shadowland with the remaining high warriors.*

Since then, Yamendo has been trapped in the Shadowland. Being the Forsaken, she's locked inside her world, away from humanity. She made an army in the sunlit realm by providing them favours. The people born out of Yamendo's curse are her demons, she treats them like her children, and when the time will come, she'll choose one of them to help her kill moonchild and Maverick by claiming the powers from the Wandering Star.

I gulped down audibly, reading further.

High warriors that settled on Earth, and mated with humans produced Shadow Walkers, humans with godly powers, warriors for the moonchild, protecting humans till she arrives.

But even though how powerful they might be, they cannot contain or command Yamendo. Only, Umbra-Mae, *or* moonchild, *can hold her. Shadow Walkers, who are spell casters, or occultists, can summon her using part of Livana and the Wandering Star together, by completing a ritual.*

Chills went down my spine. The words like shadowfiends, demon, curse, monsters, and *Forsaken* frightened me.

But the biggest question was—*'Why haven't I seen anybody there?'* and there could be only two conclusions, A: That journal only talked about legends and myths. And B: Perhaps *moonchild* already outdid me and wiped off *Yamendo* and her minions.

Wow, such a waste of power!

But that explained two things A: I was a *Shadow Walker,* and B: The place I visited was *Shadowland.*

My thoughts were jumbled up. Why was I being sucked there if *moonchild* had already arrived, and was I just hanging in there to live the aftereffects? That idea was a relief, but still, if that weren't the case, I would never want to shift to Shadowland if it still was the home of some Shadow Queen.

I didn't want to encounter anyone. I would do everything to give up this glitch.

So, I hid the book and decided to fashion the mask of a perfect daughter and sneak into shadows whenever I shifted.

Chapter 4
The Trance

I woke up in my bed feeling tired, like I had travelled thousands of miles barefoot.

My room was cozy and warm, everything seemed normal, like nothing had changed. But everything had changed. My whole life had turned upside down.

I dragged myself to the ensuite washroom, turning towards the basin to look at my reflection. My electric blue eyes were puffy and dark. My round cheeks were ruined with smudged eyeliner, and my thick wavy red hair were a huge mess, demanding a good wash.

My terrible appearance prompted me to take a hot shower, so I opened my vanity to pull out my Victoria's Secret's Frosted Magnolia body wash, a gift from Mom on my 17th birthday, a fragrance that was my forever love.

I felt a lump in my throat just looking at it. Bile rose through my chest, and before it came out, I quickly put on the hot water hitting the faucet. I want it hot, damn hot, to scorch my sore body.

My clothes sank to the floor as I gazed at my body. I was around 5'3" with curves in the right places. Everything was full, firm and even. My eyes were locked on my chatoyant necklace, the twin of what my mother had. My hands subconsciously reached to hold it, seeking some calmness, some strength. It was a gift from Noni when we first arrived here. They belonged to Leticia, the first queen of Murkwood, it was an ancestral heirloom, something I feel gratified to wear around my neck.

I checked the water on my toes, immediately making me hiss at the heat, which meant it was perfect for getting in. I closed the shower enclosures and let the water fall on my body. Blocking out the stinging and ripping pain, I continued to take a hot shower. The steam started rising in enclosures as I gazed down at my chatoyant, subconsciously spinning it between my fingers.

Questions regarding my mother's death flooded my thoughts, even though my whole body was sore, my mind kept running miles per minute.

Who wanted to kill her? And why?

Suddenly, I felt a kick in the stomach, and I choked on the last breath I took. I threw my head back, holding my chatoyant firmly, as it tightened around my throat. It emitted green light, illuminating my surroundings, and soon I shifted.

I stood in an old building. It was a vast empty hall with no furniture, only the candles hanging around the corners, enlightening the place. A strange giant painting of a woman on the front wall was split in half. Half had black wings, and the other half was burning alive with the words *'Si ingerii au demoniilor'*. I would have googled it, but I couldn't feel my hands.

Hell! I couldn't even feel my body. What's happening? It's never happened to me before, I have shifted to Shadowland numerous times, but this—never. I would have shivered if I could, but I feel far from it.

There in its front was a podium on which a bowl was kept. Walls were painted with a weird symbol of a trident over an overturned crescent moon wrapped around by a snake. It was a peculiar sigil. Weirdly, I had seen this before but didn't remember where.

The second floor had a small balcony area where I saw lanterns burning red. There were statues of angels masking their faces with hands in the corner of rooms. The walls were covered with long violet banners with the same sigil in silver.

"Take this baby out now," a lady screamed, catching my attention. "I can't bear it, Miguel. Take her out, now," she cried in pain, holding a man's hand. The sigil was painted on the floor, inside a chakra, where a woman was screaming. I stepped toward her, but I didn't feel anything. It was like I had no limbs, no body, just waggling eyes.

I floated to her in the air as her winter-grey eyes rolled back in her head, and her red wavy hair, like mine, was stuck to her face. She was tired, her breathing was shallow as she let out a heart-wrenching scream again. I flinched at her pain, wanting to soothe her, she seemed oddly familiar, but I couldn't touch her. She was just a dream, but how could I dream about someone I had never seen before in real life?

"Don't worry, Paloma, Leticia is helping you. She promised she'd save you and the child," said the man sitting on his heels, his brown hair plastered to his scalp with sweat.

"Leticia?" I asked, gasping, but nobody gave me even a stir.

He held his wife's hand tightly as she was having contractions. Her stomach was wobbly, and her lower portion was covered in a sheet. People were standing around them. They all were wearing silver robes. I just noticed them. They looked stronger than normal people. The confidence on their faces made them appear like warriors but from different times, the times they used to make black-and-white movies, but this dream was no movie because it was coloured, even though I had never seen these people, I could make every face out.

How could their faces be so clear when I hadn't seen even a single one of them?

"Mira, bring me more towels, and Maurice, help to guard the temple. Villagers are trying to burn this building, and the brethren will be arriving soon," demanded the lady between Paloma's legs. She pulled up her head, and my heart melted as I saw her. She was a slender lady, the most beautiful I had ever seen. Her face was pink, with electric-blue eyes filled with love and passion.

Leticia! She looked royal with a perfect body hidden with violet-coloured robes tied by a black belt around her slim waist. Her eyes were covered with red eyeshadows extending to the sides. On her forehead, there was a watermark as if a third eye. Her black hair was tied beautifully in a high bun decorated with small ornaments.

"Sure, Leticia," Mira, a silver-pressed hair girl, nodded at her as she scurried back behind the pillars while the brown-haired man turned to Leticia. He, too, had electric-blue eyes—my great-granddad, Maurice Hector. I had seen his paintings in an old mansion. But he was young, probably a few years older than me, but how come? How come I was here? Why was I here?

What the fuck was happening?

Before I could grasp it, the lady screamed, stealing my attention.

"Mother, I'll need only five shadow warriors, the rest of them can secure the building from the inside," Maurice demanded. He had a crooked arrogant smile as he pulled the robe's sleeves up, showing his hairy forearms, flexing his neck. It's always said he was an eccentric ruler with a twisted mind.

My head shot up at the words he said, *shadow warriors.* My ancestors knew about this? Or was my mind making this up?

"Do as you like," Leticia nodded as she ducked back between Paloma's leg. She was trying to deliver the baby. I grimaced as the blood poured down her legs, and she screamed.

"Why don't you take her to the hospital?" I flinched, but nobody reacted. It appeared as if they couldn't sense me.

Then why was I here?

"I am sorry, Leticia, I didn't know she was *the demon.* I didn't ask her. I just prayed to every power in the universe," Miguel sobbed, wiping his mouth with the back of his hand. "After four miscarriages, I knew my Paloma would die if this baby didn't come. For her," he gulped down. "For the sake of my Loma, my child's sake, I prayed to every power, and *she* was the only one who answered." His eyes were full of remorse. "How would I know she was a demon? To me, she was the saviour of my child and my Loma, my love," Miguel covered his face with his hands, ashamed of his deed. "I didn't know she'll feed on a hundred and eighty people, even the children."

I gasped. Did he ask some demon for a child? I have seen this in movies, demons grant you a demonic child, and that child brings devastation and destruction to the world. *Fuck! Is this child going to be wicked?* It appeared like some story from Stephen King's novel, but Maurice called themselves shadow warriors. This couldn't be a story, could it?

"The brethren are saying she climbs out of her womb every day to feed on villagers and then crawls back inside," He shuddered at the idea as my eyes widened. *WTF! What kind of baby is this?*

"Miguel!" Leticia snapped, looking appalled. "Don't trust made-up stories. Have some common sense. She is still unborn. It's not her. She is not the one killing everyone," she pushed him aside. "Don't distract me now, I have to suppress the darkness inside her."

Damn! Leticia was sassy, and her voice was so soft that I could hear her all day. I think she was my first girl-crush ever.

Miguel obliged. His hands never left Paloma's, glancing at doors repeatedly as if his whole life depended on it.

I heard noises outside, recognising Maurice's voice, who was trying to reason, but there was aggression from another side, roars, and soon there were screams. I wanted to go outside when a few stones flew inside, breaking the temple's windows. The glass shattered with an ear-piercing noise.

"Shields up, now," Mira ordered, and with that, all shadow warriors stood up and created a circle around us, while a few stood in line towards the entrance, and they started doing elegant actions with their hands, all of them in symmetry. It seemed like they were performing on stage, but this was no stage, and no one was there to clap for them. And suddenly, a vast thrilling red shield started covering everyone in the room.

I gasped in shock. Whoa!

They all had a red stone ring in their hand, which was pulsing with their every action, that ring was helping them to create this shield, and soon every corner, every part of the temple, was secured with it.

"Focus, Paloma, don't look outside. We'll protect you. I'll protect this child with my life." Leticia pulled Paloma's leg in the air while two shadow warriors held them in position. "Push Paloma, push. Relax now, and then push again."

BANG.

With a loud thud, the hall's doors fell to the ground. And at the same time, I heard Paloma shriek in agony with all the force she had, and the baby cried, her baby was out. I immediately felt the urge to put a hand on my mouth to prevent the food from rising in my throat, but I didn't have a stomach or hand, as the baby girl covered in amniotic liquid was the most horrific view I had ever seen. Leticia cut the umbilical cord. It seemed like a miracle, human making human.

And there goes my will to have a baby, ever.

Nope-nope-nopety-nope, I am never doing this.

"She is here. We saved her, don't worry," Leticia's voice filled with tremendous relief and triumph. But instead of handing the baby to the father, she took her to the back of the room, ignoring her parents as if she had some claim on the baby.

My eyes fell on the people standing at the door, wielding fire torches, and their eyes were all dark, petrified.

Leticia placed the baby in the bowl on the podium and called out. "This baby is born out of the curse. We must suppress her shadow before Forsaken lays her hands on this beautiful little girl. *She took what was ours. Now, it's our time to take what's hers!*"

With that, she turned to look at shadow warriors, their eyes gleaming with happiness. "The Era of *moonchild* begins from now, the bringer of *Hara* is here," she declared, picking up the bowl where the baby was lying, crying.

And every shadow warrior whispered—*Light bless us*! Their words echoed in the temple.

My heart thumped at every word she said—*Forsaken, Moonchild, Hara.*

A smile rose on Leticia's face, and with a swish wave of her hand, she created a red tomb of light around herself. The same red ring that all shadow warriors wore flickered on her fingers with the action and started whispering some enchantments.

"LETICIA, hand it over." The fat man shouted among the crowd, his red face filled with anger, as he stepped forward. With him, all his followers mirrored him, wielding torches. Seven people from the crowd made their way ahead. They were wearing skull masks, brown jackets, bones hanging down on the sleeves, and belts, sprinkled with drops of blood. Their pants were covered in sharp and small pointed teeth. One was wielding a bow and arrows. Another had a knife, and the third had a pointed spear made of bone, saw, axe, machete, and blade. All seven of them were wielding some weapons dripping with blood. They stood behind him like an army trying to take over their territory. *Are they insane? Why are they armed? What are they thinking—to begin a war?*

"Sergio, we don't want to fight your people," Maurice entered the building. He had blood on his silver robes and twin blades in his hand, covered in blood. "This child is important to us, let us have her."

FUCK! Did they fight outside? OMG!

"She's a cursed child," Sergio narrowed his eyes at Miguel and glanced at the shadow warriors. "This baby is a shadow demon, Shaman saw her in her dream. That's why she told everyone not to have a baby this year. But you didn't listen," he turned to Miguel. "This year was prophesized to be when the Shadow Queen would lay her darkness, and you, stupid man, accepted it."

I whimpered at the information. Prophecy? Shadow Queen? Cursed child? I had tons of questions while he continued.

"Moreover, nobody can perform a ritual such as to suppress the demonic in a demon, especially when the baby is born out of favour from *Yamendo*," he spat. With that name, my heart which was thumping loudly, froze like nothing was left. My face must have gone pale because I could feel the blood draining. *What, Yamendo? Do you know Yamendo? Where is she? Who is she? Is she here*? I glanced through the room for her, but she wasn't there, still, I felt a chill seeping through my bones.

Sergio's eyes were full of hatred and rage. "Now I see *you* started everything as *your* wife conceived. That's why Paloma sent for her old friend Leticia, she invited her here to save her, and you all planned her fake death!" Sergio hissed, making Miguel flinch. "You disgust me, for one unborn, you killed them all." He looked at all of them in the room.

"Those deaths are not related to this baby," mused Mira. "You are also wrong about Leticia. She *can* perform this magic and purify the baby's darkness. She's a spell caster, a seer—a *Star.*"

"Really? If these deaths are unrelated to the baby, then why did they begin when she conceived?" Asked Sergio, but nobody answered, so he continued. "Because this demon baby needed blood to survive, and every day you hunt for her because Paloma needed blood to grow this demon inside, and Leticia fed her with the blood of the innocents."

"Blood? What blood? My wife didn't drink blood, don't make things up," Miguel kept shaking his head. "She didn't bring the curse upon this town. Leticia never killed anyone. We called her to purify our baby's soul, but we didn't kill any of our people. She's just here to save my baby."

"Your wife doesn't need to drink it. She doesn't even have to know. It's a demonic blood ritual, which Leticia is performing in her temple every day on behalf of your baby," Sergio explained, as the blood drained my face.

"He is right. A human cannot carry a demon baby. It needs strength and a blood ritual to thrive in this world with powers," said an old lady with white hair. She had wrapped a hand-woven carpet cloth around her. She was way older for walking on her own, wielding a skull staff which she pointed out towards Miguel. "You asked the child and opened the gates to Shadowland. You lured a demon into our world. She wouldn't have let you raise this child on your own. She is not stupid. She would do anything to take care of this child. That's why she must have sent her monster to do the killings, feast upon us. You placed everybody's life at stake for this *cursed child*."

Leticia was standing unaffected, lost in her trance. She was humming, cooing enchantments while washing up the baby in the bowl at the podium, totally unaware of the situation. She was so absorbed in the baby that she didn't even hear when the crowd started shouting DEMON, DEMON, making the hair on the nape of my neck stand.

"I am a Shaman, and I am a seer just like your father, like you," the old, raggedy lady addressed Leticia directly. "Not as good as you are, but I also have sight, and I've seen what this girl can do, I know what *Hara* will do. You should have listened to your sister. Valerie was right. This girl should never have been born."

Valerie?

"Not all prophecies are meant to be fulfilled, at least not the one that states it will bring destruction to the world. Hara will stop the *moonchild*, don't you understand?" she growled in horror. "*Hara* will destroy you all."

"We are no one to stop any prophecy. All prophecies will take place according to time, even if we want or not, we are merely a medium, brought upon Earth to follow the path to our destiny, and this is our destiny, and we all believe *Hara* will save us." Maurice chimed, his voice was deep, sensual, but powerful.

"Your father, *Cyavan*, prophesized on his deathbed about *Hara*," the corner of her toothless lips quirked up as if she herself had heard him. "I would have never guessed that you, shadow warriors, would help demons to create *Hara*, the vessel of *Yamendo,* who'll stop the *moonchild* and bring destruction to this world. I thought you all belonged to the *moonchild*," she scoffed, but disgust flashed. "*Livana* would be very disappointed in you."

"There can be many interpretations to his prophecy, my lady," Maurice purred, cleaning his blade off one of the cult member's shirt, who tried to attack him, but the shield blocked his hand. He was showing off his supremacy. "And your interpretation isn't the one my mother made because, as you said, you aren't as good as she is." He smug arrogantly, insulting Shaman.

With that, Shaman growled in anger. She was among people who couldn't take insults. "You summoned the Shadow Queen. I can feel the demonic presence in this temple. This is no longer holy. The rotting smell I get from every dead body is so high and profound here, like somebody from here killed everyone." She was making so many hand gestures that I could feel it was much of an overacting.

Those seven people from the cult, with masks, walked forward, wielding their weapons.

"No demon can enter our temple," Maurice rolled his eyes, but Shaman ignored him this time. "Whatever we are doing is for our *moonchild* only." He cocked his head towards Leticia. "She is saving his daughter and everyone by risking her own life because she's the true shadow warrior," he was cleaning his fingernails with the knife he held, that's when my eyes fell on it. It was the knife I carried in my pocket, my penknife, the one Noni gave me. Was it an ancestral heirloom, too? Does my Noni know about Shadow Walkers?

No, she couldn't, if she had known about this, she would have helped me, especially with my mom.

"And she didn't summon *Yamendo,* she cannot be called. Don't you know she can't cross the veil to the human realm without the part of Livana and the *Wandering Star*?" His question was aimed at Shaman.

She went mute, her lips pursed into a straight line, and I knew he was right, even I had read in the journal that she was stripped of her powers and locked inside the *Wandering Star.*

Suddenly everything quivered beneath me with a rumble of power. My heart stopped, and my stomach fell, it was strong enough to make gargoyles in the room smash down. The bowl of water in front of Leticia dropped to the floor, but luckily the baby was in Leticia's hand.

What was happening? My hands were splayed on the ground, trying to stop it from shuddering. *Stupid me! But hey! My hands were back.* I looked down, checking out my body. Slowly and gradually, I was formulating my body.

"We all know *Yamendo*'s curse never goes in vain. She's coming to take this child. It's a blood moon night, and you knew she'd find a way to come here. Leticia, stop acting like you don't know the gates are open. You are a *seer.* Feel the darkness sprinkled in the air." Shaman was getting agitated. Her face glimmered in fear.

I looked at Leticia, but she didn't budge. She was unstoppable and focused on completing the ritual. I was startled by a heart-piercing shriek.

"NO!" Miguel had been shot with a fire arrow, and his shrieks were filled with agony as I watched him burn from the gap between two warriors. I was glued to the ground. I immediately shut my eyes, but the image of him burning was stuck in my mind. It sent a pierced feeling down my heart. I was trembling severely. Tears were seeping out of my eyes, hating being so helpless.

My head spun from his screams, trying hard to go back to my room, to my house, safe, but I couldn't. I turned on my heels and marched towards Leticia. Paloma was wailing behind me. Her pain and shrieks were unbearable.

Tears rolled down Leticia's cheeks, but her incantations never stopped, like she really wanted it to work, like her whole life depended on this, this very moment. Looking at her innocent face, I could feel she wasn't wrong, she wasn't doing anything wrong but saving a life. She had some specific reason to save this girl, but why was this girl so important? Why was *Hara* important?

My eyes fell on a golden-haired lady, who was among the villagers a few minutes ago, was now standing near the podium, just behind Leticia.

"STOP," Mira commanded, leaving me stunned. She spun bolas at the golden-haired lady, which entangled her legs as she fell to the ground. All the shadow warriors and cult members turned to us, but Leticia didn't budge.

Black smoke rose from her body as she screeched in pain, whimpering on the floor.

"She is the one," Mira pointed at the lady. "Look, she has two shadows. She is possessed. Her body is smoking due to *moonwater* on the string of bolas."

Shaman and others came running, Sergio in front. "No, it's impossible!" He was taken aback as he recognised the lady, his voice was taut, and he seemed broken.

The possessed lady growled and broke the tie, launching herself at Leticia, hitting the tomb of the red shield and landing on her fours. It seemed like that shield was invisible to her eyes.

"LARA!" Sergio shouted at the possessed lady. He knew her. Her revelation scared him.

That's when Shaman beckoned the cult members, which marched towards Lara, pinning her to the ground.

I heard whispers from behind. "Mira, how can she enter the temple?" Shadow warriors asked in horror, their faces were terrified, some were just teenagers, not much older than me.

"All of you grab the jars of moonwater and wash the building," Mira turned to Maurice. "Make *chakra* with lava sand everywhere, every damn space you find."

Four cult members were pinning Lara down with knees on her limbs, one had a knife to her throat while the other two-pointed spear and machete at her, trying hard to restrain her, but she was too strong for even four buff men.

Mira walked forward and poured some water into her throat, to which she growled in pain, black smoke rose off her body as she whimpered like somebody had poured acid on her, but she was restrained.

"What did you do?" Sergio cried as he fell to his knees, devastated.

"I wanted revenge," she cried and growled simultaneously. "She killed my baby, our baby. I wanted to take away everyone that called her mother." And her sob changed to roar as she growled at Shaman.

The roar was so loud that it scared everyone. A tear from Sergio's eye fell to the floor.

"I didn't know it would transform me into this," Lara spoke. "He gave me a bowl of black smokey water, he said it'll make me powerful. Hence, I gulped the entire bowl, waking up famished. I tried to control my hunger, but—" she groaned, trying free herself from the ties. "I am SO hungry," and with that, she grunted and licked the floor. Her eyes were white with no eyeballs turning black from the corner, and her skin was turning hairy.

"Darkness is taking over her. Sergio, you know what needs to be done," said Shaman walking over to him, she pulled out a dagger with her sturdy hands, but Sergio didn't accept it, he shook his head, and more tears fell. Lara was his wife, and he couldn't kill the love of his life with his own hands.

Lara groaned.

"We need to kill her," Shaman ordered. "We don't know what she is."

"A shadowfiend possesses her," answered Mira as whispers surrounded us. "But it could only possess you when you're most vulnerable."

"Vulnerable?" asked Sergio, like he was confused.

"You were pregnant, and she had a miscarriage too, right? Like other ladies in the village," asked Mira, she turned to the thin-lipped Shaman. "You fed her black cohosh root tea that led to abortion as you did with others. But she knows, a mother always knows, and now she's seeking revenge." She grimaced her face at Shaman like she could read her thoughts.

Sergio looked horrorstruck while Shaman's eyes narrowed in the slits.

"We need to kill her," she leapt forward towards Lara with a dagger.

"NO!" Mira blocked Shaman's way. "We can perform a ritual to expel this shadow from her body."

But desperately, Shaman attacked Mira, and swiftly Maurice created a shield blocking her. The dagger fell off her hands.

"You killed my unborn child, you killed all the unborn because of the half-baked knowledge about the prophecy. Look what you've caused," Sergio growled, picking up the dagger.

"Sergio!" Shaman warned, stunned and stumbling as he stepped towards her.

"You brought the curse, not Miguel. He died because you didn't know what you were doing, you killed the unborn, and your hands are soiled with the blood of our village." Sergio blamed her.

Shaman growled, tapping her staff to the ground, force erupted from it and thrashed him back, hitting the wall hard.

I choked on the last breath I took. I didn't know Shaman was so powerful as she twisted and entered the tomb of light near Leticia, smudging the circle of red sand with her robe.

"BARBARA!" Leticia growled, her eyes flung open, snapping her neck at Shaman. "You broke the ritual," she cried, and a blast of lightning fell over the temple.

The roof fell as dreadful cries filled the room. Everybody was running to save their lives, trying to escape the room. Chaos filled the temple as shadow warriors helped villagers to escape, but Leticia didn't budge.

"I am Leticia, the seer to the *moonchild*, the protector of shadow warriors," she was shaking in anger, her eyes were splitting into silver like lightning, while Shaman shivered in her aura. "And you enraged *the Star*."

Within the blink of an eye, lightning struck Shaman, burning her into ashes. Leticia didn't even give her time to scream, leaving me appalled. There was a big lump in my throat that I was too afraid to swallow.

"Careful, Mother, you cannot summon light. The baby will burn. She's a shadow demon," Maurice held his hands in the air, trying to calm his mother down. His face had gone pale.

Leticia stepped out of the circle with the baby. And as soon as she did, Lara roared, and all the cult members went flying, and she launched herself at Leticia. But Leticia blocked her charges with a shield. This time, this shield was bright as starlight, and the baby whimpered in her arms as Lara fell back, bouncing off the shield, screaming, burning.

"Mother, you're hurting the baby, give her to me," Maurice walked forward as the baby cried in Leticia's arms, but he couldn't cross the lightning shield.

My eyes widened as I wanted to save the child from Leticia's anger, her powers were rippling out of her body as if she was filled with electric charges—she was *a star, a real star.*

"STOP IT," I screamed, and suddenly the shield was gone, as Leticia had gotten it under control. She was breathing heavily, and her chest was heaving like she was holding her powers back with great difficulty.

Lara was shivering in agony. Her body was now covered in fur, increasing her size. She was twitching and turning. Her backbone clinked like they were breaking down. I saw clearly how one, two, three, and four legs came out of her body. She had four hands and four legs with two sharp blades near her mouth. Her front limbs were much more significant than her back ones, and she was walking like a gorilla, crushing the cult members under her giant feet, who were trying to stop her. Her sharp blades pierced those humans, who were now bleeding to death while they screamed in pain.

"Shadowfiend!" gasped one of the Shadow Walkers.

Soon she was freed and attempted to take the baby. But before she could do anything, she shrieked in pain.

I looked around and saw Sergio, he had stabbed her in the back. With a roar, she cried and fell with a thud with which Sergio pulled the dagger to his throat and slit it swiftly. Blood gurgled out of his throat and mouth, his eyes closed as he fell on Lara's body.

The vein in my head was throbbing, I held my head, stopping it from bursting,

Please, let me back, I want to go back. Free me. I don't want to see more, let me go!

Leticia walked to Paloma, the ground where she was lying had started cracking, and the building was crashing. The hall was shaking, the roof was falling. Leticia quickly cradled the baby, she ripped a green stone from her forehead, leaving her watermark bleeding.

The pain of doing so was visible in the tremble and shrieks of her voice, and her blue eyes had gone red due to the immensity. It was a small bright stone, emitting bright green light. Suddenly it broke in half, and two chatoyants emerged out of it. I choked. They were the same cat-eyed chatoyant that Mom and I wore. My hand immediately reached to grab it.

Leticia took a velvet pouch from her robe, placed them into it and tied it around the baby's belly, and bent down to Paloma.

"She is coming," the shadow warriors said, turning towards Leticia, their eyes full of fear, some even had tears. "What's happening, Leticia? She can't come," this time, it was Mira. Her face had gone as white as ashes.

"Part of *Livana* and *the Wandering Star* together can summon her, and they are here in our temple. She is right here, on our lands, somebody opened the portal for *Yamendo*," Leticia spoke, finally.

Mira trembled in fear. Even I was shaking.

"Go away, I'll stop her," shouted Leticia at her fellow warriors, her voice in pain, it was more of a plea. And with that, she lifted her hair from the nape of her neck, revealing a glowing chakra, which had their sigil inside it, and pressed it, followed by Mira and several other shadow warriors, they all had this chakra on the nape of their neck, and they all pressed at once, but nothing happened. "Valerie will open the gates of Umbra-Mae headquarters for you. Go now," Leticia ordered.

"Leticia," I heard shadow warriors trying to save people, but things were getting out of their hands. Some of them made a violet sparkly starry circle in midair, a portal, I think, because they jumped into it, vanishing midair.

"Mother, give her to me. I'll help you," Maurice came forward to sit next to Leticia. "Go, Mother, give me this child and save your life. Yours is more important than any of us."

"Really, and you think if I give this baby to you, I'll live?" Leticia asked curtly. "I know what you have done, I know what you're trying to do, but you are not powerful enough, *you* cannot control her son," and with that, she swiftly put hands in his robe and snatched out a shinning orb, mystical purple smoke rising in it. I had seen this orb before. This orb was there in my anxiety dream. The little girl takes this Orb and gets to the mirror. What connection do I have with these dreams?

"Why did you steal it from me?" Leticia demanded, bringing me back. "Why did you steal the *Wandering Star*?"

It's the Wandering star, the Orb, the one with the mystical purple light, that was the vessel that held Yamendo's powers. But why do I keep seeing the Wandering Star in my dreams? What does it have to do with me?

"Give that back," he stood up. "I can handle her. I have waited too long for this moment. Just don't take it away from me."

"But why Lara, why did you perform witchcraft for the baby, so much bloodshed," she cried. "I didn't teach you this ritual."

"I know, Gomez did," he smiled arrogantly. "But why are you shocked? I mean, I did it all to help you, to save the child, going against Valerie, I tried to save the bringer of *Hara*, as you wanted." He seemed confused by his mother's angry face.

What? Maurice Hector performed a blood ritual to save a demon's child? He created Lara. He forced down that shadow in her body so that she could commit all the killings on his behalf, as Shaman said. Was he insane?

"I could have saved her without it." She snapped, "These are demonic powers, Maurice. You know what happens when angels play with demons."

"*Si ingerii au demonii lor,*" he sang. "Even angels have their demons, Mother, how did you forget that?" He tried to snatch the *Wandering Star*, but Leticia was swift. She created a lightning shield which almost burnt his hand.

"Maverick loved a demon. That's why we all are here, so why would performing a demonic ritual harm me? Instead, it'll help me complete the prophecy," a wicked smile rose from Maurice's lips.

"And he has suffered much for loving a demon," She spat. "*Even angels have their demons,* but remember angels are not demons, those angels who use demonic powers are no more angels, and you, son, you are no more angelic blood," she emphasised on the last word, wiping off the smile from Maurice's face. "Why, son?" She shook her head in disbelief, ashamed of him.

"Because I wanted to prove to him that I am the *moonchild.* I and only I can control *Yamendo*, then finally he would come and meet me," his eyes were red, glistening with angry tears.

"You did all this to call *Maverick*? To prove to him that you are his *moonchild*?" She shook his head. "Who put that in your mind? Who said he is your father? You are a Hector, remember?"

"I know you and Father forged me out of the *Wandering Star*," his eyes narrowed. "I know Maverick came in your dream and handed you *the Wandering Star*, and that's how I could perform this ritual. I am part of *Livana*—I am the *moonchild*, and I have *the Wandering Star*. I opened the gate, and now I will control *Yamendo*." He opened his hands wide, deluding himself as an almighty.

Fuck!

"We didn't forge you," Leticia shook her head. "Moonchild won't be forged, she'll be born. She'll be part Cosmic, part human, and *Hara* would be her key." She whispered. "And *Maverick* gave this star to me because I'll be the seer to *moonchild* so that I could help *Hara* with its powers." She crooned. "I am sorry, son, but you're not *the moonchild*."

"What are you saying?" He was taken aback. "Then how did I open the gateway?"

"You didn't, you just performed the ritual, and her presence completed it." She shook her head in defeat.

"But—" he seemed confused.

"No, but this is not the time. Go to Dorcas, she'll fill you in," she pushed him, but he didn't budge. Instead, he fell to his knees. Devastated.

Dorcas? As in Dr. Dorcas?

Before my mind could grasp it, the floor under us started cracking up. Leticia created a magical portal beneath her son, and he fell into it.

I whimpered.

The worst fear of my life was here. *Yamendo was here*. I could feel it.

Only Leticia, baby, Paloma, and I were left in the room.

"Get up, Paloma," Leticia, now crying, carrying the baby in one hand, the velvet pouch wrapped around her, with the other, she was trying to move Paloma away from the crack.

The ground was splitting, like a gateway was opening.

"HELP HER," begged Leticia, not to anyone but me. My eyes went wide in shock. I turned around, was there someone behind me she was talking to, but there was no one.

ME?

She was looking directly at me, in my eyes. That moment, in that exact moment, I knew what to do. I immediately took the baby from her hands. I could touch her now.

"Take her, save them…save *Hara,* our only salvation," she told me as she pushed Paloma on me. Her eyes mirrored mine. There was terror but still filled with hope. "This is my destiny," she whispered, looking at me like I was some messiah. The ground blasted open with thunder, making us flinch. "And I fulfilled it."

She bowed in front of me as tears rolled down her eyes. A small smile rose her lips as she sprang into the crack in the floor, sealing the gateway with her, shining brightly like a star.

I choked, but the baby started wailing at the top of her lungs. I looked down at the baby—she was in my arms. I was really handling a baby, touching it and feeling her warmth. She had winter grey eyes, so familiar. I could feel her small heart thumping as I tucked her around me.

I looked at her sweet face and took her mother's hand, drenched in blood.

"SHIFT," I whispered.

Before that, I remember everything had gone dark. Mist and ashes surmounted us like night. Through the crack, large red eyes crawled towards me in the form of smoke. Big scarlet eyes filled with anger. She was not a woman. She was a shadow. Leticia was trying to wrap a leash of lightning around her, pulling her down the crack. But this woman was different. She had a big face, with large, brown and sharp antlers on her head. And then she opened her mouth and spat out darkness towards me. I felt piercing pain on my face.

And everything went dark.

She was SHADOW QUEEN—THE FORSAKEN—*YAMENDO.*

Chapter 5

The Escape

My eyes flashed open, realising I was panting while my heart thumped loudly. The shower was still running, and I was drenched, unaware of it, lost in my trance.

I looked for Paloma and her baby everywhere. Leticia told me I had to save them, but I was alone in my bathroom, still stuck in that weird trance as my hands were empty. All I could see was the water droplets surrendering themselves, dousing my body. What was that? Was that a dream or trance, but it felt so real! I could see all of them, in fact, I held that baby. *How come that's even possible?*

She was there, Leticia, the first queen of Murkwood, she was a fucking-real-walking-star, a seer to *moonchild* she called herself. She died saving that baby, that cursed child.

Who was that cursed child? Where did she go?

Her words—*Save Hara, our only salvation*, were ringing in my ears. What was that supposed to mean, who was *Hara*? And how would it save us, the Shadow Walkers? Where did all those Shadow Walkers go? How did they make portals? Where did they get that ring? Do they still live? Are there more Shadow Walkers like me, like J.P.P.?

The Wandering Star! There was the fucking *Wandering Star* in the dream, the same purple orb I see in my anxiety dream.

What was happening? What does it have to do with me? I had so many questions throbbing inside my head.

Leticia was a star, Maurice was a Shadow Walker, but Noni and Mom didn't know about any of this. Of course, they didn't, or else why would my mother force me to tame my powers, to hide me from everyone?

Was my grappy aware of this? Perhaps, the fire in the old mansion was connected to it. God! This was so confusing.

I closed my eyes for a while. The dark smoke with antlers and fierce scarlet eyes flashed past me. Even in hot water, that image made goosebumps rise on my body.

Yamendo! Did I actually see her? My brain was pounding harshly against my skull. I groaned, leaning back at the enclosure.

Suddenly my shower enclosure opened, and I keeled back. My stomach hollowed as I tried to save myself, but then without any mercy, I hit the floor.

"OUCH!"

"Geez, Lizzy, what happened?" Clara's face came into view, she stood just above my face, upside down, while I was lying on the floor, naked.

"I was taking a shower, and you happened," I growled, sitting up, trying to hide my boobs with one hand, and failing completely while rubbing the back of my head with the other. "Get me my robe,"

"Don't be so modest. It's not the first time I've seen you naked," Clara rolled her amber eyes like it wasn't a big deal to barge into someone else's bathroom while they were showering. Her strawberry-pink hair falls to the side of her face, framing it perfectly like she had just gotten them straightened. She wore a plaited skirt with a cami top and mesh jacket, revealing her long legs. I was so envious of her perfect slender figure, like Adriana Lima, but of course, it was a good kind of envy.

"What are you doing here?" I asked, standing up.

"I've been calling you since I landed, but you weren't answering. So, I decided to drop by, I mean, I can now, right, as your m–" she cleared her throat, handing me my blue plush robe. "Anyways, I was waiting for you in your room when I heard you scream."

"Oh! Now I am the one to blame?" I snapped, securing the robe with a knot, avoiding the subject of my screaming. "Everyone was calling you, but *you* were out of reach."

"I am sorry, grams lives in the middle of nowhere, she's a Nirvana fan. So, no signal." She cringed her nose, as I walked past her into my walk-in closet. "Are you angry with me?" she asked, worrying her lips.

"It's been a whole day, the most challenging day of my life!" My hands straightaway went to the stash in my wardrobe, which I only wear when my mother isn't home. Guilt lodged in my throat. Now, I never had to hide these clothes. A whimper passed through my body at the realisation.

"I am sorry, baby, I missed you too," she wrapped her arms around me from behind, hugging me tightly. "I hate myself for not being there with you," her voice went heavy, on the verge of crying. Finally, she was here, the one person I wanted by my side. I relaxed in her embrace and let my tears fall.

Clara Parsons was my girl, the one girl that I always hung out with, who called me bitch or slut in each sentence without making me angry. She's crazy, and I am crazy with her. She's my lifetime therapist who listens to my sorrow and stories without any complaints and tries to give me the best advice whether I heed it or not. We just love each other in any condition.

We stood there, I don't know for how long, but she let me cry till the hysteria went by, holding onto me.

"I am sorry, I tried to hurry as soon as Kayden called. He even arranged the private jet, but it took me hours due to the weather," she said in a guilt-stricken voice. "My flight landed just a few hours back, Kayden said you fainted," she examined me, her always enthusiastic eyes were all sad and worried.

Obviously, everyone knew I fainted, I did that in front of the whole media. This reminds me of the strong hands and the whiff of the oceans that saved me from hitting the concrete. They were oddly homely. I shook my head as I let go of her embrace, leaning further into my secret stash, fetching out my tonic to suppress my abilities.

I was tired of shifting, I needed some rest from this glitch, but today it felt something more than a glitch, but still, my head was throbbing, desperate for a peace out.

"Were you hurt? Did something happen after that? What are you doing?" she kept bombarding me with questions when I finally found the panacea for my glitch.

I fetched out the bottle of Chateau and pressed it on my lips. The sweet taste of cherry hit my tongue, I relaxed. The wine burned my throat, leaving a tint of resin and leather in its wake.

"OMG! You shifted." She gasped loudly as her eyes darted between the bottle of red wine and me. Yes, she knows my secret, apart from my mother, only she knew, figured it out herself.

When I was eleven, I caught Homer with some other girl at the Ruins, it was our secret place, but he took another girl there. I was crying in the washroom when I had a shifting trance. She caught me crying. Being a stranger, she held me and pumped me up. That's how our friendship began, and by the freshman year, we became BFFs.

Then one day, I was using my school locker, and she fetched out the journal by J.P.P., having no heed to give me privacy and read it. "Is this where you go when you vanish?" she gasped.

"You know?" I asked her, dumbfounded.

"Obviously, Lizzy," she rolled her eyes. "Have you heard some of your excuses? I went under the desk to pick up my pen," she mimicked me. "Oh, Clara! I just lag behind, tying my laces like I haven't seen you vanishing into thin air," she shook her head. "I got a cramp in my leg, so I sank," she laughed. "I always knew you were a weirdo."

That's when we became inseparable, and I let her borrow that journal.

"Yes, I did," I sighed, turning to face her, taking one more sip. "Not once but seven times, seven fucking times," another sip. "I have been glitching the whole morning."

"I knew it," she whispered. "You got to tell me everything about it, but not now," she walked past me to choose clothes and tossed them at me. "Your dad is downstairs, making a scene, fighting your grandmother, telling her you're better off in Caribasca."

"What?" I choked on the last sip I took. "Is he insane? Why would I leave my home to live with some stranger? He's practically a stranger to me, I don't even know him." I secured my bottle back inside, quickly wearing my clothes. Mom was pregnant with me when she found my dad was cheating on her, so she divorced him, and after my birth, we came to live with her parents. I had seen him only once when he married CeCe, the girl he cheated on Mom with, he wanted me to be his ring bearer. I mean, WTF! I wasn't his dog, but Noni made me go, and that was the first time I saw Caribasca. It was a busy city with high life and high crimes, not my type.

"Since you've pointed it out about someone else behind the wheels, he's determined that someone is after your inheritance. He practically rammed Kayden, thinking he was your boyfriend," she scoffed.

"Kayden—my boyfriend? But why?" I scooped my wet hair in a bun with a claw clip as I had no time to comb it. I hurriedly wore Bryelle 85 Jimmy Choo block-heeled ankle boots, though they had four-inch heels, they never held me down when it came to running. I took out as much cash, my credit card, and my penknife, stuffing everything down the pocket of my denim shorts.

She shrugged, observing my every action but not uttering a word. She knows I keep a knife with me all the time but never uttered a word.

"Let's go," I leapt to the window but was jerked back.

"Where are you going?" Clara pulled me from my top.

"Out, with you, isn't why you came? To help me escape?" I frowned at her, arranging my top.

"I did, but through the window?" Her eyes widened. "It's been raining heavily, what if we slip?"

"We won't," I ground out. "How else do you want to get out in this curfew?" I held the branch of the tree, stepping on another. Sometimes I thought this tree was here because nature also knew I'd be sneaking out a lot. This was not the first time I was sneaking out. I had done this a lot during my house arrests, becoming a champion by now.

I got down swiftly.

"Come," I called, but she stood on the windowsill, chewing her lower lip.

"No way, I am going to catch you outside," she shrieked. "My car is on the front lawn."

"But—"

"I'll manage," she gave me a flying kiss before darting back into the room. I rolled my eyes as I dashed across the side lawn, leaping to climb the iron fence and straight away sprang out smoothly. I was trained to climb the walls, and fences were the easiest.

I didn't look behind as I rushed down the road, waiting for Clara to get her Volvo.

It took her ten minutes to dodge Noni and get to her car when I saw another car propelling towards Hector Mansion, I hid behind the tree. It was Dr. Dorcas's car, Clara's neighbour at Sea-Witch Valley. She was single and only in her early thirties, but she adopted Neil Datye at a very young age, even though she had Crew Rai Denali, her nephew whose parents died in a car crash, to care for. She was a very good psychiatrist, I had been to her too many times, and Mom visited her regularly, but never saw her at my place before.

Before Dorcas could figure, Clara drove out, almost crashing into the mermaid fountain. I had to hold my mouth to stop myself from screaming as she scrunched the bunch of tulips. *Hannah's going to kill her.* She was a terrible driver, too distracted and driving made her edgy.

"Move," I opened the door of the driver's seat as she made it outside without trampling anything else.

"No way, you are drunk," she shook her head, her hands tightened around the steering wheel.

"I am a better driver than you, even drunk," I scoffed, pushing her.

"Fine," she swung to the other side and slammed her dashboard twice. "Go-go before Robin catches us."

"You ran into Robin?" I gasped, hitting the gas. "He'll kill me," I shook my head, Robin thinks of himself as my bodyguard.

"What was Dr. Dorcas doing at your place?" she asked me, securing herself with the belt.

I shrugged, things were changing. When Mom was there, nobody was allowed in the Hector mansion, mostly because of me, and only one day had passed, and it was filled with people, and most importantly, my dad, the last person she ever wanted to see. But right now, I didn't want to think about him. I opened the windows, letting the cool breeze hit my face, giving me a sense of freedom.

Soon, we were driving off the mountain road through the forest road that led to the Northern Circle. We had to dodge main routes to escape the patrolling, but Murkwood wasn't that of a big town. But we had an urban population of around 12000. It sat on the shores of the South Island's Lake Qualia, with a river stream arising from the Kwalien mountains. The range covered the North and West area of the town, with few floating isles and Sea-Witch Valley, whereas the East part was covered with dense forest, having a Red Pearl Glen in the middle, with a natural hot spring. Most of the population lived in the centre of the town, but we were heading towards the pier.

The pier was the heart of Murkwood, the liveliest place where everyone goes to have fun, escape their daily problems, and have a breath of relief.

I was narrating my trance to Clara.

"Are you sure it wasn't some movie?" She frowned as I parked the car behind the parking area, between the trees. "Because I think I've watched or heard something similar somewhere before."

"You think there is some horror movie featuring *Yamendo*, Leticia, Maurice Hector, and the *Wandering Star*?" I arched an eyebrow.

She shivered visibly.

"Was *Yamendo*…was she…scary?"

"She was the scariest thing I've ever seen, more frightening than the movie—Drag Me to Hell."

She knocked my shoulder. "Don't you dare mention that movie, I had to sleep with Kayden in a sleeping bag for a whole week, which was not so helping, you know how he is about someone sleeping in his bed."

I rolled my eyes, she's scared of horror movies, anything that's in the dark. I would never comprehend how she accepted my truth so easily.

"Sorry," I clicked my tongue, not so sorry myself, as I stepped out of the car.

It was a silent night as I examined the empty pier, only the mesh of star lights blinking over the shops, unlike most days when there's all hustle, people have fun with friends, go fishing, and some play the guitar near the crescent moon fountain, where kids dance to the dancing water and lights. While adults enjoy the street food as well as loud music barging out of the nightclub, but today my cheerful town Murkwood seemed to be dead, just like Mom. Only cops were patrolling the area.

The night was chilled for July. A sharp wind was gushing and growing from the sea, sending a shiver down my spine. I wore a powder blue square neck crop top, highlighting my cleavage with denim shorts, which were a bit skimpy for weather like today.

"You know legends state that the weather in Murkwood changes according to the emotions of the Hectors," Nathan remarked, making me flinch. That was when I noticed Homer's car parked two trees far from ours.

"Seriously, Nathan, tell me the truth, are you an immortal wandering in these lands from before the times?" I teased half-heartedly. He was into history and wanted to develop a game where people could learn about legends and myths while playing.

"Maybe I was the one who built this all," he winked, sauntering towards me, then his eyes softened as he read me. "Things will get fine when you feel fine," he added, placing an arm around my shoulders, enveloping me in his warmth.

"You really think it's the right time for small talk, fatty?" Homer tugged me into walking.

"Homer, behave," I grumbled while Nathan's eyes fell, and blood rushed his cheeks.

"Just stating the obvious, now shush," he rolled his eyes, while I turned back to look at Nathan, mouthing sorry, but he gave me a weak smile. Clara tucked her arm into the crook of his elbow and tugged him after us, whispering profanities.

We sneaked from the back lane, where these shopkeepers keep their trash, it's the dirtiest lane I had ever encountered. There were garbage bags all over the street, with trash spilled over. They should call it Rat Street, as all I could find were rats and cats eating out of trash cans.

"Ewww! Why are we going from the trash lane?" I cried out of disgust, barfing on the pungent smell. It was tough for me to walk down this street.

"Because the Queen just died, and we kidnapped the princess," Homer smirked darkly.

"Don't call me that," I snapped. He knew how much I hated being called princess, and he doesn't do that much, but today, things were different.

I was the poor princess that fainted due to the shock of her mother's death—that's what they were flashing on the news. He rolled his eyes at me without any further explanation, so I turned to Nathan. For a change, he agreed to Homer's bullshit.

Homer was still holding my hand and was dragging me to the back of Leonard's café, with Clara on my heels, shooting daggers at me for letting Homer hold my hand like this. She called me naïve for letting him play with my feelings, but I didn't have the guts to say no to him.

Suddenly, we halted outside a yellow door. He knocked on the door, two knocks, then one. *Was it a code?*

Soon the gate flung open, and a blonde bitch attacked Homer, sucking his life out of his lips.

Chapter 6
The blonde bitch

Homer left my hand to hold Sophie as I cringed at sight, feeling a piercing pain watching them make out.

"What the fuck is she doing here?" I hissed at Clara, my hands turning into clenched fists.

"She helped us find a place for our secret meeting," Clara winced, feeling guilty. "As our houses were a total no-go."

"Out of all the people in this world, you found *Sophie* to help us?"

"I asked for her." Out of all the odds, Nathan was the person who answered—*Nathan!* My Huggy-bear.

Oh god! The vein in my head was thumping hard, and I wanted to smash their faces till blood oozed out of their noses.

I grimaced at Nathan angrily while Homer was still eating Sophie's face. He seemed sorry, adjusting his specs as he stepped forward, pushing them inside. "Guys! Know your surroundings."

Sophie jumped, wiping her lower lip with the tip of her thumb.

"Oh, Lizzy!" she breathed.

I narrowed my eyes as she acted like she had just comprehended my presence.

"I am so sorry to hear about your loss," she hugged me, but I didn't hug her back. I knew she was pretending, and it was her fake voice. I grimaced as if she had given me herpes.

She noticed it as her eyes narrowed as if thinking—*supercilious, arrogant bitch,* but to be frank, I didn't care.

She wasn't even that good-looking. Ok, she was busty, but so was I, but unlike me, she goes bra-less, I didn't know why. Even now, she was wearing a grey romper with a deep V-neck, must have taped her boobs up because they still looked firm and locked in place. She was a fragile bimbo. I never understood what Homer saw in her.

Even though I turned into a beautiful girl and caught many gazes, he never asked me out. Actually, nobody asked me out. They treated me like I was wearing a purity ring, which confused me.

But Nathan explained—

"Locker room talks, somebody claimed you."

"What do you mean?" I asked, confused.

"I heard jocks play this sick game in which they could claim some girl as their, and none of their friends would hit on her," Clara explained.

I scowled, thinking about who could have put their stake on me and still aren't asking me out.

"You got claimed too?" I arched my eyebrow.

"With Kayden on the team," she scoffed. "I don't think someone wants to get on his darkside." But she had already lost her virginity to her current boyfriend, Zach, she had him, even though he was a jerk, and things weren't going as smoothly as they should.

"That's just jocks, what about other guys?" I raised my concern.

"It depends on that guy's social circle. If he's famous or something, he could extend the stake in front of others, too."

Was it Homer? I bit my lips thinking about it, he's got a big social circle, and mostly everyone knew him.

"Then why isn't he asking me out?" I scowled, stomping my feet.

"No offense, but have you seen your mother?" Nathan adjusted his specs. "I mean, she is damn beautiful but scary, and your grandmother is scarier, but your bodyguard is the scariest. Even a glare from that brooding man made guys pee in their pants. Moreover, you guys fucking own Murkwood. Nobody wants to attract their wrath by asking you out because if anything happens, he'll be buried six-feet under in some corner of the town." Even though I wanted to date someone and was angry with whoever claimed me, I sympathised with the guy because if my Mom ever found out I was dating, she'll rip him into ribbons just by her nails.

I knew that day—I would die a virgin.

"I asked Craig to give me the café's keys. You know Leonard's son, they live next door. He has a huge crush on me," Sophie was showing off as we entered Leonard's café. "Poor little boy always does whatever I tell him to do, he just—"

"Lizzy, sit here," Clara cut her off, giving me a chair in a small room with dim lights. It was the kitchen, and five of us crowded it. The room was full of cinnamon and coffee, sending a soothing sensation down my throat.

"This seems fine," she added, sitting on a chair beside me. "This place is safe, nobody can hear us, and we can have our group meeting here. First, Nathan, hand me the box." She splayed her hand before him as he handed her a box from his backpack. As soon as I saw that blue box, I knew she had baked cookies for me, and when she opened it, my stomach grumbled just by the waft.

"I directly came to your place, so Kayden texted me that he's sending these with Nathan," she shoved the whole box in my lap. A smile spread my face finding my favorite, freshly-baked Choco-chip cookies inside the box.

"Yeah! He came to my house, even Neil, in this curfew, they handed me the box," Nathan added excitedly as his apple cheeks got crimson and his specs did nothing to hide the glint in those moss-green eyes.

"Because Kayden did them." Clara gleamed with pride. "Sorry if they don't taste as good as mine." She winked.

Clara was never a good cook, but she had a fantastic fashion sense, she even had an influencer page, which was growing daily.

Nodding, I took one. They were still warm.

"He says sorry," Clara added, an odd expression on her face like she wanted me to believe her. *Like Kayden can say that…that too to me!* I rolled my eyes.

"Kayden Parsons bakes? Aww, he's so cute. This is like the latest hot news," Sophie said, excitedly. "Give me one, I'll post it on MyBook. All the girls are gonna get so J," she was about to pick one, but Clara swatted her hand away.

"These are for Lizzy, he made this batch just for her," she eyed her angrily. I think she lied, as Kayden would never do that for me. Perhaps she just wanted to insult Sophie. *Bro code.*

"I hope he hadn't poisoned them." Homer scoffed, scooping Sophie from her waist and pulling her into his lap. Kayden was his archenemy as he had always created trouble for him, and since he became a student council member, Homer's life had become hell. And being a prankster didn't help his case, ended up with multiple detentions. One time, Kayden reported him just because he was lying on the ground, with his head on my lap, for PDA, a hypocritical move because he himself keeps on making-out in front of the whole school, and nobody complained because he's the King.

His terrifyingly beautiful face flashed before me, how his molten hazel eyes watched me while some girl was humping his leg. Even when she was kissing his throat, his gaze never faltered.

My stomach churned.

Stop thinking about him, Lizzy. I mentally flicked myself.

Clara and Homer were bickering over Kayden. She was too protective of her brothers. She had one elder brother Jason Parsons, who was working with the military far away near Greenland.

Ignoring them, I took a bite, and they melted in my mouth. Actually, they were accurately baked. "Mmm, not as good as yours, but still mouthwatering," I told her, stuffing my mouth with more. I am not going to share them with anybody. "Tell him thanks."

"He would appreciate that," she softly held my other hand, smiling at me, ignoring Homer's frown.

"Ok guys, come to the point," Nathan squared his shoulders towards me. "Lizzy, I talked to Bert, the truck driver's son, and he claims a different story."

"Oh, come on, he was high and hallucinating," Homer turned his gaze to Nathan, scoffing. I eyed him curiously, so he explained. "Truck driver claims he saw a ghost and got distracted, and that's how the accident occurred. What an asshole!"

"Not a ghost, but someone jumped out of the car, rolled in the middle of the road, and to save him, he got disbalanced, hitting her car," Nathan rectified. "That's why they couldn't find any other body in the debris."

"Perhaps someone was trying to rob her, that's why her necklace and phone are missing, and it fit well—why we couldn't see anyone behind the wheel," I backed Nathan. "Moreover, she would never drive over the limit, and have you noticed how fast the car was going? It must be above 200 mph."

"But in the video, nobody was there. We all saw it, the road was clear. He is making it all up," Homer argued, his jaw tensed.

"Video can be tampered," Nathan pressed on it.

"Quit bullshitting," Homer spat. "C'mon, bro! You cannot believe in this ghost shit," Homer eyed me, looking for some assertion.

BRO?

Are you fucking kidding me?

Was he bro-zoning me now just because his girlfriend was sitting on his lap?

My face got red. *Don't kill him! Don't kill him!* I chanted, pretending to be deaf, ignoring his comment.

"No baby, ghosts are real," Sophie cupped Homer's face. "And cameras don't capture them."

I scowled at Nathan, and he immediately looked up at the ceiling, avoiding my glare.

"Honey! We don't need ghosts, humans themselves are scary monsters." Homer smirked, lifting her legs to place them on his thighs. He was now practically cradling her, his hands traced her romper up while he nuzzled into the crook of her neck. My heart lurched from inside, bile rising in my throat.

I turned my face. It seemed like a personal hell. My eyes burned as Clara shifted towards me, her hand snaking around my waist as I sunk to her side.

"Guys, focus," Nathan scowled at Homer, but when he didn't listen. Remorsefully, he turned to me. "It could be a glitch, or the person who was robbing your Mom intentionally avoided the camera," Nathan mused. "He must be from Murkwood to know all the cameras' positions."

"But why would he jump out of the car? Why take only the necklace and phone but not her purse," Clara shook her head. "I don't think it's the case of robbery but some defect in the car."

"If there was a defect, then Julia must have comprehended, as it was her car. Moreover, if the driver knew and had time to jump, why didn't she? What stopped her?" Homer shook his head. "This story has so many loopholes, it's definitely cooked up."

"I still think it's a ghost, or she was possessed. I've seen it in the movies. Ghosts make you do stuff like eating insects and moving things with minds," Sophie suggested keenly, sending her imagination wild.

"Everyone is entitled to be stupid, but you abuse your privileges, you know?" I snapped. Clara chuckled at my outburst, and the look on Sophie's face gave me immense satisfaction, she had gone red with embarrassment.

"At least, I have some privilege. What do you have?" she asked curtly.

"Really? She practically owns the whole town, and after her mother, she'll be the queen within three months as soon as she is eighteen." Clara scoffed, but that statement slid away as we were busy in an eye contest because Sophie just took Homer's hand and glided it further in her romper, making me jealous.

She was a bitch, she knew how I felt for him, how much he meant to me instead of the title of princess, and she always showed off that *she* had him, not me. Whenever I made plans, she made excuses so that Homer won't hang out with me. Yeah, I know they were dating, but excuse me, he had other friends too. She was like—give me all your time—don't leave me, I get scared—please drop me home—please do homework with me—please pick me up from home. For the last five months, she'd been glued to him.

"Why is she even here?" I snapped my head towards Nathan, making him flinch.

"She was the last family your mother had seen, I thought she would know something that we don't." He confessed.

"Yeah, don't forget she is the daughter of Bill Muller, manager of the museum," Homer added proudly. My blood boiled every time he tried to defend her.

"*Was* a manager," I corrected him, with a sharp voice, tilting my head. "No museum, no manager," I smirked, making Sophie fume. *Good!*

The Mullers lived down Cambridge Street, down Highway 59. Bill Muller was a small round man with little white hair on his head, a huge belly bulging out and a fat nose. He tried to be funny, but he wasn't. He had two children, Colton and Sophie, and a wife who worked at a salon.

"Lizzy, I think we should listen to her," Clara eyed me, telling me to stay calm.

"Fine, out with your story, tell us what you know," I waved my hand at her, wanting to listen to what she knew about my Mom's last day. "After that, you can just return to your home planet."

She raised her eyebrows, frowning. "You know, I don't wanna help you either. I am not here to indulge in your princess's tantrums. Homer is making me do this!" She folded her hands in front of her stomach, lifting her chest, standing up, trying to be intimidating.

Yeah, like that could scare me.

"Yes, because you are the sweetest," said Homer, kissing her hand and pulling her back on his thigh. I rolled my eyes. *So much sugar, why doesn't he just open a sugar mill?*

Sophie smiled at Homer. "Only for you, my sugarplum," she gave him an Eskimo kiss. *Ewww! I would have barfed on their face.* "Your mom was nosing into the museum's business, trying to get my father fired by blaming things on him. She called this upon her. That's what karma does, *bitch*!" she snapped. The hatred was mutual.

"It takes one to know one," I smirked. It enraged her. Her fist curled up as she started screaming.

"Your mom was framing my father," she trembled in anger. That's what I wanted. *Enraged people always spill the truth—I heard that in my mother's voice.* "She wanted to see the camera feed of the night of the breach at the museum, and my father showed her, but she was blaming him for splicing the camera. She went silent when my father asked whether she knew something about it. Even I could make out that she was hiding something. She confessed she had no proof, only that footage could help her find the truth, but there was nothing in that footage."

"After dinner, they went out, and I sneaked out in the bush to listen to them. They were arguing about something that had happened long back. She was blaming my father for everything that was happening."

"It's then she checked her phone and went to the washroom, and as soon as she came out, I didn't know what got into her, she started shouting, '*I know what you're up to, Muller, I will stop it, I'll never let you accomplish this stupid plan of yours.*' And then she rushed out, leaving us appalled. It took us a few minutes to gather our senses and process what happened, and then soon after, the fire broke in the museum."

"She screamed at your dad. Why?" asked Clara.

"I don't know, but my mom says when a person is nearing death, they lose their mind, face emotional changes, get bipolar—one second you feel fine, another second anxiety, fear, anger, sadness, guilt, loss, takes over you." Sophie completed.

"I face this emotional distress every time I am PMS-ing," I said curtly, making Homer slightly flinch.

"Maybe it's in your blood, the freaks of the Hill Road." She shrugged her shoulders.

"Sophie, shut up," Clara shouted before I could. "We are here working out on things, please, Homer," she eyed him like *make your bitch quiet, or I'll kill her*, as he tightened his hand around Sophie's waist.

"This is not some logical explanation of your mother's change in behaviour," Nathan said. "Perhaps she found some proof."

"A footage to prove what happened on the day of the breach," I arched my eyebrow. "And she shouted at Bill because she had proof against him. That's why he killed her."

Clara gasped.

"And became the prime suspect in the murder of the Queen of Murkwood? Are you fucking kidding me?" Sophie's lip curled. "Moreover, my father was with us when your mother got caught up in the accident."

"He could have hired somebody to do that. After all, she shouted at your father, he might have done it to wipe off the evidence, whatever she got against him, that's why her phone is missing." Clara concluded.

We gave Sophie solemn looks, including Homer.

"My father isn't some mob boss or a bigshot like you guys. We don't own big money to hire some snipers. If your mother found the footage against my dad, then why not call the cops at our house? Why'd she leave if she had proof? She's the leading lady, why would my father kill her, that too when everyone knew she was at our place? Why would he want to destroy his survival?" Sophie was practically shivering with rage.

"You tell us, why didn't he tell the media about what happened at your house, about her outburst?" asked Clara.

"Because her grandma asked him not to," Sophie pointed at me. "Alice Hector zipped his lips."

A shock went through my body, making me go very still.

"Why?" I choked.

"Because she's breathing down everybody's neck," Sophie groaned, holding her head. "Even Mayor is part of this and wants things out of media," she called on Clara. "You guys practically control everything around the town. Do you even think my father could have gotten out of your grandmother's bound?" She looked at me with red eyes. She knew her father was innocent, she knew someday this story would be out and people would suspect Bill. She wanted this story as much out as I wanted, *she wanted to prove his innocence.* "If my father had planned something like this, you think your grandmother would let him live?"

Of course not. She would have wiped him and his family.

"Our elders know more to this story than we know, and it's related to the day of the breach at the museum," Nathan concluded.

"What about the guard—Arthur? What does he have to say about both the days?" I asked, utterly confused. They were saying nothing was stolen, even my mom said it was some animal that broke into the museum, then why look for footage? Why blame it was spliced?

"He went on a sabbatical, nobody was guarding the museum since ten days. His alibi checked; everyone has an alibi," Homer nodded sincerely.

"If everybody's got a clean chit, then who was driving that day, a ghost?" I snapped.

"Exactly," Sophie crossed her arms around her midsection, affirmative. Her eyes fixed on me like she really wanted me to acknowledge it.

"Oh, fuck off," I threw my hand in the air, getting agitated.

Chapter 7

The Cave

I stormed out of Leonard's café, eyeing the cops, hiding in the shadows. I was good at sneaking, as I had been doing it since I was a kid.

Sophie locked the doors while Homer kissed her neck, squeezing her bums. He said something in her ear, which made her giggle, and then she turned around and threw herself on Homer, kissing him back.

"Get a room, guys," Clara pushed them aside, following me.

"What's the use, she'll post that online, too," Nathan scoffed, following me. "Her post got so many negative comments, some are saying she's pregnant, that's why she's marking her territory."

"OMG! Pregnant at eighteen. Like father like daughter," Clara laughed. Colton Muller, Sophie's half-brother, was born out of Bill's lovelock when he was just a teenager, and that girl died after giving him birth, must be a teenager too. Muller didn't know about him until the girl's family left Colton on his doorstep, that too on the day he married Sophie's mother. It was his marriage present. *Scandal!*

But he was not the reason I was on the brink of losing my cool, Sophie had made my suffering unbearable. I shouldn't have agreed to meet them, I was already deep into my grief and didn't need any cherry toppings or reality check of my cursed love life.

Homer is different with her, like a stranger. He even called me, *bro*. I mean, WTF! If he weren't my Iron Man, I would have shoved my knife into his throat and twisted it, like he does to me every time he kisses Sophie in front of me.

I beeped open the car. "I want to go to the museum," I told them, stepping into the driver's seat, snivelling angrily. "Now."

"Here we go again," Nathan rolled his eyes as he jumped into the co-seat. "Babe, don't lose your shit over that jerk."

"Yeah, he ain't worth it." Clara shook her head as she slid behind me. "You got to be home before Alice hunts us down."

"I don't care," I gritted between my teeth, smashing my hand on the wheel. "I want to investigate this driver that bloody rolled out of the moving car. What was he thinking of himself, Steve Carell?" I was seeing red. "He must have left some clues, I must look into it now. Because I know Noni won't tell me either, if they wanted to, I would have known it by now." I still remember how blood drained from Noni's face and how furious Mayor was when I told them someone else was there with Mom. They already knew, and I caught them. But why were they hiding the facts? Why was Noni hiding the reality of her own daughter's murder?

"But it's curfew out there," Clara's eyes widened in fear as she looked outside in the darkness. "No, we can try it out in daylight."

"Yeah, when everyone could see us there," I rolled my eyes. "It has to be tonight."

"No, Lizzy, you should be home, at least until they find the driver," she fidgeted, but I held the ground.

"Trust me, the museum would be the last place he'd be at, and if he'd be there, I'll be ready for him." I was high on fury and wanted to spend it out somewhere productive. "I am dropping you guys home, then I'll leave for the museum, borrowing your car." It wasn't a request.

"Please, Lizzy, he's a douchebag." She gave me a sympathising look, her hand came forward to hold my shoulder. "I don't know why you're hung up on him so much. He's not the one for you, believe me."

My head fell. But he was my Iron Man, the guy I asked to be my boyfriend, since then, I've taken him as my mate, the one who's born for me, just me. But she doesn't know about it, it was something intimate, private that I only wanted to keep between him and me.

I know I had no right to be angry with Sophie. She was his girlfriend. If he's happy with her, I should be happy for them. He wasn't mine, and being mates doesn't always mean lovers, sometimes two good friends could be mates and be happy with it.

But then why did it feel like he was betraying me?

"Exactly. He's cruel and dark at heart. We don't even like him. We just hang out with him because you're biased for him," Nathan cringed his nose. *Oh! Nathan, you don't know I've a spine-chilling darkside, only I could embrace his dark heart.*

Suddenly, we were interrupted by Homer. "Ok, guys, I am out of gas," he opened the door on our left, making Clara flinch. "So, who's dropping me?"

"Seriously, cheapskate, once in a while, get a full tank," Clara snapped furiously, her hand resting on her heart.

"Clara!" I eyed her. I know she was furious with him, but she couldn't stoop so low.

"It's no way he's getting into my car, I am not letting him, Lizzy," she eyed me back, her amber eyes filled with fury.

"Then I'll leave with him, you guys carry on," I reached for the door when she held my shoulder again.

"God! This bitch will never learn," Clara growled, Nathan shook his head, making me bite my lips. "Fine, get in, but we all are going to the museum. If you are up for it, only then can you sit with us," her chin jutted out.

"Sure, supernova, I will follow you till the end of the world," Homer's smile reached his eyes as he slid next to her, slipping his joint between his teeth.

"And I wish you get lost there, forever," Clara huffed, snatching that joint. "And no getting high in my car, my brothers will kill me." She threw his joint outside the window, scooping towards the corner, her hands wrapped around her midsection.

God! What did I get myself into?

"Highway 59 is blocked, you've got to take a shortcut from behind Mathew National Park," Clara told me the route, while *Dark Times* played in the background.

Soon we hit the road towards the Mile-O-City, crossing Mathew National Park. It was an abandoned amusement park, all rusty and covered in junk. The secret cave that led to the museum was behind the waterfall.

"But there could be poisonous snakes in that cave," Homer seemed a bit uncomfortable as he shifted towards Clara.

"Venomous," Nathan corrected him.

"What?" Homer asked, looking at Nathan like he had grown two heads.

"Venomous snake," he rolled his eyes at Homer. "If you bite it and you die, it's poisonous. However, if it bites you and you die, it's venomous."

"And what difference would it make?" Homer scoffed. "You'd still be dead."

Nathan grunted.

I interjected, "But it's guarded by that old guard. He's a gone head and always throws stones at the people trying to use the cave."

"Edward, yeah, he's insane. He was the gatekeeper of Mile-O-City, and after it shut down, he lost it and started guarding the cave, not letting anyone inside. Earlier, it was a hell-of-a-making-out spot," Homer laughed, tying his hair on the nape of his neck, looking hot. "Or I would have used it to hide my drugs."

"Seems like Edward knew your plans beforehand. That's why he's guarding caves against your kind of frat boys," Clara scoffed.

"What do you mean by my kind of frat boys?" He arched his eyebrow at her. "You date frat boys, my kind of boys only. Your Zach is a frat boy too."

"Keep him out of it, he is nothing like you," Clara grimaced her face. "He doesn't smoke joint all the time."

"Yeah, he just throws parties with naked girls and sniffs shit from their boobs," Homer snickered, making Clara flushed.

"You are lying," she jutted her chin out, pretending to be confident, but I knew she'd be grinding Zach about it afterwards.

"Ok, guys, we have to go by foot from here," I interrupted, parking the car on the side. I could hear the gush of the waterfall, the moon shone upon us between the myriads of stars. It was a beautiful night. If my world hadn't turned upside down, I'd be in my solarium, stargazing. "Moreover, we need to figure out a way to distract Edward, to enter the cave."

"Don't worry, he won't be there. It's a curfew," Nathan spoke, he seemed excited to see the cave finally. "You know, it is said to be the gateway to hell," he added as we neared the waterfall.

"Like you believe in these legends?" Homer scoffed. "Legends are made to scare people and keep them from destroying nature."

"Legends aren't just stories. They are facts that someone has experienced." Nathan persisted. "And FYI, legends were right about the caves behind the waterfall, after all."

"Tell me again, what the legend says exactly?" I insisted. I had heard Noni's version, but I wanted to know his version.

"Oh no!" Clara urged. "Don't you dare, this is already creepy," she was scared as we entered the Limestone Cave. It shone under the flashlights of our phones.

"Why? Are you scared?" teased Homer. "Will I get to hear your screams?"

"You wish," she must have rolled her eyes, but I was busy taking in the cave's beauty. It had a waxy glistening appearance with crystal-like straw drops hanging from the roof. There was a thrum in this cave, a foreign vibe. "You're the last person ever to hear me scream."

My eyes were transfixed on the drag of red on the limestone wall. It seemed like blood, fresh. I stepped towards it, examining it.

"Are you listening, Lizzy?" Nathan asked from behind.

"What?" I stepped away from it thinking it must be from some animal.

"So, the legend says, the pink tree above the waterfall—that tree is so strong that even the gush of water couldn't break it because it had fourteen roots going beneath the stones, creating a cave, and two of them were interlinked in such a way that it created a door to the other world. At night sometimes people see the light coming out of these caves, which means the door was opened. Some even heard voices of a girl crying, and the temperature here is way low."

"Yeah, because we are beneath a waterfall, and I thought you were the one with A grades," Homer scoffed, stating the obvious.

"But some people crossed over and never came back, that's why they sealed the cave," Nathan added, ignoring Homer's comment, his moss-green eyes were on me.

"Stop lying," Homer snapped. "We all know they closed Mile-O-City after a girl committed suicide."

"Suicide, who?" I asked, not knowing about this part.

"There was a girl…*Heather Reynolds,* I don't know much details, but they say she jumped into the waterfall and died," Homer answered. "After that, they sealed the area."

"What if people see her spirit in the cave, perhaps, she's the one who haunts it," Nathan looked around excitedly.

"Perhaps she is the ghost that killed Julia," Homer scoffed as my stomach twisted badly. "Dude, there can be many *perhaps,* as many as you want them to be. It's your choice which one you believe or create."

"Shut up and tell us where we have to go from here," Clara was getting anxious as we were in the middle of the cave, and we couldn't see any way out. It was getting dark as we got deeper. The vibe was getting stronger, like it held energy, some pull, and it was getting substantial with each step, making my hair stand.

"It's here, behind this rock," Nathan said, examining the route. "It has to be," whispering, his brows furrowed.

"It is here, or it has to be?" I asked him again, looking at his face with a flashlight.

He immediately shielded his eyes with his hand. "I mean, this stone was a little bit bigger last time."

"Yeah, as if the guard fucked it down," Homer snickered, taking the lead.

"You know, Nathan, my version of the legend is a bit different," I said while following Homer, who was helping Clara.

"Um-hmm, really?" he asked.

"Yeah, Noni told me the tree is a universal portal, and it charges up the cave, and when its energy is at peak, it takes you wherever you want to go."

I heard him gulp down hard.

"Lizzy, you making this up, right? Tell me you are making this up?" Clara was whimpering as she held Homer's hand tightly.

I bit my lip. "Yeah! Totally," I didn't want to scare her, so I lied.

Chapter 8
The Void

Despite the grief surmounting me, something in this Shadowland kept calling me.

It was dark, similar to our realm, but the only difference was that it was moonless and enclosed with mist and ashes, filled with a toxic smell creating an itch down my throat. The building I was staring at was a small building without any symmetry in a barren land with dead trees.

Three lopsided windows hung loose screws and were oddly placed on the building, like on the corners. Shadows and mist played tricks through them. Even through the mist, I could make out it was an old wooden dilapidated creepy house.

"Whose house is this?" somebody asked the same question that was clouding my mind, but this was not what I was worried about for now. My heart skipped a few beats to the voice that came from my right. Someone was there who could also witness these scary things apart from me.

I slightly craned my neck towards the voice, and to my utter surprise, Clara stood next to me, judging the house like I was, a few seconds ago.

She was here *in SHADOWLAND.*

"What the FUCK!" I squealed.

"What?" she asked, looking at me, tearing her eyes from the weird creepy house.

"Where are we?" came the voice from my left, this time, it was too difficult to turn back. I was frightened to my death when that voice fell into my ears.

No...No...No!

I slowly turned back to look at Homer, crying my heart out—*why? WHY?*

"Where the hell are we?" asked Nathan, who was standing with Homer, looking around while wiping ashes away from his specs. "What exactly is this place? Stupid Homer, where did you bring us? We were supposed to go to the museum. What is this?" He pushed Homer angrily.

"What the fuck, dude," Homer gasped, marching towards him furiously. "You took us to the cave. It brought us here. Now go and fetch my car keys, I can't find them anywhere." He pushed Nathan, making him stumble.

"How dare you?" Nathan was angry, and he swung his fist and clipped Homer's jaw.

I gasped.

"I am not your dog, you douche," Nathan's face was red, terrified, and angry at the same time. I'd never seen his violent side, it was as if this place was bringing out his darkside.

"Dude! Careful!" Homer bellowed. "What's wrong with you?" He wiped the blood from the corner of his lips and gazed down at his fingers in shock.

Shadowland. That's what's wrong with him, not just with him, but with all of us.

I wanted to say it out loud, but shock sank in—how could *humans*, mere humans, enter this place? The journal said only Shadow Walkers could do so, then how come they were here?

"What's wrong with me? What's wrong with you?" Nathan shouted. "You always try to bully me."

What the fuck was happening? How did we all end up here?

The only thing that could come out of me at that particular time was a SCREAM. With everything I had in me, with every single cell of my body, I screamed my heart out.

Scared, I fell to my knees, hiding my face between my knees, annoyed by myself. "What have you done, you stupid bitch!" I blabbered.

"What have I done—what have you done?" Clara looked at me in confusion.

"I was talking to myself, Clara," I turned to her, and soon as our eyes met, blood drained off her face.

"Is this S-Shadowland?" she asked. I think that was the first time I'd heard her stammering. A confident girl who handles a large crowd with a smile on her face, today, at this point, was stuttering, standing in front of me. "This can't be happening. How come *we*—humans crossed it? We'll die, the darkness will devour us." She shivered, thinking about what we'd read in the journal.

I nodded, holding my head as if it might fall. "How is this even possible?" I thought out loud. "I never brought anyone with me, but why today, why you guys?" That's when it hit me. "Something else has brought you here, not me," I concluded.

"You mean a void?" Clara asked anxiously, her eyes went wide.

"Void…Shadowland?" asked Homer. He looked at me in confusion. These words caught his attention, he stopped looking for his keys, which he didn't know must have turned into ashes.

Oh no! Oh no!

I never wanted this day to come, I knew he wouldn't be able to accept my reality. He shows he's headstrong, but he isn't. He would never buy anything unnatural. And now, if he gets to know that *I* was peculiar, someone who could walk in this stupid parallel universe, he'll walk away from me, terrified. And the last thing I wanted was for Homer to be frightened of me and leave me forever, drowning my hope of being with him someday in the ocean of fear.

"Not now, Homer," Clara snapped, she held my mouth between her fingers, a little too harsh, making me pout. "Look at me, we don't have time for him, we have to go back," she trembled visibly. Reading a bizarre journal and experiencing horror in real life were totally different things. And that difference was reflected in her voice.

"What the hell are you both talking about?" asked Homer. "What is Shadowland?" He looked back and forth, but none of us answered. "Don't you mess with me," he stepped towards me, his eyes wandering everywhere, and a hysterically nervous laugh slipped his lips. "I know all of you are bluffing. This is like your escape room gigs, right?"

I gave him a pitiful look.

"Maybe it's not a void, maybe it's you, your powers must have grown with you, and you never realised because you always shifted back." Clara tried to fill the gaps with all the gibberish coming into her mind.

"I don't know, all three of you?" I asked. "And that too, humans. It must have sucked a lot of energy from me, but I don't feel anything. I don't think it was my powers because it had never happened before, not in school, not with my mom, not with you, even though we were hugging when I shifted one time." I said, thinking about the time I shifted after a basketball match.

"You have powers, what kind of powers?" Homer cocked his eyebrows, biting his knuckles to suppress the laugh. *What's so funny about this?* I wanted to ask, but now was not the time. "C'mon, guys, now you are creating this up, stop trying to scare me. I am not scared, it's not working. You lose, let's go back."

"Shut up, Homer, stop making everything about yourself," Nathan snapped, his skeptic eyes on me, listening to us carefully, trying to contemplate.

"Everything *is* about me, don't you know?" Homer smirked at Nathan arrogantly. "Are you Jealous?" He was picking on Nathan, but I blocked them out. I needed to focus.

"I don't think my powers have grown, and they are not even powers, it's a stupid glitch," I said through clenched teeth. How could I bring someone when I couldn't even visit this place on my own will?

"Then how did a void get created?" Clara hissed, her fists clenched on her sides. "What's the difference?"

To my shock, it was Nathan who answered me. "The cave. Legends are true, it's a universal portal."

My heart which was thunderously beating against my chest till now, seized.

"It's not our world. Look at the creepy house," he pointed at the one we were standing in front of. "It's made up of ashes." His remark made me observe it closely, and he was right. "And it's not even touching the ground."

My eyes widened in anticipation, the house was hovering above the ground, at least two feet above, due to darkness and mist, it wasn't clear, but when I focused on it, the difference between the level of the ground and the creepy house was evident.

My hands started shivering as my dinner rose in my throat, but I swallowed it hard. "This house shouldn't even be here, this is where the museum blazed."

"You mean it's an illusion," Clara mused, and we both looked at each other like somebody killed our dog because we knew only *Yamendo* could create illusions in this world. She's the Queen of Shadowland—*she's real*, I just saw her a few hours ago.

"Enough, guys. Do you even hear yourself? This all sounds absurd." Homer frowned at Nathan, then back to me. "I am going back, I am not going to be a part of your stupid made-up stories or whatever the fuck you are manifesting." Homer turned around, stomping towards the cave.

"You know what, I never thought I'd say this, but I agree with Homer," Clara blinked rapidly. "Let's go back to the cave, maybe we'll find a way back home," she rushed after Homer, and Nathan swiftly joined her.

"It's not going to work," Nathan said, reaching the Limestone Cave while I followed them, formulating a plan. "None of the people who crossed ever came back, guys. I am telling you it's not possible."

"Shut up, Nathan," Clara pushed him in, our phone's flashlight was always on.

"This is insane, the legends aren't true, this isn't real," Homer shook his head.

"Homer, I know you don't have the brains for this, so keep low for a while," Clara sizzled. He flipped his middle finger in return.

"Should I tell you a place where you can shove it?" she snapped angrily, kicking Homer's ass as he snarled at her.

Soon we crossed the cave and were in the forest, surrounded by mist and covered in ashes.

"Told you it's not going to work. God! We all are doomed, shit." Nathan moaned. He sank to the ground hiding his head between his knees.

"It was my idea!" Clara whispered in horror as if something flashed in her eyes as she sank beside Nathan. "We shouldn't be here,

I shouldn't be here," she was petrified, rocking. "This shouldn't be happening," I wrapped my arms around them, somehow holding them together.

"Don't worry, guys, we'll get out of this mess, there has to be a way," I took Nathan's hand, asking him to get up. "C'mon, Nathan, let's try again, I will not stop until we all return. Get up." He didn't budge, so I bent down, levelling with him.

"What's the most important thing to do when your enemy gets you?" I asked Nathan. He was a gameoholic. "Tell me."

"Impale his territory," he shrugged, "focus on its weakness."

"Let's go with the latter, focus on what more you know about the legend," I gazed into his moss-green eyes, his brows furrowed as if focusing, I turned to Clara. "Concentrate on what we know about this land, what loophole we can find to escape it, what all we have read in the journal."

"Sophie was right, you all are freaks. I am done with you all," Homer threw his hand in the air, groaning loudly. "Enough with this legend bullshit, the cave can lead to other cities too. Maybe we are behind Kwalien mountains. Let me call someone, they'll drive us home."

Clara and I screamed. "*NO!*" but Homer had already dialled.

BOOM!

It was a sharp explosion, making Homer's hair fly, and his dark eyes flared at his phone, which caught flames and soon doused, turning into ashes. Only flashlights work, not even cameras or calls. Been there, done that.

"Geez, man," Homer threw it away, jerking his hand, shaking as if it burnt his skin. I quickly reached for his hand to observe the damage, my stomach churned, finding a black burnt mark.

His eyes were full of terror. "Homer, focus," warned Clara.

"What the fuck, guys," he backed off, snatching his hand away from me. "What is this, how-how, can it happen, w-what's going on?" His voice was trembling, now horrified.

Suddenly, thunder rolled above us, making all of them shriek, but I was stunned, this was new. Clara was hiding behind me, Nathan held my hand, and Homer jumped towards the cave as if ready to bolt. But my focus wasn't on them, it was on the lightning striking across the sky because it wasn't silver like starlight but blood red, and soon the clouds above us started changing colours, turning scarlet, as if ready to cry bloody tears.

"Holy shit!" Clara gaped, walking backwards. "We have to do something, I can't be here." She ran inside the cave, crossing it back towards the creepy house.

I ran after her, but the mist got dense, and thunder rolled again. This time, it was a roar sending chills down my body, making the hair stand in its wake. "Let's go back," I caught Clara's hand, she was shivering, tears rolled down her cheeks. My heart broke.

"How?" asked Homer.

"Just hold my hands," I told him, taking his hand, feeling guilty. "And trust me." Nathan held Homer's hand, and we made a circle, Homer's eyes never leaving me. I ignored him.

We all were together when we came in. "If this is how we came in here, then this is how we'll go back," I looked at Clara, if her theory was correct, then I should be able to take them back. She nodded at me, trusting me like always.

I closed my eyes and whispered, "SHIFT."

Chapter 9
A Cooked Up Story

I felt a jolt in my stomach like somebody kicked me, bile rose as I held it back in my throat. I knew this was what shifting back felt like. I wasn't new to this sensation.

A swift wind flew, piercing my cheeks and sending shivers down my body, the toxic smell was gone, but the hair on the nape of my neck stood up, telling me something had gone wrong.

I heard a woman scream, like Leticia, when she had towed *Yamendo* back into that portal with her starlight whip.

My eyes flashed open, knowing I had returned. Standing in front of a museum's rubble. It was still dark, but no creepy house, no ashes and no mist, and to my horror, none of my friends by my side.

I couldn't bring them back.

My eyes went wide in anticipation, looking at my empty hands.

"Holy fucking shit!" I screamed, and agitatedly I tried to shift back to Shadowland, repeatedly muttering *SHIFT*, but there was no use. All my efforts were futile. I couldn't go back, and then I remembered—*I only wielded the powers to shift home at my will but can't visit Shadowland on my own without getting sucked.*

F-U-C-K

I groaned loudly, gawking at my empty hands. I raised my hand to tear the skin out of my face. "Lizzy, what have you done?" I watched the museum in horror, I knew what had happened, and for the first time in my life, I was trying hard to visit Shadowland, and my stupid powers were not taking me, not sucking me in.

"NO", I growled loudly in misery at my helplessness. My friends were stuck up in that place where they didn't know anything about it. *How could you leave them there? How could you not remember that it was not in your hand to visit Shadowland? How could you be so ignorant?*

What am I going to tell their parents, to everyone? I couldn't tell them they were stuck in the Shadowland, what excuse would I have to cook up this time? What mask would I wear?

I had to fetch them out—devise a plan to reach Shadowland.

I was still standing in front of the museum, don't know for how long, alone, waiting for Shadowland to suck me in.

I crossed the cave many times, searching for the void, but nothing happened. Somehow, the void closed, and I was stuck here while my friends were trapped in my Darkside. Friends who always stood beside me, they sneaked out to comfort me, were now suffering because of me. It was my stupid idea to come to this museum.

Why do they always have to follow me?

Guilt struck me hard—they were suffering because of me. What scared me the most was the thunder, scarlet clouds, and Clara's tears, she was beyond terrified.

Could *Yamendo* be after all this?

My head throbbed as I was spent, and the fear of something happening to my friends was clouding my thoughts. I was trying hard to think of any person who could know about this, any person who might help me with this situation. But no, nothing hit me.

My mother was gone, now Clara. Only these two knew about this curse, yes, curse. I was cursed, as this thing took away my friends. They were in danger because of me while I was here, standing harmless, clueless, not knowing what to do. *What if somebody harms them?*

"Shut up, Lizzy, think positive," I told myself. "Think, think who can help us?" I was sitting on the street, looking at the museum, the place that took everything from me, first my mom and now my friends. *I am not cursed. This place is cursed.*

I started hurling stones at it, livid. Whatever I could find in the rubble, I trounced towards the withered-down building, trying to take revenge. I hate feeling helpless.

That's when I picked something. It wasn't a stone but a burnt phone, an iPhone which seemed to be in red phone cover made of silicon, as that silicone was now stuck on the phone due to fire.

I shoved it down my pocket, wanting to check more, but clouds were turning blue, the light was coming out, and it's been hours since my friends had been in Shadowland. I must go back home and find a way to create a portal as those Shadow Walkers did in my dream.

I must find the ring they used to create portals.

But where and how?

"Lizzy", I heard a sweet voice.

My eyes fluttered, realising I had slept in my room after climbing back at dawn. "Clara," I muttered, immediately getting up with a jerk, but it wasn't her.

"Noni, where is Clara?" I asked her, looking at her soft winter grey eyes and then at the pink netting of my square canopy bed, her brows furrowed in confusion.

"Was it a nightmare?" I asked more to myself, climbing off the bed, reaching out for my phone from the left bedpost. I was still in yesterday's clothes, covered in soot from the rubble.

"*Mija*," Noni said, her voice deep, but I ignored it. I had much more things to focus on.

I hit Clara on my phone, but it wasn't reachable.

"Listen to me, *mija*," she was trying to get my attention, getting concerned. Her hair was tied in a round bun while wearing a solid green dress to her calf. She raised her eyebrows as I worried my lower lip. I think a part of me knew what she was about to say, but I didn't want to listen to it, never ready to listen to what came next.

"Just a sec, Noni," I said, raising a finger, hitting Homer's and then Nathan's numbers, but they were out of reach.

I continuously called them, fidgeting, not accepting last night's reality. *But it was all real, not a nightmare.*

"Nobody can find them, we found Clara's car in that abandoned amusement park, and you climbed back in the morning," said Noni, scowling. "Where are your friends?" She narrowed her eyes.

I groaned in pain as I fell on her lap. Tears rolled down too quickly that her dress got drenched in a few minutes, and her gentle hands were on my hair, trying to soothe me. "It's my fault, Noni, all my fault. I shouldn't have taken them there with me," I blabbered between tears. Wiping my tears with her dress, she passed me tissues so I could blow my nose.

"Taken where?" She narrowed her eyes as I became stiff, guttering the last sob, not knowing what to tell. She pulled me up, her voice had gone all strict. "Where are the other three, Eloise?" She never called me Eloise, not unless she was furious, which was never the case till now. "What trouble did you all find this time?"

I flinched.

I didn't know where to start and where to end, I didn't know what she would think of me. *What if she thinks I have gone mad or hallucinating?* I didn't know what to tell her.

I gulped down loudly, not knowing how to frame it in words that didn't sound like a made-up story, but I couldn't word my worries.

So, I decided to pivot.

There was a commotion in the living room while I sank into the armchair, terrified and devastated. Meanwhile, I watched everyone trying to interrogate me, but Noni sat next to me, and no one would even dare to ask me again what exactly had happened to their children.

Mike Cooper, the deputy chief, was extremely furious that Homer sneaked out during curfew. He was discussing the facts with some detective. Finally, a detective was working on this case. Far away on the couch, Nathan's parents were sitting. Meghan was sobbing into Ethan's embrace while Mayor seemed intense, standing with his knuckles on the table, listening to the detective, but his gaze never faltered from me.

I squirmed in my seat.

"*Mija,* tell them the truth. Look how worried they all are," she said, taking my hand. "Lying to a cop is a felony. If they find out you are lying, it will get complicated for me to save you." She was worried, trying her best to convince me.

But I didn't budge. "Truth for the truth," I told her. "It's my right to know what exactly happened with my mother and why."

I had made a deal with Noni, I told her that I knew about her outburst and that they had known it before. I wanted the truth they were hiding, but she didn't answer. If she was stubborn, I could be too, after all, her blood was rushing through my veins.

"*Mija!* You are just a child, you won't understand," she said, looking dreadful.

"Try me," I said, my eyebrows shot up.

"Please tell them before those children get into some trouble. Tell Cooper, and he'll help you find his son," Noni kept pushing me, but I knew only I could save them.

I sat there stubbornly. Mayor's eyes continuously scrutinised me, speculating me for my lies. He twitched his lips while talking to the detective. I could feel he knew I was lying about his daughter, and I was in deep shit.

But he didn't come near me or ask me anything. *Phew!*

Thank god! I had a feeling that I couldn't lie to him. He had such a strong aura that made me go all feeble.

But I didn't know how much longer Noni could protect me from him, so I had to find a way to open a gateway before he cornered me.

Hence, I googled.

There was a hustle in the town.

It's been three days since they were searching for my friends. Nobody has taken a breath of relief since three children from Murkwood had gone missing overnight. Whispers spread around the town like wildfire, search parties were organised. My cooked up story was flashing all over the news.

My lie wasn't that inappropriate. It was scary as hell but believable.

It was driving them nuts as they hadn't heard from anyone about their whereabouts, and nobody had called for ransom. But I was buying myself time, waiting for another shifting episode because all the methods Google told me to create a portal were either impractical or scams.

Nothing was working out. I was going crazy thinking about what would be happening in Shadowland with each passing moment.

I rocked on my bed, thinking about visiting Clara's room as she had the journal by *J.P.P* with her. It was my last and only hope. Perhaps I could find some way in that journal to reach them, some loophole or a way to get sucked back again or create a portal.

Breaking into Clara's room was my last resort.

I quickly got up, opening the left drawer of my side stool to grab my penknife and shoving them into my combat boots. But my eyes went to something placed on my bedpost. It was the red cover phone I found in the museum's rubble. I totally forgot about it. I hurriedly turned on my iMac and put the wire attaching the phone, trying to charge it and google how to retrieve the data from that phone, but found nothing that I could understand though it was charging, to my luck.

I was biting my nails, waiting for it to charge at one percent, and I quickly turned it on. The screen came to life, but it asked me for the password. I frowned, but to my luck, I saw a picture on the locked screen. It was a girl. She seemed a few years older than me, with mint green pixie hair, similar tone eyes, a nose piercing in between, a black choker around her neck, and dark black lipstick.

She was with an older man, maybe her father. I didn't recognise any of them, but I focused on her surroundings, finding some clues, which was when I saw a guitar hanging behind her on the wall, and from the window, I could see a red-ish building. If I wasn't wrong, it had to be our Lumber Mills.

I shoved the phone down in my pocket with my phone and ran downstairs, looking for my car keys near the fireplace, but they were nowhere to be found, making me grunt loudly. I was about to ask Hannah but heard some voices. I carefully stepped down towards Noni's room, but the voices came from the basement.

I walked towards the stairs, finding the door open. It was the first time ever I saw Noni's office door open, I couldn't walk down as they'd see me, so I stayed upstairs, eavesdropping.

"Murder, missing children, washed up by the waterfall," Noni said. "Never thought I'd have to face everything at the same time." Ok, that's what I told them, we went to the waterfall to relax. They were trying to cheer me up by cliff jumping when they all got washed up with a gush of wave and couldn't be found. I looked for them everywhere, and that's when I discovered that waterfall had a passage behind it that took me to the museum. I waited for them, but they didn't return.

I know it was a terrible lie, but I needed to buy myself some time.

"It's Heather Reynolds all over again," Mayor added in distress. "It's the same chaos, and frankly, it involves a hell lot of the same people."

Ok! Heather Reynolds was the girl who died 22 years back, the one Homer told us about. She jumped from the cliff and died. Because of her, they shut down Mile-O-city, and thanks to that, everyone accepted my stupid story, but hopefully, my friends were not dead.

"Even I am thinking about it. Her words have been engraved on my heart since Julia told me," Noni replied, her voice going icy cold.

"You want me to get her read?" Mayor's voice was sharp. "I can tell she is lying, you read her or let me get her read, I'll call Dorcas." He knew about the lies, but why Dr. Dorcas?

"She isn't in Murkwood, I sent her to look into something," Noni's words trampled my new plan before I could even formulate it.

"I need to find my Clara, I can't just sit here and listen to her lies," he growled anxiously, desperation in his voice. "You read her," he ordered her.

"You know I won't do that, and neither would you do," Noni spoke, her voice calm. "I can understand your pain, I can feel it but give me some time, I'll try to find them." She sounded tired. "You think they are in—" she said but was interrupted by Mayor's grunt. "She smells like it."

"That's her scent since Julia died," Mayor grumbled.

"Hmm," Noni sighed. "But what would have happened to them, why isn't she telling the truth? I know she loves your daughter and Cooper's son, she's all crazy about him and won't let anything happen to them. I know Lizzy would tell if they'd be in trouble, but if she's not telling, maybe things aren't that bad," Noni suggested.

"Or there is nothing left to do anything," Mayor spoke curtly. My heart sank at his assumption.

"Shut up, Phineas. How could you even think like that about your daughter?" Noni yelled at Mayor. Even I was shocked, he thought they died? "Robin, track them."

I wanted to barge in and tell them they all were alive, but even I had no clue whether they were alive. It was just my firm belief. My breath became shallow. I couldn't breathe properly.

"Lizzy, what are you doing here?" Hannah came out, startling me. Her bright brown eyes, high cheekbones on a chubby face with an impression on one side. She tied her umber hair in a half-high bun, flashing her all-time warming smile. She was a little older than my mother but had been equally beautiful, even with the burn mark covering the right side of her face. She had a snack tray in her hand, I could sniff a salami panini, and there was a pitcher of orange juice.

"N-nothing, I was looking for my keys. I can't find them."

"Alice has them. She says you cannot go anywhere until you tell us the truth about your friends. Lizzy, tell us. We can help you," her eyes were full of care as she carefully tucked the tray between her waist and right hand while trying to put her left hand on my shoulder, but I shrugged her hand away.

"Nobody can help me or stop me," I told her, running outside the house before they could act.

I found my Segway in the garage, though I got bored of it, but I had no other mode of commute. I could have called Uber, but that would be a ton of waiting, and by then, Noni would have dragged me in. So, I stepped on it and flew past the big iron gates. It wasn't chilly, the sun was shining on me, and there was only one agenda on my mind—who was this girl, and why was her phone in the museum's rubble?

Chapter 10

The Swamp

I parked my Segway near the gate of Lumber Mill, walking past the entrance towards the swamp. This area is called a swamp, and now I know why.

The houses differed from what we have near the Northern circle, far from the Sea-Witch Valley. They were only single stories, disarrayed and old. Some were in bad shape. The area smelled like animals and sweat. Even the crowd was different, their clothes were old and tattered, and they seemed dirty like they hadn't bathed in days.

Children were laughing at each other while glaring at me. They were wearing just a vest, shorts or pillowcases. They were poor. *Why do we have such an underdeveloped area on the outskirts of Murkwood? Why hasn't Mom done anything about them*?

I hesitated to be there. Even in the bright sunlight, it felt uncomfortable. But I wanted to know more about the phone's owner, so I built the courage to go to those boys and showed them the picture.

"Hey, do you guys know who she is?" They laughed at me but looked at the phone and whispered things into each other's ears.

"What?" I raised my eyebrows, but they giggled, looking at my Dior dress. I was so overdressed for this rendezvous.

"Do you have money?" one of them asked me, taking out his tongue, licking his lips, swaying his leg and arm, smiling sheepishly.

I rolled my eyes. "Yes," I shoved my hand into my pocket and pulled out a few twenties. They immediately pounced on the money, but I pulled them away from their reach. "Hold on," I raised my finger. "I'll give you all money. First, tell me do you know who she is?"

One of them nodded, so I placed a few twenties in his waiting hand.

"Can you take me there?" I arched my eyebrow, halting before handing out any more money.

They nodded, so I handed them money as they beckoned me to follow. It made me uneasy, I looked at my surroundings. I had a tough time trusting them, but I had no other option. With a grunt, I followed them, sweeping my knife from my boot into my pocket.

People looked at me like I was an alien who had just been left alone on this planet by the troop. Some pointed at me, but I ignored them, raising my chin, I kept walking, masking my concern and discomfort. I had been wearing a mask of an ignorant feeble girl since I was a kid, but now I have to mask like a confident, feisty girl, who'll rip them apart if someone tries to touch me, and it wasn't challenging because I just have to be myself now.

Those boys took me to some narrow lane and stopped. "Second door from the left," said one of them. "Isaac lives here," they said and ran away laughing, waving money in their hands, showing off happily.

"Isaac, who is Isaac? I was looking for this girl," I scowled. Maybe it was the guy in the picture. A girl, merely seven years old, was standing in the corner with a pout on her face, her coffee-coloured hair was a mess, she was wearing a threadbare frock, but her almond-shaped sad brown eyes were what strained my heart.

I beckoned her. "What's your name?" I asked her softly.

"Lucy." She replied with a blush on her cheeks.

"That's a beautiful name, Lucy. Do you want money too?" I asked.

She didn't reply, but her stomach grumbled at my question. I felt a sharp pain in my chest.

I pulled out my wallet and took out a few hundred, her eyes shone at the vision. I placed it in her hand. "In case you need more, find me in Hectors mansion."

Her eyes widened at the mention of the name. "You—you are the princess?" she asked.

"So are all the girls," I chuckled as I booped her nose. She nodded, flashing a full smile in return, and my heart swelled with it. "Now, go, and don't spend it all, save it for later."

"Can I give one to my little sister?" she asked innocently.

"Of course." I smiled as she grinned like I had given her the whole world. She turned back, grinning as she ran away, screaming her sister's name with glee.

Mixed emotions filled my heart but soon it was waved off as I found a few pairs of eyes scrutinising this incident.

I quickly darted towards the narrow street covered with filth puddles and clothes hung outside on the street. There was no bell, only a nameplate with Lynn's written over it. I knocked on the door. "Isaac Lynn?" I asked softly.

The door was ajar. It seemed better from the inside than the outside. I could hear the loud television, but no one answered. I slid in. It was way too small and smelled like a cat. It started with the end, just a tiny kitchen and a living room. Somebody was sitting on the old couch. He had a beer bottle in his hand, hanging from the armrest, almost touching the floor, but he didn't answer.

I stepped forward, finding him snoring. He had little grey in his hair, weeks of stubble, mouth hung open, drooling, but he seemed to be the guy in the picture.

And yes, this was the house. I could see the girl's picture hanging behind this man, it was broken, but I recognised her, same mint-green pixie hair. I looked around and found some books, one had Riley written over it, with some musical notes.

"Hey, who are you?" somebody asked, startling me. I spun around instantly. She was a girl, not the same but someone older than mint-hair girl.

"Hi-Hi, I just came to meet Riley?" I was trying my luck. *What if she was Riley?* That girl had brown bags in her hand.

"She doesn't live here anymore," she answered curtly, putting down the groceries and turning to scrutinise me from tip to toe.

"Oh! Sorry, but can you tell me where I can find her?" I asked, biting my lips, putting the book down, carefully, not waking up the man. I tip-toed behind the lady.

"I don't know, she ran away with her so-called boyfriend, and we haven't heard from her since." She was rummaging through the drawer, and I had an awful feeling that she would take out a knife, so I quickly approached the door.

"Oh-kay, I am sorry to barge in like that, I'll take your leave now," I basically lunged toward the door, but she held my hand, and my heart started beating fast. I quickly put my free hand in my pocket to reach down my knife.

"Has she taken money from you?" she asked me furiously. "If yes, please don't bother us, we don't have any money, and she's the one who borrowed from you. Go and ask her or her fiddler. We are not going to pay for her drugs." She pulled me near her face, her breath smelled like cheap beer.

And she pushed me out, slamming the door in my face. I ran—I ran as hard and fast as I could, but I forgot my way. I turned among the narrow streets, but they all looked the same. It was a pretty stinking maze with puddles of sewer water. I wanted to get out, but I was roaming in circles. Even going in one direction wasn't helping me. Google Maps were confusing too.

It all seemed the same, but the sun was setting, and it had started to get darker. I couldn't determine where I had to go when I saw him.

Edward, the guard of the Limestone Caves. He stepped down to walk away from his home, but my focus was not on him but on his house. I couldn't unsee it because it was covered with *mist and ashes.*

My mouth hung open at the divulgence of the house. It was dark as if somebody poured Shadowland darkness over it. A shiver went down my spine, making goosebumps rise on my hands. I shrugged before I took a step towards it.

The darkness, the shadow smoke, mist and ashes weren't visible to anyone, it was customary to their eyes, but I could see it clearly.

I stepped forward, not attracting any attention, and I was right. That house wasn't just covered in ashes but smelled the same, toxic, as it did in the *Shadowland.*

I was scandalised. How come this house had the same smell and aura as Shadowland? Thousands of answers were enfolding my mind, but I was keening on only one… this house could be the portal.

But what if it wasn't? What if it's a trap?

But that was a risk I had to take to find my friends. I tied my hair in a bun, took a deep breath, and sneaked inside the house.

There was no light in the room, just a long lobby, no windows, and at the end was a room with light flickering from the ceiling—the burning toxic smell kept on increasing with each step. I tip-toed, to that room, covering my mouth.

It was an old room that smelled too much of an old cat lady, and the burning toxic smell was at its peak. I peered in and saw a wooden cot around which white plastic sheets hung, just like the hospitals. I flinched when I heard someone groaning in pain.

Someone was lying on the bed. She was grousing and cringing in pain. "Wat-er, w-at-er," it was a lady's croaked voice.

"Can't you give me some water?" she asked. I thought she was talking to me. Did she see me here?

"No?" she groaned. "Then what's the use of having you here? I should let you lose," she was talking to herself.

Her hand came out of that sheet, and sweat slid from my neck to my back, leaving a chilled sensation down my spine.

Her hand was stitched, her fingers and nails were all uneven and sewn very clumsily. Her trembling hand tried to grab a pitcher of water placed on a stool, but she couldn't reach it. When she tried further to drag herself towards it, she groaned loudly. She must be in enormous pain. Her head came out of a white curtain, and I gasped.

It was the most horrifying face I had ever seen. She was bald, and her baldness was sewn to her head. Too many stitches around the face, one from her left eye to head, and another eye was dangling down with a stitch from ear to neck. Her skin was dark in some places. One could even assume as if she was rotting. She heard my gasp and looked at me. I quickly hid.

"Who's there?" she asked sharply, then groaned in pain again.

My heart was thumping against my chest, feeling the sweat on my forehead, and my breathing became erratic. "Go check, who's there," she told someone, but I was out. I practically leapt out of the house. There was a point when I felt like the ash cloud surmounted me as the toxic smell was almost unbearable, but I kept running out from the tendrils of darkness, out of the aura of that house.

Was she a monster? Whom did she ask to check on me? I didn't see anyone there. Who was she talking to? But there was darkness, I felt it on my body because the goosebumps trailed wherever it touched.

There was nothing about this area that could make me feel safe. It was a wrong decision to come here without knowing about it. I was scared, but I kept running, getting out of breath. My heart was pounding louder as if my lungs would jump out of my throat, and suddenly I slammed into a motorbike.

I immediately concealed my face from the bright headlights that blinded me.

"Princess, is that you?" a deep male voice asked.

"Dim the lights," I commanded.

"Sorry, sorry," he said, quickly turning off the ignition. I looked at him. He was Colton Muller, Sophie's half-brother.

"What are you doing here, in this area?" he asked with a frown.

He was my mother's assistant, a nice guy, always giving sound advice. Earlier, he was our music teacher, but soon he left the job and started working for Mom. Homer was a big fan of his music, always hovering around him. He was the originator of their band *Blaze.*

As soon as his voice fell on my ears, I felt relief.

"I just forgot my directions," I said hurriedly, he looked past me, but I climbed on his bike behind him, grabbed his jacket tightly, and hid my face. I was shivering from fear.

"But—" he started to enquire.

"Take me home, now," I commanded again, to which he dropped his questions and nodded before turning on the ignition, taking me out of that hell hole.

The wind pierced my cheeks, but I wasn't ready to face the world. That lady's face never left my eyes, she was horrifying. I was scared to my heart. Her stitched face and different coloured eyes made her seem like a monster, she herself was the monster. My hands were shivering even though it was around Colton, but I couldn't get a hold of myself.

"Princess," he stopped. That's when I raised my head to look around. We were in front of the mansion, and without saying anything, I hopped from his bike, and before I could barge in, Hannah opened the door. Her face went white as ashes as she saw mine.

"Lizzy, sweetheart, are you ok?" But I ran past her, slamming the main door loudly, my chest heaving visibly. Behind her, I saw Noni sitting near the fireplace, adjusting cinders, phone in her hand. "She's here, she's back. I'll call you later. Where were you, *mija*? We were all looking for you, why weren't you answering your phone?—"

"There is a monster downhill," I blabbered, terrified, halting Noni from bombarding me with any more questions. "You wanted to know the truth. Go check the swamps. You wouldn't miss it, she's all stitched." Noni exchanged her looks with the Scotts, they didn't utter a word. "Her nails, her eyes, her head, it's all like it belonged to several other people," I rubbed my eyes with the heel of my hands, trying to wipe off that image.

And when I raised my head, they looked at me like I had grown with three heads.

"And she was talking to someone I couldn't see," I kept blabbering, begging them to understand.

"*Mija!* Calm down, come sit next to me, you haven't eaten in days," Noni said, putting the phone down, carefully taking my hand, but I snatched it back.

"No," I stomped my feet. "I am not hallucinating. You've got to believe me. Someone has to." I wanted someone to have faith in me so that I could share what happened to my friends, that's when the doorbell rang.

"Shhh…" Noni shushed me, soothing me like I saw a nightmare. But it wasn't a nightmare. She has to believe me. She tilted her head to look past me. "Hannah, take her to her room and give her some hot cocoa.

"But—" I started to interject, but Robin opened the door taking a stance, and Colton stood outside with my pashmina. He stepped back, a little scared, looking at my six feet tall bald mentor. Robin wore a white button-down with blue slacks, showing off his muscles clearly.

Instead of asking, he folded his hand over his chest, the action highly intimidating, displaying the bulge in his biceps. Broodingly, he just arched his eyebrow, not uttering a single word. I couldn't see Colton's reaction as Hannah tugged me towards the stairs, but I knew he must be having a hard time not shitting in his pants.

"Hannah, do you believe me?" I asked her as we climbed upstairs, but she didn't reply. Her face was blank, devoid of emotions.

Later she said, "Stay here, I'll be back." Hannah left me in my room and locked the door.

WTF?

"HANNAH," I shouted, banging on the door. "Why are you locking me up?" Didn't she know I could climb down the tree?

"Shh… stay low. I'll be back with hot cocoa," she whispered.

Chapter 11
Yellow-Eyed Monster

I was slurping on a frappuccino in Leonard's Café.

The soothing smell of coffee relieved my throat, happily reading the journal by J.P.P.

I turned a page when suddenly it fell, making a metallic sound as if it was made of a metal cover. I bent down to pick it up when the lights started flickering. I looked down at the book, it was emitting red light, and soon the room didn't smell like coffee anymore. A burning toxic smell had replaced it.

Even in the dark, I knew where I was, mist mixed with ashes filled the whole room. From the little light from the open window, I could see that this place was also burnt like everything else in this realm. Black and burnt cupboards, a fridge covered in green slime, crockery lying on the floor, broken into pieces, and mason jars in which coffee was kept were now lying on the floor shattered into pieces. Everything was a mess. Even the chair I was sitting on was lying precisely in the same position I had left, but its legs were tilted towards the floor.

Finally! I felt relief as I made myself out on the pier, searching for my friends, but suddenly, I was standing in the swamps near the stitched monster house. Somehow, I managed to get there without even walking.

Were my friends trapped here?

I made a step towards it. It was when I heard a loud shriek.

Every thought in my mind vanished. My stomach dropped, my heart was racing. Everything I just read in that journal about Shadowland was coming back to me—demons, monsters, shadowfiends, and most importantly, *Yamendo*. I stood there frozen, shivering with fear, but soon I heard that screeching voice behind me. With everything I had inside me, I accumulated it around my core and ran with all my strength without looking at what was behind me.

Suddenly, I was outside on Highway 59, pressing myself forward, feeling my sore legs ache with stress and my lungs burn.

This time I didn't notice what I was stepping on or where my combat boots were going. All I wanted was to save my ass, but I didn't know how. With every breath I took, I hoped it wouldn't be *Yamendo*. I kept running forward towards the end of the road. It was a different road, somehow, I managed to escape Highway 59, and now I was in some dark forest.

The ground was dark, with no grass. It was a shadow of someplace, covered with mist but no ashes or toxic smell. It wasn't even *Shadowland* anymore. I was in a place I'd never seen before.

I shifted elsewhere.

The same shriek fell on my ears. That monster had followed me here too. I started running again, without looking back, because I knew if I would, I will face the biggest fear of my life, the nightmare I was not ready to face. The fear, the curse of my life bestowed upon me, was now taking a bad form. I knew one day it would crash down on me. Suddenly, I heard a slithering sound, but I knew looking back would slow me down, so I kept running.

I could hear the crackling of the ground as it hustled behind me, and it kept getting loud. My eyesight blurred from all the tears, and somehow it made me trip, and I dropped like a ton of bricks. I cringed and groaned, trying to stand but slumped again, feeling an agonising pain shooting through my ankle. I knew I wouldn't be able to stand up again. I knew running from that thing had come to an end. I wanted to live more, do so many things, find my mother's murderer, rescue my friends, and most importantly, I never wanted to die a virgin.

But I knew my time had come. I looked up, wiping the tears that were flowing down my face.

I saw a black shadow of a woman, it was dark, and it seemed like a silhouette instead of her body. A shadowfiend, I thought, but when the yellow eyes opened brightly, it was the only lit thing in this place. She was hovering over me. Looking at her made me think whether it was

Yamendo or something else. It was a strange place, nothing familiar, and I was dying in that peculiar place, my body wouldn't even be found. Like my friends, I'll be lost forever.

All my desires and aspirations would be buried with me, and no one would find me. Those big yellow eyes were staring down at me.

"Please, leave me, please," I begged that shadow monster, dragging myself away from her, but she cocked her head to the right as if sizing me up.

"Yamendo?" I asked the monster as if she would understand. Her yellow eyes burnt in anger with that word, making them bloodcurdling. It seemed like she was scared and angry—both at the same time. It pressed down at me, sending chills down every part of my body.

I whimpered as I made the monster angry. I closed my eyes, begging her not to kill me.

"Stay away from that house," she hissed in my ears, it was a cold sound tickling my ears. It was a voice of many but none, sending thrills in my bones. "If you want to live, don't go back to the swamp."

My stomach dropped when I felt warm hands around me, covering my mouth, holding me around my stomach. My eyes went wide, I turned to look at yellow eyes, and then they changed into a pair of emerald-green eyes, a sort of amazement in them. He seemed handsome but jaded, covered with years of stubble and messy long blondes. His eyes were new to me, but he seemed to know me like he had known me for years, looking at me like I was some accolade.

"Nice to meet you again, princess," he whispered sweetly and then hissed "Shift" in my ears. At the same time, I thought—SHIFT.

His voice was still ringing in my ears, someone else was there, someone who knew how to shift, just like me.

"NO," I heard that yellow-eyed monster scream behind me.

I woke up in my bed.

My heart was thumping rapidly, my breath was still caught in my chest. I raised my hand to check my throat, finding my voice when I felt my locket stuck between my boobs. I took it out, it was all drenched as I was sweating like bullets. I looked around. I was in my room, and all windows and doors slammed hard due to the storm. A Cornish Rex white cat was sitting on the windowsill, mewing loudly, terrified of the thunder crashing outside.

I quickly got out of my bed, putting my feet down on the cold floor, it soothed me. I hid my face inside my hands, trying to calm my mind. It was a nightmare, just a nightmare. There is no one like me, no one can shift like me.

My nightmare and cat's mewing were creating a headache. The vein in my head was thumping wildly as if waiting to pop. I wanted to stand up, close the windows to keep the cat and storm out. But I sat there for a minute, grabbing a few breaths. I was so relieved it was just a nightmare, but it felt so real, I could still feel goosebumps on my hands.

I rubbed them off and went towards the headrest, looking around for cold water, but there was no water bottle. It was kept on the windowsill. I got up to grab it as the cat leapt outside on the tree. I twisted the cap, watching the cat, still mewing as if stranded.

I gulped down a few sips, feeling relieved as water travelled down my throat. I downed half the bottle like an elixir before tossing it on my bed.

I kept my gaze locked on the stray cat, which was asking for help, as it was raining heavily.

"C'mon, Wonton." That's the first name that clicked my mind when I saw it. "What made you think people will listen to your cries and help you?" I sighed. "No, nobody will help you. Nobody believes in us," I told her, leaning against the wall. For a moment, I thought she paused, but she didn't turn to look at me.

Whoa! Now a cat was giving me attitude. So instead of rescuing it, I sank onto the windowsill. The wind blew a few droplets in my direction, and I accepted it on my face. It was soothing, but my body still felt stiff as I thought about my friends, Mom, and dream. *What does it mean?*

It all seems connected—that monster and the creepy house. This has become blasphemy in my life. "What if that yellow-eyed monster has my friends? I must find that journal," I told the cat. "There must be something inside it, I should go to Clara's place, and there I would find the answers to all the nudging questions in my head."

My head was bulging with the happenings in my life. Mostly, I had no friends to share my doubts with. No one trusted me, but my gut was compelling me to believe in the happenings as if they were indicating to me the reality, the truth that I was hovering for.

I was angry at Noni and Hannah for not understanding me. '*Tell me the truth, my foot!*' as if they could handle it.

I had to search for the journal. *I must know how to create a portal before my friends get into any more trouble.*

I was about to wash up, but Noni called me downstairs. Hannah said she had to discuss something with me. I could feel butterflies in my stomach. Finally, would they believe me?

"Dinner, I hope?" she asked me. It was almost eight, and I had no appetite, but I felt she wanted to talk to me about what I had told them about that stitched monster. So, I got excited because finally, I'll be able to tell them the truth, I could tell her about the journal, and she could ask Mayor so that he could bring it over, and I could go to fetch my friends. It was a simple plan, and I was very confident about it.

I smiled wildly, excitedly, holding my head up while sitting at our royal dining table. Robin was making kung-pao chicken, I could sniff it, even from here. My stomach grumbled with its whiff, but I held it, telling it to stop—*you won't get any soon.*

Hannah was serving tea when Noni asked. "Ready to talk about it?"

"Yes," I nodded.

"We found out your mother was not murdered, it was an accident indeed."

"W-what?" I was taken aback, not expecting this conversation.

"CIS has found the girl, who was driving your mother's car that day," she told me, *her part of the truth.* "She was at City Hospital getting treatment. That's why she couldn't come forward till now, but yesterday she was discharged."

Riley Lynn! I thought.

"She is a nurse and was returning to her place when she asked for a lift, and your mother asked for her to drive as she was disturbed. But soon, a bottle rolled under the brakes, so she couldn't press them. Your mother tried to pull the bottle out, but the girl panicked and jumped out of the car. She didn't realise a truck—" Noni closed her eyes like it pained her physically, even to imagine it. "The truck hit the car before your mother could jump or shove the brakes." Noni took out her specs and pinched the tower of her nose with her right hand's forefinger and thumb. "The girl got many scratches, Poor Lea."

"Lea?" I asked, confused.

"Yeah, her name is Lea Perker," she answered.

But then who was Riley Lynn? How come her phone was in the museum's debris?

It turns out that my downhill trip was a merry chase, *Argh!*

"But why did she scream at Muller?" I pressed.

"You're well aware of your mom, *mija!* She had schizophrenia, her insecurities pushed her over the edge, and that was one of her episodes," I know about her episodes, I was the main victim, she once chained me into the cell because of the same. "She had created some scenario in her mind that something happened on the day of the breach when nothing happened, the videos were clear, and even her phone held no evidence of anything as such."

"They found her phone too?" I gasped, she died because of her stupid schizophrenia? That was too lame for the Cobra Queen.

"Yes, Lea held it. She returned it to the cops. There was nothing suspicious in it. CIS checked." Noni pressed the bridge of her nose, sighing.

Oh God! It wasn't a murder, the mystery had been solved, and here I was, thinking about how to reach the culprit. CIS was working way too fast. Obviously, that's why it's called CIS.

"I told you to trust me. I will handle everything. I am here for you, *mija*! You can tell me anything," she said, reaching out for my hand, she looked jaded. "I will always be there for you, we only have each other now."

To my shock, she started crying in front of me. Hannah excused us, leaving us alone. I looked at this old woman, she had shed so much weight since Mom's death. How could I be so cruel and selfish that I left her alone to cry, not take care of her? Her hands were quivering when I held them back. "I am sorry, Noni," I walked up to her, wiping her tears. "I am so sorry for what I am forcing you to go through, but I am…"

I had no excuses. I was so lost in my trance that I forgot she had also lost her daughter. I was the only person she looked up to.

"Tell me, Lizzy, tell me, what's going on with you? What happened to your friends? Where are they?" she begged. "No lies this time, I gave you my truth, I want your truth now."

I bite my lips, nodding at her.

Just then, Colton Muller, the mauve-haired dude, interrupted us. "Ma'am, everything has been arranged for the funeral tomorrow. Oh! I am sorry, I didn't realise you were busy, I'll come later," he apologised.

Chapter 12

The Music Teacher

"Princess?" A hard knock on my door startled me.

For a while, I was curled up on the floor, thinking about getting up and taking a shower, but my legs were numb, and my knees buckled under me. Wonton, the cat, also seemed to leave me at my mercy.

The thought of my mother's funeral had thrown me off beat.

I didn't want to attend it. I somehow wanted it to be a big ugly lie, refusing to accept it. I know I was being unreasonable, but I hoped it was all just a nightmare.

But giving her a farewell would make it concrete that she was gone and I wasn't ready. She was my mom, and how could I bid her a final goodbye?

I got up and opened it slightly, finding Colton standing outside my door. What was he doing here, in my house, at this hour?

"What?" I asked rudely, not in the mood to be a perfect princess.

"I have something for you." He narrowed his eyes, as he tapped the manila folder in his hand.

"What is it?" I enquired, sweeping off the wetness from my cheeks before snatching the file from his hand. As soon as I opened it, my stomach dropped, it was an autopsy report of my mother. Tears welled my eyes, and my lips quivered as I closed the file, tossed it onto the bed, storming to my window, letting the chilly air hit my cheeks, burning the freshly flowing tears and searching for breaths.

"You were terrified earlier like you'd seen a ghost." Colton broke the silence, trying to make small talk. I turned to look at him, finding him sitting on my bed, folding my blanket.

"Nothing, it was nothing," I told him, feeling awkward—why was he sitting on my bed? "I just got scared of the darkness." *Like I could!* Darkness was the reality of my life. But I didn't lie to him. For one second, I thought, darkness did surmount me, trying to catch me, but it couldn't get hold of me.

"Ah! Darkness! Nobody is afraid of darkness, Princess." He smiled. "But everybody fears not being alone in the darkness."

I rolled my eyes at his philosophy. I wasn't in the mood.

"My name is Eloise, don't call me princess."

"Your wish is my command," he nodded. "So, Eloise, what were you doing in the swamp? It's a downgrade area, especially for a girl like you." He gazed at me, tip to toe, a compliment that made me smile a little. "I've never seen you there before."

"I was looking for my friends," it was part truth, I did think that house was a portal to *Shadowland.*

"But you said they drowned in the waterfall."

"I said *washed up*," I snapped, frowning at his words. "Not drowned, they are not *Heather Reynolds.*"

His head shot up, his shoulders got locked, grinding his teeth. "Seems like I am not the only one listening to the rumors," but within a blink, he relaxed. "You can't do anything to what people think or talk. You can't stop them. If you want to live in this world, you've got to ignore them. That's what your mother taught me."

No, my mother said always keep your ears open because people often give away true intentions through words.

But he doesn't have to know that. So, I looked away, not ready to talk about her.

I kept looking outside the window. There was neither moon nor any stars. It seemed like it was going to rain again.

That's when I realised he would have been there. He was also the last person who saw my mother. After all, she was having dinner with *his* family.

"Did she say something…anything before she…" I cleared my throat, turning to look at his reaction. "She was with you all having dinner just before the accident."

I still couldn't believe she died because some bottle got lodged under the brakes, and her outburst was nothing but her schizophrenic episode. It was all so palpable yet so obscure.

"Sorry, Lizzy…can I call you Lizzy?" He bit his lips.

Didn't that escalate quickly?

He continued assuming my silence as my consent. "I wasn't there with my family, Lizzy. As it was Sunday, so I was out with band practice."

"You were with Homer that night?" I arched an eyebrow.

"Yeah. He's your friend?" he asked politely, reaching for my Iron Man Mark III action figure. My hands curled into fists as he touched it.

"Don't touch my stuff!" I snapped.

"Oh! Sorry, I didn't mean to." He took a step back, returning it to its place. "It's just that you didn't seem like a girl who's into the Avengers," he smirked. "I mean, princesses don't play with action figures. They generally are the ones with barbies."

It made my insides groan, but it wasn't his fault. That's who I pretended to be in school.

"How many princesses have you met to know what they are into?" I sank to my windowsill.

"Not princesses, but I have a half-sister," he hunched his shoulders.

My mouth twisted at the mention of Sophie. I wanted to tell him about his sister dating Homer, but I didn't know whether he already knew. That would be a waste of outbursts, plus I didn't want to get into Homer's bad books by being a tattletale. *What if he tosses him out of his band?* I couldn't harm his career because of mere jealousy.

So, I preferred to seal my mouth as he came to my side.

"May I?" he took permission to sit next to me on the windowsill.

I shrugged as rain droplets tickled my back.

He put his hand around me. "Are you feeling cold?" he asked. "Should I close the windows?"

"No," I felt uneasy at his touch as blood rushed my cheeks, but he didn't remove his hand.

He sat there quietly. "I know how it feels not to have a mother around you, I can feel your pain," he whispered. "But it's the truth of life, one day or the other, we have to go through all this, rest is all made up lies by us humans. Death is the only truth."

"Mm-hmm." Though I wanted to shut him down, but my whole focus was on his hand around my shoulder. He kept talking politely like it was nothing, but my skin crawled under his touch. When he was a music teacher at my school, every girl swooned over him, and he mainly had an amicable relationship with girls. He listened to their problems and solved them. They said his soothing voice made them calm. I'd sought comfort this whole week, and today this stranger offered me that.

I wanted to lunge at the opportunity, but it felt awkward. So, I shrugged and pulled away, craning my neck, tucking my hair behind my ears, and wiping my face. I felt his eyes lingering on my face.

"What?" I asked, frowning.

"Your mascara is all smudged." He whispered, his voice a little breathy.

"Oh!" I blinked, embarrassed. Brushing my cheeks with my palm, but before I could stop, his hand was already raised, brushing the corner of my mouth. I flinched. I was about to thank him when he suddenly leaned in and planted a kiss on my lips. It was quick, like a peck.

I went stoic, stunned by his action. What was he doing?

He looked into my eyes, waiting for my permission, a slap, a scream, or me to tell him that I was too younger than him, he was 23, and I was just 17. But I didn't do anything, I froze in shock. A guy just kissed me, my enemy's brother, a guy who's my mom's assistant. He should be in college, dating college girls, but instead, he kissed me. My first kiss, my first kiss ever, was in my room with someone I didn't even know much.

I flushed as he filled the space between us, and soon, his lips were on mine. My heart rate sped up. I couldn't believe it. My eyes were still open in shock. I could feel his hands sliding under my top from the back, his fingers tickling me, kissing me, trying to get my full attention. But I was too astonished to revert it, and when I did, I felt it was a little bit sloppy as it was my first kiss, and I didn't know what to do. My hands were still on my sides, shaking, not knowing where they should go, so I closed my eyes, going with the flow.

Unlike me, he seemed very confident and swiftly unclasped my bra. My eyes snapped open, pulling away. I didn't know where it was going, he was in control right now, and I hated losing control over my life. It triggered my insecurities. I quickly got up from the windowsill, taking two steps back.

"I think you should leave."

He was taken aback. He waited a beat before brushing his hands through his mauve hair, "Oh-Kay."

I looked outside, where a car was parked near the fence, waiting for him to leave, but he didn't budge.

"Sorry if I have done something wrong," he said after rubbing his face with his hands. I felt his gaze on my face, but my eyes were outside, ignoring him.

"Go," I ordered, pursing my lips and crossing my hands over my stomach.

"You didn't like it?" he asked. I didn't know what to answer. But I always wanted my first kiss to be with Homer, obviously, exceptionally. I mean with someone special, someone I love, but life was no fairytale. It never gives what you ask for. So, I tried to pivot.

I shook my head, masking my flush with an irritated look. Who talks about this stuff? I mean, I could have blurted it out in front of Clara, but I felt nervous about confronting him.

"It's ok to be uncomfortable, Lizzy." He took my hands in his, and I let him, still unable to face him. "It's totally fine to step out of your comfort zone. I know it's not that easy, but give yourself to it, you'll feel calm, and it'll help you." He tugged me, pulling me between his legs. I finally glanced at him, shocked.

Geez! He's being so pushy.

"Relax," he whispered sensually as he moved my hair away to kiss in the crook of my neck. And this was it. I moaned, craning my head back. His cold lips brushed lightly over my skin, making me weak in my knees. I couldn't bear the sensation. He realised my weakness and pulled me down to his lips.

It started raining heavily, and we were kissing on the windowsill.

He hauled me until I straddled him, with my hands fisted in his hair. It was better than last time. This time, I knew what to expect and could gain control.

His hand crawled over my back, lifting my top. I pulled away, catching some breath, but he wasn't breathing at all. His eyes were wide open like I had caught him doing something nasty.

"What?" I asked, but his hand immediately left my top.

"N-Nothing," he said, smiling bizarrely. "Now put your hands in the air," it was like a command.

An order, really? I arched my eyebrow while he waited for me, holding the hem of my satin top.

"And I thought you only had a thing for good boys," said a cold, masculine voice echoing in my room, sending a shiver down my spine.

Chapter 13

Gasoline to my fire

Startled by his presence, my eyes widened in shock. *What the hell?* I didn't have to look at him to know who he was. Like always, his voice sent a shiver down my spine, a zing, a sense of fear and pleasure furled in my bones. I quickly got off Colton, rearranging myself, flushed.

"Kayden!" I turned to him nervously. *There he was, in my bed!* A drenched black shirt and denim hugged his muscular body as if waiting to be ripped off. Water droplets shone in his brown hair, making them appear like dark chocolate. His legs were straight on my mattress, with Salvatore Ferragamo's derby on. His left hand was tucked behind his head, resting on the headboard, while the other held the water bottle I had chucked on the bed earlier. He was doing nothing, but the authoritative aura rippled from his body like he owned my bed, my house, and everything in this world.

He turned to me slowly. His expressions were odd, his jaw was locked, and his hazel eyes were icy cold, making me gulp down hard.

"What the hell are you doing here?" I asked, baffled.

"Saving you, perhaps, but it seems like you rather enjoy being a part of a scandal," he glared as he gracefully raised himself in a sitting position, his eyes wandering all over my body. A creepy feeling crawled my spine as his raging gaze fell on my bare thighs under my satin shorts and lingered on my breast. My mouth went dry under his gaze.

"Hook yourself up," he ordered, unscrewing the bottle's cap.

My breath hitched at his audacity. I quickly hooked myself up, cursing him.

"Such a filthy mouth," he spoke in his icy cold voice, *rage,* I could feel it till here. "But still tastes delicious," he raised the bottle to his lips, taking a swig, and this time rage wasn't the only thing in his eyes, but desire.

I strode toward him, trying to snatch my bottle, but he pulled it far from my reach, taking advantage of being a giant. "Give it back," I huffed.

"Take it," he challenged me, always challenging me, knowing I wouldn't back off. It was hard to ignore his alpha-male personality, but it was much harder not to indulge him. He was gasoline to my fire, always an extreme.

I climbed my bed to reach out, still not even a single hint of amusement on his face. I arched further, but my action was erroneous as I felt his breath on my neck. Shuddering, I retracted back. I was about to fall when his strong hand caught me, snaked around my waist.

The zing I always felt around him was no longer just a sensation, it was electricity, a spark that jolted me from where his warm hands held me. My eyes widened in shock. Colton stepped towards me, but Kayden lifted his hand, waving him off as if he was a house boy, halting him.

Kayden's gaze never left my face as I tried to get out of his strong arms, but his grip tightened around me, holding me put. Envy was rippling from his body in the form of heat. I wanted to snap at him, but his scent wafted through me when I opened my mouth. Fuck! His raw smell, mixed with rain and sweat, was utterly masculine, making my core clench.

Colton's eyes narrowed, but I wasn't focusing on his irritated expression. I concentrated on Kayden because whenever things come to him, nothing else matters, as anger consumes me. I hate him so much that he sucks all my attention, unwilling to take my eyes off his arrogant, beautiful face.

"So, Eloise Valerie Hector," he took my full name in a specific tone that tingles every bone in my body. "Do you like straddling strangers on your windowsill? Does it turn you on taking control?" I felt his breath on my lips, my body hummed under his voice. I immediately flew back, tearing myself from his daunting aura as blood rose my cheeks at his filthy words.

"How did you enter my house?" I asked, ignoring his question, trying to mask the shivers. But he gracefully rose from my bed, ignoring my question as if it didn't matter, striding closer to me. My mask faltered as I stepped back.

"Do you moan when someone kisses your neck?" His eyes travelled from my mouth to my neck, which must have turned red. "Or you just love creating chaos?" He cornered me like the devil had come to claim my soul.

Argh! Why this judgmental ass has to see me kissing? Out of all the people in the world, why does it have to be him?

I scowled at him. "Go. To. Hell."

"Oh! Believe me, this is my personal hell," he glared at me, taking all the space in my room. Dark shadows behind his vast hazel eyes were my grave concern. I had never seen him so furious, his fists clenched, but his voice was cold, like he could barely keep his temper aligned. He was drenched in rainwater, water droplets in his hair shining like a star in the night sky, his black shirt sticking to his chest.

I could tell he was mad at me, perhaps because of Clara.

My eyes shifted at the commotion behind him. Robin and Hannah had entered my room while Kayden was still towering over me.

I mouthed *'what happened?'* at Hannah, who stood near the archway of my room, but she shrugged and shook her head.

But I knew he was mad at me because of his sister.

"Listen to me, G-Kayden," I was about to call him Gigantor. *But this was not the right time.* I wore the mask of a sweet girl and added softly. "I am sorry, I tried to find her but couldn't. I know you are mad at me for being reckless. But I didn't know she'd wash away. If I had any idea, I would have stopped her."

He narrowed his eyes as if reading me, so I sugar-coated it more than what was required. "Dude, I love her, I really wish her to be with me, I know you are angry, but I am devastated too."

"So, you will go around kissing some random shit just because you are upset?" he frowned impudently.

I gasped.

"How dare you?" I was shocked. My mask fell off my face. Hannah and Robin stepped forward to stop him, but he shook his head, telling them not to interfere.

Whoa! Who do you think you are, giving orders to my staff?

Fine, it's one on one. I'll take this jerk. I'll handle him alone. I wasn't a kid, and neither was I scared of him. Enough being overbearing, I was ready to kick some ass. No masks, just me and him.

"Dare I?" he asked curtly. "Dare you, how could you be so irresponsible climbing upon some guy you barely know? Do you even know his true intentions? Or you just don't care."

"That's none of your concern," I pushed him. His chest was as hard as his personality, not budging even an inch. I turned my palm into a fist that was clammy because of his drenched shirt. I couldn't lose this fight, so I kept staring into his eyes with all the strength I could accumulate.

"It's none of my concern?" He raised his hand. For an instant, I thought he'd touch me, but instead, he brushed his hand through his hair, grunting loudly. Suddenly, he ducked near my face, levelling up with me, sucking all my oxygen. He's going to explode. The anger behind his hazel eyes was so dark that I knew he was barely holding himself back. "It's none of *my* concern that this guy—" he pointed the finger at Colton, not tearing his gaze from me.

But I cut him off. "What, this guy…? It's none of your business whom I kiss or not. Who are you to judge me?" I asked breathily, trying to overcome his dominant personality but failing miserably. We were standing just a breath away, and my heart was beating fast due to anger. "I never judge you when we all know we can't even count how many girls you have kissed or fucked." I said bluntly. His eyes narrowed when I used the F-word. "As it's not my fucking business, likewise this is not your fucking business, you are Clara's brother, not mine."

"I am very well aware that you are *not my sister*," he cringed a little at the last word.

"I'll decide what I can and can't do. You stay out of it," I jutted my chin out. "And how dare you come to my house at this hour, making a scene. Did you sneak in? Pervert," giving him an ugly grimace.

"Don't you call me names!" he growled. "I was minding my own business, but you're naïve enough to invite chaos into your life. You've always been in your little magic world in your magical castle that you don't know how bad the outside world is, but looking at you right now, I could tell you don't even want to know it. You have been hiding behind this mask of being feeble so long that you have become one." How does he know about my mask? *No, it was just a figure of speech. He doesn't know me.*

"I am not feeble," I screamed at the top of my lungs, having never been humiliated so much. "It's you, a narcissistic cyborg, who ignores other people's feelings," I snapped. "Controlling everyone in school wasn't enough that now you are barging into my house, threatening me. What do you want to become, a criminal?" I was fuming, but he growled at me in exasperation, making me tremble, but I kept screaming. "With a father as Mayor, you think you can get away with anything? I'll call the cops right now,"

"Fine, go away, call them. They should know what this pedophile was doing here to you." He crossed his hands around his midsection like the cocky bastard he was, taking a step back, giving me space to make a call. "I don't mind when everything comes out." He gave Colton a murderous look like something I didn't know was going on.

"Wait, Lizzy," said Colton as he stepped forward to stand near me. "Let it be, I'll leave. I don't want to create a scene." So mature. I turned to him with my phone in hand.

"Your ass is on fire, jerk," he shot at Colton, then turned to me. "What are you waiting for? It's 911," raising eyebrows, jutting his chin out, nudging me to dial, but I didn't. I was furious, but I decided not to call the cops. I couldn't go against Clara's family behind her back. Somehow, I felt it was my duty to take care of them in her absence. So, I closed my eyes, taking a few deep breaths—*for Clara.*

"Kayden, I think you should leave," I opened my eyes. "You can't just barge in my house and affront me. Once, you told me that you didn't want to be my friend, and two people who aren't friends don't get to interfere in each other's life," I told him sternly. "You're Clara's twin, her family. Before I forget that, leave."

"HECTOR," he growled my last name, making me flinch, like we were strangers, stating that we weren't friends, but even though I knew it, it still stung. "Ask him what he was doing." He ordered me, narrowing his eyes, there was something else in his eyes, was that agony?

"I won't," I straightaway denied, crossing my hands over my stomach, the coldness in my voice surprising us both. He went stoic like he wasn't breathing. "I don't want you anywhere near me, Gigantor."

"Don't be difficult. I am trying to save your goddamn ass," he hissed through clenched teeth.

"I am not yours to save," I retorted with the same coldness.

He winced back, shocked as if I had slapped him. Colton placed a hand around me, making me flinch, but he ignored it, and pulled me to him, tearing from Kayden's aura. "Where were you hiding this fire, little princess?" He licked his lips, closing the distance between us.

Was he trying to kiss me in front of everyone? My heart froze in anticipation. Robin—Hannah—Kayden, all were watching.

"Hands off, Colton, not *this one*." Kayden snarled. Anger was rippling from his body like he was profoundly powerful and dominating, on the verge of exploding.

One second ago, he was standing next to me, but instantly he was between Colton and me, very smoothly taking me off his grip, and then he wrapped his fingers around his wrist. His jaw was tense. His arm muscles flexed as I could see them through his black button-down shirt sticking to his body. His chest went wide as he twisted Colton's hand, who groaned in pain.

And within a blink of an eye, Kayden swung and clipped Colton's jaw, making him stumble back.

Woah! That was some swing! My eyes were fixated on the bulge of his muscular biceps. I should give that to Kayden, *but no, Lizzy, stop them.*

"Fuck you, man." Colton jerked back, holding his jaw. Blood oozed out from the corner of his lips.

They both looked at each other like they would tear each other apart.

"Woah, Woah!" I squeezed between two angry guys. "Seriously, in my room? Get out of my house if you want to fight, I am not interested."

"I am sorry, Lizzy." Colton immediately backed off, wiping the blood off his lips. "I understand how vulnerable you are right now."

Then he turned to Kayden, "You should leave, man. This is her house, her life. Why are you intruding?" Colton was being polite, "Wasn't spreading words that she's lesbian enough that now you're forcing her away from someone she likes." He smirked with a glint in his eyes.

"What?" I gasped, shocked. Colton's words went down as if he had poured acid on my body. Kayden's silence was agonising. My insides were screaming over the top, enraged with him. I wanted to rip him into ribbons with nails, a knife, anything.

I shoved him back, and this time, pain reflected in his eyes. "Why, Kayden, I mean, what have I ever done to you?" I fisted his shirt. "You tell guys I am a lesbian?"

I always thought it was because of my powerful family, Cobra Queen, but that wasn't it. He played a significant role in forcing me to remain single. It was because of him that nobody ever asked me out, not even at the freshman party, spring dance, or prom. OMG, this guy is why nobody ever showed interest in me—Kayden Parsons—the biggest nemesis of my life.

"I'll kill you," I growled, punching his chest. Robin stepped forward, but Kayden raised his hand as Robin halted. My eyes narrowed as I groaned, striking him.

"I didn't say you're a lesbian," he held me. My wrists burned under his touch as his grip tightened around my hands, stopping me from hitting him.

I yanked my hands away from him, freeing myself to punch him in the face. I wanted to dive my knee in his crotch, like right now, breaking him, squeezing his balls so that he could never get to have sex with anybody. But Colton interrupted.

"I specifically remember you told Lucas, one of my students, that she always hangs out with your sister, and you sounded it in a way you were implying that she's gay."

"I just told him the truth. I don't care about his assumptions." He brought out his famous monotone like nothing affected him or was important enough for his consideration. He turned to me. "Lucas is a player. He was thinking of having a hook-up with you, so someone has to protect you from a bad influence. You're too naïve to judge people."

"I am going to decide whether I want a hook-up or not," I growled, pointing the finger at my chest.

"You're not a hook-up kind of girl." His jaw clenched, losing his monotone as if he disliked the idea. Hypocrite.

"When your locker room claim didn't work, you manipulated the facts. But you can't win like this." Colton's eyes sparkled with malice.

Locker room claim?

But before I could process that, Colton stepped toward me, and Kayden exploded. "I always win," he hissed, slamming his fist in Colton's chest so hard that he was about to fall off my window, but he grabbed the curtains. He stumbled but was back on his feet, but livid.

"What the fuck is going on between you two?" Colton snapped. "What are you two, friends with benefits? Do you fuck her in private? Is that how she got great boobs?"

I flushed in embarrassment. Kayden was about to launch at him, but he dodged it and flashed his phone.

"Nuh-uh," Colton raised his finger, stopping Kayden. "One click and this slut show will be out. I'll spread it so wide that people will spit on her."

I gasped.

Did Colton call *me* a slut?

Chapter 14

A Close Encounter

"DON'T YOU DARE CALL HER THAT," Kayden's growl was so loud that it echoed in my room. Suddenly the ground rumbled beneath me. *Was Murkwood experiencing an earthquake?*

"Careful," Robin grumbled, but Kayden ignored his warning.

Colton's tar-black eyes widened as he stumbled back. "Don't raise your voice at me, or I'll just click on upload, and it will spread on the dark web," he threatened, pulling out false bravado.

I stepped forward, looking at his screen in disbelief. The ground slipped under my feet as my eyes widened in horror, looking at a video of us making out.

"OMG! This is… fuck…Are you nuts?" I was appalled. "Are you sick or what?" I flipped, stunned by the video. "You recorded us making out, I mean, who does that? Are you a psychopath or something?"

"Psychopath?" he gritted through his teeth. "Do you even know what a psychopath can do?" he reeled towards me. I stepped back as Kayden gracefully slid between us, hiding me.

Instantly, Robin tossed a cloth on Colton's face, making him stumble, and before he could act, Kayden grabbed him with his throat and flipped him over, crashing him to the ground, and started punching his face. Blood was running down Colton's nose. Soon, he was out without any fight.

"Lizzy," Hannah held me tightly, her mouth hung open. She cupped my face. "Don't worry. It's over, relax," soothing me, but I was in shock.

"He. Made. A. Video. Of. Me. Kissing. Him." I said every word so slowly as if trying to grasp my mind around it. "He. Was. Asking.

Me. To. Take. Off. My. Clothes." Kayden and Robin rumbled simultaneously at those words.

Kayden pressed his shoes on Colton's nose, trying to block oxygen, Robin placed his hand on his shoulder.

"Don't," Robin shook his head. "He ain't worth any piece of your soul."

Same time, Hannah crooned to me. "Shhhh... Lizzy, nothing happened. Everything is fine now," but I had gone icy cold.

"He. Was. Going. To. Post. It. Online." I added in the same tone. "He. Wanted. To. Create. A. Scandal."

We are the Hectors! I have always been taught to stay low away from media, to mask my real emotions, to hide my true self, and I have done everything I could till now. But today, my seek for comfort, a little slip, would have destroyed everything.

Hannah crushed me into her arms as if protecting me, stopping me from breaking.

"There won't be any scandal. Look, Kayden already handled him. He wouldn't let anything happen to you," Hannah whispered.

My eyes fell on Kayden, who was flipping through Colton's phone while Robin was hovering over Colton, checking his pulse while he was immobile. His knuckles were broken, and blood dripped from them, but he gave no heed.

I had to physically stop myself from reaching out to help him.

"What was he doing in your room, Lizzy?" Robin asked me, in his uptight voice, a frown on his face as he brushed his bald scalp angrily.

"He-he came to give me the autopsy report, Noni sent him," I looked at him, breaking the hug, biting my lips, embarrassed about letting my mentor down.

"No, Alice left the house just after dinner. He was supposed to leave too." Hannah mustered, "She wouldn't let any outsider in the house with three children already missing. She didn't even let Moores stay in here."

"He must have come here on some mission," Robin nodded, looking at Hannah. Something passed between them.

"And we know what it was," Kayden's fingers tightened around Colton's phone, a muscle jumping in his jaw.

"Call—" I was about to tell Robin to call the cops, but Kayden cut me off.

"Nuh-uh, he's mine to punish," He announced.

I bit my lips, taking a few steps back. Kayden loves punishing people. He had given Homer so many detentions that his life had become hell at school.

"It's my house, I make decisions here," I pulled up a fake bravado.

"Enough," He whisper-yelled. "You should listen to me sometimes, but why would you?" he asked, irritated. "*I am Eloise Hector, the princess of Murkwood, so nobody can tell me what to do,*" he mimicked me as I scowled.

I don't sound like that.

"So, a word of advice, princess, if you want to survive, get your claws out because princesses are always the first ones on the target list," he said, showing me Colton's phone.

My phone fell out of my hand when I quickly yanked it out of his grip. I was too embarrassed and didn't want anyone to see it.

"What are you looking for, just smash it." He tried to snatch it away, but I refused.

"No, I want to know how many he had."

He didn't argue back but flashed his eyes at me, making me shiver.

Shit! I couldn't believe I was saying it, but Kayden was right, and I was relieved of his existence for the first time in my life. He saved my ass.

My first kisser turned out to be a psychopath. "Why does this keep on happening to me? Don't I deserve happiness even for a split second?"

"Perhaps, you're looking for it in all the wrong places." Kayden strode toward my Avengers collection, but I let his comment slide, busy scrolling through Colton's phone. That shitty dude even has his dick's pic on them. I feel disgusted, wanting to puke out his taste from mine.

"I urgently need a shower, a very thorough and deep cleansing one, for the rest of my life." I shivered in disgust, feeling soiled.

"I'll get it ready," Hannah said, nodding. "I'll put on some scented candles and your favorite cleanser." She strolled towards my ensuite washroom.

But I stopped listening to her as my focus shifted to other girls' pictures. I was not the only one. There were more pics and videos of making out, even having sex with numerous girls. He had a folder, and I just realised there were also a few from our school. "She is Aisha, Kayden, check, isn't it Aisha, the cellist?"

Fuck! It was a close encounter. He tried to warn me, and I thought he was just here to torture me again, but hey! Given our history, I wasn't the one to blame.

I bit my lips, sneaking a gaze at him, he was holding my Iron Man action figure.

I arched my eyebrow at him, but he ignored my glare, observing it. "Jason told me he was a jerk and was rusticated from the school for leaking nude pictures of some classmate. That's why he never went to college, as he hadn't even graduated. Rumors are that he even had illicit relationships with girls from our school last year, but nobody came forward, and now we know why. He blackmails them by recording their videos." He grimaced.

I gulped down audibly, turning to Robin. "Don't tell Noni. She'll be disheartened. Tomorrow, after the funeral, let her know that Colton isn't working for our company anymore." He gave a firm nod without peeking into the phone. "And hold his company account or any other incentives he was receiving," I added. Colton should know with whom he was messing.

"I'll handle everything from here," Robin assured me. "How could Julia hire such a guy? She always runs a background check."

"He was working for your mother?" Kayden interrupted with a crease between his eyes.

"Yeah, he was her second associate," I told him reluctantly. I didn't want any more lectures about getting involved with an employee. *You don't defecate where you eat*, I knew it well, but I was stupid and grief-stricken, but that shouldn't be any excuse, and what's done is done. And this should remain among four of us only, Kayden must keep his mouth shut.

"Give me that phone." Instead of yelling at me, he reached for the phone, yanking it from my hand.

"What are you going to do with that?" I asked, trying to snatch it back from him. "Let me delete my pictures." But he secured the phone inside his back pocket.

"I found it. I will keep it," he told me blandly, his monotone was back.

"It's my photos, you jerk," I snapped at him angrily. He was back to being an obnoxious narcissist cyborg.

"Don't worry. I'll delete them. I have no interest in looking at your make-out session," he rolled his eyes like he was least interested.

"Hey, where are you going?" I asked as he opened the door and stepped out of my room, ignoring me. Argh! I followed him. "You can't just enter and leave my house at your own will. It's my home, not yours. This phone was found on my estate, so it's mine, give it back, and my Iron Man too."

But he was already descending the stairs, still ignoring me. He was in the hall when Robin asked. "Should I put him in the back?" I halted, and so did Kayden. We both turned to look at Robin, who dragged Colton out of my room.

And to my shock, his eyes were not on me but on Kayden. *Whoa! Now he was taking orders from him? Was Kayden the new king?* I frowned at Kayden.

"Have you roofied my staff?"

"I am not Cooper," he grimaced, making a jab at Homer.

My nostrils flared as I turned my back to him stubbornly. I crossed my hands over my stomach. *It's my house. He's no one to give orders.*

"Throw him out," I ordered, disgusted even to talk about Colton.

"I think we should—" Kayden was about to say something.

"Nuh-huh!" I raised my finger, craning my head back. "Nobody cares what you think," I smirked pretentiously. "This is my house, and Robin will do whatever he's been told."

Kayden scoffed. "Bring him to the vaults," and to my shock, Robin nodded.

My mouth fell open. Did they make a pack to humiliate me? *BTW, how does he know about the vaults?*

I flinched as he closed the doors loudly, Kayden had strolled his ass out. I groaned at his exit, stomping my foot down, aggravated to the extent of pulling my hair out.

I wanted to punch him hard. "Come here, honey," crooned Hannah, standing near the last staircase. "Don't worry. He's a nice guy. I know he'll delete those photos."

"You do? Do you even know what kind of jerk he is?" I asked them, confused. Why do these people trust Kayden so much?

"Sweety, we've known him since he was a child, and he's one noble boy," she tugged my hair behind my ears. "Alice is so fond of him." She smiled at me.

"Urgh!" I rolled my eyes. "He is just a manipulative jerk who knows how to put up a show to control others. He is the Devil,"

Hannah chuckled. "Don't worry, this devil won't manipulate you. And if he does, you can call me anytime, and we'll kick his ass."

"Swear?" I asked.

"Pinky swear." She smiled, hugging me. I felt her sigh in my hair. "How cruel is Light, making my little girl suffer so much." She rubbed my hand, soothing me.

"I don't know, Hannah, she probably hates me," I hugged her back.

"Don't say that, honey. She loves you, it's just dark times, keep hope in her."

Seriously? After all this? My mother was gone, my friends were suffering in that demonic place because of the stupid shitty glitch, and now the person with whom I was looking for escape turned out to be a sex addict. A jerk who would have posted them on the dark web if Kayden wasn't there.

"But where did he hide?" Robin asked. "I checked every room before going to my room."

"Did you check in Mom's?" I asked. Blood drained from his face as he shook his head.

Chapter 15

A Psychopath in Town

My mother's room was nothing like mine. It had withered rose walls and a king-size black bed on which black satin bedcovers were neatly wrapped with too many pillows. A white fur carpet was on all three sides of the bed, with an old typewriter on the right-side table and black candles and dried lavender in a silver tray on the left. A glass terrarium for her tarantula lay empty in the corner. A large chandelier in the middle gave enough light to brighten a dim room. A glass table with fresh purple lilies in a crystal vase was placed in the centre. I could see photo frames in the back, mostly belonging to us before grappy died.

I couldn't see anything moved or messed up.

"The room is a mess," Hannah spoke, to my shock. "He tried to cover it, but everything is not as perfect as I make them."

"Seriously, like what?" I arched an eyebrow, not able to find any flaw.

"Look at that flower arrangement, it's all disrupted and pillowcases, they are not arranged as per Julia's choice and look at the drawer, it had that string coming out of it. And books, some of them are kept reverse. Only psychopaths keep the books that way," she groaned and pointed out everything like some detective who had covered the crime scenes numerous times.

She's good, better than I thought. I was impressed.

"Fine, let's check," but I didn't know what to look for, something Colton wanted from my mother, and what could that be?

I looked through her drawer. It was the usual stuff, cigarette, pens, pins, papers, make-up, just regular stuff.

"I think he was looking for this." Hannah took out Mom's laptop from her wardrobe, which was a mess, but that laptop was in a wooden compartment under the drawer, which no one could have found. "Why her laptop, what does he want from it?" I asked, turning it on.

"Password?" I mumbled, biting my lips. I wasn't that close to my mother to know the password to her laptop. I put Mom's birthday, name, and Noni's, but nothing came out.

"Try your birthday," Hannah nudged. "It has to be yours."

"Are you sure? Who wants to use Friday the 13th as a password?" I asked, typing the grimmest date, but to my amazement, it worked.

I went to Chrome and looked for the history, I wanted to know what she had Googled lastly, and there she had many names searched on MyBook. It seemed like she was going through various profiles on MyBook. It was an outdated social site, who uses that till now?

"All of them are girls." Hannah pointed out. "It has to do something with Women Empowerment Club." *Whoa! She should be a detective. Why was she wasting her skills in taking care of me?*

"You think?" I read all the names. They were mostly seniors, passed out. I clicked on their profiles when I saw Riley Lynn. Mom had searched for her name many times.

Riley Lynn, I know she had something to do with my mother.

I opened her profile and saw she had several pictures of her with Colton, and they seemed to be in a relationship. I recalled her sister saying that she ran away with a fiddler. So, Colton was the fiddler who was kissing me even though he was in a relationship. He disgusts me. I looked at the other girls' profiles and most had Colton as a common friend.

I quickly slid to the desktop, searching for these girls' names in documents, and I found them in a common spam folder.

I opened it, and it had many more folders, each with a particular girl's name. I opened the first one, it was a copy of mail from her, with a video and some photographs, and I didn't have to open those photographs to know what they were. I read her email. It was a request from my mother to act against him. She was going on about how he lured her, made a video without her consent, and was blackmailing her.

God, I was ashamed, a psychopath was running among us, and we weren't doing anything. I felt terrible for all these girls and somehow blessed that I was saved from this humiliation.

Thank you, Kayden!

I read other emails, and each one was mostly the same.

"Such a monster. If she knew his truth, why hire him?" I asked, turning to Hannah, who was still reading the emails.

"I don't know, but your mom works in a mysterious way. She had her own unique style."

"What's the use of a style if he's still roaming openly?" I huffed exasperatedly.

"If Julia had acted hastily, he could have uploaded these videos on the dark web. She had to tread carefully." Hannah answered, contemplating.

"Are you forgetting she was Cobra-Queen? She would have wiped him off this town in a snap." I arched my eyebrow.

She hummed. "Something was stopping her. You think Colton was blackmailing her too?" Hannah raised her eyebrows too.

"What could he have over, Mom?" I frowned at the laptop, checking out more folders. "She wouldn't have fucked him." I shrugged.

"PRINCESS!" Hannah hissed.

"What? I said *she wouldn't.*" I bit my lips.

"But how did Colton learn about these emails, because he was definitely here to wipe them off. Do you think he had something to do with your mother's death?" She arched her eyebrows in concern.

"No, he was with Homer that night. Moreover, I think his girlfriend Riley must have chickened out and told him about the mail after my mother's death." I cringed my nose. "Thinking she might get into trouble if cops find her video on Mom's laptop," I shook my head. "And Noni told me they found the girl who was driving. It was someone named Lea Perker."

She nodded, not meeting my eyes.

"I think he was here to delete them, but as he couldn't find her laptop, so he thought about blackmailing you, but Kayden sabotaged his plan." She was joining all the dots.

I groaned loudly. How could I become a stupid pawn in his plan? I was so angry with myself. How could I be so naïve not to judge his intentions? I should have known why a twenty-three-year-old artistic dude was interested in me.

My mouth fell when I heard Robin.

"Hannah," Robin called her from downstairs. "I need your help."

"I'll be back." She tapped my shoulder and gave me a timid smile.

I was checking all the folders when I found my mother's childhood photographs. She had received an award at school. I clicked on the next, in which she was laughing while cutting a birthday cake. I chuckled at her photograph. She seemed so lively in these photographs than ever in her life. Mom was beautiful in a smart kind of way but looked carefree in bellbottoms and sweaters.

In this one, she was sitting on some boy who crashed to the ground, showing off her muscles. She seemed funny. *Why haven't I seen this fun side of her?*

What happened, Mom? Why did you become so heartless? Why aren't you ever happy?

The following was a group picture. I gasped, amused as I could recognise most of them. Mom was in the middle, red-haired with freckles. With her must be Mr. Parsons, as he looked a lot like Kayden, wrapped his hand around her shoulder. They seemed like close friends. Next to him was a boy with black hair, he seemed small and slender, but his blondes gave away—Bill Muller. Then was Mike Cooper, looking precisely like Homer with a cigarette in his mouth and black shades on his eyes. There was a couple as the girl had two ponies, and her head was on the boy's shoulder, it must be Ethan and Meghan. Were they school-time lovers? I never knew that. Next to Mr. Parsons were two girls, one had these dark eyes with similar tone hair, a heart-shaped face, a bit shy, and the other seemed haughty, a bit older than the rest of the group. This photograph seemed to be of some birthday party, in some fair.

That's when my phone beeped. And suddenly, all my hopes went up. Maybe it was from my friends. I quickly took it out of my pocket and realised it was a text from Kayden.

I frowned before opening it.

K: *Want to go out for a walk?*

Was he crazy? He rushed out of my house, and now he wanted to go for a walk. He was so confusing.

I shook my head. It was all too much for me. I needed to get ready for tomorrow, and it was already 11:15 pm, though I wanted to tell him all about Colton and the girls, but I was tired. Moreover, he would never listen to me. I closed Mom's laptop and put it back where it belonged, carefully closing the door.

E: *We don't hang out together. We aren't friends.*

K: *Walk. Now!*

Geez, man, how could someone be bossy through messages also?

I groaned loudly. '*Fuck off,*' I wrote, but I deleted it. It would've been too harsh, he did save my life today. I wrote—'I have to write a eulogy,' but this seemed too explanatory, so I deleted it and settled on the basics.

E: *Busy. Bye!*

K: *Cut it out. I am waiting outside, be there in five.*

Argh! I didn't reply, as I got out of my clothes, urging towards my shower.

My phone pinged again, making me roll my eyes.

K: I received a message from CLARA.

E: WHAT?

I typed hurriedly, but he didn't reply. Instead, he went offline.

"Asshole," I groaned. I quickly jumped in the shower, scrubbing out Colton's waft off me as I reached out for fresh clothes, my eyes wandering from clothes to phone, in case he replied, but he didn't.

Clara messaged him. How? What?

And that's what stopped me from shattering into pieces, drowning in embarrassment and getting lost in the thought of what would have happened if Kayden hadn't come.

Chapter 16

A Control Freak

I dressed before going out to look for Kayden, to kill him, of course. He left me on read. No one ignores me as he does. But today, it'll be over. I'll retrieve the message and kill him. His arrogant ass will be lying somewhere in Hector's estate or in the vaults where he took Colton to do God knows what.

I'll probably be the first murderer who smells like litchi and magnolia with a hint of jasmine, ginger, and a dash of pepper. It was Hannah's mix of herbs for cleansing my aura, and protecting me from the evil eye, even though Noni told her the chatoyant I was wearing around my neck would be enough. But after recent events, I needed better luck.

I brushed around four to five times, still feeling soiled, but it was better. But right now, my focus was on Kayden—his last message made me curious. I have been looking for a way to reach my friends. Perhaps a clue from them could show me a path.

There was another message from him telling me to grab a jacket as it was cold outside, but I read it when I was already downstairs, so I ignored it.

"Oh my gosh! It's chilly," I said, rubbing my hands while standing on the porch of my house. It was surprisingly cold for July.

You know legends state that the weather in Murkwood changes according to the feelings of Hectors—Nathan's words hit me, and I shivered, thinking it might be true.

Though it had stopped raining, but there were no stars, and the moon was peeping from the back of the dark clouds. The cool breeze compelled trees to dance to its rhythm, and water droplets on their leaves shone like diamonds reflected by the streetlights. A trail of flowers planted across Hectors estate, dazzled in the moonlight.

The smell of wet ground was refreshing. Crickets chirped somewhere in the background, adding music to the ambience. Everything was perfect despite my day. My day had been terrible, and the events made my life miserable. I fucked up really bad.

I held my chatoyant between my palm, asking for some strength or calmness as I walked down the paved path finding him standing near the mermaid fountain. He must have heard my footfalls as he said—

"I said five minutes. You took forty-five. Don't you—" His words guttered once he turned to me. His eyes widened, darting from my face to my clothes. His shoulders went rigid like he had stopped breathing, not taking my scent. He closed his eyes, cursing, brushing his hands through his hair as if I looked gross.

I was wearing a noodle-sleeved ditsy coral front twist crop top showing good cleavage and skinny denim shorts just below my navel, I didn't think it was hideous, but it's Kayden. Everything about me disgusted him.

I frowned at him, thinking of punching him in the face for giving me that look. *You need the message first.* I had to remind myself.

"And I suppose you are used to that as you date so many girls," I stride towards him.

"I don't date any," he said, clearing his throat.

"Of course. You just do hook-ups, you don't have time for relationships," I sang it like a litany, rolling my eyes.

"Perhaps I am saving that for someone special." He eyed my arms, where goosebumps trailed.

"Yeah, still didn't stop you from fucking everyone on display," I scoffed, rubbing my hand over my arms.

"I told you to grab a jacket," he frowned, ignoring my jab. "But when have you listened to me?" His gaze fixed on me as he strode forward, towering over me.

Why would I? You cocky bastard. I know you saved my life today, but that doesn't change anything. You're still the devil, and I hate you. I wanted to say it out loud, but I need that message first.

"Come on," he grabbed my hand as electricity shot through my bones, but he seemed unaffected, leading me outside the iron gates. It felt weird—him holding my hand, we don't do that. We don't touch each other. I performed CPR on him once, which doesn't even count as touching. That didn't give him any right to hold my hand the way he was holding it as he marched me down the paved path.

"Where are we going?" I asked. "And what the hell was the message?" He ignored me. *How could someone ignore me while holding me?* I looked at him, his jaw was locked, and his grip tightened as I tried to yank my hand away.

So, I leapt and stood before him. He halted with a jolt, letting my hand fall.

"Give me your phone," I splayed my palm out, asking for his phone. "Show me the message," I demanded, asserting that I wouldn't go with him anywhere. I wouldn't trust any guy after tonight.

I should stick to Homer. At least he hasn't done anything like this with me ever. Or perhaps I should consider dating girls because I was done with boys from now on. *Maybe I will date some girl and rub that in Kayden's face, proving that his games no longer affect me, but can I? Can you change your preferences like that?*

"I don't have it on my phone." His monotone was back as he walked past me, retaking my hand. We kept marching on the wet street outside the iron gates towards a white Merc parked near the iron fence, just where my room was. It wasn't his car, but Mayor's. What happened to his Hummer? I thought he loved his car way too much, *I mean, who doesn't, it's smooth AF.* Whenever Clara was in a crisis and invited me to her house, he was mostly washing or polishing it, with his eyes fixed on me as if forcing me to bolt.

"Were you keeping an eye on me?" I asked, looking from his car to my window. Anyone could see anything from here. I had to keep in mind, no more making out on the windowsill, or I'd be colossal news someday. Only if I got to kiss again, as my chances were negligible because this jerk told everyone at school that I was lesbian. "You could see he was recording me from down here?"

"No," he said flatly in his famous monotone.

"You assumed because he was Colton?" I asked. He knew about Colton's reputation. He said Jason told him. That's why he was up in my bedroom?

"I didn't know which jerk it was," he hissed. Of course, he presumed him to be a jerk because *I* was kissing him. As if I couldn't kiss a good guy. *Though he was right today but I cannot give him that kind of satisfaction.*

"Then why did you come to my room?" I frowned. When he didn't answer, I added, "Stalker,"

"Not everyone revolves around you, Hector." He growled darkly at me, being obnoxious again.

"But you do, control-freak." My eyes flashed. His need to control my life was too much to contain that I could feel his hatred towards me rippling from his body. "I am not going anywhere with you until you tell me what Clara said in the message." I yanked my hand from him, and he let it go as I crossed them firmly over my stomach.

Kayden rubbed his face before turning to me. "Would you please just get in the car?" His heavy voice, creased forehead, and glistening eyes told me he was in pain.

"Where are you taking me?" I asked him without getting in the car. I couldn't trust him. What if he also tried to take advantage of me, though I know he won't, but that's what Colton had been—'a good guy.' And then he turned out to be a psychopath.

"Get in the car first," he demanded, sliding inside the driver's seat, but I held my ground, tapping my foot. *If he's stubborn, I am more persistent than him.*

"Just get in the car, Hector," he commanded, making me go weak in the knees, but I stood tall. "Fine, I'll find her on my own," he said, hitting the ignition. "I don't need your help anyway. According to you, she died," he snapped.

"No," I retorted. "Not dead—never dead—I never said that" I was shivering. The idea of them dying was already killing me. "Leave me alone," I broke down. "I can't take all this yelling," I told him, stepping back. "I am too tired now, tired of everything that is going on in my life, tired of everyone," I spilled. "First my mom, then my friends, stitched lady, Colton, and now *you*." I sucked a long breath. "My life is already chaos, I want a clear head. I just want to reach her…find her. I don't deserve all this, Kayden." I almost choked on his name, my mask slipped, and the fortress that I built around me to safeguard my feelings, broke down.

His facial expressions changed as he got out of his car and came to my side, his hands inside his pockets as he gazed at me without saying anything, his eyes reading me, trying to tell me things he couldn't mouth, but I didn't get him. He lifted his hands and then curled his fingers into fists.

He sighed. "I won't yell," his voice went velvety soft, to my amazement. He stepped forward, closing the distance between us, leaning in. My eyes widened in shock as I stepped back, thinking he was about to kiss me, but instead, he opened the door. "I want to help you. Believe me."

Blood rushed my cheeks as he spoke those words so softly, filled with determination that if I'd been any other girl, I would have followed him blindly.

"But I don't need your help, I just need the message," I told him, blinking his charming aura away, not falling for his trap.

"We both know, Hector, you're too supercilious to ask for my help, so cut it short and let's not waste any more time. She's already been missing for a week."

He was right, he'd be the last person I would have gone for help, but I was not that desperate to accept help from Kayden Parsons. *It was dark times, but not that dark*—I heard that in Moira's voice.

I looked up at him. He had bluish marks under his eyes, like he hadn't slept for days. "Get in. We need to hurry. The message is not here. It's at home." There was a hint of agitation in his voice that he was trying hard to hide.

At home? Really? Did she send a letter or a telegram? I looked at him skeptically, finding any hint of malice, but he seemed genuine, and he wouldn't use Clara against me. He loves her, they were twins, and he was too protective of her. Their mother died after giving them birth, so they're close to their *abuela* and too many cousins, who always celebrate all the festivals together.

"Fine," I agreed, getting into his car. "But if it turns out to be some trap, I'll kick your stupid ass. I know how to take care of myself, I do have claws." Making myself clear as Kayden closed the door. His words—*if you want to survive, get your claws out* were ringing in my ears.

I took in his car's leather and ocean cologne scent. It was masculine and highly swooning. Even the car's aura made me feel like it belonged to a powerful person.

"Yeah!" he scoffed as he got in, turning on the ignition. "As if you had it all under control today," he shook his head, hitting the road while I secured myself with the seat belt.

"It was all happening because I wanted to," I scowled at him.

"No, babe, it was all happening because HE wanted to," he spoke through gritted teeth, but my body went through some foreign shivers as he called me *babe*.

He continued. "This is exactly what I am talking about. You are so naïve that guys tend to take advantage of you. You shouldn't just kiss anybody." His words were clipped and full of anger.

"I wouldn't if you didn't freaking hate me so much. It's all your fault!"

He gasped.

"You really think I hate you?" He seemed taken aback, like it was some hot news.

"Of course, why else would you spread fake rumors about me? Why would you act so repulsed by me?" *What else was the explanation for his behaviour?* "You must be delighted about what happened today. It would have been good riddance for you." After this scandal, Noni would have sent me somewhere else, far away from Murkwood, perhaps to Caribasca with Dad. Even the thought of it made me cringe.

"I guess I am not done with you," he smirked, and I arched my eyebrows. What was this Devil planning for me? It had to be something worse. Chills spread through my bones thinking about it.

"Asshole," I huffed, a little scared, he was highly intimidating, plus I could never read his mind, he was highly protected with these concrete walls around him that I couldn't reach him. I never knew what he was thinking, which made him dangerous.

"Stop name-calling me," he warned. "You don't know me."

"I do. Everyone knows you are the mean candy boy who just likes to fuck everyone and win every time."

You are a manwhore Kayden—I wanted to add, but I bit my lips at those words. People don't like to be called slut or whore, somebody called me that today, and it hurt. It sank in deep, even though I was slightly out of the line, but that didn't make me a slut.

"Jealous?" He narrowed his eyes.

"No," I scoffed, but something inside me burned. His knuckles whitened on the steering wheel as his lips thinned. "I don't care what you do with your life."

"At least I don't play with someone's feelings, everyone knows what they are getting into with me, I am upfront with them. Have you ever seen me walking up to anyone and asking for a kiss or convincing them to make out with me? No, I don't. They decide to make out with me *willingly*. It's their choice to be a part of a hook-up. They all want me, and I am just fulfilling their desire. It's a kind of social service." The corner of his lips rose. *What a pretentious jerk!*

"Yeah, right," I rolled my eyes. "I don't need any kind of social service from anyone. I already have one, and I'll stick to him."

Homer's terrorised face flashed before my eyes, the one he made when his phone caught fire. I flinched at that memory, pulling my knees to my chest, holding onto myself, and controlling onto tears.

I felt Kayden's gaze on me and then back to the road while taking a right turn from the central library towards the Sea-Witch Valley.

Finally, he retracted himself from arguing with me, which was good because right now, I wasn't in the mood to bicker anymore, tired of all the drama in my life. He filled the silence by putting on the song—T*reat You Better by Shawn Mendes.*

My stomach coiled as I felt the words. *Why this song?* Was it intentional or just random? I turned to look at him, but his jaw was locked, and his knuckles were still white as he held the steering wheel too tight. *It has to be random.* I was about to change the song, but instantly he rolled down the windows, and my hair was talking to the air. I have curly hair. The wind was the last thing I wanted. I held my hair, pulling it back in a bun and scowled at him.

He shuddered due to the chilly wind as he was all drenched. "Do you want to catch hypothermia?" I glared at him. He gave an astonished look. "Roll up the windows," I ordered, tapping on the heat segment of the AC.

"You're too bossy for someone who doesn't like to be called princess," he murmured, but he rolled up the windows.

I kept staring out the window. There was a deep silence for a few minutes. Only Bruno Mars—*Grenade* raged through the speakers.

I tapped my shoes with the rhythm, closing my eyes—as today's events came crashing onto me. Adrenaline was washing off, leaving me shaken. Fuck! Things could have gone worst. I have seen what he does. All those videos—how he had recorded his sex sessions with all those girls without their consent. I could be one of them. I would be one of them.

Tears rolled down my eyes as I hid my face from Kayden, I didn't want him to see me weak and broken.

"Come here," he said softly. *What? Was I delusional?*

Before I could act, I felt a warm hand snaking around my waist, pulling me towards him, crushing me to his side. I gasped as my hand immediately fell on his chest, a thrill zinged through my body.

Fuck! What the hell was wrong with me? Why was my body reacting like this to his touch? It's not that I hadn't been touched by any boy before. *Nathan does it all the time, but he's gay. Even Homer does, but it never sends electric shivers. It never reacts the way my body is acting now.*

He shivered and then took a deep breath like he had finally breathed after a long period. I arched my neck to look at his face, but he was looking at the road, driving with one hand, while his other was around my waist, drawing circles on my bare skin, from the split of the front. I should have asked him what he was doing, but no words fell from my mouth. His touch clouded my mind, making my heart beat faster, and for some reason, his pounding matched mine.

He looked down at me, his eyes met mine, and for the first time, I felt him. He was scared. He let his walls down, and Kayden Parsons, the winner, seemed defeated. My heart lurched as my hand fisted his shirt. Even though he was my nemesis, I still wanted to take his pain away, and before I could, he broke the connection to look at the road.

"Why did you go to the swamps alone?" His chest reverberated under my hand, somehow, it felt like the most real thing in this world.

I should have pushed away from him and stopped myself from swooning into his masculine scent, but I was drained, exhaustion weighed down heavily on my bones and TBF, his fingers were extremely soothing, so I let myself give into him for the first time, and the last.

Sighing, I placed my head on his broad shoulder. "I am cursed to be alone, Kayden." His grip tightened around me. "I was never supposed to make friends, but I didn't listen to my mom and look what happened, my darkness consumed them." Tears fell from my eyes, one after another, drenching his already wet shirt, but he didn't push me away. To my amazement, he stayed and listened.

"Perhaps, you need someone to evade your darkness and let you shine," he whispered, caressing my hair to my shoulders, and rubbing his cheek on my head.

"No," I shook my head. "I am no Damsel in distress, I don't need a prince-charming."

His muscles stiffened like he was shocked by my answer, and then he relaxed. "Then what do you want, baby girl?" he purred.

My heart flipped, *baby girl.* I had never been called that before.

Acceptance.

But I didn't answer him. Instead, I chose to answer his first question. "I was looking for the girl who was driving my mother's car," I finally spoke when my tears subsided, fumbling through my pockets for Riley's phone. "I found this in the museum's rubble."

And then, I couldn't stop myself, I told him how I tracked that girl down and went to her house, bribing children.

"And you did it all by yourself?" He smiled in amazement, brushing his cheeks on my hair like he couldn't stop himself.

"That part was pretty easy," I closed my eyes, snuggling into him further. I was in terrible danger because I found sanctuary in the arms of the devil. "But it was a bootless errand. It belonged to some girl Riley Lynn, but Noni told me the girl who was with Mom was Lea Perker, but Riley was Colton's girlfriend, I found her mail in my mum's laptop," telling him about the emails and videos.

He listened to me quietly, but his grip tightened around me, crushing me to him like I was the only thing that was stopping him from turning the car around and killing that bastard.

Chapter 17

Bad Boy of Murkwood

The first thought I had when sunlight fell on my face—*my room doesn't smell like this*. The mixed scent of oceans and gardenias wafted as nostalgia hit me. *Clara!* I snuggled more into the blanket as a fresh breeze brushed my face.

The first time Clara invited me, she had a beautiful house with the latest technology but not even a single plant. So, I took it into my hand to provide my BFF with filtered oxygen and planted gardenia in her room, followed by every other room. Then I planted more flowers all around her house, and now she had more than a hundred potted plants, and Mayor never gave a damn, too busy to even acknowledge it.

Her house was on the cliff, edging the ocean as we had beach rocks instead of beaches in Murkwood, and the rest was covered with forest area.

I rolled back onto my back, stretching, a smile spreading through my face as I opened my eyes, expecting to meet Clara.

But the first thing I saw was writing on the ceiling—*I have to protect the one thing that I can't live without. That's you.* My heart fluttered. This was from an Iron Man movie, I had seen that movie more than ten times.

But suddenly, I bolted upright. It wasn't Clara's room.

Fuck! Where was I?

I looked around, grey walls, black curtains, opened balcony with potted pink gardenias and white bougainvillea creeping all over the edges of the wall, and an extensive collection of books colour-wise arranged on the bookshelf with certain basketballs kept on the side plank with equal distance between them. I frowned. This room seemed to belong to some control freak.

There were trophies, a vast collection of action figures from Marvel and DC and various artwork, but my eyes squinted on the Iron Man action figure, which looked exactly like mine, not just looked like mine but was mine, sat next to an action figure of wonder woman.

I narrowed my eyes, but I totally forgot about it when my eye fell on the jerseys that were framed and hung on the side wall. It had the number thirteen written on them with his name—Parsons.

FUCK! It was Kayden's room.

I quickly whipped my head to the side as if expecting him naked, but God saved me from the series of heart attacks as I found it empty, but to my horror, it was messed up, like someone did sleep with me last night. I made a strangling sound as I looked under the sheets.

By God's grace, I was wearing my clothes, *good—that was a good sign—right?* My boobs were a little out of place, but I rearranged them back in my bra, thinking about what happened last night.

"What's wrong with you, why can't you mind your own business?"

My head shot up as muffled voices fell onto my ears. I tiptoed towards the door, tying my hair up in a high bun while eavesdropping. *Yeah, I give zero fucks about the rules of society, so sue me!*

"This *is* my business. You let a girl sleep in your room for the first time. It's like a milestone," A heavy voice spoke. It wasn't muffled, and I recognised it because it was filled with mischievousness and belonged to one and only Jason Parsons, the bad boy of Murkwood.

In school, he used to get into fights every day. He spent most of his days in detention and rest, driving his Harley. He's got a powerful aura like he could crush somebody's skull with his bare hands. Clara was always worried about him, as he kept getting stitches every month, but he never cared. Fighting was his MO, and he was living life stating *carpe diam.*

I was devastated when Mayor sent him to military school, and later, he joined the same, far away near Greenland.

When did he return?

"Lower your voice. You'll wake her up," Kayden hissed through clenched teeth.

"Aww, look at you, Kiddie, you're already pussy whipped, but it's past three. She can wake up by now, or did you not let her sleep all night? Is she that hot?" he teased him.

Kayden grumbled something about not calling him by that nickname. I felt commotion outside as I quickly turned to hide, and before I could launch towards Kayden's washroom, the door flung open with a bang, making me flinch.

"Eloise Hector?" Jason choked. I halted, biting my lips. *Was my name written over the back of my head?*

"Oh! Hi BJ," I chimed, turning to him, masking the uneasiness behind my wide smile as Kayden ground his teeth. Clara and I used to call him Big-Jay, as he'd been a big brother to me. Helpful and protective, he taught me how to play video games while Kayden used to pull the plugs. He was four-years older than me. People think of him as a brute, a bad boy with anger issues, but he's a total goofball and had so many funny incidents to tell that made us laugh rolling on the floor.

Right now, he looked like a Gypsy with a month-long scruff along his jawline and mocha brown beach hair falling onto his shoulders casually. He was taller, around 6'4" and buff with a broader chest than Kayden, and his smile was more natural. He had amber eyes like Clara with a scar over his left eyebrow. He wore a black co-ord set with two buttons undone, showing off his man-cleavage

His eyes went wide, and the menace in them turned into fury, growling at Kayden.

"Are you fucking kidding me? You screwing Lizzy?" He launched at his brother, pounding his giant hand at his chest, which I now realised was bare.

"What if I am?" Kayden challenged. I would have countered, but I was busy gawking.

Holy mother of God!

Kayden wasn't just fucking gorgeous, he was beyond that… he was GOD! Even Jason looked nothing in front of him.

It was a mesmerising sight, I don't think I could ever undo this... his broad shoulders… the perfectly chiselled chest… his wet abs, which I think were made of steel, made me want to weep, but what made me swoon was the lower V that was going deep in his ripped denim. Water flooded my mouth. I was practically drooling all over the pulsing veins of his strong hands, blocking his brother's charges, who was shouting at him, but I was busy ogling at his flexing muscles. I wish I could touch him to check whether he was real. I should say his shirt wasn't doing any justice to his body. He shouldn't wear anything. He should roam around shirtless, showing off his flawless body.

Now I realise why every girl wants him, even if it's just a hookup. This was the sight that every girl wanted to wake up to—*he was beautiful.*

Both the guys halted and looked at me, arching their eyebrows like I had grown with three heads. Did I mumble it out loud?

I bit my lips, clearing my throat. "C'mon, BJ, he's not my type," I rolled my eyes. Ok! That took enough courage, and I was hyperventilating inside but masked it, stopping Jason from murdering his brother.

"Yeah, because I am neither a druggist nor a psychopath," he crooked his eyebrow as a dark smirk rose his lips.

My nostrils flared. "But have commitment issues," I snapped, wiping that smirk off, and before I could feel proud, I was crushed into a boulder, which sucked away all my air.

"God! I missed you so much, gorgeous." Jason picked me up, giving me a bear hug, smelling like woodsy.

Why were these Parsons so giant? My lungs were deprived of air, and my breasts were aching when his hand grabbed my ass. "You've become fuckable, Lizzy," he slid his giant hand on my waist, laughing his animalistic laugh, shaking me throughout. I went scarlet. He's always been like this, bold and blunt.

"Ok, that's enough," Kayden announced agitatedly with his hands on my shoulders. He pulled me away from Jason, making him frown. "Now that you've met her, why don't you act like a grown-up and bring her lunch. She'd be starving." His grip tightened on my shoulders.

Jason would have commented, but something passed between brothers, and he mumbled, "Not so imaginary are we, NOICE." The corners of his lips curled with a glint in his eyes.

Before I could ask what he meant, he added. "I should have known you were there as he made Nutella churros with smothered Burritos," he shook his head in disgust. He wasn't a dessert person and constantly lectured us about eating healthy and staying fit. "Let me get that."

"Oh!" I whispered, as Jason stepped out, but kept standing there, controlling every single raging hormone that urged me to spin and look at the masterpiece of God, the bare-chested devil, but I knew if I did, I would touch him or, to my horror, lick him, because that's all I could think about.

You should get yourself checked, Lizzy.

Giving in, I turned to Kayden, and my eyes widened, finding his hazel eyes bore deep inside mine like he was searching for something, but couldn't find it. Water droplets shone in his hair like he had just come out of the shower, and his nose was perfect for his face. I'd never thought about that, but his nose was beautiful.

"You didn't have to do that," I whispered to him.

"I know, but I wanted to," he said, leaning in, sucking all the oxygen out of my lungs. I could feel his breath on my lips. For a second, I thought he would kiss me, making me forget how to breathe, but he didn't do anything, nor did he reply. We both stood there looking at each other while I fought the urge to lean in and kiss those extremely inviting lips, but I controlled myself.

"But I am not hungry," I breathed, but it was barely audible. He felt it on his lips because suddenly he shivered. His hazel eyes widened, and he instantly stepped back, bursting the bubble.

"Is that how Hectors say *thank you*?" He cleared his throat, as there was an immediate shift in his demeanor.

My blood started boiling. He always made me feel like a debased human. "*Fuck you*," I stompe off towards his washroom.

"Sure, would you like me to join you in my bathroom, or you like to do it on my bed, where you couldn't keep your hands off me last night," he smirked, teasing me.

I had a hazy memory of last night, my cheek over his chest, falling steadily, while his hands wrapped around me, and I didn't know whether I was being delusional, but I felt him sniffing me as if assuring himself I was real. Who would have known Kayden was a cuddly sleeper?

"Last time I checked, *you* couldn't let go of me, or else you'd have taken me to the guest room instead of bringing me here," I flipped him before slamming the door shut, hyperventilating. I banged my head twice on the door before sighing, and growling.

Kayden was my enemy, who loved to create chaos in my life, his words shouldn't be affecting me so much, but it's always been *his* words that brought fire out of me.

I found a spare toothbrush in the well-maintained vanity, which made me smile wickedly.

I brushed my teeth, washing my face, trying not to think about bare-chested Kayden. If he would have kissed me, I would have slapped him hard.

Liar.

Chapter 18
Duty Calls

As soon as I opened the door, a whiff of Nutella made me swoon, my stomach grumbled due to craving.

Jason's eyebrows raised questioningly, making me embarrassed, but before he could say something, Kayden handed me a Nutella-covered churro. "Have it. You going to need it."

They sat on the couch, playing a tactical shooting game while devouring burritos. Kayden had slipped into an olive jacket with sand-coloured pants and brown leather boots. Fuck! He looked smoking hot, hotter than the sun shining behind those curtains. Now that I have seen him bare-chested, nothing looks more sinful than him. I wanted to rip off that jacket and frame him.

Careful, Lizzy, getting too close to the sun will burn you.

"No thanks," I said, shoving his hand away as I sank between them, not breathing, not taking any of it. "I am not hungry." Picking a wireless controller as the introductory narrative story continues.

"Really? Your mouth is saying something, but your stomach said something else." Jason arched his eyebrow. "Since how long have you not eaten?"

"Since our sister has gone missing, she is fasting for her return." To my shock, it was Kayden who answered.

Cocky bastard.

"Seriously, dude! Did you bug my house?" I asked, confused. How in the hell did he know? But he didn't answer me, ignoring me altogether.

"Geez! Stop doing that to yourself." Jason playfully pinched my side bum, as Kayden became stoic next to me. "I know you love our sister, but she would kill us both if she found out we didn't feed you well."

And he was right, Clara would whip their asses, and I was really starving, so I grabbed the churro from Kayden and took a bite. "Mmm." OMG! I moaned as the food touched my taste buds.

Kayden groaned as he squirmed uneasily beside me, enclosing me from the side, but I ignored the zing of heat that enveloped me because it felt like I had forgotten what food tasted like. The Nutella pleased my tastebuds.

"Atta girl!" Jason exclaimed as Kayden shifted the plate of Burritos in front of me while they both devoured theirs. We started playing. Jason's player walked by, burning Merc 1 with a smirk while Kayden put him out of his misery. The game soon got intense, I was throwing grenades while they took over the shooting. They were swearing over the top, shooting instructions, fighting, and screaming while I kept them from coming to blows.

"Fuck! I am late," Jason announced, just when we were looking for the north-side tunnel to escape.

"Seriously, not now," I hissed.

"But Daddy's got a date," his smile touching his eyes.

"Wow! And you guys claim you don't think with your dicks." I scoffed. Both the brothers passed a look behind me, but I was too busy with the mission. "Fuck all you want, but right now, your team needs you," Just then, his player got attacked by a missile. I sizzled, whispering profanities.

"Great going, *my princess*, but duty calls," he chuckled as Kayden, and I took over. I am generally a sweet mouth girl, which I pull off easily as I don't talk to many people, but the Parsons were like a second family, Clara and Jason were always inviting me over, and most of my pre-teen memory belonged to this house until I stopped visiting them to avoid Kayden after the swimming pool incident like Clara would let me, but I tried to avoid him most of the times. "Lea Perker would be waiting," he added.

"WHAT?" I whipped my head to his side, getting a kink.

"Careful brother, if she dies, the world would be in grave danger," Kayden grumbled, and at the same time, my player got killed. He took over the campaign alone, crazy about winning.

"Yeah, she was a senior, and Kiddie told me you're uncertain about her authenticity, so Daddy's back on the job," he smoothed his shirt. How did Kayden know I was uncertain? I thought I only told him the facts.

"I pinged her last night, and she was totally up for it," Jason winked at me. I couldn't believe he was doing that for me. If he knew what I had done to his baby-sister, what kind of monster I was, he'd never help me. He was just there because he thought I was a feeble girl who had just lost her mother and friends and was extremely scared.

But I was extremely scared, and I needed someone to listen to me.

My chin trembled as I immediately wrapped my small arms around him as he tucked me under his.

"OMG! Thank you so much, BJ. I feel something is fishy. I mean, why did she come just after I pointed out someone else was driving the car, why'd she rolled out, why didn't my Mom pull handbrakes if bottle rolled under, and the emails I found—" I broke the hug to look for my phone, wanting to show him Colton's emails.

"Your phone is plugged in. It had no battery left." He nudged his chin towards the side table, frowning, his eyes darting to where Jason's hand was still wrapped around me.

I arched my eyebrow. Did he plug my phone? Really?

"You did right that you spent the night away from the Mansion," Jason nodded. I gave Kayden deadly stares, to which he winced a little and shook his head, implying Jason didn't know my dirty little secret.

Whoa! Did he hide my truth? Why was he being so benevolent with me? What was he playing at? Was he going to punish me later? I shuddered at the thought.

"I can't believe that mouse got the guts to sneak into the lion's den. I would have crushed his head with my bare hands if I hadn't gone down to look for that stitched lady in the swamps, but we didn't find anything." Jason bore his eyes into mine, thinning his lips as if trying to pass some secret message.

"Really, but she was there, in Edward's house, the old guy who guards the Limestone Cave." They couldn't see the mist and ashes around the house, as they were not Shadow Walkers, but that stitched lady, was she visible to me only?

He hummed, promising me to look into it. My heart melted at his faith in me. I felt ashamed of hiding the truth about their sister, but it'll be easy for them to understand Shadowland once they find out about the stitched lady.

"And this Riley Lynn is a shady person," Kayden fetched out the burnt phone from the side drawer, in between the narrative story. "I searched about her last night, and Neil collected dirt on her. She is a peddler who sells drugs in the garage where she runs some cult called *Blaze*."

"It's not a cult. It's a band," I corrected him.

"The one with red hoodies?" Jason asked, his eyes darting from Kayden to me. "You know any among them?"

"Yeah, Homer is the lead guitarist," I added pompously.

"And a drug abuser, he must have known this Riley very well," Kayden added, busy completing the mission.

"And if he had been here to answer my questions, then this is not even the last place I would rather be," I glared at Kayden, crossing my arms, feeling so relieved to throw this in his face because I knew it'd hurt him.

He twitched his face, his eyes locked into mine, frowning.

"Does he sell drugs too?" Jason asked, looking from me to Kayden and then back to me, sensing the tension between us.

"No," I said flatly, tearing my gaze. "But Riley had mailed Mom for help. She was being blackmailed by Colton too."

Jason hummed. "Don't you think Colton went Ted Bundy on your mother?" He arched his eyebrows. The concern was all I could see in his eyes.

I squealed at his suggestion. The idea of Colton being Ted Bundy was daunting. Could he have gone Ted Bundy on me? If Kayden weren't there, I would be lying limbless in his basement. Fuck! I felt beads of sweat trailing down my neck as I gulped down, it was then that I felt a warm hand squeezing my thighs, and I turned to Kayden, who was eyeing me instead of playing. His player got killed too, but he didn't care.

His eyes were soft as if telling me I was safe. I exhaled for over five seconds and then pulled a smile on my face.

"No, he was hanging out with Homer that night. They were at rehearsals, preparing for the freshman's party. Homer—" Whatever I wanted to say guttered into my throat as I felt Kayden's hand trailing up my thighs before removing it, sending shivers in their wake.

Fuck! Why was my body reacting to his touch when he seemed casual, like he hadn't even noticed? Why couldn't I take it so carelessly?

"Who is this, Homer?" Jason asked, grimacing his face.

"My b—" I was about to tell him, but Kayden interjected. "Cooper's son."

"That bad?" Jason grimaced.

"Next level." Kayden chuckled. They made fun of Homer, which I didn't like.

"Hey, he is my friend and a good guy," I frowned at them. "Moreover, we need to find Colton's computer, where he is keeping all these videos. I don't want someone to leak them."

"Don't worry, Robin is working on extracting information out from him," Kayden smiled darkly, making my stomach twist. My mentor was ruthless. An image of Colton strapped to a surgical table, and Robin working on him with different kinds of tools made me shudder.

Lizzy, you need to stop watching gore movies.

Kayden's hand slipped past to the backside of the couch, warming me up with his heat. "And Neil corrupted the hard disk of the laptop that Crew found at his home, Sophie was far more than happy to hand it over to him." He chuckled as my eyes flashed at him. Arrogance was dripping from his face. "But there was nothing on that laptop. We need to locate his office."

I started to open my mouth. "And we didn't find anything at the garage too, not even Riley," he ended his sentence. I pursed my lips. "Look for that stitched lady, find Edward," he ordered Jason like a boss, who nodded and stood up. "And drop these phones at Neil's, he'll look into them," he handed over Riley's and Colton's phones. "And check whether Crew was back from the search party or not."

"Why don't you do that, they just live next door?" Jason asked.

"I got to babysit, her majesty," he snickered.

My nostrils flared as I threw a cushion at him, but he smirked darkly, acting like a feather touched him, while Jason again roared his animalistic laugh.

"Okay, guys, I am leaving, will stop at Hector Mansion. Want to have a look at the mouse," he smiled sheepishly. He's bonded nicely with Robin as he'd been to our house many times and loved my training room but avoided confronting my mother. This two hundred and ten pounds guy was scared of my hundred and twenty pounds mother. "Do you know when Dad will be back?" he asked, gulping down a pint of cold beer without offering us like we were little kids.

"Why—what?" I asked, startled by the mention of Mayor. "We aren't doing anything. We are just hanging around. I just came to get the message. Why does he have to be here?" I mumbled nervously. Kayden held my waist immediately, sending a jolt down my body, and I stopped mumbling, too shocked even to breathe. I looked down at his hand, where we were connected.

Jason looked at us skeptically.

Shit.

"He went out for a day-drink," Kayden shrugged, crushing me to his side. His giant hand splayed on my bare stomach, sprouting tickles wherever our skin touched. "You know he doesn't talk to me nowadays, busy becoming a raging alcoholic," added curtly. I was too busy not to feel the shivers travelling down my legs. It took a mountain of courage to avoid it and focus on the conversation.

"Kiddie," Jason's voice softened. "He's disturbed. Moreover, he's trying to protect you. We all are trying to protect you, kids."

"I am not your kid!" I snapped, but they ignored me.

"Yeah, by taking my car and telling me to stay at home and zipping my mouth." Kayden rolled his eyes as his grip around my waist tightened a bit, his muscles flexed again, getting uptight, and at that time, I realised he was in pain. It was like his body was transferring that pain into mine because, putting aside our enmity, I worried about him.

Why was Mayor doing this? What did Kayden do?

"Which you aren't listening." Jason eyed me, cocking his head, smiling.

Kayden flipped his middle finger.

"Oh, baby brother, make it two, or even better, three. It'll make her scream," Jason winked-laugh as he slipped out of his room. "Bye, gorgeous, and Kiddie, use precautions. I am not ready to be an uncle," he teased before slamming the door, leaving me stunned.

Blood rushed my cheeks, my heart beating rapidly inside my chest as I tried to get out of his grip, but Kayden didn't budge. Instead, he seemed pissed off, his eyes gazed into mine with an intensity that left me defenceless. They narrated a tale of his agony, but his tongue was restricted from shedding words about what he was going through. I wondered why Mayor took his car. I mean, Kayden was his favorite child. He's everyone's favorite child, the one who makes us feel lame in front of our parents.

I softly rubbed his arms, trying to calm him down, to which I thought he would diss it away, but instead, he closed his eyes, which gave me certain confidence. "Kayden," I whispered. He sighed, his shoulders relaxed a bit, his eyes still closed, but he took a deep breath. "Are you alright?" I asked, biting my lips, wanting to ask what was happening in his life. I wanted to soothe him, hug him but felt I shouldn't.

"Yeah, let's get back to our mission," he opened his hazel eyes, which once showed the vastness of the universe, were now blank. Once again, all his pain and emotions were shoved somewhere behind, locked in some corner, and his walls were back, making him appear like a shell of a person.

Chapter 19

A Message from the Other Side

Striding off to his walk-in closet, he called softly. "Follow me,"

To his closet? Why? What if he tried to be funny in there, *but he could be funny here too, there's no one in his house.* But still, it felt like invading his privacy. What if he hangs his underwear out on display? That thought made me flush and scared.

"I won't. You can show me here," I called with all the contempt I could muster. A bit shaken. It wasn't a good week for me, nor did Leticia's chatoyant provide me with any relief.

He cocked his head out from the door frame.

"Now she's scared," Kayden rolled his eyes. "I should find you attractive enough to touch you," he said, examining me from tip to toe before turning his back.

My mouth pops open. *What did he just say? How could he insult me like this?*

Blood shot up in my head. Shocked, that steam wasn't coming out of my ears as I stormed after him, ready to kick his ass, but instead, I said, "It's kind of relief to my ears. Thank God for making me less attractive to keep me from your attention."

"Who says it's going to hold me at bay?" He smirked darkly.

"I say because I don't find you attractive either. Instead, you're repulsive. You're the last person I ever want to be with." I wanted it to be affirmative. Instead, it came out loud and squeaky. But nobody has insulted me like this before, *'don't find you attractive enough' to hell with you!*

Within a blink of my eye, he was towering over me, taking up all the space, depriving me of any air. I quickly stepped back but hit the mirror, too intimidated by his aura. His hand held my jaw, the dimly lit closet playing tricks on his face. One side shone brightly, while the other was covered with shadows.

"Keep smart-mouthing, and I would love to punish this mouth of yours," he growled, believe me, I felt the air around him rumble. He was sinister. My heart was thumping hard against my chest, too scared by his demeanor. It was like I made the devil angry.

My chest was heaving. "Try me, and I'll rip you into ribbons," I hissed. He was trying to intimidate me with his alpha-male aura, but there was no way I was losing this fight, at least not after his insults.

My warning went unregistered as his hands trailed down my jaw towards my throat. I whimpered as his thumb pressed on my fluttering pulse. "The day I'll try you. I'll destroy you, break you, and remould you around me."

My breath rushed out of me as my stomach tightened at his voice filled with dark promises.

"Why, what have I ever done to you?" I gulped down hard as his gaze darkened.

His hand trailed down my throat to my side, tracing every inch of my body. Electricity exploded wherever he touched, slowly taking his time, he rested his hands on my waist, and when I thought he'd lean in to kiss me, he spun me.

I gasped, placing my hands over the mirror, too afraid to ask what he was doing.

"I'll punish you for every torture you'd laid down on me. I'll hurt you for every single time you've hurt me." His nose traced the shell of my ears, making me shudder. "Your tears will be my elixir, and your screams will be my salvation."

His words were full of hatred, but there was a hidden sting behind them.

"Kayden," I wanted to threaten him, but it came out all wrong in the form of a moan, deep-throated.

"Open your eyes, *princess*," he breathed on my neck, invoking a hunger inside me that I never knew existed before pulling away, leaving me starving.

I had to physically stop myself from leaning back in search of his warmth, the frenzy that consumed me. I opened my eyes, feeling depraved, but my eyes fell on something written over the mirror in hot red.

!EREH GNIDIH

I didn't get it at first, but it's the message. Kayden wasn't lying. It was here, something that didn't make any sense. He took a step back, away from me, as if giving me all the space to work on it.

I grazed it, but I couldn't touch it. "It's written with lipstick, but it isn't smudging," I wiped my hand over it to prove my point.

That's when I realised it wasn't written from this side. It was written from inside the mirror, *a message from the other side.*

My senses woke up with a jerk, deciphering what she wanted to say. "It says—HIDING HERE!"

OMG! I got it now. "Brilliant, Clara! You gave me the gateway. Fuck, I love my bitch." I got all excited and relieved, feeling proud of her.

My eyes fell on Kayden through reflection, finding him already looking at me.

"Um!" I said, contemplating what excuse I should tell, how to hide this, how to explain this. Should I tell him my secret? A secret between two nemeses. *Fuck! It even sounds forbidden.*

Even ordinary people couldn't handle it, and Kayden, he'll laugh in my face and make fun of me or go to Mr. Cooper and put me behind bars. No—no, telling was not an option, but what excuse could I give him? I need to use his mirror as the gateway. Could I excuse and tell him to stand outside while I use his dressing room? No, that would be a terrible excuse. Should I ask him to make out with his girlfriend, but why would he leave me back in his room? Fuck! Excuse, Lizzy, find some fucking good excuse.

Fuck! Why does it have to be his room? Why couldn't it be my room? CLARA!

I took a long pause. But if I consider it, the portal in the devil's room does make sense. He might use this to visit his underworld. I should ask him to open it.

"You don't have to say anything, I know your secret." There was a dark glint in his eyes, corner of his mouth rose like he had finally trapped his prey.

What? No, I didn't hear him right?

"I–I don't know what you are talking about," I stuttered. Obviously, he was messing around. How would Kayden Parsons know my secret? I looked at him skeptically, and he seemed pretty serious. *NAH! He is faking, or is he?*

"You know exactly what I am talking about, Shadow Walk—"

"Shhhh…" I shushed him down, my stomach dropped, and my heart bounced up in my throat, choking me. "Somebody will hear you."

OMG! He knows.

I held my head, gasping at him.

Kayden Parsons, my nemesis, the hotshot devil, called me a Shadow Walker. *He fucking knows my secret.*

I went cold and numb.

"You know?" I gulped down hard, finding my voice. "How? When? Who told you?" I asked. "Clara?" No, she would never betray me. Oh God! He'll tell everyone. My secret would be broadcasted on wide screens—*Glitching Princess, cursed or boon?*

I had to go into hiding, maybe with my father. Nah! I would rather stay in Shadowland than go and live in Caribasca.

What was I going to do? I was screwed.

He will reveal it to everyone, and they would laugh at me. They might get scared of me or would throw me out of school. Or even from the town, perhaps they'll send me to people who'd love to make me their lab rat.

ARGH!

Kayden turned to rummage in his wardrobe and handed me the journal, *Shadowland.*

Fuck my life! He read that.

"Who is this J.P.P.?" he asked. "Sounds like a girl."

"Seriously, ain't you a bit sexist?" My subconscious was sassy, but my conscious was still trying to wrap around—how? "Where did you get this?"

"Where did *you* find it? That's the more pressing question," he pursed his lips into a thin line, but his eyes gave away his excitement.

"Under Leticia's bed when my mother chained me to the vaults for shifting," I muttered without thinking, subconsciously rubbing my wrists. It was his snarl that made me realise what blunder I did. I accepted that I was supernatural and dangerous.

Now, he'd go running off me, but instead, his expressions were odd. His eyes went wide, gleaming with rage, his lips curled over his teeth, heaving, clenching his fists to his side.

"How did you know it's mine?" I bit my lips, pivoting.

His eyes never left mine, as if musing something, finding answers in them. I closed my eyes, not giving him any. He groaned, slamming off a drawer made me open my eyes back.

"I saw you doing your vanishing hoax the first day of your junior year." He rolled his lip between his teeth. I remember I was too busy enjoying my new ride Audi R8, enjoying a little limelight, but as soon as I reached the lockers, I shifted. I thought nobody saw me that day as no one questioned me, nor were there any rumors.

"You did?" My voice cracked as my throat went dry. *He saw me shifting?* Even Homer or Nathan never noticed. No one else in school noticed except Clara. What's up with these twins? Why were they so exceptionally good observers? "You knew since last year?" I gulped down hard. "Why didn't you say anything?" It must be befuddling for him to see me swishing. Probably he had already shared everything with his friends or girlfriend. *Oh God, what else is remaining in this life for me?*

"Didn't know how to confront you," he said so calmly, like we were discussing the weather.

"But I don't understand," I shook my head. "How are you behaving so normally around me?"

"Then how do you expect me to behave?" he asked, amused.

"I don't know, freaking out, leading torch-wielding villagers to my home," I shrugged and flinched at the idea. It reminded me of Leticia and that cursed baby.

"Freaking out is a huge understatement for what I've been through—you left me horror-struck—I thought you Hectors were into some dark magic or what," he brushed his hands through his hair, distracting me. "I thought you were in some trouble, and then I found this journal." He shivered outwardly, I know it was bothersome to read, but these were only myths. Shadowland held no monsters or demons. "It's a pretty scary journal, except this entry about Cosmics."

I remember reading that part, flipping through some pages. I found the entry about him. It's easy to find because it's the last entry. After that, all the pages were torn off.

It was an entry with lots of hearts around it, even a red lipstick kiss mark. "Girls do this stuff," he chuckled.

I rolled my eyes at him. "Boys do stupid shit, too," I snapped and snatched the journal from his hand.

They walk everywhere freely, never grazing the ground.

They'll touch you like you won't belong anywhere else around.

And yet they'll show you what it means to have something you can never hold onto forever.

Everyone will reach out to them, but they cannot be anchored.

Little do we know, Cosmic belongs to no one, to nowhere, won't be bound.

They are a free spirit that lives all around.

Looking for them is like remembering an erased dream,

Finding them is more like losing yourself intervene.

"Every time I read these lines, I get goosebumps," I grazed the lines with my hand, feeling every word.

"J.P.P. worshipped them," he whispered, but his gaze locked on me.

"Or one of them," I muttered, lost in the world of her words.

Suddenly, a trail of goosebumps rose on my body due to the zing Kayden was transmitting.

One-sided love. I shrugged and shut the journal, but my eyes fell on the symbol on the book's backside. It was a trident over an overturned crescent moon wrapped around by a snake. Fuck! I knew the Sigil in Leticia's temple was familiar, it was here in the journal.

"That's where I had seen this symbol," I whispered. "I knew that trance was weird."

"What trance?" he asked, looking interested and worried at the same time. I bit my lips, deciding whether to tell him or not. *Oh god! He'll think I am a crazy person.*

"Seriously?" he raised his eyebrows, folding his hands over his chest. "As you wish, but you know, I am all you got now, and time is ticking," he smirked. "You're stuck with me, *only me*."

I didn't miss the dark caveat, but he was right. He was the only person who could help me right now. The only person in this universe to know my secret. *But why would it have to be Kayden Parsons?*

I groaned inside.

"Fine."

So, I told him all about my trance, everything, every little detail I remember was laid down in front of him. He listened to me attentively, nodding, grasping every little detail I had to offer.

"You saw all this in a trance?" he asked, dumbstruck.

"Yes," I nodded. "It all seemed so real, I mean, I have never seen a shadow in Shadowland, but I saw it there, a shapeshifter shadowfiend and the *Forsaken* itself, she was looking for the *Wandering Star*," I blabbered out.

"Hmm, interesting," he held his chin, his eyes narrowed as if he was calculating something.

"Oh God! finally," I groaned, feeling so much better, wanting to hug him, but I kept my hands to myself. "You won't believe how relieved I am to talk to someone about all this stuff. I've been burning inside to ask for someone's help but didn't know what to tell these people." I took a long breath, feeling so relaxed.

Finally, there was a person in whom I could confide about my tragic story, the person who would believe me when I talked about Shadowland sucking us in, so I told him about Clara being trapped in there with Homer and Nathan.

"I am sorry, I lied about Clara getting washed away, but you understand, don't you?" I sucked a deep breath, desperate for someone to believe in me. "I was freaking out. Not knowing where to start or what to tell. They would've sent me to mental asylum if I had told them the truth. Moreover, they couldn't even see that stitched lady or her house covered in mist and ashes. They can't even see what I can. How would they believe me?" My eyes fell while I played with my fingers. "I think they already take me a lost case after my outburst."

"Ok! Whoa! This is more than what I was expecting." He scratched his forehead. "But don't worry, we'll figure it out." He was trying to relax, but he was taken aback by my truth. "I wish I reached out a little early, I wanted to come to you before, but I didn't know how to initiate," he whispered, biting his lips.

Wait a minute, Kayden was nervous because of me? I arched my eyebrows. *Was he afraid of me?* I felt my stomach drop. *He thinks I am a monster. Fuck!*

"Did you tell anyone about me?" I asked in a small voice, silently praying he didn't.

"Are you seeing any torch-wielding villagers outside your house?" Kayden scoffed. "Take a hint, *Voodoo Lady*," he smirked.

"What?" *WTF is Voodoo Lady? I am not some witch.* I frowned. "Don't call me that," I snapped. "EVER!"

But he kept smirking.

"Fine, smirk all you want while I focus on rescuing my friends." I flipped through the pages of the journal, finding out any entry regarding portals.

Chapter 20
The Gateway

"You're useless, J.P.P.!" I grind my teeth, unable to find anything about creating portals. Kayden snatched the journal, flipping through the pages.

"Now, how are we going to get there?" he said, touching his chin.

"WE?" I squeaked. "There is no WE—WE aren't going, I am going. You'll stay here and cover up for me." I ground out.

Reading about some place was different from experiencing it, I remember Clara's reaction, terrified face, and welled eyes. It still coils my stomach into knots, thinking about what would be happening with her, with all of them.

No way. I'll not give him any tour of Shadowland, I wasn't a concierge. Moreover, Shadowland wasn't the place to hang out. It's filled with darkness, not that it could harm Kayden. I mean, he was pretty shady himself, but being practical, it wasn't the place for the mundane.

"Perhaps, we should wear something appropriate. It's a cold place, right?" he said, rummaging through his closet, totally ignoring me. He almost had everything in blue or black, other colours were stacked in the corner, like forgotten. It made me think he wore the green olive jacket on purpose, as if masking his true self. *What was he hiding?*

"Kayden, I am serious. There is no *we* here. There could never be." Clearing things, he passed me his basketball jersey jacket. My words got swallowed in my mouth.

Seriously, his jersey jacket? I mean, girls would kill to wear Kayden's jacket. It was the most hyped thing in our school. Number 13 and his name written on the back in white over the navy-blue jacket with white sleeves and a striped collar.

I couldn't take it, neither I wanted to leave the privilege of wearing it. I would gain so many Instagram likes if I posted even a single photo in it. I couldn't bring myself to deny it even once, even for formality.

He's a jerk. What if he changes his mind?

I bit my lips, sliding my hands into them.

Whoa! I felt great as I wore the basketball jersey jacket. It was too big for me, almost covering my shorts, but it felt amazing, warm and comfortable.

"Now I see how you feel wearing it." I chuckled, feeling a rush of confidence. It smelled like citrus fresh detergent.

He smirked, folding his hands on his torso, his head slightly tilted and resting on the closet door. His hazel eyes went luminous as a smile lingered on his face.

"What?" I asked.

"This a bribe for taking me to *Shadowland.*" He clicked his tongue as blood rushed his neck.

"Listen," I said very calmly, pulling the dangling sleeves up. "I know that place through and through, and I have never encountered any monster, so I don't need your help. Not that you could help me otherwise, but alone, I'll be swift."

"I am not going in there to help *you.* Why do you make everything about yourself?" he scoffed. "Geez! I am going to rescue my sister."

"I am not making it about myself," I hissed through clenched teeth. *How dare he? I have never been insulted so much. He always treats me little, hurting me. Why's he always so rude?* "If you get stuck in there, I'll have to risk my ass to save you," I argued, placing my hands on my hips.

First my friends, then him. I don't want to keep doing this all my life. I have other work too. Moreover, if he also gets stuck, Mr. Cooper would definitely put me behind bars this time if his father didn't send me to the juvenile centre first. I swallowed hard.

"*I am not yours to save*, right?" he quoted me, trying to hurt me, and it did. I didn't know why, but his words pierced me. It's like he didn't trust me. I'd worked a lot to gain people's trust. I'd lived my whole life in a lie to have them like me, love me, but his words shoved everything down in the gutter.

I pouted as he sucked in a deep breath. His wide eyes were locked on my lips with shadows behind them.

I shivered. "Fine, I'll leave your ass there."

"That's all I expect from you, princess," he said, shaking his head. His cheeks flushed too.

"Argh! Stop calling me that," I yelped, stomping my leg on the floor. "Why are you so irritating?"

"Because your eyes lit up when you're irritated, revealing the real you," he answered without thinking. "Which is much hotter than the one with the masks."

My world stopped. I gazed into the infinity of his eyes. Did just Kayden Parsons call me hot? *Seriously, he thinks I am hot?*

He clicked his fingers in front of my face. "Get out of your princess world and do your voodoo. Open this gate."

I jolted, blinking rapidly. "I don't know any voodoo."

"Then how are you going to open it?" he asked, again clicking fingers.

I batted his finger out from my face. "Stop doing that, let me focus."

"Sure," he said, again clicking.

I gave him a sturdy look, ready to break his fingers.

"Fine." He folded his hands as if reading my mind. "Feisty little creature," he murmured.

A smile rose my lips at his comment, I was looking at the mirror, at the handwriting. "How do you know it's from Clara?"

"Who else is going to write a message in my bedroom?" Kayden answered, flipping through the pages of the journal. "But J.P.P. says only shadows and Shadow Walkers can visit without creating a void."

"Believe me, I've been thinking about it every second of my life, and I just reached one conclusion that someone laid a trap."

"Who?" he asked, dumbfounded as I hunched my shoulders.

"You think one of the demons or monsters?" I could hear the fear in his voice.

I just shrugged outwardly, closing my eyes, not trying to imagine what that scarlet thunder meant.

"You didn't run scared?" I asked after a beat. If I were in his place, I would have refrained from such a person.

"What?" he said, confused, our eyes met through the mirror. "Why would I be afraid of you? You are not a monster," he scoffed.

My heart inflated with so many emotions that I felt it was going to burst out of my chest.

He didn't see me as a monster.

He didn't realise it, but his words had spread warmth throughout my body. They meant so much to me. It built up my courage, courage that had shattered for a few days. To him, I was just a human with a glitch, and he could understand that. He was being empathetic, which was a total upgrade. Surprisingly, I found it easy to talk to him about my shifting.

Clara also took it in so quickly. She wasn't scared of me either. She was scared *for* me because she's my best friend, but why does he fathom? When he could have used it against me anytime, he could even have told the cops or media. Instead, he came to me. Yesterday he hugged me, let me cry on his shoulder, and even put me on his bed, the one he never shares with anyone. He saved me from becoming a gag among the media—*a slut among Royalty*—I could imagine their headlines.

But it's Kayden Parsons, the devil. He must be planning something bigger, an act of revenge, a game in which he could beat me, or why else would he keep my secret? This benevolent act from his side was fucking with my head, I didn't know what he was thinking, and that scared me.

"You thought I'd be scared of you?" he asked, amazed, turning me to face him, his finger under my chin. I shivered at his touch as he raised my chin to meet his gaze. "It's not your fault that you're dangerously chaotic," he chuckled.

I frowned as I batted his hand away. "I am not chaotic."

"You are, and by what happened yesterday, I am affirmative."

I bit my lips, okay! That could have been a total chaos. I could give him that.

"I'll be careful next time," I nodded.

There was a crease between his eyebrows, and his jaw tightened. "There isn't going to be the next time."

"I am a big girl, the one with the claws. I can make my own decisions," I rolled my eyes, ignoring how the shadows behind his eyes returned.

"Yeah, big girl, first try to rescue my sister from the demon realm, then focus on the monsters of this realm," he scowled. But he was right. I should look for my friends first.

But right now, my problem was this gateway, which wasn't opening.

"So, mirror-mirror on the wall, it's the other side I want to crawl," I murmured softly, but Kayden heard it. He chuckled, flipping the pages again.

"Wait until all three come through this and then smash this mirror. Even if I'm not with them. Don't wait for me. Close the portal as I can shift."

He sighed but didn't reply, focusing on the journal.

"How will I turn this mirror into a gateway?" I asked myself. I closed my eyes hard, imagining what it looked like and spoke. "SHIFT." I expected a cold breeze, but nothing. I didn't even budge.

"Then how?" I groaned, tired of being stuck in boring Sunlit land without my friends.

I tried with both hands, but nothing happened. I closed my eyes and focused, blocking everything out, just me and mirror and pin-drop silence. That was when I heard something. I quickly opened my eyes. The voice didn't come from the mirror, but Kayden made it when he lifted the journal again.

"Maybe that's what that dream was about." Curiously, I snatched the journal from him, remembering the dream about the yellow-eyed monster.

"What are you doing? I was reading that." He scowled.

I shushed him down. "I had another dream, or maybe it was a trance again, I should really know how to distinguish between dreams and trances," I shook my head as I blabbered about my trance where the yellow-eyed monster's warning to stay away from the swamps while looking at the journal carefully.

"Someone shifted with you?" he gasped. His eyes went wide in horror. "He knew you?"

"Tsk, that's not important," I waved my hand. "You know, being a girl, if I bought a diary to write in it. What'll be the first thing I'll look for?" I arched my eyebrow, examining the journal.

He seemed confused.

I saw it, hidden behind a scrap of leather. The corner of my lips rose at my accomplishment, "A secret compartment," I beamed, loving every second of his dazzled eyes. But soon, it waved off. "But I don't have a key to it."

"Seriously?" he asked, shaking his head. He took the journal from my hand and hit it on the shelf at a particular angle. The cover broke, and a ring bounced out. I caught it before it could hit the ground.

My face lit up, examining the ring lying on my palm. It was a Turkish gold ring with an eagle claw wrapped around a red zircon stone with dragons on the side. The ring every Shadow Walker was wearing, the ring with which they were creating big protective shields.

"What is that?" Kayden was flabbergasted.

"I've seen this ring with Leticia and others too." I got excited, feeling the urge to wear that ring as if it was calling me. I couldn't wait to put it on my finger, and as soon as I did, I felt a strange tickling running down my hands, spreading through the veins. I flipped my fingers and saw a red light pulsing out from it as if accepting me.

I turned to Kayden. "You think?" I asked. Can every nightmare I had, be true? Was it possible that I was more of a Shadow Walker than I give myself credit for? The powers I took as a glitch were yet to be explored. "Is it possible?"

"Everything is possible," Kayden smiled, placing his hands on my shoulders as he bent down to whisper in my ears. "You just have to believe in yourself."

A warmth spread throughout my body. His words went like a spark through my veins. Accumulating all the confidence I had in my hand, I took a deep breath, closing my eyes—placing my hand on the mirror, letting my base instinct take over. I felt the mirror wiggling under my hands. Butterflies fluttered in my stomach.

Taking a deep breath, I took a step forward in the mirror. It didn't collapse. Instead, I just walked through it like some icy cold door.

Finally.

Chapter 21

The Darkside

My heart was thumping loudly. I was finally going to Shadowland to rescue my friends through a fucking portal that I made through a Shadow Walker's ring, that a yellow-eyed monster showed me in a dream. None of this made any sense, but still, I had a broad smile on my face as I stalked forward.

But my smile vanished when I felt Kayden's hand around my shoulders. They never fell back. I quickly opened my eyes.

I stood in Kayden's room, all burnt up. Ashes and mist surrounded it, covered in green slime everywhere.

I turned back furiously. "What did I tell you?" I snapped loudly. "This is no place for humans. You cannot sustain the darkness here. Why don't you ever listen to me? Anything can happen here. You should—"

"Whoa!" Kayden exclaimed, his eyes widening in amazement as he examined the darkness around him, walking around his burnt closet. "So, this is real?"

I felt relief at the coolness of his voice because he wasn't running scared. Instead, his eyes sparkling, excited to know about this place, I could say he's different or a maniac. Because ordinary people react like Clara did when she realised we were here. On the contrary, Kayden wasn't terrified, but, to my horror, he was content.

A little smile formed on my lips as my shoulder relaxed. "Cross my heart and hope to die, welcome to my Darkside," I sang to him, grinning wickedly.

"This is going to be interesting." he strode towards me with the grace that of a king. "So, it's not happening inside your head," it wasn't a question.

"You thought I was making this up?" I raised my eyebrows.

"There was a little hope, as it would have been a much better explanation," he chuckled, brushing his hand through his hair, getting flushed.

Suddenly, I heard a slithering sound making me freeze. He placed a finger on his lips, as my ears followed the sound.

My eyes widened. "Clara?" I mouthed.

He shook his head slowly, his eyes widened, and the blood drained from his face like he had seen a ghost. His hands immediately reached out for me, pulling me to him. My heart stopped as the slithering sound neared.

To my amazement, he hid me behind him. His breathing had gone hard as I gulped down the rising bile due to terror. I slowly turned around to peek at what he was glaring at, still standing behind Kayden, his arms secured around me as if protecting me, shielding me.

My eyes widened in terror, and my heart froze in place, meeting big black eyes with no pupils or eyelids.

It was an enormous brown-green reptile with a colossal head bearing a large bony frill and one horn on the nose, on its sizeable two-legged body. His hands were much shorter for his twelve feet long body, with only three fingers. It even had a long tail, sharp like an arrow. His mouth opened, glaring at us, flashing his sharp pointed teeth.

"It's a *Grovetile*," Kayden grumbled. They were mindless flesh-eating shadow monsters, the most commonly found in the Shadowland, and their bites were infectious. I had read about them in the Journal, and the beast here matched their description.

Its eyes drifted off us to our left, where the portal glimmered in darkness, filled with violet light and stars.

I wanted to scream, but nothing came out. My mind was running a thousand miles per minute to calculate what would happen if he jumped into the portal.

Before I could do something, Kayden picked up a trophy from his wardrobe and hurled it towards the mirror, shattering it to the ground with ear-piercing noise. My hands sheltered my ears as the violet-black cloud of portal vanished, and the monster growled so loud that the ringing of a shattering mirror seemed timid. I was already being dragged out before I could figure out my next move.

"Run." Kayden grabbed my hand tight as the monster launched at us, but we dodged him and were out of his room as he slammed into Kayden's wardrobe, splintering it into pieces. We dived towards the stairs, helping ourselves out of his house.

He was way taller than me, so his strides were much bigger. I had to run fast to catch him. Thank God I was wearing Bottega Veneta black bounce leather ankle boots with contrasting heels, giving me an edge and comfort. *Grovetile* was slithering after us, but Kayden closed the doors swiftly by putting an iron bar from fallen curtains between the handles, blocking the beast.

"So, this place *is* swarming with monsters, but how come I haven't met any before? What's the difference now?" I asked, frowning my brows. "Did they sprout with the blood rain?"

He hunched his shoulder, looking around. "We have to look for Clara, fast. Where could she be?" he asked, concern in his eyes palpable. We were standing in front of Dr. Dorcas' house, under a flickering streetlight. Red clouds shone over the nearest floating isle as I saw some shadows flying in them. They had wings.

"I don't know. I thought she'd be at your house," I said as kayden grabbed my hand and started walking away from the isle. "But if that monster was there, she'd be hiding somewhere else."

"Possibly."

"Let's try the museum. There was a creepy house instead, where I left—" I cleared my throat. "Saw them last," I quickly reframed my sentence. I didn't leave them there. It wasn't in my hand to bring them back like that but still couldn't help feeling guilty.

"You know, it wasn't your fault what happened to them," Kayden put his hands inside his pants pocket as we walked down the streets, observing my reaction, reading me like an open book.

"It doesn't matter. I did it. I left them here," I bit my lips, not meeting his eyes.

"According to what I have understood till now, it wasn't your powers that brought you all here. You didn't know you'll shift alone. You even went to a house filled with mist and ashes in the swamp, thinking there would be a portal." He teased, but I did that.

Before I could respond, a growl came from our right. We quickly hid behind a tree to see what it was. There was a different *Grovetile*, searching for something, sniffing around.

"How do you think we are going to reach the museum? It's far from here, and I don't think cars work here. Can they?" he asked, confirming.

"I don't think so," I answered, scrutinising *Grovetile's* every moment. He sniffed towards us, my whole body trembled, but Kayden held me tight from my waist. Again, the electric shiver passed down my body. Argh! Blood rushed to my cheeks. *No, not now, Lizzy. It's Shadowland. You're surrounded by monsters.*

"It's heading this way. Let's hide inside this house." He whispered, bending down, slowly we got inside the nearest house. My heart was thumping against my chest due to mixed feelings—terrorised by the shadow monsters and Kayden's touch, which was, to my surprise, having an assload of impact on me.

But I shook my head, gazing around the burnt house, focusing on the elephant in the room. "Do you think it's *Grovetile's* boogie?" I asked, feeling disgusted, but I needed to distract myself.

Kayden chuckled. "Take a hint."

"Ewww!" I said, jumping around, but it was everywhere.

"Shhhh," he shushed me down, glancing outside the window. "He is lurking close. Duck." It took me a few seconds to work on what he said, but he had already pulled me onto him.

I slammed into him, taken off guard, as he keeled back with me. Our lips brushed for a fraction of a second, and I quickly turned my face. Blushing! My heart froze for a few seconds. *No, no, nothing happened, it was nothing, just a mere accident. Act casual.* "Where is it?" I asked, lying on him, not looking at him or his lips, behaving as if nothing happened.

I could feel his eyes on me, the intensity of his gaze pierced a hole inside my sides as he smirked. *Oh my gosh! Don't you dare smirk. It was merely an accident. It wasn't even a kiss. Argh!* Flustered.

"Don't act like you're enjoying all this." I snapped, my heartbeat matching his, "I disgust you."

"Why do you keep saying that?" he asked, frowning, his voice reverberating through my body. *He's got to be kidding me.* I turned to him to search for the menace in his eyes, but he had his one eyebrow arched up, genuinely surprised. "I am not repulsed by you," he claimed, and to prove his words, he wrapped his arms around me, which I resisted, but he was too strong and stubborn to let them fall as he crushed me into his chest.

"Then why do you start brooding every time you see me? When I pulled you out of the pool, you ran away. I saved your stupid ass, I didn't give you herpes by performing CPR, I am not a piece of garbage." I hissed-screamed. His body got tensed under me, but I needed to relax and focus on my job. "You know what, it doesn't matter, you don't owe me any explanation, we're not friends." I jutted my chin out. "And I hate you," I added rudely, trying to get out of his grip.

"But I don't hate you," he licked his lips. "Let me kiss you and prove it to you, okay?" His eyes, filled with menace, darted to my lips.

I gasped as he arched his neck to kiss me. My eyes widened as I squirmed in his embrace. I know he was bluffing. I tried to free myself, to which he chuckled.

"Let me go, Kayden," I battled.

He groaned, trying to control me. "Keep wiggling, and soon you'll be moaning my name."

I froze in my place as his words settled inside me, raising the heat around us. But the slithering sound increased, too, distracting me. I glanced in the direction of the noise while my breathing was coming out heavy and rasped. Kayden pressed his hand on my mouth. His eyes followed his ears on our left, listening to the shadow slither by.

No noise. Everything calmed for a few seconds, it seemed like everything just stopped, but I knew it was the lull before the storm because, at that instant, *Grovetile* barged in, destroying the whole house. We didn't get time to get up, as he was already upon us.

A scream waited in my throat, but it never crawled out as I quickly swayed my left hand, rolling over to my left. I was trusting my base instinct too much, begging it to work, and it did. A red tomb of an electrifying shield got manifested upon us, just like those shadow warriors fashioned in my trance. And soon as the shadow monster touched it, it burnt to ashes. Whoosh!

WOAH!

"That. Was. Freaking. Amazing." Kayden's mouth fell open as his eyes widened. We both were lying beside each other on the floor, breathing heavily.

I kept on blinking, "Did I just kill a monster?" I asked in shock. I could feel powers surging through my veins. Killing a monster was something I never thought I would enjoy so much! It was much better than playing video games, even more than my training, because it was real, pure adrenaline. I had a taste of power, and believe me, it's delicious, more than anything in the world.

Finally, I was using my powers to do something right.

"You do have *claws,*" Kayden drawled, looking awe-struck. A smile rose on his lips, but I was shivering badly, trying to gobble down my breathing.

If you want to survive, get your claws out—that's what he told me, not to develop them but to get them out.

"You should have seen yourself how hard you used to try to hide your abilities," he chuckled like it was every passing day incident. "And with your fake mask of being feeble as if nobody could see you through,"

"Nobody did see me through," I corrected him. Only he could tell I was wearing the mask. Even Clara didn't know, but he did because he was an obnoxious observer who kept finding flaws in me. "All are not weirdos like you. They wouldn't have accepted my truth," I shook my head.

"Why do you need *everyone* to accept you?" he asked. "It's better to lose people than to lose yourself by trying to please them. You'll be surprised by some of us." His eyes glimmered with something I didn't recognise.

What does he know about being a pariah? He was widely accepted and adored while I was trapped in a cage, like some wild animal.

"When did you realise I have claws?" I asked, pivoting.

"Remember the time you jumped from the cliff behind my house?" He propped himself on his elbow to look at me better.

"Yeah, the time you pushed Homer down, and he twisted his ankle," I remembered Homer's red face. He had to take off for three weeks and missed basketball team selections.

"You were spending too much time with that sloppy guy," Kayden shrugged like it was his right to choose with whom I should hang-out. "But you didn't climb it down like we normally do, but just sprang after him."

"So?" I arched my eyebrow.

"It was a fucking 9-metre fall," The corner of his lips rose as his eyes sparkled. "And then you pretended not to bag even one basket," he rolled his eyes, remembering I purposely failed the selections. Rule no. 2, no extracurricular activities.

"I wasn't allowed to be in the limelight."

"But if you had tried to control these powers, then maybe you'd have mastered them by now," his voice got soft. "You could be yourself. You could be happy." His eyes reflected concern, but I didn't need his pity.

"And why do you think I haven't tried to control it? My mom caged me almost my whole life to control this glitch," I grimaced.

He pinched a strand of my hair that came loose on my face and placed it behind my ear, electricity buzzed even from this minimal touch. "She shouldn't have done that. There is a difference between controlling it and suppressing it. Your mom tried to suppress your powers, but I am asking you to accept and control them," he suggested with a soft smile. "You deserve nothing but to be yourself. Nobody should take that away from you." His voice was filled with promises of the fantasy world.

My heart fluttered at the anticipation of controlling my shifts by accepting it, to be myself, no masks, no hiding? It all seemed so lucrative. My whole life, I wanted to get rid of this glitch. I always thought of my power as a waste because Mom used to think that I had some problem. But what if I had worked on it? Would things be different if I had accepted my fate rather than running away?

"You think I could do that…control my shifts?" I bit my lips.

"Of course, after all, you're a Voodoo lady," he chuckled as he brushed the tip of his finger on my nose.

I cringed my nose and was about to bite his finger in anger when he quickly retreated. His eyes widened. "Feisty little creature," he murmured.

"That's not even a title. I should get myself a fancy name," I thought as excitement spread through my body. I looked down at the ring. I didn't know it was so powerful—*I have powers,* and if Kayden was right, then I could control them. Even my shifts, I must work on it. "What do you think I should take as Wonder Woman is already taken, but I need something classy that matches my personality." I blabbered while he strolled out the thrashed door, ignoring me.

"Hey-hey, where do you think you are going?" I leapt to him.

"I thought I'll look for my sister while you're busy in princess world," he teased. *How rude!* I saved his life too, and instead of gratitude, I was getting an attitude, typical obnoxious Kayden.

"You can't even sustain for two minutes without me," I scoffed. "*Grovetiles* are going to eat your obnoxious ass."

He halted with a jerk. I thought he was about to comment on something, but instead, his eyes went wide, grabbing my hand and uttered. "More *Grovetiles*, Run."

Chapter 22

A Trickery

Kayden swayed a metal rod, hitting the *Grovetile* that neared us, but it growled angrily, ready to charge at us again. He again swayed his rod, now hitting it on its flappy ears. The beast shrieked in pain, green boogey dripping out from its ears, but that angered it more. So, I quickly ran and pushed Kayden aside as I created a shield in between. It was a wall dividing the monster and us while Kayden stumbled and fell to the ground. "Geez."

But as soon as that monster touched the shield, it disintegrated into smoke and ashes.

I turned to Kayden, impressed by my skills. But his palm was bleeding. He might have hit the ground hard.

"Shit," I said, springing at him.

"I know you're enjoying the ring's powers, but please don't hurt the help," he said, closing his fist and jerking his elbow. The way he was stretching his arm, I knew he was hurt.

"I am sorry. I didn't mean to hurt you. I was just protecting us," I sank, feeling bad, telling him to take out his jacket to examine his wound.

He flinched at my touch. "Let me be."

"Don't be a baby," I scowled when we heard a growl again. I was startled and looked around us, finding a silhouette, and I felt Kayden's hard breathing beside me. His hand gripped my biceps tightly.

"I wonder," I whispered, swaying my left hand, manifesting a bubble shield around us.

"What are you doing?" he asked, looking at my extended hand and pulsing ring.

"Shielding us, dumbass!" I told him. "I hope it'll block our scents and voices."

The corner of his lips rose. "Only *you* can call me a dumbass and get away with it."

My eyes narrowed at this pretentious jerk, but he was right. Everybody treated him like a King, his words were their command, and disrespecting him wasn't an option. "We need to hurry up. At this pace, we can't reach the museum in days," he said, holding his arm. My face fell, feeling terrible for hurting him. *Why was I so chaotic?*

Which was when I remembered the passageway. "Let's take the cave in Mile-O-City. It'll lead us there quickly."

Getting excited, I bolted towards Crow Lane but was pulled back.

"We need some vehicle to reach there," he said, holding my hand.

"Oh! Yeah, right," I said, figuring. "I think bicycles will do." Ignoring the way my cheeks were flushing as his hands twined with mine.

We found a bicycle a few houses down, and soon we darted towards the forest. It was a great plan to use some vehicle as it was a long way, but the rusty bike gave away after the Northern Circle. From there we had to walk. But to my luck, the shield was working, blocking our scents and voices from the monsters.

"I can't walk anymore," I bent down, heaving, halting in the middle of the forest. We had been talking and walking for a long time. He shared so many stories of himself with his friends that were totally normal. I didn't know Kayden leads a normal life. All I thought was that his life was revolving around basketball and fucking, but not once had he mentioned any girl's name, but basketball indeed was his life, and his team was his safe place. I felt him opening up to me, even though we weren't friends. It was an icebreaker between us, but I knew he was doing that to distract me because every time I hear even a single twig cracking, I get jittery.

He rolled his eyes at me. "Next time, I'll keep a hoverboard ready for you, my princess," he said sarcastically.

"There isn't going to be the next time. I am done with Shadowland and *you*," I raised my hands.

"We'll see," he scoffed, wrapping his hand around my wrist, hauling me into walking like I weigh nothing.

There was nothing to see. I would control my powers and stop shifting. Everything would be easy and normal. The idea was so tempting, but I still didn't know how to control them. By *accepting them*, Kayden had already given me an answer, but I still didn't know how to implement it.

"Give me your phone," he asked, splaying his hand.

"Why?" I asked, pulling it out of my pocket. "Where is yours?"

"Low battery." He answered in his monotone. I squinted at his smartwatch, but there was no point, smartwatches didn't work here. "I am thinking maybe we can call Clara."

"But it will burn," I told him, hiding my phone, but he snatched it. "Fine, you have to buy me a new one if it catches flames," I warned him.

Ignoring me, he dialled Clara's number, but instead of burning, the ring went, but nobody answered.

"Pick up, damn-it," he sounded worried, but I was appalled. "How come it didn't burn?"

"Because it isn't a cross-connection, we all are in Shadowland," words rolled out of his mouth like he was a Shadowland Major.

Smartass!

"Try Homer's," I suggested. "Maybe he'll pick up, he's always glued to his phone."

A frown touched Kayden's lips but didn't say anything as he dialled his number.

"Switched off," he told me in a taut voice.

"Give it to me," I filched my phone from his hand. "Oh, I remember, his phone got burnt," my face fell as I saw his picture on my phone.

I caressed my phone, it was the day he got the lip piercing. He was so excited.

"You like him?" Kayden asked, his shoulders straightened visibly.

"What?" I asked. "Whom?"

"Cooper boy," he said with his clenched teeth, his eyes blank.

"Oh," I arched my eyebrows. "No," I lied.

He grimaced while shrugging as he started walking ahead. "Good, because I heard he's already taken."

I frowned.

"Yeah, I know," I said through clenched teeth. He doesn't have to rub that information in my face.

"Why don't you express your feelings to him?" he suggested in his monotone, without looking at me.

"We are just friends," I rolled my eyes.

"You know you can't be friends once you're in love," his hands clenched into fists, and I sighed because he was right. "He deserves to know."

I sighed. *Kayden knows.* There was no point in denying anymore.

"And ruin our friendship? No, thank you," I trembled a little, scared. "That's the risk I will never take."

"Maybe he likes you too but cannot say it out loud, just like you." There was an edge to his voice.

"What if he doesn't?" I bit my lips. "What if he runs away because of the guilt that he doesn't feel the same?" I shook my head. "I don't want to create a mess for him to push me away. I am not strong enough to lose him."

"You just killed monsters. I think you are strong enough," he gave a dry chuckle, shoving his hands in his pocket. "You just need to fix your priorities."

I crossed my hands over my stomach, shaking my head.

"But you're not happy." It wasn't a question. He turned to me with concerned eyes.

"But he is."

"Oh, come on, Hector, don't be so naïve." He threw his hands in the air. "Fight for what you want. Why are you being so feeble?"

I grimaced. "I am not feeble, but I lose all my strength when it comes to him," I whispered, looking down at my hands.

"Why? I mean, how come that guy has so much control over you? You hate being controlled, but this guy, he walks all over you." He was searching for answers in my eyes.

I sighed, looking at the ground. "He was the first person who thought I was strong enough to fight the darkness." And then I let it out. "I don't think it was a big deal for him, but it was for me. It was my first interaction with someone outside my small world." I smiled, thinking about that moment. "It was nothing, just a small meeting, and he was this cute little boy trying to be Iron Man."

I chuckled, thinking about that memory. Kayden halted, getting stoic. He raised his eyebrows, wrapping his head around my words.

"But he helped me with my fear. I didn't know it was him back then, I didn't even ask his name, but when I started school, I found him wearing the same Iron Man suit. So, that's why I feel so close to him, because he was the one who believed in me. He was the one who was there for me when nobody was, who thought I could stand up for myself when everybody in my life thought I was dark and tried to hide me. He embraced me." I turned to him with a twinkle in my eyes. "And whenever I think about this, it provides me strength."

Kayden's eyebrows went so high that they were touching his hairline. He looked at me like I had grown three heads.

"Just because he was wearing the Iron Man suit doesn't mean he was the same guy," he said through a clenched jaw, stepping towards me, closing the distance, his dazzling eyes filled with the whole universe never left mine. They were so deep, like he was trying to tell me something, but all I could hear was his erratic breath.

"You think I don't know that," I tried to roll my eyes but couldn't due to the intensity of his gaze, of the zing I always felt around him as it heightened, leaving goosebumps in its wake. "I confronted him, and he said yes."

"He did?" He blinked, and the zing was gone. He cocked his head to the side, processing the information. "He's a hell of a trickster!" Kayden exclaimed, and with that, he turned around, clutching his hair and burst out a roar of laughter.

I gasped. *What the hell?* He was being a jerk, making fun of something so important to me, something so special that his mocking laugh was ruining it.

"Shut up." I snapped, turning him over with his elbow. "It's important to me, you don't get to ruin this for me, not this memory," I scowled. "I know I was too young, but it's a significant part of my life, it's my first pure memory, and you won't make fun of me about this."

But he couldn't stop laughing, tears glistening in his eyes, he bent down to place his hands on his thighs, trying to control it, but he couldn't, and it infuriated me.

"ARGH! I hate you, Kayden. You don't understand people's emotions. You are this narcissistic cyborg that only gets to boss us around." I stomped past him. "I regret telling you something so intimate about me, I never told this to anyone, but I told you."

What was I thinking? Empathy? From Kayden? That was so stupid of me.

"I trusted you, and that's what you are giving me in return, a fucking mockery?" I was screaming when I slammed into something like steel but warm and stumbled when his hands caught me, snaked around my waist.

"I wasn't mocking you." He was back, grinning widely, showing off his cutest dimples, taking my breath away. I didn't know he could smile like that, the one that swoons you and makes him look like an angel. His eyes were way softer than before, like my story lightened up his mood. Obviously, who wouldn't be alleviated by a good laugh? "I am sorry if I hurt you, *ever*," he said in a velvety voice, his grin reaching his eyes.

Kayden Parsons is sorry? It was like Ross accepting that he and Rachel were not on a break.

"Get lost, you obnoxious jerk." I shoved him back but failed miserably. Instead, he pulled me flush into him. I gasped.

"One of us has to, but it wasn't enough, I guess." His fingers threaded into my hair, bringing our forehead together, making my breath catch hard in my throat. My heart almost stopped beating. It was such a tender act that it unnerved me.

A growl made me jump, and I realised our shield was gone. I quickly created another one as I walked, creating distance from him.

My heart fluttered. What does that forehead touch supposed to mean? It wasn't normal. It was highly intimate, a romantic notion. No, I was overthinking it, but why did it give me goosebumps? I rubbed them from my hand, walking silently with my weak heart thumping against my chest. I restrained my hands to visibly hold my heart to calm myself down.

He followed me with a wide grin like he had found his long-lost happiness in this Shadowland.

Chapter 23

Déjà Vu

I wasn't going to share any of my secrets with him. He didn't deserve that. He was still that douche, so I chose to ignore him. It will be strictly professional between us from now on, two colleagues on a rescue mission, that's it.

But I could feel his gaze on me, building up tension between us.

"Can I ask you something?" he asked softly, breaking the secluded silence.

I sighed.

"Spill it," I nodded, keeping my voice even.

"If you feel so strongly for him, why don't you do something about it? I mean, how come you're sitting on a backhand, that's not the Eloise I know." My eyes widened in shock as I halted. My heart somersaulted.

"You called me Eloise," Not Hector, not Eloise Valerie Hector, not Voodoo lady, but Eloise. My name seemed so different from his mouth. There was a zing to it that made my happy muscles go all tingly.

"That's what you get out of it?" He couldn't stop grinning, showing off his cute dimples. God, I hate them, they were so distracting. It was hard to think straight when all I could wish was to stick my tongue in them.

I shook my head, hiding my heated face. "I don't know what to do."

"Win him over, entice him," he answered like it was a piece of cake.

"It's not that easy."

"C'mon, do your voodoo thing, make some love juice or put some spell on him." He was again mocking me.

I rolled my eyes. "I wish I were a Voodoo lady. Half of the guys would have been dying to ask me out if you wouldn't poison their potions." He would do anything to make my life miserable.

"That seems like something I could do." He rubbed his jaw, thinking.

"Ha! I knew you couldn't see me happy. You hate me." I grimaced, pointing my finger at his chest.

"I don't hate you," his eyes lightened. "I was never able to," he sighed. His voice went too soft, as if caressing me.

I arched my eyebrow, pursing my lips in a straight line. *What about all those threats about destroying me? Punishing me?*

"Trust me." He gave a small smile.

"Please!" I rolled my eyes. "Trusting you is like trusting the devil with your soul," I scoffed, but he gave me an intense look.

"Ok, let me prove it to you, let me help you to win him over," he offered. Even though he says he couldn't hate me, he still hates Homer. Then why was he offering to help us?

"How?" I asked, confused.

"Tell him that you're dating me. This way, he'll get jealous and try to win you back," he offered, his eyes sparkling at the mischievous plan.

"Yeah, right," I scoffed again, sarcastically this time, thinking he was kidding, but he cocked his head, pursing his lips. "Come on, you can't be serious. Homer would never believe me dating *you*."

"Sweetheart, everyone's going to believe," he purred, making my hormones act funny. My heart flutters at his word—sweetheart, it felt so good falling from his mouth.

"He's not the jealous kind," I pursed my lips.

"Oh! You don't know what jealousy does to guys," words sizzled out of his mouth like he had felt it himself.

We were about to reach the waterfall, the sound of water gushing down seemed louder and eerie in this dark world.

I ignored him, not taking him seriously, but what if it worked? What if Homer did get jealous and tried to win me over?

"Why do you want to help me?"

"Just like that," he shrugged, but there was excitement in his voice.

"Yeah, right," I ridiculed. "You never do anything without reason. So, tell me, what's in it for you because whatever you say, the last time I saw you, you hated us."

"I don't hate *you.*" He corrected me again, this time firmly. "But let's just say I want to get back at Homer," he bore his eyes on me, a mischievous smile never leaving his face.

"What's up with you and him?" I asked. He does hate Homer. Fuck! Every time I thought he mistreated Homer because he wanted to get back at me wasn't true. It seems like Homer and Kayden had their own personal rivalry that didn't connect with me. Perhaps, he was right, I do think everything revolves around me. Whoa!

"He stole something from me, something that was just mine." He spoke with a locked jaw.

"Homer—stole something—no, no, he would never do that," I shook my head. No, Homer wouldn't steal from Kayden. I mean, he has a habit of borrowing things and not returning them, like all my gadgets. "Perhaps he forgot."

Kayden shook his head. "I don't think so. He abuses it every damn day," he looked at me. There was pain on his face. It had to be something important to him.

"What is it?" I bit my lips. "Maybe I could ask him, or you could ask back."

That was when I heard a roar startling me. It was louder than I expected, like the monster was somewhere within five feet. I spun hurriedly to look, but my feet got stuck between the tracks of Hot Wheels Nitro. I didn't realise we had reached the old, decaying, abandoned amusement park where I twisted my ankle.

"Ouch," I shrieked as a sharp, piercing pain stung my ankle.

"Shhh..." He bent to free my foot so smoothly that I felt nothing with his clever hands. "It's out, don't worry," he said as he placed his hands under my waist and knees to haul me up in a swift motion.

"What are you doing?" I almost shrieked, with my eyes wide open. I wasn't used to this kind of treatment. I was strong, but I immediately locked myself around his neck. "If you throw me in the river, I'll kill you."

"Your mistrust in me is disheartening," he spoke with a clenched jaw as his eyes tightened around the edge. His grip got firm around me.

"And you cannot blame me with our history," I bit my lips, was he hurt?

"I'd never hurt you." His brows furrowed.

"Not directly," I murmured. All his actions towards Homer made him livid, and he took out his anger on me by either fighting with or ghosting me, like somehow it was my fault.

But right now, it felt nice to be cradled and taken care of. I melted in his jacket when I sniffed. I don't know why, but I took in his scent, and he smelled like oceans, a familiar scent. God, I love this scent. It swoons me.

Déjà vu!

That's when I remember. This scent was the same from the day I passed out in the hospital, my eyes wide open in anticipation, strong hands, ocean's smell. It was Kayden, he was there when I passed out. I'd felt these strong arms before.

"Is it hurting?" He carefully placed me on a bench and bent down on his knees, examining my feet. My heart froze in place. Kayden Parsons was kneeling before me. I didn't know why but at that very moment, I felt powerful, watching Kayden, the strongest guy I know, the candy boy of our school, next head of the student council, captain of the BB team, the guy for whom all girls go down on their knees, was there kneeling in front of me, removing my boot with his own hands, examining my ankle. His touch sent a sensation down my core and I clenched my thighs together.

"Nope, it seems fine." I breathed as his soft fingers brushed my feet, I felt a jolt in my body as I quickly tried to retrieve my feet, but he held me firmly.

"Are you sure? You twisted it badly," he raised his brows with a glint in his eyes as he observed me. It made the corner of his lips curl up, giving me his devil look while caressing my ankle, tickling me. My eyes rolled back in my head as his touch was featherily soft.

"I heal fast," I spilled my truth as everything around me became hazy. I couldn't remember anything, just his soft touch, but soon he let it go, helping my shoe back—my insides groaned at the lack of his touch.

Whoa! Calm down, Lizzy. He's Kayden Parsons, control your hormones.

"Fast healer, huh! Did you heal my knuckles too, Voodoo lady?" he asked, pulling me to him, sliding me with my leg till our noses were brushing.

"It was you who brought me home when I passed out in the hospital?" Our breathing merged, making a moan rising in my throat. "You saw me shifting that day too."

He got stiff, suddenly, his walls were back, as he got up and turned his back on me. "We need to go." He tried to walk away, avoiding this conversation.

"You know, you can't leave without me. It'll break the shield," I said, my brows dancing. I got him, finally.

I felt him squirm, and I like it.

"It was you who held me," I was enjoying his uneasiness, taking him off-guard. "I remember the scent of oceans."

"You liked it?" He turned to me, grinning, *Argh! I hate this grin.* "Sniffing me?" He offered his hand for me to get up.

"I'd rather sniff an old lady's carpet," I rolled my eyes, batting his hand away, helping myself up.

"Do you want me to carry you the way I did that day? You know I can do that if you like *sniffing* me so much." How could he turn the tables like that?

"In your dreams," I scoffed, as blood rose on my cheeks as I walked past him.

"In my dreams, I do *so* many filthy things to you," he purred at me as he grabbed my hand and tugged me to him. The movement was so quick that I didn't realise it when he wrapped his hand around my waist, burning me. I arched back, but suddenly I felt something warm and wet gliding up my neck making me shiver. I gasped as he licked me.

"Should I give you a demo?" he whispered sensually. A wicked smile rose on his face like a predator sizing up his prey. I felt a jolt between my legs. My traitorous heart was thumping hard as I placed my hands on his chest, creating distance. His coquettish words made me go weak in my knees as he caressed my cheeks with his knuckles.

"Jerk," I yanked out of his grip, frowning at him. All of a sudden, he was flirting with me, grinning, I didn't know what changed him, but I felt a shift in his demeanor. He seemed more open, more accepting now. It was like the wall he had built around him to safeguard himself had disappeared. I shifted out of his way, getting out of his body heat, avoiding the burning and tingling feeling on my neck, flipping him my middle finger.

In return, he flipped me his but then pulled out his forefinger too, gesturing to finger me. My core clenched, perplexed at how much havoc one gesture could cause. My breathing quickened as I whispered profanities at him, getting out of his licentious aura. Fuck! I must be sweating because it got heated so much. I was nervous. My hands were shaking. I tightly clenched them into fists, not giving away how much he affects me. *Stop it! He's just flirting.*

I should find you attractive enough to touch you—his words ringing in my ears.

"Then what do you want, Eloise?" He sighed, walking behind me.

I turned to him. "I want to know the truth. Why were you there?" My tone was surprisingly even for someone who's experiencing chaos inside.

"Truth?" He raised his eyebrows, rolling his teeth on his lips. "I wanted to make sure you were okay." His eyes went soft and warm. I searched for a hint of malice in his eyes but couldn't find any. I blinked in shock. He was telling the truth.

My heart flipped. What? *Kayden Parsons was trying to look after me!* It was bad, very, very dangerous. It was so unlike Kayden. Why was he saying these sweet words? He was supposed to snap a comeback or a fight, but '*make sure you were okay*' was not something *we* say to each other. We were the ones standing with daggers in hands to rip each other apart at the first chance.

But this? Care? How? Why?

"Even though you know I hate you?" I raised my eyebrows.

"Yes, that's why I maintained my distance." The corner of his mouth twitched.

Whoa! He was looking after me from afar. That was very bad for my heart. This was a very dangerous game that he was playing because it gave me hope. I couldn't have him coy with me like that.

"I think you are wired erroneously," I scoffed, trying not to hyperventilate.

"Oh! You are the one to talk?" he exclaimed, flipping around and laughing sarcastically.

I stomped my foot. "That's not fair."

He chuckled, looking at my face, and I just noticed how much I liked his chuckles. His eyes lit up, his cheeks glowed as he smiled, and creating those swooning dimples—*he's so handsome.*

"Nothing is fair in this world, *baby girl.* You just have to fight for what's yours." He smiled as we walked beside each other, brushing his arm on my shoulder. I felt all kind of butterflies anyone could ever feel, fluttering inside my stomach with his *baby girl* because he didn't just say it. He purred it, like he was caressing me with his words.

He was looking after me from afar. *Is that why he was outside my window?*

"You know we could have avoided this whole Colton situation if you wouldn't have chosen just to be my stalker," I chuckled, and with that, he halted, closing his eyes, and shook his head as if shaking off the memory.

"I know," he said through clenched teeth. "I was too absorbed with other things that I miscalculated the threat. But right now, I don't want to think about killing Colton. Let's focus on Clara." The agitation in his voice was palpable as he bent to take my hand.

I looked down at our entwined fingers, raising my eyebrows. "You can't keep your hands off me, can you?"

"And let you go? What if you vanish and dump me in this eerie place?"

"No matter how tempting it sounds, I can't do that to Clara," I laughed.

"I like that sound," he looked directly at my mouth. "That sounds haunts me in my nightmares."

Me laughing haunts him? And he likes it? Does he know how confusing he sounds right now?

I would have pressed further, but I was busy observing the waterfall with black water. It seemed super cold here and eeriest. My eyes were glued to the dark water, the darkness of this world. I stood on the cliff and listened to water gushing, just black water, no moon, dried-off trees, and swamp ground. It was a dark night. On my right was the waterfall, around 1600 yards away, and behind it was the Limestone Cave. The smell of the water was disgusting, like sewer water. That rotten smell was torturing my nose. I put my hand on it, blocking it. I don't want to inhale it.

I saw my reflection in the water. Suddenly, I felt something about the water calling me.

Kayden was still rambling about something I didn't know. I had stopped listening long ago. My whole attention was on that waterfall and its magical black water. The foam rose at the surface where the waterfall met the river, and it soon started swirling.

I should have run, but it was so mesmerising that I couldn't. The water was creating a doorway. I wanted to jump in it, it was like a siren's call. Even the rotten smell from the water was gone. I found it alluring for a change.

"Eloise." Kayden's voice called me back as if he tugged me, waking me up from a long sleep.

"Huh?" I asked, looking at him, blinking, like not knowing what had happened.

"Are you ok?" he asked, closing the distance, looking into my eyes, confused, concerned.

"There," I pointed at the dark water from the cliff we stood on. That rotten smell was back.

We both looked down as the swirling increased. With a shriek, many skeletons crawled out of the water. Their sockets without eyeballs fell on us as they started climbing the cliff on their two giant talons while their tail of vertebrae slithered behind.

Chapter 24
A Claim

I was frozen to the ground, there was nothing mentioned about them in the journal, I guess, J.P.P. never encountered these kinds of shadow monsters.

"Eloise, we need to run," Kayden whispered, tugging my arm. I couldn't move, not believing my eyes. Undiluted fear knocked into me, whooshing air out of my lungs. *How is this even possible?* So many skeletons. This waterfall was swarming with them, as if they were the Merfolk of Shadowland—Mer-skeletons, as per their appearance.

Their shrieks pierced my eardrums. "How come they have vocal cords? They are just skeletons?" I asked, on the verge of losing my mind.

"Stop freaking out, run!" He jerked me into running. I felt like Nemo being chased by a shiver of sharks, that too on land. We bolted behind the waterfall and entered the dark cave.

"Why are we running?" I asked him, panting. "I have protected us with a shield."

"They could feel us beyond the shield. Your reflection arose them." He told me, hiding inside the Limestone Cave, which was all dark and decaying. We never stopped running. My phone's flashlight flickered as we reached the middle.

"But they don't have eyeballs, they can't see us."

Kayden halted and turned to look at me, baffled. "And skeletons don't run around like that. They are shadow monsters, like *Grovetiles,* and we don't know whether their bite is infectious. What's up with you?"

I gulped down, but suddenly the shrieks drew onto us. I cast a full shield around us. I even created a wall, blocking them to the other side.

"Out—we need to get out—I can't fight these many, we need to run and find a way to hide." My hands shook, freezing the blood in my veins while my heart ratcheted into thunderous beats.

I don't want to be eaten. I don't want to die a virgin.

Kayden nodded. "Let's go." He took my hand as we started crawling out of the dark cave. It reeked in here like sewer water and burnt meat. But I had no time to acknowledge that, as the temperature dropped down by many degrees, even while running, my teeth were clattering. But soon, the smell got suffocating. I wanted to get away from those weird Mer-skeletons as soon as possible.

I kept glancing back, looking at the shields I created, hoping they could hold those monsters. A sob built in my throat at the rising cacophony of Mer-skeletons shrieks and squeals. The whole cave was reverberating under their dominance. I could see them crawling toward us, their white skeletons in the darkness shone like pearls, propelling towards us. Gravity doesn't affect them. They were everywhere on the cave's roof and sides. Their jaws vibrated, making nerve-chilling shrieks, ready to rip us apart. Infectious or not, they'll soon chew us like a lump of juicy meat.

It was a horrifying view.

They vanished in thin air as they touched the wall of shield, burning into ashes like *Grovetiles*. A small smile raised my face but it was short-lived as more monsters crawled in. Slowly the shield started to diminish. I cast layers of shield after each step I took.

"FUCK!" Kayden groaned, taking me in his arms, his hands tightened around my waist, crushing me to himself, every part of my body was touching him, feeling his fear. I arched my neck to look at him. He was gone pale, making me scared to my toes. His eyes were fixed on the exit of the cave. I followed his gaze, finding more Mer-skeletons blocking our exit.

Dread crushed in—*we were surrounded.*

"We need to hide…we need to hide." I kept mumbling, finding it hard to breathe. We were stuck in the middle of the cave with no way out. I started casting shields on both sides, trying to block them, but they vanished within seconds, and the distance between them and us was diminishing. I tried my best, but it seemed impossible to hold these many.

"We can't, there is nowhere to hide," Kayden answered against me, his voice filled with fright.

"What are we going to do now?" I asked, feeling agitated.

"Don't worry, I'll save you." I could feel his body fidgeting through my body, looking around us, searching for a way to get out. He slammed his fist above us, trying to break the limestones.

"It's impossible," I told him, but he kept slamming his fist until blood started oozing out of his knuckles, but he kept aiming for it, ignoring the pain. There was desperation in his movements, purely in survival mode.

The shrieks became unbearable, I felt like my head would explode. I looked around, finding all the shields had diminished. I cast more shields while Kayden kicked and punched the wall, groaning in pain.

"Stop it, you're hurting yourself." I swiftly tugged on his hand. Monsters were trying to bust my last shield—the last one around us, leaving me scared to death.

No, no, no, no, no—

I cast a full shield around us.

"I don't want to die," I whispered as Kayden took my face into his palms, tilting my head to look into his eyes.

I could see he was afraid, more than terrified, looking at me like he wanted to tell me so many things, but instead, he whispered. "You won't." He said with complete confidence. "I won't let anything happen to you." He placed his forehead on mine, closing his eyes.

"How?" I asked, knowing I wouldn't like it because it felt like a goodbye.

"Go, shift," he whispered.

My whole world froze around me. I couldn't believe my ears as I came undone by his words. Something glimmered in his eyes, something that shifted inside me too. The walls between us demolished to the ground invoking the whole turmoil of emotions, and I felt warmth—I felt *him*, his true nature, his gentle care.

"SHIFT, ELOISE." He groaned, kissing my forehead. I felt his plea against my skin, making my whole body tremble.

"Fucking—NO." I snapped, pulling back. *How can I leave him alone and shift back?* I'll leave him alone to die here—How could he even think like that? He saved my life. How could I betray him?

"GO NOW," he ordered sternly, but I shook my head, and our last shield vanished with that.

He groaned as he wrapped himself around me, cornering me into the cave wall, trying to protect me from those monsters. I tried to cast the shield, but it wasn't possible, monsters were already upon us. I felt Kayden whimpering in pain as their tendons scratched him. I couldn't bear it. His pain pierced my heart, but there was nothing I could do.

Even in pain, Kayden's hands never left me.

We were going to die—such a horrible death. Poor Kayden, he didn't deserve this. I couldn't think about anything. Kayden was dying. He was losing his strength. I could feel it. I held my hands to my heart. "Please help me save him," I just prayed, asking for help. My hand hit my chatoyant, and a green light flashed.

SWISH

A green beam zipped through the cave, slaying all the Mer-skeletons into thin air within a blink, leaving me appalled. No more reverberating sound, no more clinking, silence fell over, and so did Kayden.

WHOA! What just happened? How did my chatoyant work? How many mojos was I carrying? I looked down at the necklace, it was still glowing, emitting green light. It belonged to Leticia. Was it possible it held her powers inside it?

"Thank you, Leticia," I might sound crazy, but it was a miracle, and I knew it wasn't something of my doing, kissing it, feeling blessed. I looked around, stunned, still not believing my luck.

"Kayden, they are gone," I whispered, still waiting for some more monsters, but none of them came. But neither did he answer.

"Kayden?" I turned to look at him, but he was lying on the uneven ground, unconscious. My smile vanished as panic took over me. I quickly dipped to check on him, but it was too dark. Even my phone got smashed in the ambush.

"Please, wake up, Kayden, please," I brushed his dark hair, his face, which was covered with something dark and clotty, which I knew was blood, knotting my stomach. The only ray of hope was that he was breathing, but they were shallow. I tried to lift him, taking his hand, but he was too heavy. "Please wake up, Kayden, help me a little," My heart was lodged in my throat as guilt washed over me—he was in such a state because of me.

I am a horrible person.

I winced as he whimpered in agonising pain, but he tried to get up. "Yes, please, let's get out," I said, wrapping them around my shoulders and walking him out.

I made him lie on the forest ground, across the street was the creepy house, we were so close, yet so far.

He grunted. "I got you, Kayden," I told him while the tears blurred my vision, drenching my cheeks, feeling guilty. "You shouldn't have followed me. I told you this isn't a safe place."

I shielded us, looking down at him. Tears welled in my eyes, seeing him in this condition. He was lying on the ground, covered in blood, all scratched. I examined his wounds, which weren't turning blue, which was a good sign, he wasn't infected. His front wasn't that affected as he was shielding me, but his back was all scratched, including his hands and handsome face. I couldn't even wash them, as the water here was unsafe. I felt helpless.

My hands brushed his silky soft brown hair, trying to soothe his pain, wanting to take his pain away.

A gush of emotions overcame me, wanting him back with me. He was protecting me. He even saved me from Colton. Nobody has ever done what he did—*risking his own life*. Even in the cave, he was shielding me instead of protecting himself. *He is so selfless, so beautiful.*

"Please get up," I whispered, kissing him on his cheeks. He had bite marks on his chin. I gave him a peck on that mark. And when I lifted back, that spot slowly covered itself, healing.

"Whoa!" I exclaimed, taken aback. "What was that?" I wiped my tears, clearing my vision. "Did I just heal you?" I said incredulously, there was a scratch, a deep wound a few seconds ago, but now it was gone.

Can I even heal people?

I wasn't just a quick healer. I could heal others too. Wow, I was totally on a roll, next level—throwing shields, blasting monsters, and now healing. What else was left?

A smile rose my lips. I quickly started kissing him everywhere he was hurt, on his legs, arms, sides, his knuckles, turning him over on his back, kissing every inch of his body, where he was bleeding from, and as soon as his blood touched my tongue, the copper taste filled my mouth.

A shiver rolled down my spine with awakening, multiple electrons tickled my bones like my body was charging. But I didn't have time to check what was changing, as my prime focus was to save Kayden. So, I kept kissing him, didn't stop, or felt disgusted, not even once. At that moment, all I cared about was him—*The boy who wanted me to shift, to protect myself, leaving him at the mercy of shadows.*

I rolled him onto his back, placing my palms around his face. Slowly and steadily, blood from his wounds cleaned as they started vanishing from his body. It was a fast, quick way to heal somebody, not that I would run around kissing and licking people. He was just the exception.

Blood filled his pale face as his eyes fluttered open, looking at me in confusion.

"Why didn't you shift?" he asked, terror filled his eyes at the realisation, and he sat up with a jerk. "I told you to shift," he frowned, taking my face between his palms, glaring at me like I was the one who was scratched by the monsters.

I chuckled, as his voice was a chime to my ears. I took an aching breath which was caught in my lungs, more tears rolled down my eyes. He wiped them from my cheeks as I leaned into his warm, calloused palm.

"I know you think I am a supercilious princess, but I am not a horrible person." I raised my hand to wipe dirt off his chin, and with that, his eyes softened. He gulped down hard, looking at me like he would devour me any second.

"Are you okay?" he asked, still seeming concerned.

"Kayden, you took the major blow and are concerned for me?" I chuckled, snivelling, examining his face for any hint of injury. He kept observing my every action.

"Yes," he declared, making my heart flutter. His eyes were tensed, stating that his concern was genuine, while I was in shock over his declaration—*he was concerned about me, over himself?*

I had no words, nothing to snap at Kayden for the first time in my life.

"What happened?" he asked. His eyes followed my hands to my body, I had a few scratches, but they were gone red, already healing. The blood had dried.

"Those Mer-skeletons… they scratched you," I cleared my throat. His eyes examined his hands, arms, surprised as every wound had vanished. Only his olive-green jacket was ripped apart from the back and sides, along with his sand-coloured trousers from the sides. "But it wasn't deep enough, nor were they venomous."

"I am asking, how did I survive that?" He raised his eyebrows, studying me.

A smile stretched widely. *Finally, a proud moment, and he couldn't take this away from me.*

"Voodoo lady!" I chuckled, my eyes dancing happily. His lips parted, but no words came out, revealing a cut on the corner of his lips. I bent forward and kissed him on the wound.

I quickly pulled back as soon as I realised what I had done.

"I am sorry." Blood rushed through my cheeks at the anticipation of what I had done. My eyes went wide, and so were Kayden's. He went stoic. I think he forgot how to breathe.

Oh god! What have you done? You could have avoided it, stupid.

What would he think about me kissing two guys back-to-back in the same week? *Shit! I didn't want to give him any wrong ideas.*

"Oh God," I babbled, beyond humiliated. "I am sorry, I was just—I mean, oh man," I was fumbling in front of him. "It's just that's how I heal—there was a cut—wanted to heal—oh no—I mean."

It was when he took my chin between his fingers, I stopped breathing as he leaned in and kissed me. As soon as our lips met, something weird happened. I saw sparks all around. The whole Shadowland faded into the background, and firework land replaced it. A huge gush of fire ignited me, and my heart melted at the warm sensation of his soft lips as I gave into him.

And there in Shadowland, Kayden Parsons claimed me.

At that moment, I lost all my senses. I forgot everything—I forgot we were in Shadowland, forgot shadow monsters just attacked us, forgot we were here to save my friends, forgot it was Kayden—the devil, forgot he was the guy because of whom I was still single, forgetting he was no one to me, I just kissed him back instantly. His hand wrapped around the nape of my neck, tilting my head back, ravenously working on my lips as if he would devour me. I felt a kick of joy inside my stomach. He was awakening all my senses as I moved closer, tangling my hands in his silky soft hair.

I couldn't believe this was happening, between us, between two nemeses. *Was I dreaming?*

His tongue touched my lips, asking my permission. I could have stopped it there and pushed him away, but I opened my mouth a little, letting him explore me more, wanting him to deepen the kiss. As his tongue touched mine, he let out a throaty groan that reverberated through my body, travelling from my mouth to my neck, to my breasts which got tight and were aching now as the vibrations travelled south. His grip got tighter around my neck as he kissed me desperately as if he couldn't control it any longer.

His lips were unravelling me, breaking all the bounds inside me, point by point, till I was free from everything and everyone, and I just belonged to him. My hands caressed his broad shoulders, holding onto him, holding myself from floating into the clouds.

It was surprisingly comfortable, just following his lead, to get lost in him. Just when I wanted this to never end, I felt a string of zing, but this time it was alive and sparkling with an intensity so high and overwhelming that I wanted to get lost in it. It was sliding down my body, swiveling around us, wrapping us together. It didn't feel tangible, but its warmth glided down my body.

I pulled apart, catching my breath, feeling dizzy, my chest heaving, lips feeling tingly. My hands left his hair as I examined where I felt the touch of the string, but now, there was nothing.

"I wish this were my first kiss," I blurted out, lost in his magic. *Shit!* "I mean, it's not that I haven't kissed anyone before. I have, I mean—" I didn't have any words to cover myself up. I looked down, far, humiliated. I wished the Earth would swallow me.

A smirk played at the corners of his lips, his eyes sparkling at me.

Oh, God! He's laughing at me, this obnoxious jerk will think I wanted him when he had already told me he didn't find me attractive enough. *Argh! But the worst part was that I did want him.* It was not like an old kiss with Colton. It was profound, the one that sweeps you off your feet. We shared a moment of ecstasy that nobody could ever take away from me.

I immediately buried my head into my hands, blushing. *Fuck you, Lizzy. Can't you keep your mouth shut for like two seconds?* I had broken my cover, there was no mask on my face, and now he was going to think I was hitting on him. *Well played*, I thought sarcastically.

He took my hands and suddenly pulled me to him. I choked on my last breath as our bodies touched. He was emitting an enormous amount of heat, making my hands clammy even in this cold Shadowland. I was leaning on him, both of my hands tucked to his side, firmly. I closed my eyes and instinctively moved closer, anticipating another kiss. Even the thought sent a shiver down my body, his breath on my lips was playing with my hormones, but the kiss never came.

"If you want that, you can have that." He just whispered in my ears, his cheeks brushing mine.

My eyes flashed open. He looked down at me, smirking devilishly. "What do you mean?" How could I have *that,* once done—it's done, could I reverse time too? *Yeah, and you can be a goddess one day!* I told myself sarcastically.

"Your first kiss was not with that psychopath," he stood up, taking my hand with an entitlement this time. "You had your first kiss way before that."

We walked with entwined fingers while I was thinking about what he said, but nothing struck me. No, I haven't kissed anyone before. "You are wrong this time, Kayden Parsons," I snapped. Have I kissed anyone before Colton? My mind wavered—no, never.

He nodded. His eyes were sparkling with menace.

"What?" I asked. "You think you know everything about me? Even about when I had my first?" He was being that obnoxious jerk again, playing with me.

"Yep," he said, popping the P while walking towards the creepy house.

"No, you don't," I yanked my hand back, halting stubbornly. He thinks he's always right, but this time he wasn't.

"Yes, I do," he drawled, enjoying teasing me.

Argh! I stomped my foot loudly on the ground.

"Then when?" I asked loudly. He was already on the street when I tried to catch up with him. He and his long legs! "CPR isn't counted as a kiss," I told him if that's what he was implying.

"I know." He hunched his shoulders.

"Then when?" I asked like he owned me.

But he kept on laughing without answering me.

Chapter 25

A Fall into a Rabbit hole

We both were standing facing the creepy house.

He was looking at it, meanwhile, I was trying not to think about our kiss or what he meant about my first kiss. I was still blushing, unable to look at him. I was probably imagining all the awkwardness and tension in the air, making a big deal out of it because he seemed pretty casual, teasing me.

He had already clarified that I wasn't attractive enough to him, he even called me gay in front of Lucas.

Still, *he* kissed me.

I didn't know whether it meant anything to him. After all, he was a player, but I could feel something rushing inside me. *What could one kiss with me mean to him?* Possibly, he didn't even like it. That's why he wasn't saying anything.

Fuck! It was a mistake, Lizzy. How could you make such a huge mistake?

Still, my mind was going miles per minute, just thinking about him, our kiss, confused about why it was affecting me so much. Betraying my love for Homer, I wanted to kiss Kayden back again. I would like to have his soft lips back on mine.

In this ungodly world, at these ungodly hours, I was craving for this devil to wrap his hand around my neck and kiss me again. I wasn't a saint, but lusting over a boy was something I wasn't used to.

Shut up, Lizzy. He is a jerk, a Playboy, to whom you don't mean anything more than a spoilt little girl who is best friends with his sister, a girl he is repulsed by. He goes around. He makes out with so many girls. Why would this kiss mean anything to him? Moreover, you hate him, right? Remember?

It didn't help telling myself that.

Was it possible to hate someone so much that you started craving their attention? If it was, that's what was happening to me right now. I still wanted to kiss him again, reassuring myself that he liked it. Somehow, I wanted to prove to him that I was attractive enough that he wanted to touch me again, to kiss me as much as I wanted to because, after all, he was the one who turned it into a French kiss.

But he seemed distant and unmoved by the current events while I was trembling from tip to toe under the heat he was emitting.

After everything that happened today, his flirting, concern, and protectiveness, I was sure there was something between us, or was I deluding myself? *Maybe another kiss will give me all answers.*

No, Lizzy, remember you love Homer?

Do I? I asked myself.

I doubted my feelings for Homer, which was not a good sign. Obviously, I loved him, and it's better not to kiss Kayden again or anyone. It's leading me off track.

It felt like an eternity standing in front of this creepy house, his eyes measuring every inch of it while my eyes were travelling down his body, on his tattered clothes, his athletic arms—strong and defined, his firm legs, basketball suits him. I was ogling at him when he turned to me, catching me. I flushed and looked away.

"Are you sure this is the last place you saw them?" he asked, confused. *Hello! We just kissed, say something!*

I was burning inside, whereas this guy was acting normal, chilled out as if nothing happened, focusing on this stupid creepy house when he should focus on the conversation that was buzzing inside me.

Fine, if you'll act as if nothing happened, then I can mask the same, CHILL OUT! Huh.

"Yeah!" I wore a mask of being bored, "Perhaps they went inside," I said as I strode toward the creepy house. "C'mon, buckle up. I don't want to attract any more monsters." I was overconfident like I was just going to knock, they'd flung open the doors, hug me, and we'll leave.

I know I was being silly, but I was hoping that was it. I didn't want any kind of a mess, no more trouble. I already had a lot going on for such a young age.

"Where are you going?" He took my hand as I halted with a jerk.

"Inside, saving them," Du-huh! I yanked out of his grip. "That's what we are here for, remember?" *Not for making out and then not talking about it or pretending like it never happened. HUH!* I silently added as he frowned at me, and I gave him a hateful smirk.

"But it's just a hologram."

"What?" I asked, turning to the house.

"Oh!" I whispered. "Even Nathan noticed it. The house was just an illusion," I pointed at the foundation that wasn't touching the ground level. "This is where the veil was broken, you know, because of the fire at the museum."

Kayden gave me a baffled look. "How can a fire create a void, a hole in the veil? Unless…the fire was unholy." He held his chin, thinking. "But J.P.P. states you cannot douse it with normal water. It needs moonwater, and the fire at the museum was doused by normal water. It couldn't be unholy, it couldn't be the reason for the void."

I bit my lips. "But something near this creepy house created the void."

"Look," he pointed at an outhouse just at the side of the creepy house. It wasn't a hologram, and to my shock, it was the same kind of outhouse I once hid in, where I met Iron Man. And without thinking, I just sprang toward it.

"Eloise, wait," he called out, but I didn't stop. I had this gut feeling that Homer would be there, and as soon as I pushed open the door, Kayden caught me, panting. "What the hell are you thinking?"

I stepped in with my heart swelled in hope, but my mouth fell, finding it empty. I sighed loudly as disappointment washed over me. I brushed my face with my hands before examining the wooden walls, the same wooden floor and a pail where he had his candy. A weak smile rose on my lips. I didn't dare to lift that pail, it would turn into ashes, and I didn't want to change anything about this memory of my life.

He closed the door behind us, his gaze never leaving my face, reading my every expression very carefully.

It was too much to be in this outhouse. The nostalgia was so hard that I felt a burning sensation in my eyes. I was missing him. I was dying to look at his pretty face, to laugh with him. I hugged myself, gathering all my memories with him, and sucked in a deep breath, holding onto tears.

His hands grazed my shoulders as I whispered. "It's the day I felt what being accepted means. I thought things would stay exactly as they were in this outhouse, all warm and wrapped in love and happiness, just him and me, in our own bubble. But I was wrong, people change too fast, and I think that warmth was just my delusion. Perhaps I fell in love at the wrong time." My face fell.

Right after the words were out of my mouth, I realised I just kissed Kayden and was babbling about Homer in front of him, that was super shallow of me, but I couldn't stop myself from feeling while standing in this outhouse.

I thought he would be angry, but to my surprise, he hugged me from behind, his hands sliding down my front from the face, wiping off my tears to my neck, surfacing on my breast till my hands that were wrapped around my stomach. He wrapped his hands around mine and kissed my hair, sending shivers down my neck. I stepped back to lean into him, melting in his warmth.

"Love is pure and feeble. It doesn't understand the concept of time. It just happens anytime, anywhere. Sometimes it doesn't take more than a beat to fall in love with someone who makes you feel accepted, gives you home, and defines what it means to be happy together."

Kayden poured honey into my ears like he knew what it meant to fall in love, but to be frank, I never felt that with Homer. He was never home. Perhaps it was a different kind of love with Homer, not the one Kayden knew, but I want to hear more about his type of love. "Perhaps he isn't—" Suddenly, the ground shook under us, making us jump.

"Whoa! What was that?" I asked, holding him tightly as his grip tightened around me, my heart beating into my ears. It was when I heard a scratching sound.

It was like somebody was scratching their nails on the wall, the screeching sound was nerve-chilling, and I felt goosebumps all over my body.

I turned towards the sound and peeked at the wall behind him. As he craned his neck to look at the wall, he got stiff as our eyes fell on the carving in the wooden walls and fresh blood dripping.

'*I spy on your dreams and thrive on your nightmares.*'

Somebody just carved it. Somebody else was here with us, right here, right now.

I shivered, and without further warning, the wooden floor beneath us broke.

"ARGH!" I screamed while skidding down that tunnel. I tried to grab his hand when suddenly we hit the ground. I fell upon him, making him grunt.

"Sorry," I whispered. Though it wasn't bad for me, he was a good cushion, and his muscles saved me from getting hurt. My lips were just inches away from his chest. A shirtless image of Kayden flashed before my eyes. NO, *Lizzy, don't go down that road, not now. Ooo, but I so want to go down that road.*

I put my hands on his iron-clad chest and pulled myself up, trying hard not to look at him as the heat rose in my cheeks.

"About what?" He winked, I bit my lips as he helped me stand, and then he allowed himself. "What is this place?" he asked, brushing his hair with his hands. Seriously he was concerned about his hair, now also?

I observed the place where we were. We were trapped in a small vault, a confined space, my heart lurched, and my eyes widened.

"We must be 15 feet down," he exclaimed, glancing up the hole where the outhouse stood.

Suddenly, the walls started closing onto me as I realised we were trapped down a rabbit hole.

I hurriedly tried to tap around the vault walls to find some doorway, but we were trapped with mild yellow lighting and no way out.

"What does that writing mean—*thrive on your nightmares?*" My breathing increased. I was trying, but it was getting hard for me to breathe. This had to be a trap.

"Hey, are you alright?" Kayden asked, grabbing my face with a tender touch, trying to look into my eyes as he noticed my ragged breathing.

"Air pressure is low here," I huffed, trying to grab a few, but it was unsteady.

"Eloise, look at me," he told me sternly.

"I can't breathe," I whispered-gasped, getting out of his hands and jumping around to grab oxygen.

"Shhh… don't panic," he said, examining my condition.

I had already started bloating. "I am dying, I-I need more air, please help me." I was already seeing white in the corner of my eyes. It seriously felt like I would die there only, not by some shadow monsters but by lack of oxygen.

My survival instincts kicked in, and I quickly unbuttoned my shorts, helping myself breathe, then my hands fumbled with the zip of the jersey jacket. I reached inside my top to unhook my bra. I didn't know what I was doing, all I wanted was to stay alive.

"Stop it," he grabbed my hand as I started removing my jacket, but I was sweating like bullets already. I had no other option.

I tried to push him away, tossing the jacket on the floor. My hands wrapped around my top, trying to take it off.

"Listen to me," he sucked in a deep breath, his face all crimson. "Breathe," pushing my top down forcefully. "Close your eyes and fucking breathe." He ordered, but I shook my head.

I wasn't listening, so he spun me around in a swift action, taking me off-guard. His giant hand splayed on my bare stomach, electric waves shooting at his touch, while the other was on my eyes, blocking my sight. I didn't know what he was doing.

"Trust me," he whispered in my ears, desperation in his voice. "Breathe in with your belly, not with your chest." His fingers played with the hem of my top as if thinking whether he should reach up to cup my breasts, but he didn't.

I tried to do as he said. "Think about your happy place, the greenhouse, the gardens, every damn corner, where you love to plant flowers," I imagined everything he was saying. "Try to expand your belly with air rather than your chest." He was helping me patiently, and soon I was breathing through my belly.

"Good." His muscles relaxed a bit around me.

"Think about sitting on your windowsill gazing at all those gorgeous stars that light up your face, the calmness of the moon that provides you peace," he changed my happy place. I was imagining it now. I was feeling better. "Now, remember dancing to the song—*Only Girl*," his lips brushed my ears, his breath sending a tingle down my spine. The last time I danced to that song was at the concert.

"Inhale slowly through pursed lips, one, two, three, four, now exhale." His nose caressed my neck. I shuddered in his arms, his sturdy body was emanating a tremendous amount of heat, while his breathing became erratic as mine, but he continued.

"Now think about the night of your last birthday. You were wearing that amazing blue dress that accentuated your curves, barely covering your thighs," his hand slid from my stomach to the waist, following the curve of my hips to my thighs. His touch awakening the volcano inside me as if imprinting on my skin. I have never been touched like that ever before. "You were dancing alone in the middle of the crowd, too high to control your legs…,"

Then it came back to me—

My seventeenth birthday eve, when I sneaked out with my friends as Clara had gotten us Rihanna's concert tickets at Meghan Complex. Everyone was going, and I took advantage of my mother's business trip to Ontario. It was fun until Clara was all over Zach, and Homer was in the bush with some girl named Annie, leaving Nathan and me alone. The first birthday I celebrated with friends outside turned out to be a bummer, so Nathan and I decided to play a drinking game, and we drank a lot.

That's all I remember till now, but today, standing here with Kayden, it came back to me like an erased dream. It hit me like a gush of a wave—*the truth of that night.*

I remember dancing in the crowd and feeling dizzy when somebody caught me.

"Easy, baby girl." His hands caught me mid-air. He was amused as I frowned at him, blinking. Why was he here?

"Am I still blurred?" Kayden asked, chuckling. "What did you all have?" He bit his lips as he observed me, his eyes filled with humour. I was too high to tell him what I had, what all I mixed. And before I could get out of his arms, he hauled me up. I choked audibly, but he didn't notice. I even asked him to put me down, but it was all murmurs as the music was so loud, and everything was spinning.

We were in the parking lot when he carefully made me stand, but my legs had become jelly. I grabbed his hand tightly. "Whoa! Careful, it's an earthquake."

"No, it's not," he chuckled. "Come, sit in the car," but I climbed the hood of his Hummer, safeguarding myself from the earthquake, to which he laughed, showing off the perfect dimples on his cheeks.

My eyes blurred, and my hearing went sharp. A bead of sweat dripped off my forehead as I lifted my dress to wipe it off.

"NO!" he gasped in shock. He looked at me wide-eyed as he shoved my dress down, turning crimson.

I remember asking him. "Do I still look better than Annie?"

He looked confused, as if he was figuring out who Annie was, but then his eyes went soft, they glimmered with something I never knew he could feel.

"None of these girls holds a candle to you, baby girl." He cupped my face, biting his lips, seeming nervous. "But you are wasted. Let's go home."

"No," I shook my head. "It's my birthday. I want to dance to it." I started getting off his car, but he stopped me. His hands fell on my waist, holding me still.

"Fine, dance here. You've already punished me enough by letting those random guys touch you," he growled, as his grip tightened around me, as if afraid I'd vanish. "If anyone of them touches you now, I'll rip their hands off."

"Kayden!" I gasped. "You are a possessive caveman." I frowned, sliding down the hood and getting imbalanced as he caught me. My legs wrapped around him, and my arms were around his neck as I giggled for no reason. "You smell so good, like oceans," I bent to sniff him.

"Just like your eyes." He smiled, tucking me carefully around him, still sitting on the edge of his car's hood. He tucked my hair behind my ears. "But you smell like vodka, whiskey, and is that tequila?" He cringed his nose. I threw my head back, laughing. Everything seemed funny. I don't know why?

But then, my eyes fell on the sky. I let my hands fall from his neck as I arched back to look at the night sky, lying on the hood, unaware as his hands slid on my back, never leaving me.

"Do you know the moon is the sun's mate?"

He chuckled. "What?"

I was officially drunk.

"Yeah," I smiled as I looked at the moon shining brightly above me. "Sun always desired the moon, but he never went to her, thinking she didn't need him as myriads of tiny, sparkly stars always surrounded her, presuming she was full in her life. So, he used to watch her from a distance, never making a move, but little did he know that she had no one to understand her. Even surrounded by so many stars, she was all alone. So, she eagerly searched the skies for a friend, perhaps a meteor, to discuss her life's joys and sorrows. But nobody listened to her. Then one day, she vanished from the sky, which scared him." His grip got tightened around me.

"Sun searched for her everywhere, under the sea, over the mountain range but couldn't find her. He even asked her friends—the stars—but they didn't know what happened to her, and then one star told him about her sadness and loneliness. Sun thought it was his fault that he couldn't save her, glorify her as he does to everything in the world. All he wanted was her, to make things good for her, so he didn't give up and searched until he found her, waking up from a long slumber, dizzily looking at him."

"But she was sad. Her light was gone as she had cried through the night. He tried to reach out to her, but she ran, afraid that he would hurt her, but he kept on chasing her till the day when he finally got her. That day he gave her all his spark, light that blotted out of her loneliness, happiness that erased all her pain from the past, love that showed her that there was someone who cared for her. She went dizzy in the wonders so much that, look at her," I pointed at the sky. "She still speaks of the night they met, still lights up beautifully among all the stars, showing off the loving sun gave her, only her."

With a jolt, he hauled me up to look at my face. His eyes were molten lava. He gulped down once, twice, but still, he had no words to speak. I reached out to touch his face, tracing his forehead to his nose to his lips which were trembling. "You know, every Moon waits for its Sun."

He grunted as if he would devour me, leaning in close. Just then, I felt bile rising in my throat. I pushed him back with all my strength and hurled my guts out all over his shoes as he didn't step back in time.

I slid down from the hood to puke the alcohol out of my system. I felt large hands pulling my hair back. "It's ok, breathe," Kayden told me as he sat beside me, stroking my back, carefully tucking my hair in one hand.

"Go away," I told him, trying to shove him, but I felt my head spinning, so I gripped Kayden's hand tightly instead.

"I am here, don't worry, I got you," he whispered, gently stroking my back. He handed me a tissue as I wiped my mouth, trying to get up, but I felt no strength in my legs. They were numb and stuck as Kayden slid his hands under me and hauled me up, cradling me.

He made me sit in his car. I was drenched in sweat, and my hair stuck to my face as my dress clung to my body. "It's getting hot in here," I murmured, removing my arm from the sleeves.

"Jesus," he stopped me. "Can you just not take off your clothes!"

"But it's hot," I frowned at him.

"No stripping," he ordered as I huffed and crossed my arms around my midsection, turning my face away.

He sighed as he opened the back door and brought two bottles of water, he offered me one as he splattered water on his shoes, emptying the other one, but I rejected it, still frowning and angry that he was trying to control me.

"C'mon, take a swig," he offered again, but I shook my head.

His eyes widened in surprise as he twisted the cap and stepped towards me, towering over me. "Do you want me to shove it down your throat?" He arched his eyebrow.

I sneered at him as he placed a finger under my chin, and I batted it away.

He sighed. "Please, baby girl?"

I grimaced at him as he placed the bottle over my lips, holding my jaw, but I was determined. I batted the bottle away and held the water in my mouth, stubbornly not drinking it.

He groaned, looking at me in disbelief. "Stop crawling under my skin, spoilt brat."

I got furious when he called me a spoilt brat, so I splashed it all over his face. He flinched, closing his eyes, taken aback by my actions. "I am not a spoilt brat," I snapped at him, wiping my mouth with the back of my hand.

It took him a few seconds to realise what have I done. He raised his hand to wipe off his face before opening his eyes, which I knew would be filled with wrath, but instead, they were soft and filled with amusement. He shook his head as he let out a roar of laughter, making me arch my eyebrows, and without saying a word, he pushed my legs inside his car, tying a safety belt around me.

I was shocked that he was still laughing when he claimed the driver's seat as he turned on the AC, rearranging the vents towards me, and as soon as the cold air hit me, I sighed, getting relaxed.

But this wasn't all. I wanted to dance, so he took me for a ride. I was shouting, standing from the sunroof, feeling the air on my face. I made him play—Only Girl on repeat for over two hours, and I was screaming that song to the world in my horse-like voice. He patiently rode by my side, then spoon-fed me enchiladas. We laughed till I was tired and slept in his car.

My eyes flashed open at the memory. I spun around. My heart was beating crazy against my chest. He was breathing heavily now. His predatory eyes were filled with dark desires as I pulled him with the front of his ripped jacket and smashed his lips on mine. *This is my happy place—kissing him.*

Chapter 26

Caveman

I lost all my senses as his soft lips touched mine.

I kissed him demandingly with all the hunger I had in me as he returned me with the same passion. His hands grabbed my ass, hauling me up to his level. I immediately wrapped my legs around his hips, securing myself to him. He pinned me against the wall, flushing his body against mine. The pressure of his weight felt indispensable as he kissed me roughly, like he was yearning for this. My heart was beating crazy as I reached to dig my fingers deep inside his brown hair, telling him to kiss me harder, begging for the pleasure they filled me with.

He moved his lips away from mine, kissing his way down my jaw. Goosebumps formed on my exposed body. My legs were getting numb, losing all their strength. Thank God Kayden was supporting me, or else I would have fallen to the ground. The zing heightened as I again felt it in the form of string around us, but Kayden didn't let me see, he kissed me like he desired nothing else in the world.

"I told you my story, I never told anyone this story," I whispered, out of breath. He licked the hollow of my throat too generously. A soft moan escaped my lips, making him smile against my skin, disarming me.

"Everything about you hexes me, even that story. It felt like our story," he swarmed back to my lips, licking the corner of my mouth. *Is that why he calls me a voodoo lady?* But my every thought vanished from my head as I felt his hard-on against me, my core clenched at the touch. A gasp left my mouth.

"I don't think you're having any difficulty finding me attractive," I whispered—at that second, I didn't think he found me any less attractive. Kayden Parsons finds me as attractive as he should. A victory smirk rose my lips, but soon it vanished as my words triggered something in him. I felt a shift in his body as he pulled my head back with my hair and smashed his hungry lips on me while he grinds his impressive length against my core. I whimpered as I let out a throaty moan, unable to bear the excitement. He smiled against my lips.

"Even I don't think you are finding me repulsive, *Voodoo lady*." He bit my lower lip, squeezing my ass and grinding, driving me crazy.

I hate being so vulnerable in front of him, under his control, I hate wanting him more, but there was nothing I could do to repulse him anymore.

"Kayden." His name left my lips in the form of a moan, and he crushed me on the wall with a grunt. I was getting damp between my legs, enjoying that he wanted me back as much as I wanted him. "It's you who started it. You pulled back from me when I saved you." I told him between the kisses. My clit had swollen and was aching for more. I had never fooled around with anyone, even in our land, and here I was, getting dry-humped by Kayden in *Shadowland*. The copper taste on my tongue made me realise I had bitten him, as I love his taste. It's like his blood ignites me, sending waves of need down my body. I wanted him more. "I didn't pull back because you felt repulsive," he mutters against the soft skin of my neck. "You electrocuted me."

"What?" I mumbled, lost in the friction, reaching towards something.

He halted.

I almost groaned from missing pressure, but his finger traced my spine, a little touch on my bare skin, and I arched, squirming in his arms, as it sent electric shivers down my spine. "Electrocuted," he whispered against the skin of my neck as he nipped it between his teeth.

Oh! God! He felt the same shivers years back that I was feeling now.

"I didn't understand at that time, but now I do," he confessed between the kisses, his hands tracing my back as I arched until I crushed myself into him, baring my neck, his lips followed to my neck, leaving wet kisses, sniffing the dip of my cleavage, taking in my raw scent. I shuddered in his arms as he wedged his nose in my cleavage.

"You know how hard it is for me not to grab you every time I see you, how much control I have to gather not to touch you, to sniff you, to taste you." He licked my cleavage, popping my chatoyant, wedging his tongue between my full breasts. I came undone, moaning so hard that he swarmed back to my lips. He tasted like my sweat. My heart fluttered at his revelation. *He didn't repulse me, he never did. He is exquisitely attracted to me. Oh my god*!

"But you don't like me. You don't even want to be my friend." I broke the kiss, looking into his insatiable molten eyes.

"Like? No, baby girl," his voice went gravely as he shook his head, clicking his tongue. "What I feel for you is more dangerous, more lethal than *like*." His friction increased, and the seam of my shorts rubbed against my clit, and I felt a wild sensation building in my core. "I don't want to ruin *this* with the word *friend* when I can give you so much more." We hadn't even gone to second base, but his grinding had ignited me to a level where there was no comeback. "When I want you so much more."

"More…," I breathed with an open mouth as my legs trembled. The deep ache in my core reached its high. It felt like I was going to explode.

But—what? Was it possible to come like this? I don't know, I'd never touched myself, it always felt odd to do that next to my mother's room.

But is it possible?

Oh!

OH!

OOOH!

"Kade," I moaned as I came. My orgasm surprised me as I dug my nails into his shoulders, that sensation was so unique and highly addictive. It felt like nothing I'd ever felt before—it was amazing.

"Luna Mia!" Kayden grunted as I crashed on him. My head fell on his broad shoulder. What did just happen? Did Kayden just make me come without even touching? My thighs trembled as he held them firm with his giant warm hands.

I always knew there was something between us, some spark, that made me so mad when I felt him repulse me, and now that spark was pushing me towards him. I triumphed that he liked me. One person I thought wasn't attracted to me was wholly and highly spellbound by me.

"I had a dream about you that birthday night," I confessed, a little out of breath, easing my grip from his shoulder, licking my swollen lips.

"That wasn't a dream." He slowly put me down, putting his forehead on mine, grabbing some air now, hyperventilating.

I looked at him cynically, confused. "But how could you—how did you—but I was in my room."

Obviously, if it was Kayden who brought me home that night. If Kayden was the one I was out on the drive with…it was Kayden with whom I made out in my room.

Fuck!

"Kiss me," I demanded, my hands on the collar of his coat that he was wearing as I pulled him towards me while he was tucking me in my bed, which Noni allowed him. His eyes went wide as if I had taken him off-guard.

"No," he chuckled in amazement. "You should sleep." His hands uncurled my fingers from his coat but didn't let them go.

"Please, kiss me," I practically begged him.

"You're drunk, Eloise," he chuckled softly, as he tried to push me onto my bed, but I didn't budge.

"I don't care," I frowned, reaching out to wrap my arms around his neck. "Please, just for one time, I don't want to be a 17-year-old kiss virgin," I said, looking deep into his eyes. He gulped down hard, I could see his gaze on my lips, but he closed his eyes, holding onto control and shook his head.

"Just go to sleep," he told me sternly, pushing me down.

"Please," I gave him my goo-goo eyes. "Please give me my first kiss ever," I batted my lashes at him.

His eyes widened as he sucked a deep breath as if breaking all the controls he had over his mind.

"You're a viciously irresistible creature, Eloise Hector," he grunted before taking my chin between his thumb and finger.

And kissed me softly, thinking it'd be just a brush, but he couldn't stop it, nor could I. Instead, he turned it into a passionate one, like he was waiting for years to do so. I could feel his desperation, fear, hunger, claim, everything to make me smile against his lips.

We pulled apart, breathing heavily. "Happy birthday, baby girl," he whispered, kissing my forehead before tucking me in.

"I am going crazy. I am dreaming of kissing Kayden Parsons." I mumbled and soon drifted off.

As that part involved Kayden, I always thought it was just a dream because if someone had said that this super-hot devil would like to kiss me before this night, I would say I had a better probability of surviving the Bermuda Triangle than him kissing me.

So, I never thought that it could be real.

Oh no! "Perv!" I snapped at him. "You kissed a drunk girl."

"Hey! You begged me," he chuckled. "To be your first kiss ever."

OH MY GOD! I did. I begged him to kiss me. "HOLY SHIT!" I gulped down hard, ashamed of myself, I had the urge to shove my face in my palm and hide, but he didn't give me any option.

But somewhere, I was happy that at least Colton was out of the picture.

"I must be a joke among your friends!" I practically whimpered.

"It's going to be a hell-of-a-gossip, isn't it?" he teased. "The supercilious self-absorbed princess begged someone for a kiss."

I hissed. "I'll kill you, Kayden Parsons," I threatened in a deep voice.

"C'mon, try me," he smirked, his eyes filled with mirth, arching his brows as if enjoying the show.

"I hate you," I pushed him hard, but instead, he slid his hand on my waist and pulled me to him, slamming me into his chest. I was taken aback.

"No, you don't," he grumbled, his eyebrows frowning. "I haven't told it to a single soul. Haven't I done enough to gain your trust? What else do you want me to do?"

"Caveman," I pouted. I'd never been scolded so much in my life as he does. He was so dominating, but the irritating part was that it was hot. He was right, he didn't spill about Colton to Jason. He has already kept *me* being a Shadow Walker as a secret, and this was merely a trifle.

A groan passed his lips before he leaned in and tugged my lower lip with his teeth softly. And he kept sucking on it until I moaned, "Kade."

Suddenly a spark went inside him as he hungrily went for my upper lip, desperation in his kiss, teeth, lips, tongue, everything was making my heart thrum faster, seeming it was going to explode. God! He was so good. I couldn't believe kissing could be so amazing. Why didn't we do it before? This was like heaven.

But as an answer, Clara's angry face flashed before my eyes.

What will she think about me? Will she understand this or not? Will she accept that Kayden and I made out? What if she didn't? What if she gets mad at me for fooling around with her brother?

And Homer. Oh God! Homer, how was he going to react if he ever got to know?

However, the main question was—do I want it? Do I want to leave Homer and move on to Kayden?

What if I did? I moved on, but Kayden took me as some random girl with whom he just wanted to have a fling. I didn't want a fling. I wasn't that kind of girl, but he just made me come, which was fucking intense.

He must have felt the shift in my demeanor because he let me go. His eyes were studying me.

But I didn't know why we were doing this. He's not my boyfriend. He shouldn't make me come like this. This was not right. But he was so addictive, his words, his touch, everything was turning me on, and I knew if I didn't stop now, I wouldn't be able to stop ever. *I have to save my dignity.*

So, I gathered all my courage and pivoted.

"We should look for them," I bit my lips, hiding my face from him.

He ran his hand through his hair, a bit frustrated, but he nodded to my relief because if he had pressed further on this topic, I would have given in. I quickly rearranged myself, hooking back up as he helped me with the jacket.

But I didn't know how to behave, he just made me come, and I didn't know what to do or how to be around him anymore.

"How are you feeling?" he asked softly.

"A little woozy," I told the truth.

He grinned wickedly, showing his dimples, making me all swoony as if I could take it anymore. "I have my charms," he said, shoving hands down his pockets. "But I was asking about your panic attack. Although, it's good to know I can put you in a swoon."

My cheeks heated, but he continued.

"So, what does that make me—The Savior of the Shadow Walker or The God of Orgasms that can make you come even *without touching*?" he asked, his eyebrows dancing in mirth.

Pretentious jerk.

"Seriously? Has anyone ever told you that you are obnoxiously self-opinionated?" I rolled my eyes.

"Of course, I have two siblings breathing down my neck all the time but don't change the topic. So Voodoo lady, has someone else given you such an orgasm before? Has someone ever given you an orgasm before?" He folded his arms over his midsection, smirking pompously like he won some trophy.

My body flushed at his question.

"Of course," I hunched my shoulders, lying easily. "I liked him feasting between my legs, he was better than you."

Instantly, his hands were in my hair, scraping my roots, roughly pulling them back, licking my lips. "Lies taste sweet on your lips, Voodoo lady," he spoke darkly.

I gasped. *How did he know that I was lying, was it obvious? Was it written on my face? Or did he make it out of the kiss we just had? Was my inexperience palpable?*

He chuckled, his whole chest reverberating, making my nipples hard, as he buried himself into the crook of my neck. His free hand roamed my waist to my ribcage, tracing my lacy bra with his thumb. I waited for him to squeeze my breasts and give me more, but instead, he took a step back, and I groaned because of the missing euphoria.

"Your punishments just started," he smirked, too satisfied with himself. Arranging my top, he gave me the lightest peck on my lips.

"Something is shining behind this wall," he whispered against my lips. "I thought you'd like to know."

I spin around to look. It seemed like the burnt wallpaper was coming off. I quickly ripped off the wallpaper from the corner and saw an iron door with no handle.

"Get back," he pulled me aside by my arm as he kicked it, and with that, the wall pounced open like a lid.

Chapter 27

Nightmares

The archway leads us to an old-fashioned corridor, covered with an old rug and scones on the walls that flicker every time we walk past them, but the weirdest thing about this corridor was there were no doors or windows, just burnt rug and torn wallpaper.

We kept on walking, it seemed like an eternity, but there was no end to it.

I looked around. There was a red mark behind a torn-off wallpaper, which seemed like a handprint of a person in blood. EW! Ignoring it, I kept searching for more.

"Geez! It's like a never-ending corridor," I told him. My voice seemed raspy, panting.

"You are tired," he said, stepping forward. "Stay here. I'll just check it out."

"What are you talking about? We are not separating," I ground out. "Haven't you seen horror movies? Whenever they split, somebody dies." I felt chills crawling up my spine.

"We're not splitting," he rolled his eyes. "I am here only, just taking a few steps ahead. Stay calm," he added, his voice soft and resolute at the same time.

He walked forward, and I saw him walking and walking, and then he vanished.

"What the fuck!" I gasped as I jolted to my feet.

"Eloise?" Kayden asked. I was about to run, but I heard his voice from behind.

"When did you?" he asked me, looking to and fro. "What's going on?" he asked, frowning, puzzled.

I was baffled, too. "I just saw you vanishing," I told him, walking forward and slowly outstretching my hand, where Kayden vanished. My hand was unnervingly steady as it vanished as if it went inside some invisible wall, widening my eyes.

"Eloise," Kayden growled in disbelief. "It's a loop," I turned behind and saw my hand hanging in the air near Kayden, at my back. "It's a fucking space loop."

"Interesting," he murmured, closing his distance to reach me.

"I knew something was wrong. Someone is messing around with us." I trembled in horror. "Homer's always loved sci-fi movies, but space and time loops creep him out, as he finds them impossible to break."

"You think we are in Homer's nightmare?" Kayden grimaced. "That writing on the wall said *I spy on your dreams and thrive on your nightmares*. You think it includes your friends?"

I hunched my shoulders. "At least it confirms one thing," a smile rose on my lips.

Kayden raised his eyebrows.

"They are alive,"

"Oh! Smart-ass," he winked. "But that's a relief," he said, as his shoulders relaxed a bit. "Believe me, till now, I was thinking what I'd tell my dad if Clara was…you know," but he shuddered and shoved that thought out. "It's not important now. So how will we break it?" he asked, examining the corridor's walls. My eyes fell on the same handprint on the right that I left a few metres back.

"Do you think this handprint had to do something with this loop?" he asked me, pointing at it as he placed his hand on it.

"Ewww! It's someone else's blood." I grimaced, feeling disgusted, while I stepped forward to check whether the loop had ended or not, but I reached behind Kayden. "Nothing happened," I told him.

"Wait," I figured. "I need something, something sharp." I looked around for something. That's when I remembered my penknife, fuck, how could I forget it during a fight with Mer-Skeletons. *But it was an ambush. I was taken aback. I shouldn't be the one to be blamed.*

I took out my penknife off my boots. It's an antique schrade cutlery square and jackknife. I unfolded its beautiful, jigged bone handle, which felt cold inside my palm. The old carvings on the sharp blade were glowing as if it was a brand new one. But it wasn't brand new, I had seen my great grandpa Maurice holding the same, it was a family heirloom.

"You keep a penknife?" Kayden asked in horror.

"Yeah, people's *abuela* give them pepper spray. Mine handed me a penknife," I grinned pompously.

He seemed impressed as his eyes examined every inch of the knife. "Interesting. You're much more than what I anticipated. You surprise me, Eloise Hector."

My chest filled with air as he praised me, which was so uncommon to come out of Kayden's mouth, but he added. "Now do your Voodoo and get us in. This place is giving me chills," he said, rubbing his arms.

He couldn't let me enjoy even a second of gratification.

"Fine, just get out of my way," I pushed him aside with my shoulder, making him chuckle. "I hope this works," I whispered, and with that, I slit my palm with the sharp blade. "Argh!" I cringed as it stung. Hot blood oozed out of my palm, filling my nostrils with the smell of copper, carefully not letting it drip to the ground.

"ELOISE!" Kayden cussed, concerned. "What's wrong with you?" He quickly reached for my hand, but I snatched it back before he could wipe it off.

"No," I shook my head. "I am a fast healer, remember?" I told him. The blood pooled in my hand, but he wasn't convinced. He was still looking at my hand, worried, but he didn't say anything, just held my hand with my elbow as if holding me was the only indication for him that I was real.

As my hand got drenched in blood, I placed it over the handprint.

Soon after my blood touched the handprint, it glowed under it. A red beam covered the corridor, warming my hand.

With a pop, a lift appeared, levelling from 3…2…1… and when the doors opened to the side, a massive wave of water gushed toward us.

"RUN!" Kayden growled, with horror in his eyes.

I didn't need a second command to understand. I quickly sprinted forward, hoping the loop had ended. We darted together, but I slowed down as he vanished.

"Kayden?" I screamed. My heart froze as a sudden fear of losing him surmounted me.

"I am fine," I heard him, warmth spread through my body as his voice hit my ears. *Kayden was fine!* "A wall separated us, keep running." He added as a wave gushed towards me, waiting to drown me.

I ran forward and reached the end of the corridor where three doors appeared from somewhere. I quickly took the right door, thinking about meeting him there, but instead, it was the same corridor, I was led back to the place where we started running, and the water was still gushing towards me, but this time Kayden wasn't with me. I kept running as I reached the doors again.

I hastily opened the front door, and instead, I stepped into the left one, dodging, letting that water flow inside the front door. I heard no sound of flowing water, but I had no strength to open this door again.

Later, I realised I was again in the same corridor, standing near the hand imprint, panting heavily.

"What happened?" I asked, turning around. "Did I do something wrong?"

I ran again, realising I was trapped back—it was so tiring, so confusing. The water was again gushing towards me. I again reached the doors. This time, I opened both the doors from the right and left and hid behind the front door, panting heavily.

But I was back in the corridor.

"FUCK YOU!" I swore loudly, getting agitated. I didn't know what to do.

Running away from the gush of water was getting tiresome as all three doors were not the way out, but the water wasn't giving me time to think about it.

This time I opened all the gates, and suddenly the wave of water hit me hard, slamming me to the door on the right, which opened with a thrust, and I fell to the floor. But I wasn't wet, it didn't feel like water, it was just an illusion, but I didn't know how to escape it, so my first instinct was to create a bubble of shield around me, but it didn't come out.

"Don't you do that," I snarled at my ring, which was not pulsing anymore like its powers had drained or blocked. "Don't you betray me, now."

My heart was thumping loudly against my chest. I didn't know what to do as I looked down at my chatoyant, even it seemed dead.

I was stuck here, my eyes looking at the illusion of water. *Can it drown me?* The room was filling up while I was swimming with it. Suddenly, I felt Kayden's presence. I couldn't explain how, but my body felt the zing, and I searched for him. He was lying at the bottom of the pool.

Why wasn't he swimming up? Doesn't he know how to swim?

At that moment, I remembered the incident where Kayden drowned in the pool, and Clara thought he had died while I gave him CPR. My eyes went wide, and fear crossed my heart as I descended towards him, but out of nowhere, a black shadow-like monster climbed over him.

My heart stopped beating.

It had an upright body like a humanoid with no legs, just an upper part. He had his large intestine and small intestine dangling in the water, it was like someone ripped down half of his body, and he was flying therein water with his floating internal organs. It was disgustingly creepy. He was hovering over Kayden.

I quickly dived to examine the monsters. He had no eyes, just a blank, pale face with sharp teeth and a large, disgusting tongue with enormous blisters. And that tongue was inside Kayden's mouth. That was no regular tongue but a huge, red-coloured tusk. I wanted to scream, but the water didn't let me.

Kayden was whimpering in pain. His words—*if you want to survive, get your claws out,* were ringing in my ears.

My hands fumbled with my knife, and I hurled it in the beast's direction with force. I knew my weapon, its weight, and how to use it. And with my experience, I aimed my knife at the monster's tusk, and it went piercing.

With that sudden stroke, the monster fell back, retreating his tongue, and soon became black ash. I quickly snatched Kayden with the front of the jacket and swam to the surface. It felt like *déjà vu.*

The illusionary water dispersed back into the walls, and we both fell to the ground with my knife near my feet.

But this time, I didn't have to give him mouth-to-mouth. He started coughing a laugh. "Eloise Hector!" I was relieved to hear his voice.

"This was your nightmare, wasn't it?" I asked him, still agitated.

He tucked both hands behind his head, lying on the floor. His eyes were watery and red due to tears.

"And you saved me again," he said without looking at me.

"You mean, you saw this monster that day too?" I asked him in shock.

"Yes," he closed his eyes and whimpered. "He haunts me every time I am near pools or lakes or any water body, that's why I couldn't join search parties when you told everybody that Clara washed away." Tears rolled down his eyes. That's why he was so afraid the day I saved him. He was too shocked to thank me, not repulsing me. *Shit!*

"Hey, don't worry," I got up, hovering over him, wiping his tears with my fingers. "I'll always be there to save you," I smiled, laying my head on his chest, a relief passing through me as I heard his heart thumping loudly against his chest—*he was fine.*

"And I thought it should be the other way round," he laughed, his chest reverberating.

"Always a sexist," I rolled my eyes, as he kept laughing, I couldn't help joining him. I didn't know why, but I was laughing, maybe because we both were safe. We were about to get out of this lunatic loop. I raised my head to look at him. I couldn't have imagined he could look so much more handsome, but right now, as he was laughing, he looked like the most beautiful man I had ever seen, with his cute dimples that I would love to stick my tongue into.

"I don't understand, why did you even throw my shoe in the pool that day?" I asked curiously as he said he never hated or repelled me.

He hummed. "You took Cooper's name while fake marrying Clara, making me livid."

"You're crazy, you know that?" My mouth hung open.

"Well, what can I say, you make me crazy," he smiled, giving me a kiss, a fervent one, the one that made my toes curl.

Chapter 28
Demon's Den

We exited the room after a while, entering a cold hall, temperature dropped various degrees, making me shiver as goosebumps trailed down my legs.

A huge skull, around 10 feet tall, was placed in the centre with loads of white ashen tendrils splayed on the floor. It was nerve-chillingly creepy, but what stunned me the most was three figures sitting on those tendrils, rocking on their heels as if praying to it.

Not just any three figures but my friends, Clara, Homer, and Nathan.

"Guys!"

Thrilled, I quickly leapt to hug them, but they turned to me with a jerk, shooting me a deadly look.

"They are shadows," Kayden held me mid-air, stopping me from climbing the mountain of tendrils.

Their eyes were molten tar with no trace of white, and their hair was a mess, gone all silver. I saw Clara whose strawberry-pink dyed hair had gone silver too. Their skin was deteriorating, breaking from places, falling off like ashes, their lips were cracking white. They were so pale.

I stumbled back on Kayden in horror. "What happened to you?" I asked them, holding my throat, feeling his grip tighten around me.

"You left us to rot," they said in sync in a cold voice. It was their real voice, but too cold that it made me shiver.

"No, I didn't." My stomach dropped.

"You did. See what we have become." Clara showed me her hands, white deteriorated.

"You made us into monsters like you," Nathan grumbled.

I was on the verge of crying, looking at them like this. "I didn't," I whispered, trembling, but Kayden pulled me flush into him, providing me his warmth, his eyes scrutinising everything.

"Why does everybody you love have to suffer?" asked Homer. "You should have stayed away from us. Look at us, what we have become. You are cursed, Elmo. You should have told us. We would have run away from you. At least we would have our lives, the life we deserved."

"You are a terrible person Lizzy. You killed us," Clara snarled, making me flinch.

And for a fraction of a second, her tar eyes changed to bright red.

I choked, standing there. "You are not dead," I cried. "Please, I never wanted you to suffer like this,"

They all were saying everything I used to think, sitting alone in my room, my worst nightmares.

"We are dead, Lizzy. Look at us. We are decomposing in this land where you left us. The land nobody can visit except you, you brought us with you. You killed us." Nathan said, cocking his head to the right.

"I didn't bring you," I moaned. "I don't have the powers to bring humans to this land." With that, they all turned to my left.

Kayden's grip became one of steel. "What?" He looked aghast. "I came through a portal."

"You shouldn't have." said Clara. "You will now face the same fate as we did. We all have to suffer because we loved this monster."

"No, he won't suffer," I said, trying to get out of his grip, but he snarled at me, telling me to stay put.

"He has to," growled Clara. "You are cursed, Lizzy. You shouldn't be loved." My heart shattered into million pieces. I knew that already, and that is why I was sobbing heartily. It was all my fault. I was whispering sorry between my sobs.

"Thank God I chose Sophie over you," Homer said. "At least I had a good time with her, I know it was a short time, but it was the happiest time of my life," playing with his lip piercing.

"I have loved you all my life," I sobbed as my knees buckled beneath me. "I waited for you every day," I wanted to reach out for him, but Kayden shook his head, his jaw taut.

"Liar, you loved the guy you met in the outhouse, and because of your obsession, you pushed me into this DOOM." His eyes also flickered bright red, returning to black again.

I flinched at his words, my stomach dropped, and I could feel sharp pain filling my chest.

"Yeah! Even I should have chosen Sophie to be my best friend. I would have been alive," Clara said. "Wish we had never met you," Nathan added in a low rumble.

"This is just your fear, Eloise," Kayden whispered, his nose tracing my jaw. "Remember, this is not real. It's all illusionary."

But I was whimpering in despair.

"No, don't touch me, or you'll die too. Stay away from me," I tried to push him away, terrified.

"ELOISE!" He spun me to face him, his hazel eyes bearing into mine. "Look at me," he demanded.

"No, I don't want you to face all this. You should leave me alone. They are right. I am your doom," I gulped down, shivering visibly.

"Whether my boon or my doom, you are mine, Eloise Hector," he growled, holding my jaw, forcing me to look into his eyes. "Trust me, everything is an illusion. Just me, just us, this is only real," he told me authoritatively.

"No, they are telling me the truth. I should be left alone. I don't deserve anyone," I was trying to get out of his grip, tears rolling down my cheeks. "I am a MONSTER!" I screamed at him, but I was telling it more to myself.

"No, you are not," his voice went soft as he placed a wet kiss on my forehead. He held my face between his palms as he licked my tears off my cheeks, taking me off-guard.

"Nothing is real here, except this, except us," he whispered, against my cheeks, forcing my hands to wrap around him so that I could hear his heart beating under my skin, his breath tickling on my cheeks as he licked the fresh tears, a warmth spread through my body at his gesture.

"See, this is real, now relax, and I know this is too much to grasp, that's what you have been told, but it's not true. *You're not the monster, you're the one these monsters fear. You'll become that, right?"* A smile rose on his lips, my eyes widened as his words went like a spark through me. My heart swelled with confidence.

He thinks I am powerful, of course, I am, I killed monsters, I healed him, I was strong, and I must stay strong.

Clara growled. "You both will die." And with that, Clara put her hand on me, which was icy cold. I tried to push her, but her grip was too tight.

"Leave her," Kayden snapped at Clara, but she didn't budge. "I said *Leave. Her. Now*," he snarled as his lips curled up, baring his teeth.

Clara's eyes went wide like she got scared of Kayden and stepped back, leaving me. "You can't be alive," she whispered in terror in a foreign voice. Her eyes never left Kayden's.

Suddenly, she started vibrating, shivering in terror as the tendrils started moving like snakes, the skull started cracking, and the façade fell apart, revealing a white-coloured brain with no blood in it, attached to tendrils.

A ten feet tall single-eyed brain was bobbing with a small body, like a baby, hanging with it. A tiny penis was hanging out with small balls. It had teeny legs that weren't even touching the ground, standing on the tendrils sticking out of its brain. A scream stifled into my throat when my friends flew and went inside the brain, but within that moment, a tendril wrapped around Kayden, and before I could save him, they were enclosing me.

They felt cold and wet, slithering around my body.

Kayden was right. They weren't my friends. It was this brain with his little thing. This monster was doing everything till now.

I heard Kayden screaming my name. I tried to look at him but couldn't move even an inch. It was getting hard to breathe, I tried to use my ring or chatoyant, but it didn't do anything.

"Argh!" I screamed, trying to break free with all my strength. My breathing was getting uneven. I kicked it in desperate need of air. It budged for a split second, its grip loosened, and instantly I grabbed the opportunity, taking out my knife and slit the tendril wrapping me.

The blade of my penknife glowed as it pierced the tendrils, and I fell to the floor, breathing heavily.

"Whoa!" I exclaimed, looking down at my penknife glowing like a lightning bolt. Soon, I heard Kayden's groan. A tendril was crushing him. He wasn't even visible. More tendrils tried to grab me, but I danced away, slicing them with my blade. It was swift, like chopping veggies for burritos. My grip was tight while swinging my knife. It was like tap dancing with the knife. I have done this many times while fencing with Robin, but instead of a knife, I had a Sabre.

One by one, I sliced the tendrils off, trying to make my way towards Kayden. I slashed the one wrapped around Kayden. He fell with a thud, blood coming out of his nose, and his face was gone white due to lack of oxygen.

I got distracted by Kayden's white face, and the monster growled. His tendrils wrapped around my legs and swept me off the floor, hanging me upside down.

I groaned as he spoke in a heavy voice. "Finally, I met you," there was no mouth, only one red eye continuously watching me while that brain throbbed as it spoke. I was hanging upside down, making it too hard not to look at its baby penis. "I was waiting to see who was being stupid enough to enter the den, but now I see it's not a shadow, but it's *you*, raw, who doesn't even know about Demon's Den."

"D-Demon's Den?" I stuttered. "Are you a demon?" I asked, gulping down hard. Blood was flowing in my brain, the adrenaline and my breathlessness were making it quick.

But that wasn't my biggest fear. It was the monster standing in front of me—he was a demon, not shadow monsters, beasts, but a demon, an actual fucking demon.

"You seem very curious…hmmm…I could feel…there are so many questions in your mind…you need answers…hmm…just lost your mother…how harsh it would have been for you to give her up…and your friends too…hmm…you are curious about this world…thirsty for knowledge…thirsty to find yourself," he read me like a book like I was standing in front of him naked. "We didn't know about your existence, neither did you," he said in a curious voice.

"Who are you?" Kayden asked, but he didn't turn to him. His red eye bore into mine.

"Every question demands a sacrifice," he said in his low, grumbling voice.

"What kind of sacrifice?" I asked curiously, twitching my body and trying to free myself from his hold because my position was extremely uncomfortable.

"I am the keeper of Demon's Den, *Thamex.* I have an answer to every question of this world," he said. I've never heard of this demon before.

Yeah, right, like you've heard about so many demons. I shook my head, giving myself a mental eyeroll.

"And I could feel you have so many questions in your mind," it slithered towards me. "I can fill you with my knowledge." He hangs a bait in front of me.

Instantly I swayed my hand, trying to build the shield around me, but it didn't come out. He gave out a laugh, the devil's laugh. His brain was rumbling, making my head numb.

"Innocent child, you're standing in the Demon's Den. *Moonstone* doesn't work here," he scoffed.

Moonstone? The red stone in the ring I was wearing was a *moonstone.* Every Shadow Walker in my dream was wearing it. Perhaps they got this ring to safeguard themselves, to create the shields, it was working till we were above the surface, but here in Demon's Den, something is jamming its powers. This Demon's Den is more potent than moonstone, than Shadow Walkers, that's why J.P.P. didn't mention anything about it. She might not even know about its location.

Fuck! We were screwed.

Ok, no shield, no portal. I have to work beyond that, but how?

I looked at Kayden, raising his eyebrows as if asking, '*What are you doing?'* As I was acting recklessly, instead of killing this demon, I was talking to him, who had his tendrils enveloping my hand but never touching it.

I gazed down at my hand. The penknife's blade was still glowing.

"If you kill me, you won't be getting any answers," *Thamex* said like he was reading my mind, "There is so much to you other than just shifting to Shadowland. You're born for greater deeds, deeds only I can tell you, deeds only you can do—deeds for which you always had been called to Shadowland, here, where your blood calls you. Don't you want to know why you're being sucked in here? Who calls you here? Who are you exactly?"

And with every fact he told, he crawled up to me, feeding on my curiosity, and he was right. I wanted answers for everything, and it seemed like he knew a lot about me. He could give me the answers I've been searching for all my life. Who else could do that if I killed him? No, I needed to think more about my next step, but blood was flowing into my brain, and it started to hurt.

He was standing near me. "Sacrifice your Cosmic blade, and I'll tell you answers to your question." He was hovering near me. My palms were getting clammy.

"Cosmic blade?" I asked, at which he rumbled in laughter, his body bobbing with him, but the tendril holding me up from the ground never moved even an inch.

"You don't even know what powers you hold, not even your weapons. Poor child, the blade you carry never rusts, never needs cleaning. It's a Cosmic weapon—*Livana's* blade. Sacrifice it, and I'll give you all the answers,"

He was right. I never cleaned it or oiled it, not even once, and still, it's sharp as new, even though it's a family heirloom. I gulped down hard. He was telling me the truth, he knew about things and held the answers to my questions.

I raised my eyes, and all I could see was the red-eye. "Are you ready?" he asked me.

"Eloise, first he was triggering your insecurities, and now he's feeding over your curiosity, do not let him get you," Kayden spoke very carefully. With every word, I saw the demon's eye seeing red. Kayden was in huge trouble. I knew he was about to harm him. And as soon as his gaze darted toward Kayden, I jammed my knife in his eye.

It felt like piercing an egg. Its black blood spurted on my face. *YUCK!*

"You, stupid girl!" shrieked *Thamex*, growling in pain, his eye bled with a black tar kind of liquid, and he melted on the floor, soon turning into ashes. As I fell to the ground, my neck would have cracked if Kayden hadn't caught my head.

My body hit the ground, but my head was safely cushioned over Kayden's hand—always protecting me.

We are one great duo.

But my mind was on something else, the thought of which made me quiver—I just killed a demon, a real demon, not Mer-skeletons or *Grovetiles*, no dream monster but an actual demon.

I was shivering in comprehension, fuck! That was close, and I almost thought I had lost myself to him. I looked down at my hands which were shivering. My penknife was covered with black tar, which soon evaporated, leaving it glowing.

Cosmic blade.

Suddenly Kayden's giant hand filled mine perfectly, providing me warmth. "For one second, I thought you would give him this." He chuckled, facing the blade. I knew he was terrified too, but trying to lighten the mood.

"Do you think I am that stupid?" I looked at him sideways.

"No, but you wanted answers," he said, smiling, as he hauled me on him, locking me in his arms. Why was it so easy with him? How come it never felt awkward, like this was inevitable? I was wrapped up in his warmth. His touch calmed me down and made me feel secure and protective in his soothing embrace. *Most of all, he makes me feel desired, filling my heart with hope. And he sparks me up every time I feel low or lose it. He gathers me up and boosts my confidence.*

You're not the monster, you're the one these monsters fear. You'll become that, right?

If you want to survive, get your claws out.

"As if you know me so well," I said sarcastically, rolling my eyes.

"Oh, hell yeah!" he said, chuckling, his chest reverberating beneath me. "I know you better than you know yourself. That's a fight you can never win," he said, but before I could tell him otherwise, he added, "Let's get going, get us out of here, then you can ask me out on a date, and I'll tell you everything." Hauling me up with him, carefully making me stand on my feet like a gentleman.

I must have gone crimson red, blushing. Did he just offer to go on a date with me?

Whoa!

Does he want to make it official? My heart flutters.

"Let's find others," Kayden dragged me to the window, figuring out where to go from here.

Ok, I need to focus here first. I stretched myself, cleaning my face with the jacket. My body was getting rigid, examining the room. It was filled with darkness with just one window, and there was nothing but darkness behind it.

I pouted, confused about how to escape a room without a door, but Kayden came to stand behind me, his hands placed on my shoulder as he whispered. "Darkness is what we have inside us, the darkness that sometimes takes over us, creeps us, scares us, and forces us to forget the light inside us, but we should never forget that we have the choice to rise above it."

I bit my lips as he traced his nose on my neck, making my breathing hitch. Even though I was drenched in a demon's filth, he didn't care. "When darkness surrounds your life, you can either wait for the light, look for the light, ask for the light, or if you want, you can *SHINE!*"

He said the last word like a chime, kissing my lips.

His confidence in me filled me with a spark, a smile rose my lips as I had a hunch, and following that, I slammed my knife in the window. If this blade could tear shadows, then it could tear *Shadowland* too. And with it, the Cosmic blade started to shine.

He hugged me from behind as I closed my eyes and let the room be filled with light.

Chapter 29
Good things await

A smile formed on my lips, and my body relaxed as a room with three pods with my friends appeared. It wasn't a room but an abandoned lab, with barrels lying in the corner with the word 'Danger' written on them, rusty and covered with algae. There were huge pipes leading deep into the dark corner of the room, but my focus was on the three pods with yellow vile.

I walked forward with trembling hands to examine them as my vision blurred. Kayden sighed loudly in relief, but we both didn't utter a single word, like it would jinx our happiness. My chest ached as I blinked tears away to see my friends' pale faces through the pods. These pods were made of a jelly kind of substance. Kayden jammed my knife into the pod where Clara was preserved. He pierced the slimy pod with a squishing sound as the yellowish liquid flowed out like somebody opened an amniotic sac.

He passed me the blade as I jammed it in the pod where Nathan was and pierced it, and soon the yellow liquid was hurling down on the floor as I pushed my hands inside to pull Nathan.

Kayden was trying to pull Clara, her hands were already out. With one more tug, she pushed her legs out, stumbling on the floor, coughing. *She was alive.*

My heart swelled up, while my lungs were filled with air, finally. A sob built in my throat that I couldn't control anymore.

I reached out to Clara. "Hey! Are you ok?" I snivelled, wiping my tears with the back of my hand while rubbing her back. I turned to

Kayden, while he helped Nathan climb out, who came out coughing too.

"Clara," Kayden came running, wiping her eyes, rubbing her hands, warming her up, while I lunged at Homer's pod, tearing it down, calling out for him.

His eyes blinked open. "Elmo," he croaked, looking around. It startled him. He was beyond terrified as he hurriedly pushed himself out of the pod, but instead, he slipped and fell on top of me with all the slime in the pod.

"Yuck, it's disgusting." I groaned, trying to spit on the side. "Move," I told him, he was heavy, and all the slime was getting inside my mouth. Now I was drenched in vile liquid too.

"Eloise." Kayden found my hand and shoulder, lifting me up to my feet. He wiped my face with his hands. His touch was soft, like that of a lover. "You fine?" he asked, concerned.

"Never better," I smiled, beaming, as he looked down, and I followed his gaze. "Sorry, your jacket got all dirty, but don't worry, I'll ask Hannah to clean it for you," I told him, while brushing his jersey jacket with my hands.

"No, it's ok," the corner of his mouth lifted, making my heart beat faster as he scrubbed some slime himself off the jacket. "It looks better on you."

Really? His jersey jacket—He wants me to keep that? I was wrapping my head around his words when he—*pat my bum.*

My eyes went wide, and I froze, pursing my lips. "It was just some slime," he said, trying to act natural, hiding his mischief.

"Yeah, right," I nodded sarcastically, and with that, I took some slime off my cloth and rubbed it in his velvety hair, laughing.

"YOU!" he grunted, his eyes filled with nefarious glint. He leapt towards me, but I jumped out of his way. I kept dodging him, hiding behind Clara, laughing.

"Lizzy," said Clara, turning towards me. She was a mess. "Oh my god!" She held my hands, looking at me like I was a dream. "Is that you? Is that really you?" She was slowly recovering from the trauma. "You came back for us. You really did." She kept blinking as if I would disappear, literally jumped on me, grabbing me hard and hugging me tightly.

"Obviously, I came back. How could I live without you?" I asked, hugging her back tightly. "Shhh..." I soothed her back while she cried. It must be terrifying down here. I know now.

"I knew… I knew you always had my back. You can never leave me," she looked at me again, her amber eyes filled with tears. She was happy to see me, unlike that ghost Clara who made me feel like a monster.

I reached to wipe them off her cheeks.

"That world held nothing for me without you," I told her as I brushed some slime off her strawberry hair. She was still in her plaided skirt and mesh jacket, drenched with slime. It was even sticking on her long slender legs, which she unconsciously scratched off. Her manicured nails were filled with slime, but she could get them made afterwards—no, we need a whole-body rejuvenating package this time.

"But how did you come back? Did you shift again?" Her eyes widened in horror as she worried her lower lip.

"No, we came through a portal."

"We?" She looked confused. It was when her eyes fell on Kayden.

"Kayden… it's you… really … you are here too … OMG… Kiddie, my Twinnie-winnie!" She leapt to him like a koala bear. Her hands wrapped around Kayden's neck while her legs wrapped around his torso. My heart fluttered at seeing their joy. The smile that rose his face was worth capturing. His hazel eyes were warm and filled with love. He brushed her hair and patted her head, soothing her. He was finally relaxed.

Tears welled in my eyes when a hand reached out for me. I turned around to look at Nathan. A warmth spread through my body as he pulled me in his bear hug. "Huggy-bear!" I screamed with glee, so happy to see all of them alive.

"Shadow Walker, really?" Nathan asked me, his voice reverberating through his chest. I chuckled in between my tears. Clara must have told them everything. Obviously, they needed an explanation about what was happening to them.

He pulled back, looking at me like I was something exquisite. "If you had told me earlier, I would have created a whole fucking game on you." He beamed. "We would be billionaires, think about it—Lizzy, the Shadow Walker, fighter of the demons, saviour of humankind, the knight in shining armour, rescuing her friends." His eyes were somewhere else, dreaming.

"Shut up," I punched his shoulder, as he made me blush.

"Ouch! It hurts…I am dying…you are so strong…mercy Ser Lizzy, mercy," he mocked me.

"Stop it." We all laughed except Homer, who seemed confused.

"But what happened to you?" Clara asked, sniffling, examining Kayden's tattered and wet clothes.

"She did it. She tortured me by trapping me into a vault," he nudged at me, amused. "Till I give her an—"

"Oi!" I screamed before he could say orgasm, blood rushing to my cheeks. "You incorrigible ass, I didn't do anything." I hurried to him, punching his arms, which he clearly was enjoying, grinning.

"What? I was just stating that you named me God of—" I smacked him on his arm, wanting to wipe that grin off him, which I so much hate to adore.

"I didn't call you that. You gave that name to yourself even though there was nothing special about it," I lied, crossing my hands over my stomach and stomping off toward Homer, who seemed skeptical, and was being distant from me.

"Liar." His lips quirked up with the mirth.

"Homer," I called, ignoring him. "Are you alright?"

But before he could reply, I felt hands around my waist as Kayden lifted me right off my feet and spun me around. "C'mon, I was kidding." There was a contagious grin on his face. His eyes gleamed with pure joy due to his reunion with his sister. "After all, we found them."

How could I be angry with him when he's grinning like that, with two dimples?

"We sure did," I excitedly laughed with him as he spun me around so many times that I got dizzy. He kissed my forehead as he carefully placed me back on the floor.

"OMG! Kiddie, are you laughing?" Clara went aghast, and I was suddenly aware of the gazes. Everyone was staring at us, even Homer.

He was still quiet, his eyes fixed on Kayden and me, where we were linked.

OK! That's a part I never thought about.

Uh-oh! I let my hands fall, zipping my lips in a thin line, not knowing what to say. I looked into Kayden's eyes, he was expecting me to say something.

"Hey, Homer," I drawled. "You remember Kayden, he helped me reach you all. Yay!" I cheered, but nobody cheered with me. They stared at me for a second, and suddenly, Clara leapt at us.

"I knew something was up with you two," Clara said, rolling her eyes.

"What?" I asked, turning to Kayden, but he hunched his shoulders, shaking his head like he had no hint about what Clara was saying.

"I could feel that spark between you, and with Kayden always hovering around and your bickering." She shook her head, punching his shoulder. "I am your twin, we have twin telepathy."

"No, we don't," He frowned.

But Clara ignored him, turning to me. "And Lizzy, you. I never expected you'd hide this from me. I am angry with you both. You didn't tell me that you both were dating."

"No—" but she cut me off.

"Just kidding, like I can be angry with you both, you are my favorite people, and now you are together." Making an awe sound. "I am so happy for both of you." Uh-oh, she was getting all wrong. I tried to shake my head. "Don't try to hide it from me. I could totally tell, you guys made out."

My eyes went wide, I must have gone crimson red, how the hell does she know?

Why does Clara have to know everything from my face? Why does she have to observe everything? But that's what best friends do. They're a mirror for you. Lying to them, hiding anything from them, is like lying to yourself.

Especially Clara, because she always knew everything about me.

"CLARA!" I groaned, shushing her down. Denying her was no use because she could read me anywhere.

"See, you're blushing. It was just a hit and trial but look at you," Clara laughed, mocking me.

"Stop it, Clara," Kayden said firmly. "You are making her uneasy." He brushed my cheeks with the back of his fingers. My breathing hitched. His touch was so soft it made me swoon, but this wasn't helping my case.

"Aww! You guys look so cute together," Clara squealed and jumped on her place with joy. She was all about rainbows, bright colours, flowers, and unicorns.

Excitement dripped out of her aura. "Hey, wait a minute," her eyes went wide. "The imaginary—"

"Clara," Kayden said sternly, cutting her off. "How did you guys get here? What happened after she shifted?" His grip tightened around me, pivoting, avoiding my eyes.

"We were at the cave, trying to find the void or a way to return home, when I heard a growl, and I was out. It was a series of nightmares or weird dreams. And now it's you guys. It feels like years have passed, but sometimes it's just a fraction of a second," she furrowed her brows. "How long were we stuck here?"

"A week," I murmured, but my eyes were on Kayden, he was hiding something.

"Just a week, really?" Nathan asked. His brows were together behind his specs. "It feels like an eternity," he brushed his hair, wiping off all the slime he could.

"I am sorry for leaving you guys here. I shouldn't have shifted," I pouted, feeling guilty.

"Why are you sorry? You didn't know you would shift alone, you tried to take us with you, but it was our hard luck," she grimaced. "But nothing matters. Now we'll get out. As you both are here, and you are together, good things await." Clara grinned. She had always been like this, she loved to dance, dress up for every occasion, and always smiled like she had an unlimited supply of joy. She was a freaking ray of funshine and almost loved everything, even us in Shadowland, the place that must have tortured her, but here she was, happy for me. I couldn't tell her that we weren't dating, I couldn't break her heart.

She was all excited about how we would spend time together, suggesting places where we could go on dates, and Kayden was trying to shush her down, but being Clara, she couldn't control.

But my eyes were on Homer. He hadn't uttered a word.

He was still looking at us, how we were tugged together, and his eyes met mine. His mouth was hanging open. He took a deep breath as if he was about to say something, but no words came out. He was in shock as I reached out for his hand, but he jerked my hand away instead.

It hurt.

Chapter 30

Eloise's Choice

"No, no-no," I strode towards Homer, getting out of Kayden's grip. "It's not like what you are thinking," I told him. I don't know why, but I felt guilty about sabotaging this friendship and betraying his love. He stepped back, crossing his hands across his midsection, blocking me, pretending nothing happened, like I was not even there. But I knew he was hurt, and I didn't want him to feel that way.

"Please listen to me," I begged him.

But with that, he started moving away from me, deep into the lab. It was dimly lit, but still, I could see him walking away from me.

"Wait!—Homer," I called, but he seemed so mad that he didn't stop. Suddenly, I was finding it hard to breathe.

I leapt after him, but then I felt Kayden tugging on my arm.

"Leave me, Kayden," I told him, trying to get my hand back. "Let me handle this," I ordered. He had no right to come between us. "Alone," I eyed Clara and Nathan, who were trying to follow us.

Kayden's eyes tensed, but he left my hand.

I sprang away from him, tripping over my own feet and staggering to regain my balance. My entire body had turned Jell-O.

"Kayden Parsons?" Homer screamed, abruptly turning back, his voice taut, his eyes fixed on me, distraught. "Seriously? Out of all the boys in the world, you had to choose Gigantor?"

I flinched as he referred to Kayden as Gigantor, which was strange because I had never cringed at this word before, but things had changed. We fooled around, and he confessed he was attracted to me. Moreover, he was there protecting, shielding, and helping me remain sane and differentiate between what's real and what's illusionary. His words filled me with confidence and strength. I only reached them because of him.

"It's not like that. We are not together," I told him, shivering. I didn't know what else to say that wouldn't just make this thing worse than it already was.

"Then why was he holding you like that? Why is he kissing your forehead? Why are you wearing a jacket with his name on it? It's like he has already claimed you. Tell me this isn't what it looks like. Tell me that Clara is lying." His dark eyes bored into mine. He walked towards me, his footfalls heavy and slow, but he stopped a few feet away. "Tell me you guys didn't make-out," his eyes looked for answers in mine.

"I—Homer, I—it's not like that. I am sorry, Homer, I am so sorry…." I tried to hold his hand, but he reeled backwards, looking hurt even more. He was stirring away from me like he was physically repulsing me.

Tears welled in my eyes, and a lump rose in my throat, but I tried to blink them away. He turned around, his hand scrubbing through his hair, letting out a loud groan. "How can you do that to yourself, to *me*?" he asked. I heard the pain of betrayal underneath his voice. "You are fraternising with our enemy, the worst guy I could ever think of, and that too behind my back."

I had no answer. He was right. I had betrayed him, betrayed my love for him.

"I can't lose you," I sobbed, looking into his eyes, making him understand that it's him I love. Him, and only him.

"Lizzy," Clara held my shoulder, turning me to her. "Stop it now." She wiped my tears while my eyes were glued to Homer.

"You need to believe me, Homer, nothing is going on between us." He had to listen—he had to forgive me.

"Then why did you make-out?" he shouted, making me flinch.

It was the first time he had yelled at me. I was terrified, and my whole body had gone numb.

"Oh! C'mon, don't make a big deal out of it. It's not like you two were in a relationship," Clara backed me.

Homer was taken aback.

"She can fool around with anybody. It's her life," she told him. "You never gave a damn about that before, then why now?" she asked. *Oh no*, she was making things worse.

"You stay out of this, Clara," Homer snapped at her. "You're such a hypocrite. She calls you her best friend, trusts you more than me, and you're pushing her towards your brother, the biggest player, who will use her and hurt her like he does every time, to everyone. You know he's not boyfriend material. He's the guy with the worst reputation in dating girls. He just likes to get into their pants." He twisted his face as he looked at me. "He just wants to get into *your* pants."

"Now you'll judge me?" Kayden scoffed, but I could see the dark rage in his eyes. The shadows behind them were back, his fingers flexed into fists.

Fuck! He was angry, and his rage was not something Homer should ignite.

"What are you going to do? Hit me for looking after her back. What else can you Parsons boys do?" he snapped at Kayden, fuming. "Stay away from her. She is not your type, she's not some random girl you can fool around with. She doesn't deserve you."

"Then who does she deserves, YOU?" Kayden grimaced at him, his eyes enraged, with his hands in his pockets as if controlling his urge to hit Homer. "A trickster, a lying bastard."

Lying? What was Kayden implying?

"Manwhore!" Homer spat at Kayden.

"HOMER," Clara screamed, pushing him back. "Don't talk shit to my brother. He's a much better human than you are. He never used her and ghosted her."

"Don't touch me." Homer snarled as he reeled towards her, but she didn't step back. Instead, Kayden stepped between them. Homer growled at him. "She's my friend, you have no right to speak between us." Homer's finger flips from me to him.

"You call yourself her friend?" Clara scoffed, rolling her eyes dramatically. "Then tell me whom she loves?" She crossed her hands over her stomach.

Homer didn't reply. He looked at her curiously.

Oh no, she was about to tell Homer the truth about my feelings for him and everything. Fuck, no!

"Shut up, Clara, don't be a tattletale." I eyed her. She needs to slow down. I didn't want Homer to know anything.

"No, let me tell him. He should know that *he* is the hypocrite who has always hurt you. You have yearned for him almost since we know each other, but what has he given you in return—pain, tears? I have seen you almost every day being dreadful because of him. He's the one who shouldn't be trusted. The one who had never understood his own friend's feelings. Every time he kisses Sophie, it kills you inside," she looked at me with sad eyes. "When he can go around and kiss anybody in front of you, then why is he fussing about you kissing someone else?"

Homer didn't say anything. His face went blank.

"And when she is moving on, why are you pulling her back? She has her own life. She deserves so much better. She deserves someone who loves her. I am not saying it has to be Kayden, but it's not even you, never you." She kept going like she was my mom. I couldn't bear it. It was all too much. Homer was staring at her, clueless.

"She is not your *backup*." She yelled. With that, Homer's nostrils flared. "Definitely, not your last choice."

"How dare you?" He clenched his fists.

"Enough is enough," I stepped in between, taking charge of things. "It's my life. I get to choose what I will do with it," I snapped at Clara. "I am not a prized possession that you people would decide who will get me in the end."

There was pin-drop silence. Nathan came to stand by my side as I felt his warmth behind me. Kayden looked at me with his frowned brows, his jaw locked tightly.

"You love me?" Homer whispered. "You had feelings for me?" He seemed shocked.

"Oh no…no…no… she's just kidding," I tried to lie, holding my stomach, trying to get hold of myself. I felt I was going to break half from the middle. So fragile.

"Since when?" he asked, his face went blank, devoid of all emotions.

"Since outhouse," I confessed, looking down at my fingers. He stepped back as if somebody had pushed him, guilt slapped on his face.

"That's absurd," Kayden stepped in between, but I raised my hand to stop him.

It was between Homer and me.

"Homer, you don't have to feel guilty about it," I walked up to him, taking his face in my hands, making him look into my eyes. "It's not your problem. It's mine, really—you don't have to feel bad about all this. I never expected you to return my feelings." Ok, this was a lie, but right now, I wanted to make sure he was alright. He shouldn't feel guilty about hurting me or not returning my feelings.

"You loved me," Homer spoke, narrowing his eyes. "And you kissed him instead?"

I was taken aback. I thought I heard him wrong. My hands fell from his face, taking a step back, stunned.

"That was *HER CHOICE*," Kayden snapped, pushing Homer away from me like he'll give me Ebola. I saw Homer's eyes flit past Kayden to me. His eyes darkened. "Don't play your toxic cards like you always do."

But instead of replying, Homer swung a fist and whacked Kayden on the left jaw, but he didn't budge, not even an inch.

"Tell your boyfriend to stay out of this," Homer snapped at me, his mouth twitching at the word boyfriend.

It hurts. Oh! It hurts me profoundly.

Kayden rubbed his jaw, looking ready to explode. But I jolted between them. "Please just don't make things worse," I begged, *I don't want to lose Homer*. I looked into Kayden's eyes. The shadows behind them were beyond terrifying. He gazed into my eyes till they became soft, he swallowed all his anger and took a deep breath.

"Give him time. He'll get over it," he wrapped his hands around my wrist, trying to calm me down. I was fidgeting, tensed, not knowing what would happen now.

"Maybe I won't," Homer spat from behind. His voice was calm and cold, and it terrified me. "You have to choose Elmo," he spoke the barbarous words I had heard. "Who is important to you—him or me?" He cocked his head to the right.

My heart stopped. Kayden's hands fell from me like he already knew my answer.

What? No. *How can I choose that? How can he even ask for that?* I love him and will pick him, but I didn't want to hurt Kayden either. He practically saved my life. It's because of him only that I have reached them all. He offered his help when I was at my lowest.

"Please, Homer, please…don't let me do that, please, I…" I stuttered, not wanting to hurt Kayden.

It seems serendipitous that this question found me for tonight. For the first time, I thought I could be happy, but it was like God didn't want me to.

"I am sorry, I can't," I said, looking at neither. This was insane. One side was the guy I loved, and the other was my protector. I respect him, and I've kissed him. It seemed like an eternity had passed chasing Homer, expecting him to love me back. It's unbelievably painful to be the one that cares more, to wear your heart on your bloodied sleeve over and over again. And Kayden had given me the happiness, attention, and affection I craved, but still, I didn't love him. He was not Homer, he was not the boy I met in the outhouse, *he was not my iron man.*

"It has to be this way only, Elmo, either me or him." Homer twitched his mouth.

How could he do that to me?

I took a deep breath and looked back at Kayden. I wanted him to understand that Homer meant a lot to me.

"Don't let him manipulate you." Kayden looked into my eyes, towering over me. He was telling me to take charge, but how could I, it was Homer. He was the most important person in my life.

He understood what I wanted to tell him. His soft eyes went blank within a beat. He seemed taken aback, hurt, betrayed. *I am cruel. Maybe I don't even deserve his affection.* I've always judged him for using girls, but today it seemed like I used him.

But that wasn't my intention when I kissed him, I just kissed him without any motive, it just felt right, natural, but it shouldn't have. I shouldn't have kissed him.

And he was Kayden Parsons. We just made out, that's like nothing for him. He had done this a million times with hundreds of girls. *It wasn't special.*

My heart lurched at the thought.

Argh! There is something wrong with you, Lizzy. It was just a one-time moment. Focus on Homer, the love of your life, your soulmate, the one you claimed a long time back.

Kayden stared at me for a few seconds, waiting for me to change the answer, to tell him otherwise.

"You cannot win the game with people who can play it better," Homer smirked at Kayden.

"But I already did." Kayden's voice was low and soft but intimidating, followed by a scoff. His eyes shifted from me to Homer. His confidence wiped off Homer's smirk. "I marked her, claimed her. She was always mine, and you know that. But if you want to continue this game, let's play, *but*," he stressed the last word, narrowing his eyes. "Only until you don't touch her." He cracked his knuckles as Homer's face went white as a ghost.

What game? I wanted to ask, but Kayden winked at me, making butterflies in my stomach dance, and I was so lost in their triumph that I forgot Homer was staring at me.

He cussed.

"Stop looking at him like he hung the moon for you," he snapped at me as I blinked, embarrassed.

"Raise your voice at her again, and I'll rip your tongue off," Kayden growled, stepping forward, making Homer take a step towards me, he looked so small before Kayden.

"Stay away from her," Homer pointed his trembling finger at him, pulling up a fake bravado. "Let's go."

Chapter 31

Abandoned lab

"What is all this?" Homer asked me furiously, walking away from Kayden and Clara.

"What? The lab?" I furrowed my brows.

"Don't be so immature, Elmo," he scowled. "What's up with you? And what's this Shadowland? Is it a made-up story or what?" he asked. Oh! He still wasn't sure about this realm. "And since when is it happening with you?" He sounded concerned.

"It's a long story. I will brief you about everything once we reach home, but for now, you take it as another world parallel to ours, but its inhabitants are monsters and darkness."

"Yeah! I've seen them," he cut me. "But why *you*?"

"That's the very question I have been asking for a long time," I grimaced, looking down. "But it seems like it's in my bloodline."

He frowned. "Can't you stop this?" He rubbed his temple.

"Believe me, I have tried to hide and suppress it a million times, but it's not in my control." I groaned.

"How did Kayden get into the picture?" he asked, his lips twitching.

"He helped me open the portal," A smile formed on my lips as I almost defended Kayden. "He even suggested that my powers were never in my control because I just tried to suppress them. Perhaps I have to accept them to gain control."

"Act mature, Elmo. These are just words. It's not even practical. How can you control something you don't know about, and you're just seventeen-years-old. You can't do this. This shouldn't even be an option—accepting this is like accepting death." I felt him shiver a little as his eyes observed the room. "This is just his scheme. He's manipulating you to help his sister out. Don't you realise he's Mayor's son, Parsons—they all are manipulative asses. What if he tells the truth to his father? I am sure he is just using you as he does with other girls. He wants you till you can get his sister out. But once we are out, have you thought about the consequences, your reputation? What if he tells other people, his girlfriend, his friends, the student council, or the media?"

"But he knew my truth long before and never told anybody." Yes! I was defending Kayden.

"Knowing and experiencing are both different things, Elmo. Do you think he'll act solemnly after experiencing this world? No one in a sane mind would ever accept this. No one would willingly offer their help to come here. How can you be so naïve, trusting someone who just knows how to control people? Do you just want to be another notch on his belt?"

"No, obviously not," I was taken aback. Homer was right. It was wrong of me to bring Kayden here. *What if he spills my secret to everyone after getting out of here?*

"Then grow up and learn to say no," he put his hand around my shoulder, shaking his head, disappointed.

"I am sorry, but I had no way to reach you. I was scared, and he was the only one who offered to help." I felt embarrassed, but it wasn't my fault. *Beggars are not choosers.*

"But from now on, stay away from him. The less he knows, the better it is. He's just Clara's brother. Let him be. Don't try to get too involved."

My mouth fell.

"Hey! I am just looking after you," he pulled me close. "I don't want my best friend to get hurt," he said, shaking me as I frowned.

Just a best friend? Still? Nothing else?

In our hustle, I didn't realise when Nathan left my side and went towards the dark end. He had opened one door on the right but, oddly, was standing on the archway, frozen.

Homer and I strode toward him.

"But—" I was about to ask him about our relationship status when I felt a pull, a hard tug, as if someone was calling me or watching me.

I bit my lips as I flipped to look at Kayden, who was shooting daggers at me, while Clara whispered something furiously in his ears. His eyes were focused on where Homer held me. I bit my lips as an uneasiness squirmed through my veins, I quickly got off Homer's hold, placing one hand on Nathan's shoulder, but he didn't budge. His body was unexpectedly cold, and when I traced his gaze, I knew why.

This room was filled with rusty cages hanging from the ceiling. Each one held naked humans—naked girls. Or were they shadows? I didn't know, but they all were severely wounded and in bondage. One had dark stuff dripping between her legs. One had a neck collar on her which seemed so tight that liquid dripped from her throat. One had nipple clamps, pressed so hard that dark squishy liquid came out of the bud. And so on.

I stifled a scream looking at the horrific view as my eyes fell on the opposite side of the room. It had ten screens, all smashed. It was like a control room, but suddenly I saw something moving behind those screens, lurking in the shadow. My whole body froze. My survival instinct triggered, warning me that I didn't want to entertain it. And at the same time, I felt Kayden's hand around me.

Was he thinking the same thing? He nodded at me.

Fuck! How was it so easy with him?

He tugged me towards him. We both backed off as silently as we could. I poked Nathan, beckoning him.

He started retracting, but as soon as my hand reached Homer, he whipped his head at Nathan. "Fatty, couldn't you warn us?" He cringed his nose.

My eyes went wide. Kayden hissed a string of profanities in my ear because Homer had asked that question out loud, and his voice echoed through the room, making all the cages quiver. Nathan huffed angrily, but my focus wasn't on him. It was on the cages, which, one by one, started opening.

All the girls jumped out on the floor like cats, their boobs wiggled, but nothing was sexual about them, as they were broken, covered in shadowland filth, and seemed blank like zombies.

Suddenly those girls started quivering, and each one of them began to turn into *Grovetiles* like that possessed Lara in my dream.

But my horror wasn't these girls who were shifting into shadow monsters. The sharp-bladed beast that had stepped out from the shadow and now was glaring at us with his scarlet eyes.

"Shadowfiend," I announced, swaying my hand with that, but nothing came out. Moonstone wasn't working, still. Kayden hissed, looking at my worn-off ring.

We all darted out of the room. Nobody needed an explanation as we all ran. Kayden closed the door and nodded at me as if nudging me. I pulled out my Cosmic blade before he pushed Clara towards me, who I just realised was screaming and shivering.

Tears were oozing out of her eyes as she sang in a litany—*we are all going to die*. I grabbed her hand and sprang forward, pulling her out of her trance. Kayden joined me, his strides were longer than ours. That door couldn't hold any of them, but still, we needed time because the stupid moonstone ring wasn't working.

"What do we do now?" Homer whimpered, on the verge of crying.

"We need to hide, but there are some rules you got to know," I heaved, tying my hair up. "One. Stay away from water or any kind of liquid. Second. Don't take anything from Shadowland. It'll be cursed. And lastly. Shadowfiends can possess you. Instead of killing you, they'll transform you into one of them."

Blood drained from Homer's face, but I had no time to soothe him because Nathan was lacking behind, and *Grovetiles* were hot on his heels. There were three of them. I had to do something because I knew Nathan couldn't make it.

I was scared to my toes, my hands were shivering.

It was just a split-second decision, and I halted. Kayden, Clara, and Homer kept running unaware of my plan.

There were three monsters.

Taking them together wasn't an option.

Robin had taught me this.

I can do this.

Lizzy, keep your training in mind.

The weapon I held in my hand was not for fighting but for murder. All I got to do was stab or slit.

Calculating my moves, I screamed at Nathan. "Duck." His eyes went wide, but he didn't need a second command as he bent down. I aimed at the first *Grovetile*, hitting it directly in his eye. It growled before turning into ashes, but I was fast.

I launched myself at the nearby rusty pipe, which was wider than my waist, and caught my blade before it fell to the ground. I put my step on the red valve and stirred myself to reach second *Grovetile's* height. Its hands were too short to attack me, but the tail and horn could. I had to avoid both. I held its horn with one hand, and before his tail could hit me, I stabbed it in the head, making it shriek in pain.

I swung using his horn till my leg connected with its head before it could evaporate, and I launched myself towards the monster on the right. It leapt at me with its mouth open, flashing its sharp teeth, but I slit its jaw, holding my blade with both hands, gliding till the throat as I thrust my legs in its chest, shoving it backwards. Its shrieks filled my ears as one came from nowhere and thrashed me on the side with the flick of its tail.

ARGH! I hit my forehead on the electric control panel box. It stung, resonating in my ears, and for a second, I was seeing white patches.

"ELOISE." I heard Kayden growl. I quickly whipped my head at him. Oh no! I know what he was doing, he was trying to get the *Grovetile's* attention, and he did, as the beast turned to him, ready to attack.

The anticipation made me roar. I was on high adrenaline as I pushed both my feet from the ground, leaping high and taking support from the barrel nearby. I wrapped myself around the monster, my hand blocking his view while I jammed my blade into his throat. He threw me forward as I rolled from him, landing on my feet sturdily.

Everyone watched me with wide eyes, and their mouths hung open while Clara clung to Homer.

I didn't move, nobody moved, and everyone looked at me in utter shock. They looked terrified. I couldn't help noticing shivering Homer while Clara gazed at me with amazement, wrapped around each other.

But my eyes were searching for him, who, to my amazement, was smiling, showing his dimples, swelling with pride. He sauntered towards me, placing his finger under my chin to raise my face. "You are beautiful," he whispered as he bore his gaze into mine. My heart made a squishing sound that I didn't understand.

His eyes wavered to my forehead and frowned as he wiped something hot dripping off it. I winced. He grumbled, making a sound from his chest.

"I am fine," I told him, still heaving, placing my hand on his iron-clad chest, trying to relax him. He seemed to warm under my touch. I wanted to hug him but thought I shouldn't.

Homer's hand fell from Clara as she got out of his embrace, a little flushed. "Whoa! That was freaking amazing," she exclaimed. "Please remind me not to provoke you, ever."

I was about to let out a chuckle when Homer stepped forward.

"Beautiful…Amazing…Are you kidding me?" Homer fumed. "That was terrifying," he shuddered.

My mouth fell on his words, but instantly Kayden's hand squeezed mine as if giving me a hand hug. "How did you take four monsters—all that flipping and lunging—your moves were so clear—you were not at all sloppy, not even for a single second—how was your aim so perfect and that too from so far?" He was out of breath and in utter shock.

Kayden's hand slipped around my waist as if supporting me. "Robin taught me a little self-defence," I bit my lips.

"A little?" Homer scoffed in disbelief. He frowned at Kayden, who was now studying my hand. "You're a freaking weapon."

"Oh! Definitely, she is," Kayden's smile widened as he traced the length of my spine with his knuckles, making me arch as my eyes rolled back into my head. What was he doing?

"Don't forget deadly," Clara chimed. The over-excitement returned to her face, making me a bit relaxed. Watching the gleam in her eyes gave me confidence because she knew what I was and still *trusted her life with me.*

"There is nothing to be proud," Homer spat at her before turning to me. "You're a princess. A girl. You should be delicate and stay out of trouble."

Kayden's attack halted. I felt humiliated by Homer's words. They shattered the confidence Kayden had just sparked. He reminds me of my mother. She always told me nobody would accept me as I was. I was a monster, and Homer's reaction proved it.

"Don't you dare belittle her," Kayden growled, his voice rumbling through his chest, my whole body vibrated with it, not that I was scared by him. No, he warmed me up and silenced Homer instantly. "She is here to rescue you when she could leave all of us here and protect herself any time she wants," he eyed Homer, who gulped down audibly. Suddenly, Kayden became alpha male, his daunting aura covered the expanse of the room. "She's a princess and acts like one, protecting her people. She has earned this title by putting all your life ahead of hers, facing all the monsters single-handedly." He turned to me. His eyes filled with glimmer, and his words caressed me. "You're so brave, so caring, and he doesn't get to disgrace you. I won't let him do it."

Homer was gaping at us, dumbfounded.

His words rang in my ears. I'd been fighting my own battles since I was a child, I'd always been alone, but with him next to me, saying all these perfect words, protecting me, filling me up with confidence, with respect—it felt glorious to be admired for something you thought was a glitch of your life. After a long time, I felt accepted, like my Iron Man did all those years back. It's the same feeling. It feels good to be taken in your rawest form. It sprouted *hope* in my heart.

"Exactly," Clara nodded. "And I am definitely going to thank-kiss Robin when I meet him," she added, bouncing happily.

"Your taste in men is degrading," Homer grimaced at her while she rolled her eyes.

"C'mon, the bald man is hot. He gives mafia vibes." Nathan added as he stepped forward to thank-hug me, but Kayden ignored his hands and crushed me to his side. He was indeed a caveman.

"Then why don't you blow that bald man? Or do you prefer bending over?" Homer spat at Nathan.

Ewww! I didn't want to visualise anyone blowing Robin. I was busy grimacing when suddenly, a huge cage came out from nowhere like a wrecking ball and was about to hit Homer, but Kayden was swift. He pushed Homer out of the way, wrapping his hands around me, rolling us over.

Chapter 32
Revelations

Everything happened in a fraction of a moment. I didn't realise how I reached a storage room and crouched behind the boxes. My chest was heaving, my hands were shivering because Homer was just attacked, and my heart was beating into thunderous beats, thinking about what-ifs.

While Clara was giving Homer the third degree, pompously showing off how Kayden saved his life. I was thankful to Kayden, who was now holding me tight. My back flushed to his chest while we sat on the floor, and he was wrapped around me like my personal human shield.

The dimly lit room we were in was filled with storage boxes that reeked of a dead animal. There was a vast steel vent over us. While outside, I could hear *Grovetiles* slithering.

"Shhh…" Kayden whispered, rocking me. "Nothing happened. Everyone is fine." He brushed off the goosebumps from my arms, providing me heat. I was cold, but his hands felt good. "Breathe, baby girl, breathe." At his command, I took a deep breath that strained my lungs as if I wasn't breathing for a few minutes.

"What the fuck was that—How…?" I asked, but he buried his face into the crook of my neck, kissing me. All my questions and worries subsided as I felt his warm lips between my collarbone and shoulder. I moaned, to which I heard a cuss and a throat clearing.

"Geez, guys, get a room," Clara created a distance from us.

I opened my eyes. Heat rushed through my cheeks as I tried to escape Kayden, but he held me still, locked into his arms. I totally forgot we were with friends. *Why does he keep doing PDA?*

"Did you drug her?" Homer asked as his eyes followed me to Kayden, discomfort in his voice.

"Nope, it was better than drugs." Kayden lifted his face and smirked wickedly as my breathing hitched. He was talking about the orgasm he gave me. Fuck! My flush deepened as I elbowed him, but instead, his laugh grumbled, reaching his eyes, making him so dreamy and addictive. He should always stay happy like this, much better than his brooding aura.

Homer looked confused at our inside joke. But my mind flicked, remembering an old conversation. I turned to Homer.

"Hey, do you know Riley Lynn?" I asked while Kayden went back to kiss my neck. Argh! He was so distracting.

"What—yes—why—how do you know her?" His eyes widened.

"I just know," I didn't want to repeat the whole story about her phone, Colton, and everything, so I decided to pivot. "You know where she lives?" I asked him out of curiosity.

"Whistler Lodge. She's shacked up there." he nodded, his eyes still jolting between Kayden and me. Kayden's hands tightened around me, but he did nothing to give away that he was listening.

"When was the last time you saw her?" I was firing questions.

"Mmm…It's been a few days. Sophie and I went to the garage to celebrate our anniversary, but bitch left, driving off hastily, ruining our anniversary evening." He seemed angry. "Sophie was distraught and went home without celebrating. We got into a fight because of that stupid Riley."

"Wasn't your anniversary on Sunday, the day…" Clara asked him, biting her lips. *Yeah, the day my mom died.*

"But you said you were with Colton. Your father says you're his alibi." Kayden halted his attack on my neck and raised his eyebrows.

"Yeah, I was with him. After Sophie went home, I went for the band rehearsals," Homer's tone clipped.

"And Riley wasn't there. Isn't she your lead vocalist?" Kayden pressed further.

"Nah! She's a dud. Sophie is our lead vocalist. She keeps hanging out there in the garage because of Colton. That girl seems obsessed with him, even though he doesn't give her a second glance." That was a contradicting statement about what I read from her mail, I thought she wanted an escape from Colton. What was happening?

"Cut it out, why do we have to worry, CIS will figure it out soon." Kayden rolled out, seeming bored.

"But CIS—" I was about to remind him that they already found Lea Perker, but Kayden licked the length of my neck, distracting me again.

"C-CIS is looking into m-matters?" Homer stutters as if he saw a ghost. "But why? My father was monitoring the case."

"Your father couldn't even figure out her mom was driving a right-hand drive car," Kayden scoffed.

"Hey! Don't you say a word about him," Homer growled.

"Guys, guys," Nathan crawled back to us. "*Grovetiles* are moving. Now we can go to the adjacent room," he seemed excited, maybe high on adrenaline.

"Why?" Clara asked.

"Because this vent will lead us out and its entry is from there." He crawled away towards the door, I started to follow him.

"Right or left?" Kayden went stoic, he wasn't breathing.

"Right," He answered, and as he did, Kayden pulled me back from the nape of my neck and crushed his lips on me. A gasp escaped from me, but he greedily sucked all the air and darted his tongue inside in a deep hurried stroke. His hand went to my thighs, holding me to him, moulding me like he wanted me to be.

Homer hissed and cursed, but his words didn't fall on my ears as I was on cloud nine, away from this world. I was darting away from everyone towards Kayden, where I just belonged to him.

I should stop him, tell him I chose Homer, and learn to say no to him but A. I didn't want to say no to him, and B. *I don't want to say no to him.*

His kiss was greedy and utterly dominating, but there was something else about the kiss that I couldn't figure out because his body was tense. His shoulders were tight, and he held me as if I would shatter.

I broke the kiss to catch some breath. "What was that about?" I asked, my chest heaving heavily, my hand still holding his shoulders as I took the surroundings in. Homer and Nathan had left the room, and Clara—

"I think Nathan is possessed," Kayden bombed me. I took a double take as if whatever I heard wasn't true. I stood up. He tried to get hold of me again, but I was out, there was no *Grovetile* in sight, and Nathan was walking towards the adjacent room, and to my horror, there was not one, but two shadows sprouting out of him, and the one on the wall had big thorns.

I gulped down hard.

Clara turned around, and whatever was on my face made her frown and glid towards me. "What happened?" she asked, taking my hand. "What did you say to her?" she asked Kayden over my shoulder. "I thought you guys were busy making out. BTW, you guys look super-hot, and Homer's ass was totally on fire. That's for every time he kissed those sluts in front of you, he deserves—"

"Nathan is possessed," I told her as she was divulging. Right now, my concern wasn't my love life but my Huggy-bear, who was entrapped by a shadowfiend.

"WHAT?" Clara screamed in shock.

"Shhh…" Kayden shushed her down, holding her by the back of her neck, shaking her.

"B-but, what?" she whisper-yelled, I could see her hands trembling. "Fuck man, and I thought finding *Alice is the cursed child* was the only worst news I could ever get." Clara blurted out as my eyes went wide in anticipation of what she said.

"WHAT?" I gasped in horror. Bile rose in my throat as Kayden looked from Clara to me. I could see he knew what Clara was telling me.

He quickly turned to me. "Remember your dream about a girl whom Leticia was trying to save," Kayden spoke in agitation. "We were discussing it, as our grandma used to tell us that as a bedtime story, with little facts changed, but the girl's name she mentions was—"

"ALICE, your Noni," Clara said in horror.

"There can be many Alices in this world!" I mused.

"No, she's the one, Alice Miguel Flores, now known as Alice Miguel Hector. She's *Yamendo's* daughter," Clara grimaced. "Light who saved her gave the cursed child and Paloma Flores to our gram's mother. Your Noni and our grams are soul sisters."

I gasped. "Are you out of your mind? What does Noni have to do with *Yamendo* or Shadowland?" I shook my head. "She doesn't even have any fucking hint about this," I hissed. What was happening?

"Actually, she has," Kayden answered. "As you know, I held you at the hospital when you fainted."

I nodded.

"She was the one who told me to hide you like she knew you would shift, and as soon as we turned, you vanished from my arms." His hands turned into fists, and pain and dread flashed in his eyes. "And within a second, an image of you appeared in my arms. It wasn't you. I could see you but couldn't feel you, no warmth, no scent," he closed his eyes, shaking his head at the terrifying memory. "It was an illusion of you that Alice manifested using her magic so that nobody could notice your disappearance."

"She hurried me to an empty room, explaining that you'd be back soon in my arms within a few minutes as it was the last place you vanished into. So, I waited, it took you long as you were unconscious, but she told me to relax as no harm could be done to you. She was sure you'd be safe, and you were. When you shifted back, I felt you in my arms again—your body, warmth, scent, everything was back, and nobody had noticed you vanish because of Alice's magic."

"We brought you back home, and you shifted again," his hands shivered. I could tell how terrified he was. "You were not even awake, and you kept on shifting back-to-back. Everyone was tensed."

"Everyone?" I choked, holding my throat.

"Yes, Alice, Hannah, Robin, and Dad."

"Mayor too?" I gasped. Now my head was spinning. I always thought I was good at masking and made a fool out of everyone, but it seems like they all knew, they just didn't admit it, they all acted. It was I who was being fooled. But why?

"Yes, after all, they all are Shadow Walker's kin," Kayden seemed hurt. I could feel his jaw tense as if he was angry with his father. "All of them were tensed, but none were as terrified as I was. They all knew what was happening with you as Robin tried to calm me down, but how could I have—*you vanished from my arms*," he said through clenched teeth, looking at me as if that memory brought him too much pain, looking at his empty hands.

I was frozen. Noni manifested after me, and now it makes me wonder how often she did that for me—covered up my mess.

And it made me wonder. "What powers does she possess?"

Kayden didn't seem to have words as he watched me sink to the floor.

So, Clara decided to continue. She crouched in front of me. "We found a photograph of our grandparents together, and with a similar tattoo on their hands that was at the end of the journal, they all got this tattoo on Leticia's death anniversary. My grandparents, your grappy, they all were Shadow Walkers."

Clara nudged Kayden, who fumbled through his pocket and found his phone. He showed me a photograph. A tear rolled down my eyes, looking at his beautiful white face. I didn't look at his phone. Instead, my eyes were on him, his glistening eyes. He was terrified for me, he was scared not of me but for me. Our eyes met each other when more tears filled my eyes, thinking about why our families eluded us.

I held my hand out to take his phone, sniffing, but he didn't hand it over. His eyes widened.

"What?" I asked, wiping my tears, arching my eyebrow.

"No swiping," he bit his lips. He was scared, but this was a different kind of scared. "No flipping through my phone." He looked afraid, and it hit me differently, all my pain, all his pain that I thought he felt for me, vanished in a second, turning into anger.

A sound slipped from Clara's throat as she looked at him so fast that she would have gotten a jerk in her neck, her eyes widened as she slowly shook her head, but he didn't notice. His eyes were on his phone.

"Fine." I snatched his phone, eyeing him angrily. Why was he behaving like that? Was he hiding some chat with his girlfriend or his pics, which he was afraid to show me because he was hitting on me? My insides filled with rage. Was he flirting with me to kill time?

Because he seemed so scared that I don't act like a tattletale in front of his girlfriend, whomever the fuck she was, or was he trying to double date us?

Oh no! I thought Kayden changed, but he didn't. He was still that playboy of the school. And all his words were just his charms that I was falling for. Argh! Why was he so perfect with his charms? It all looked genuine. *You can't fall for his charms. You're not going to be some girl trapped in his stupid games.*

But right now, it wasn't him I should worry about. Noni, a cursed child, and grappy being a Shadow Walker, was clouding my mind.

I glanced at the picture.

It was them, Grappy, young and handsome with dark hair, and Noni, young in bright red straight hair, with big eyes and a shy kind of lady.

I remember that baby's winter grey eyes were so familiar when I saved her, of-course they were Noni's eyes.

Leticia gave her life to save Noni. She was the cursed child.

Fuck!

I looked down at the photo again. Noni was standing with Clara's grandparents. They were sitting together, showing off their tattoos and smiling.

"But I saved that baby. How is that I saved my own *abuela*?" I asked, befuddled.

"You time travelled," Kayden whispered. "That's the only explanation I can get. You were thrown back to that particular moment to change it."

I shot him a deadly glare, wanting to rip him into ribbons, to which he flinched.

"But according to my grams and all other Shadow Walkers, Alice was saved by the Light. That's why no Shadow Walkers killed her. Even being a demon, the Shadow Walker community accepted her. And also because Leticia suppressed her powers, making her futile. Grams said a green light saved your *abuela*." Clara told me, quickly catching my attention as if stopping me from killing her brother.

"No, it was me. When you found me in the bathroom, this chatoyant emitted green light, and I was sucked in," I spin my cat-eyed fire chatoyant between my fingers. "It even saved Kayden from Mer-skeletons, it belongs to Leticia."

Clara looked confused, but Kayden's eyes went wide.

"It's a chatoyant?" Kayden carefully took that in his hand, his eyes careful as I'll bat his hand away, but I let him observe it because he had some insights that would help reach the truth—why my family hid it from me.

He was sitting so close to me that I felt the zing vibrating between us, urging me to lean in and kiss him. But now, I'd rather not. He does not tempt me anymore. He couldn't trap me in his games. So, I stopped breathing, not taking him in. "Jason told me about such stuff. You know he's a stone collector. He has some with him."

Really, I didn't know that, but I didn't speak, just shook my head.

"These stones keep memories. Whatever they see, they store them. It's like a camera, watching and capturing with unlimited memory." He explained.

"Do you think Jason is a Shadow Walker too?" I bit my lips, to which Clara's eyes widened with realisation.

But before we could discuss it further, Kayden reached out to take his phone from my other hand, and I noticed it before he could lay his hands over it. Jealousy surged through me. All his words, his care being just part of his games, irked me.

So, I tossed his phone aside. It may look like it was casual, but it was so forceful that it would definitely hit the wall behind, which was only a metre far and

SMACK

Kayden's eyes widened in disbelief while Clara gasped as I slid back, getting up swiftly, and as gracefully as I could.

"Oops," a cruel smug rose on my face. "It slipped," I shrugged, batting my eyes innocently. Strike One.

Rage, I was waiting for cold rage, but it didn't come. Oddly, he went flabbergasted, and it was Clara who spoke. "Well, I didn't see that coming." Faking her innocence, while sarcasm dripped from her lips, and I smiled with her, my best friend, she knows me.

I was hurt, and some part of me wanted to hurt him too. I'd been jealous before, but with Kayden, everything has to be extreme.

Ignoring him, who still seemed stunned looking at his shattered phone, we walked past him. My mind was rolling, having thousands of thoughts. They knew about me, everyone knew about me, then why didn't they say anything? Why didn't they help me with my neurotic mom?

Mom!

Was there a probability that Noni didn't even tell her daughter about her being a demon or about Shadow Walkers? Was my mom mundane? Then how come I had powers?

I still remember asking Leticia—why was this baby important. Why so many deaths?

That's why the cursed child was important. *She was my Noni. She was important to me.*

"So, Noni is a shadow demon, she has dark magic. That's why she could convince my mom every damn time. She could put glamour on things. I've never seen Robin or Hannah cleaning our house. Our house is always dustproof as if some cleaning charm has been imposed on it." I gulped down hard. How could I have never noticed all these things?

Silence fell for a few minutes. I tried to grasp the information I had just received about my family. Even Clara and Kayden belong to Shadow Walkers' family, we had the same blood flowing through our veins, but somehow, I have powers, like healing and shifting.

"But why couldn't I see these monsters till now? Why today?" I asked. "Homer said you guys encountered monsters that day too."

"I don't know. Perhaps this moonstone ring enhances your powers. That's my theory," she hunched her shoulders.

"But it's a Demon's Den. Moonstone magic doesn't work here, look," I told her as I swayed my hand, and nothing came out. "I should have created a shield. *Thamex*, the demon I killed, told me it won't work here."

"You killed a demon?" She gasped, her eyes on the verge of popping out.

I gave a wide grin. "A story for later."

"O-kay! Whoa! But then, what's new?"

I shook my head.

"We should address the elephant in the room. Nathan is possessed, and every time your boy-toy gay shames him, monsters lurk out." Kayden's voice was taut, and my nostrils flared.

Boy-toy!

"Don't. Call. Him. That." I growled, threatening him with my knife. I pointed it at his chest, his eyes flashed in anger. I was waiting for some fear, but nothing came.

He glared at me. "Don't you dare defend some other guy in front of me," he growled, taking one step closer, and before I could press on this topic, the knife went through his jacket. My heart stopped as blood pooled out.

"You're deranged." I immediately retreated my knife, and my hand replaced the spot, trying to stop the blood, FUCK!

"I can be anything for you, baby girl."

He had totally lost it. Who does that? Who takes a step forward when a knife is pointed at their chest? You move back, always back, but Kayden, he was wicked. I didn't know what was going on in his mind. What kind of twisted games was he playing?

But I was trapped.

Chapter 33

A Trap for the Bully

Nathan and Homer were already busy moving the boxes out of the way, clearing the vent entrance.

I gulped down hard. My eyes were fixed on Nathan's second shadow. I somehow needed to exorcise it, which I didn't know how to do. But I couldn't take him with me to our world like that. What if he went Lara? The girl who became a shapeshifter during Leticia's time and wiped off the village. I didn't want him to convert into a full-time shadowfiend.

I had to find another way to eliminate that shadow—but how? I didn't have any moonwater or knew how to make one.

But most importantly, I had to keep Homer away from Nathan because his comments were triggering him. My hands were clammy as I wiped them off my now dirty shorts. I opened my mouth to call Homer, but Kayden quickly hopped inside the vent. His athletic bod distracted me. Even though I was angry with him, I couldn't stop ogling behind him, his bubble ass looking so delicious, when Clara whispered in my ears, "Are you eye-fucking my brother?".

Blood rushed to my cheeks as I shook my head.

"The vent is going up," Kayden's voice echoed from inside as he climbed back. "I think it's an escape out of Demon's Den," he turned to me. "We can create a portal once we are out and let the elders handle things afterwards." He eyed me. Oh! Of course, Noni and others would know what to do with Nathan. Till then, we have to keep Nathan and Homer separate.

Before I could even contemplate how I would do that, Homer slid his hand around my waist. "Let's go."

Whoa! Our heads whipped at him at once. My eyes widen at his touch. Were his feelings changing towards me? But right now, my mind was on Kayden, who was standing with a locked jaw, and I liked it. He wanted to hide his pics from his phone. Enjoy the show now! *Strike two.*

I turned to Homer, wrapping my hands around his neck, batting my eyes at him. I knew how to wear a mask, even though this mask was something I had never modelled before, but how hard could it be to be something glamourous?

"Lead the way, sweety," I sing to him. Even Homer was taken aback by the chime in my voice. I saw Clara flinch from the corner of my eyes, knowing it was fake.

"Wait for a second, *sweety*," Kayden said through clenched teeth as he shoved Homer away with one hand like he was merely a scarf I was wearing, making his hand fall from me. His giant hand replaced my waist, sending a tingly sensation down my core. He seemed so powerful. "How are you going to do it? You're claustrophobic." He looked annoyed, filled with cold rage. I could see shadows dancing behind those hazel eyes. My heart flutters. *No, Lizzy. He is just playing games. You have to keep your mask on.*

"She is not claustrophobic," Homer said, holding me with my shoulders, trying to pull me out of Kayden's grip.

But his grip tightened, crushing me into him. I could feel his heat on my entire body, "You're just her *boy-toy*. That's why I am tolerating you because I don't want to take away her weekend fun. But don't mistake it as my weakness. Touch her, and I'll rip your hands off, touch her again, and I'll kill you," he snarled at him. Clear. Honest. Dark.

Homer's hands fell off my shoulder instantly.

My heart fluttered inside my chest. His words were so powerful that colour drained from Homer's face.

"Stop being an alphahole," I frowned at Kayden, placing my hands on his chest, trying to push him, but he didn't budge. "You're such a devil."

"*You* bring the devil out of me," Kayden glared, leaning in. "Retaliate again, and I'll show you what this devil can do. *I don't like when anyone touches you.*" His breath brushed my lips, and a moan built up in my throat, but I shoved it down with force. Whatever I wanted to snap at him guttered down with it, too.

"Got it?" he asked in a stern voice.

I might have nodded because the corner of his lips tugged upward. "Good, now move your ass," he said softly this time, freeing me. His hand fell on my ass, tracing it, making my eyes roll back at his soft touch, and then gave it a gentle smack. My eyes snapped open as my heart fluttered, wanting more.

Oh God! Something was definitely wrong with me.

Homer was standing white as a ghost as I turned to him. Even I was shaken and a bit dizzy.

No, Lizzy, don't fall for his words. He's trying to distract you from that phone incident. He did tell you not to swipe. Remember that.

"C'mon, fat-ass, move," Homer snapped, turning to Nathan and taking our anger on him. My eyes went wide. *Oh no! There goes my plan.*

"Homer, behave," I warned.

"Fucktard!" Clara snapped as she held Nathan's hand. "Let's go, I'll help you," she tried to pull Nathan away, who was now heaving in anger, but he didn't budge. Instead, he dodged her hand.

"I don't need your favour," he snapped at Clara, making her flinch. Nathan had never raised his voice at anyone. He's always the sweet one, laying low.

I was worried. What if he hurt them?

"Yeah, you don't need anyone's favour, just do yourself a favour and stop eating, like now, you're so fat already." Homer's mouth was out of his control, and my focus was on the shadow that was expanding throughout the room with each insult.

The lights in the room went off one by one with a spark as the shadowfiend was waiting to unleash.

"You do yourself a favour and go eat your shit." Clara snapped, but I quickly sprung at Homer, blocking Nathan's glare from him. I held his face.

"That's enough. Please stop fat-shaming him," I shivered, begging him to stop. The darkness was enveloping us all. I was terrified, not knowing how to stop it.

"Stop holding me, Elmo." He snapped at me, uncurling my hands from his face. "Are you planning to unleash your boyfriend on me?" Yanking my hands away angrily.

"Hey!" Kayden growled, stepping in, but I stopped him, shaking my head, *not now.* My eyes darted towards the darkness that encompassed the entire room.

Kayden's jaw tightened, but he brought his temperament down, looking at me, closing his eyes, saying. "Fine," he tugged me to him. "Clara, climb up, and don't look back."

Homer held my wrist, but his gaze was on Kayden. "Don't pretend like I cannot see what you are doing here."

"What's your problem?" Kayden snapped, but his eyes were darting towards the darkness. His one hand reached out for Clara as if trying to shield both of us. My heart was beating into a thunderous beat. The whole room had gone dark. Only one unit remained.

"You are my problem. You all are my problem," he was feeling out of space. I could feel it. That's why he was freaking out. But it wasn't the time because the last unit went out, and Nathan let out an inhumane shriek, sending chills down my spine.

At the same time, Kayden pushed Clara and me towards the vent, Clara quickly darted inside with her boney bod, but I remained frozen to the ground because Homer was choking on the darkness.

His eyes had rolled inside his head, his hands trying to push past the darkness that had enclosed him. I quickly darted towards him to somehow protect him, but he was raised in the air, wetting his pants. Ew!

I had no shield, just a Cosmic blade, but I couldn't kill Nathan. He was my friend. Even if he was possessed, still he was somewhere in there, I couldn't do that to him. My hands trembled thinking about my sparse options.

I cannot kill Nathan, even to protect Homer.

I cannot kill him.

"Blind him," I screamed at Kayden, who was holding my knife in his hand. He connected my blade's pommel to his head. Nathan's eyes rolled back in his head before he could realise what I was talking about. His hand shot up to hold his head, Kayden grabbed him by the shoulders before he could fall.

"Sorry, Huggy-bear," I whispered to Nathan. Kayden's eyes fell on my face, and his expression turned sympathetic, but instantly, Homer fell, and the darkness eloped.

"Argh!" Homer screamed as he hit the ground.

"Hey, hey, are you ok?" I sat next to him, but he pushed me back, scared.

"What the fuck was that?" he asked me, wide-eyed, scrambling on the floor, hiding his soaked pants with one hand while pointing at Nathan with the other, who seemed unconscious. "How was he doing that? It was him. I know it was him."

I looked at Kayden, who shook his head.

"ELMO?" Homer seemed angry. "What are you two cooking? It's you two, isn't it? You both are doing this. You both are trying to kill me."

"NO," I screamed in horror. He was getting it all wrong. "It's happening because you always torment Nathan, and now he is possessed, so his subconscious is trying to hurt *you*." I frowned at him. "He's trapping his bully."

"He's possessed?" Homer's already paled face went white as a ghost. He scurried from the floor, getting on his legs and tugging at me. "Let's get the fuck out of here," his hands were cold as ice.

"But Nathan?" I asked, biting my lips.

"Fuck him. Stop being benign," he snapped, tugging me towards the vent. "You know, he's possessed. Leave him here."

My heart sank at his words.

"Are you crazy?" I yanked my hand back. How could he even suggest that? "He's just possessed. Nathan is still inside, somewhere."

"Don't you try to justify him. He just tried to kill me," Homer pointed his finger towards Nathan. Kayden was hovering over him, and disappointment flashed his face.

"He's not doing that on purpose," I bit my lips, trying to explain. "What—"

"Fuck it," he snapped. "You're coming with me and creating a damn portal. That's it, we're getting out of this mess, I don't give a fuck what happens to him, and with your so-called boyfriend."

I heard a shriek as chilled as ice.

"Shadowfiend is coming," Clara called from the vent.

Kayden nudged at her. "Keep climbing."

"But Nathan," she called out.

"Fucking run, Clara," Homer growled. "Survival of the fittest, haven't you heard? He brought this on himself. Elmo is naïve," he grimaced at me. "But you're mean enough to understand, there is no one here to judge whether you're good or not, just save your ass. I know who you are, I see through you, and this is not you."

Clara went quiet for a beat and then spoke disappointedly, "Lizzy, please help Nathan."

Homer let out a string of profanities, tugging on me.

"I am not leaving, Nathan," I growled at Homer.

"I hate you, Elmo," Homer scowled at me, making me freeze. "Don't come to me running after he breaks your heart because he will." My heart dropped to my stomach, and suddenly it was getting hard to breathe. My limbs got numb. *How can he say that?* I just told him I loved him, chose him over everyone, and he said he hated me in front of these people. I felt humiliated beyond par.

"Oh c'mon, you don't hate her. You just hate the fact that you can't control her anymore." Kayden shot him an angry look before his gaze fell on me. "You need to fix your priorities," he was damn serious.

But the moment I nodded, a shadowfiend was in my face. His scarlet eyes bored into mine, his toxic smell filled my nostrils, and his giant blades were at my throat. But, with a sudden jolt, I was pulled back. I opened my eyes to see what had happened at that moment. Whatever was there, it went at the speed of light, and I couldn't realise the happenings.

I was lying on the ground, and Kayden was standing over me, a black chalky liquid splashed all over him and me. He had pierced one of the monsters, splitting it in half with the Cosmic blade.

And we were drenched in black blood. I sank to the ground, shivering.

That was close! That was freakishly close. Its blades, scarlet eyes, eight limbs, I couldn't get off its image towering over me. One second, he was there in my face, next, he dismantled into black liquid. Food rose in my throat, but I pushed it back with difficulty.

Homer was just behind me, trembling as fuck, sobbing like a child.

Kayden closed his eyes and wiped his mouth. "That was pretty easy," I looked around, the shadowfiend was gone.

"Ewww! You just ruined my favorite bandana," Nathan was lying near me. I turned to him, he was wiping black liquid off his specs. "My date gave me this bandana. Do you even know how he's going to react if he gets to know that it's drenched with some monster's—" he gave a pause. "Is that blood? Gross!"

Tears rolled down my eyes as a chuckle-cum-sob skipped my throat, crying because I knew he was back. Nathan was back as Kayden killed the shadowfiend that possessed him. The glint in his moss-green eyes was back. There was no shadow behind them. Moreover, his innocence had returned.

"Well, you're welcome," Kayden smirked, drenched in a black liquid. His chocolate brown hair was clammy, his already ruined jacket was now ruined beyond repair.

"OMG! Is that Kayden? Whoa! Dude, you look hot with that chalky liquid dripping off you. Can you open your jacket so it could drip on your chest too?" Nathan was ogling over Kayden, making him a bit uncomfortable. He turned to look at me, flushed, as if asking me for help, and I let out a chuckle, spitting the remains of shadowfiend blood, wiping my face with my jacket.

And soon, Clara sprang on Nathan to sit on his belly, wiping off the liquid with her sleeves and kissing him on his cheeks. Her eyes were red too, but she seemed happy now.

"Ewww! Stop it, Clara," Nathan felt disgusted, and I laughed. Clara beckoned me, and we both started kissing him on his cheeks, head, and nose, and he seemed irritated by us. Oh! He was so Nathan. "Guys-guys," he was screaming. His chubby cheeks turned red like tomatoes as I held his hands, and Clara tickled him.

"Get off him, Clara, let him breathe," Kayden cleared his throat as he pulled me up from the back of the jersey jacket. He seemed uneasy, even of our platonic affection.

I realised my top was torn from the front, and my bra was visible. I tried fixing it when he immediately blocked my way. "Are you ok, Voodoo lady?" he asked, as his eyes darted from my rack to my face.

"I saw you looking," I told him as he went red, turning to look back at Clara and Nathan, but I think he was trying to hide his flushed face while blocking me from their view.

"They're very much hard to ignore," he gulped down hard. His eyes again flashed to my boobs, and he closed his eyes, shaking his head. This was the same reaction he always gave me whenever he looked at me. Till now, I thought he was repulsed, but now I know he's trying to control.

I didn't know I affected him that much. Whoa!

"It's ok. They are my best friends. They have already seen me naked." I mean, except Homer, of course. If he had seen me naked, things would've been different. I tied the strap to the top to make it hang in there, beaming, but Kayden's eyes narrowed. "I mean, Clara had seen me naked and Nathan, almost." I chuckled.

"Define almost," he raised his eyebrows, not finding any amusement in my words as he clenched his jaw.

I rolled my eyes. Nathan was gay! Didn't he figure that out?

"Almost means I go shopping with him," I smile, thinking about shopping. It seemed like a decade since I'd shopped anything. "He's got an awesome taste when it comes to lingerie."

"Yeah, that's not happening again," Kayden's frown deepened, being controlling again, then shook his head, zipping me up as if hiding me, a possessive move.

"Can't you control yourself, territorial caveman?" I asked him, pursing my lips.

He hummed before answering as Clara and Nathan walked past us, climbing the vent. Homer followed them too, like a zombie, too shocked to say or feel something, but my focus was on Kayden, whose humming reverberated through my chest, tightening my breasts.

"I don't care whether it's Shadowland. If my sister wasn't here, I would have taken you right here, right now, in front of your boy-toy and made him hear how good my name sounds from your mouth, especially when you're moaning it." He grinned devilishly, rolling his thumb down my lower lip, giving me thrilling vibes, making me shudder. I felt a jolt between my legs. *Fuck! He was turning me on, even the idea of Homer watching us.*

Something was drastically wrong with my head.

No, Lizzy, don't fall for his charm, but how couldn't I? He was doing everything a girl wanted. *Exactly! That's what makes him a playboy. They always know how to play well.*

Urgh! My angel and devil sides were fighting over Kayden.

"Pig," I snapped at him. The heat reached my cheeks as I strode towards the vent.

He chuckled after me.

"I know you're very sensitive about this topic, but you cannot save someone who doesn't want to be saved," Kayden spoke candidly.

"He doesn't mean that. He was just scared." I tried to explain Homer's side.

"C'mon, stop covering for him." Kayden pulled me, tucking some hair behind my ear before placing his finger under my chin. "Even if he was good to you when you were a kid, it doesn't give him the right to be coarse to you. I don't like how he treats you, he shouts at you, he's toxic." His chest grumbled at the words.

"This is all too much for him to accept. Moreover, he is harbouring an emotional trauma from his past, and his dad doesn't treat him right." I shook my head, blinking away his charming aura.

"Aren't we all?" he asked, raising his eyebrows. "That doesn't give him any right to take you for granted." He whispered. My eyes caught his. I think he sought to tell me more but held onto his words. I wanted to snap at him and tell him he was wrong, but I couldn't find my words because he was right. Homer does take me for granted.

And today, he had crossed his limits.

"I think this needs a key to unlock the door," Clara called from the top. "It seems like your moonstone ring is the key."

What?

But I was too tired to think about it.

"Do whatever you want, just take me home, Clara." I removed my ring as we passed it to her.

"Your wish is my command, princess," she teased.

Chapter 34

A Betrayal

It was a *Deja vu*.

"I've seen this room in my dreams before," I said, swivelling around the room, wearing my moonstone ring back, stepping up from the vent, which Kayden helped me with while flirting and calling me *baby girl*, knowing how much it distracts me. Even though it was dark every time in my dream, but this time, it was lit. I could observe it clearly.

It was a big room with gilt alter and the antique, carved-cedar, pine, and rosewood bookshelves were nothing short of enchanting. The decorations, barrel-vaulted ceiling arches, and marble busts had transformed the library into a heaven of books. There was a priceless collection of artefacts and paintings.

I didn't have to be a bookworm to be transfixed. Far in a corner was a mahogany desk, where Homer was sitting with his legs resting on the table, hands tucked back of his head, eyes closed as if relaxing.

"I think I am going to cry," Nathan said, looking at the books, running towards the right shelf, and reading the names of the books.

"Go on. I won't judge," I mumbled.

I turned back, and there was a centre round table but no Orb this time. It was the *Wandering Star* I always saw here. The same *Wandering Star* Maurice Hector used to call *Yamendo*, the same *Wandering Star* that the journal talked about, Orb was a vessel to *Yamendo's* powers. And then my eyes fell on the large, crowned mirror with baroque angels and symbols, but it was contained in a glass cage. No light was coming through it. It was like someone pulled out its plug.

It was my anxiety dream. *Oh no! Is this my nightmare?*

But I killed *Thamex*. How come we were still rolling into nightmares? Who else was creating these?

Clara walked past me, making me jump. "We shouldn't be here," she stood in front of that mirror, examining the glass cage.

"Look at that portable charger," Nathan screamed in excitement, lounging towards it, pushing me out of his way, making me fumble on my feet, and canoodling it. "God, my YouTube followers must be missing me," he took out a phone from his pocket and put it on charging.

Classic Nathan.

"You have a YouTube channel?" Homer scoffed. "How many followers do you have?" unmoved like he didn't care that we nearly skipped shadowfiend, like we didn't have a near-death experience.

"NEC gameplay," Nathan's eyes fixed on his phone. "Seventy-five thousand approx." He was checking his phone. "Damn-it, I lost three hundred followers."

Seriously? Seventy-five thousand? I was impressed.

Homer turned to me. "You owe me a phone, Elmo."

"Why does she owe you a phone?" Nathan asked. "You used it at your own will. She stopped you. You didn't listen to her. You ignore, you lose more."

"Still, it's her *Shadowland*, and my phone got burnt here, so she has to buy me a new one," Homer snapped at Nathan, who shook his head in disbelief.

"It's ok," I told Nathan. I didn't want to fight over something worthless.

"You owe me a phone too," Kayden smug, elegantly walking towards me with a glint of mischievousness in his eyes. His devil smirk played at the corner of his lips. I was scared of this glint because I knew he was planning something wicked whenever he had it, making my heart thrum faster.

"I don't owe you squat," I snapped at him, holding my heart in place. Nathan's eyes observed us very carefully. And just like that, he stirred my whole focus to himself because right now, all I knew was aggression and Kayden.

"Oh! You do, when you don't mind giving away phones just like a spoilt brat, I think you owe me one for smashing it down the wall," he narrowed his eyes. "And don't say it slipped because we both know you were jealous," he added as I opened my mouth to say exactly what he told me not to say.

"You told me not to flip through your photos just after kissing me, you jackass!" My palms clenched into fists, trying to contain my rage. What else do you conclude from this scenario?

"I told you he's a player. You have to stay away from him," Homer strode towards me with a told-you-so look on his face.

"Did she ever talk to you like that?" Kayden turned to Homer with a smirk, shoving his hands in his pockets. "With her filthy mouth and true self," Homer frowned, making Kayden click his tongue in joy. "She won't because she knows you can't handle her."

"Holy shit!" Nathan bit on his knuckles. His eyes went wide, darting between the three of us.

"At least I didn't cheat on my girlfriend with her," Homer snapped, standing next to me.

Kayden was playing with the wrong girl—*I am the one with claws.* I'd strike back.

"Because you ace at trickery." Kayden smouldered, as if implying some secret between the two of them. I frown, wanting to know, but it was Clara's scream that stopped me.

"Guys, stop fighting," Clara trembled. Our focus shifted to her as she seemed scared. "This is a gateway," she pointed at the mirror. There were things that we had to focus on. This thing with Kayden could wait. Or there was nothing to wait for. We were done. I jutted my chin as I walked towards the mirror, examining the box it was in, ignoring Kayden.

I took a deep breath, focusing on the mirror.

"You mean it's a portal?" I asked her, figuring out how to open the glass box.

Clara nodded but gulped hard. Instead of getting excited, she was scared.

"But isn't it good, Clara?" I asked, raising my eyebrows. "We can finally leave this nightmare."

But she shook her head. "This is not a nightmare, this is a memory," she spoke in horror. "She called me here again to complete what I left in-between," she turned to Kayden. "I shouldn't be here, I have to go back," she took Kayden's hand, whimpering visibly.

"Shh..." Kayden sweetly caressed her hair. "We'll leave this place as soon as we open this portal, don't worry, Eloise is here, she can do that."

"No, you don't understand, it's not a way *out*," she stomped. "It's a way *in*."

"You mean we are back in our realm?" It was Nathan who realised what Clara was about to say. When Nathan mentioned it, I gathered that this room had no mist or ashes, no toxic smell either. Though there were no windows, we couldn't look out.

But how is it even possible? I didn't create a portal, then who did? Unless there was a hidden portal in this memory.

"Clara," I arched my eyebrows, realising. "I started having this dream after we became friends. I thought this was my anxiety dream. How could we both have the same dream?" I asked, raising my concern.

She went stoic. "You-you shifted in my memory?" she asked, stuttering, and then she started crying. "I am sorry, I am so sorry, but I didn't mean it." She took my hands. She was cold, and her hands were trembling.

"She showed me this place in my dreams, she showed me your house, that's why I became your friend," she gulped down. "She said she could return me my mom, and I believed her. I didn't know the toll it would have on me."

"You're a portal," I didn't even ask. I just said it to her face in disbelief.

She closed her eyes as fresh tears rolled down her face, and her pierced lip trembled.

"I didn't know what she had done to me, I didn't know how she planted herself in my mind, but I feel an opening in my mind through which she spoke to me." Tears oozed out of her eyes.

"*Yamendo* reached out for me, claiming she could return my mom if I brought her the *Wandering Star*. I was too small to understand, I cracked a deal with the Demon. But then I was stopped. The opening in my mind was closed so she couldn't reach me, but it opened again." She turned to Kayden.

"I didn't want you to suffer. I didn't know what she meant, but you know I love you more than anything," Kayden seemed confused. "I love you. That's why she took you." Clara threw herself on him, sobbing in his chest, but he was gone stoic, wrapping his head around his sister's confession.

"I was caught before I could give her the *Wandering Star*. It fell from my hand after getting struck by lightning, though I didn't know who stopped me, Light blinded me, and I fainted." She winced at the memory.

"And when I woke up, I was in my room. I almost forgot about all that. It was like an erased dream, but it came back. When you died that day, it came back to me. I felt a breeze in my mind. The portal didn't open completely but just cracked a bit to pass a whisper, an air, a smoke, and through that small opening, I heard her laughing maniacally." She shuddered, and I went still, not feeling anything.

"The second Lizzy hauled you out from the pool, the demon was laughing. I could hear her in my mind. Perhaps the fear of losing you ruptured the wall on the portal in my mind, but I knew what had happened. She was punishing me for going back on our deal. She took you away because I couldn't give her the *Wandering Star.*" Kayden's hands brushed her hair, but his jaw was taut.

"I stopped you," I spoke in terror. "It was me, like I saved Noni, I stopped you that day from going into the mirror, I pulled you back as you were handing the star to that shadow." Everything was getting clear, but I was hurt. I couldn't speak her name. I was terrified of even taking *Yamendo's* name, knowing what she had done with my friend.

"Alice must have found you and erased that memory. They closed the portal in your mind," Kayden mused, his eyes far beyond.

Noni, of course, would have tried to clean up the mess.

"That's why you were so adamant that he died," I whispered, remembering the day Kayden almost drowned in the pool. "A shadow monster was trying to suck the life out of you," I whispered to Kayden, remembering his nightmare. "That incident had become a nightmare in your life," I looked around.

"I again went back into memory. Not just chatoyant stored memory, I can also shift into people's memories and alter them." *FUCK!*

That was a freakishly disturbing revelation. The more I learned about my powers, the more scared I became because I didn't know my limits. *What if I create a paradox?*

"Why didn't you tell me earlier? Why didn't you tell me when I showed you the journal? You were freaked out when you read about *Yamendo*," I asked Clara, rubbing my face.

"Because you couldn't see anyone, you hadn't seen a single shadow, and I was not even sure what had happened to me, but I didn't want to scare you either. You were glad, thinking there was no monster, that *Yamendo* already died." She held her head.

"We are best friends. I am supposed to help you," I moaned.

"I know, but there was nothing left to help. The portal inside me was closed. You saved Kayden, she was defeated, I didn't know she'd come back," I felt the desperation in her voice. "I thought things got under control as Alice would have hidden the *Wandering Star* by now, I didn't know she would haul me back."

"Why didn't you tell me before that you were being haunted?" Kayden asked.

"I thought you would hate me and leave me." She looked down at her fingers, holding the hem of her jacket.

Kayden hugged her tightly. "Are you insane?" Caressing her hair, "I will never do that. You're my sister, my family, and believe me, nothing is more important to me than my family," he declared.

"I thought you wouldn't understand," she sobbed in his chest.

But my mind was travelling somewhere else, I didn't want to go down that road, but I couldn't stop thinking about it because it was hurting me. The pain was unbearable, the realisation was imprinted on my heart, so I spilled it.

"You became my friend because *Yamendo* told you I had the *Wandering Star* in my house?" I asked. I thought one thing in my life was pure and had no bounds, but it turned out marred and was stolen away from me.

"Lizzy, she didn't know about you or whether it was the *Wandering*

Star. She just showed me the orb, this veil, and your mansion." Clara looked at me, she tried to take my hand, but I jerked it away.

"You used me to get into my house?" It was even worse.

"Eloise," Kayden's voice went solemn.

"Shhhh…" I didn't want him to interfere. "This is between my so-called best friend and me."

It was getting hard to breathe. I felt a massive pain in my stomach like someone had kicked me in the gut. It would have been better for Nathan's monsters to have eaten me alive than to live through this betrayal. I took a few steps back.

You know, when you're seventeen, everything seems important, but your best friend is your lifeline. You can survive through all the problems, family, relationships, studies, everything just by having a best friend by your side, but *Yamendo* even planted that into my life. My whole life seemed like a joke.

I started laughing, thinking I was a joke, tears rolling down my eyes, and laughing like a lunatic.

"Elmo," Homer held me. "Are you ok?"

"Do I look ok?" I asked, having hysteria. "I am having the best time in the world. My best friend is not my best friend but the demon's gift to me. And she is here not because she loves me, but because she wants to meet her mother through me." I felt so naked and used that I wanted to run away, to disappear.

"It's not like that," Clara walked towards me, her lower lip trembling with each word she said.

"Na-uh-uh," I shook my finger at her. "Go on, free your soul, complete your deal with the demon. I'll be standing here, not interfering this time. I'll be here like I am no one."

Clara shook her head.

"You know, I spent my whole life being invisible like I wasn't wanted by the guy I love," I turned to Homer. "Like I wasn't enough for any guy to ask me out," I looked at Kayden. "Like I wasn't the daughter anyone wants," I turned to Clara. "Like people thinking of me as a side chick, they can be friends with to get to you. I was useless, but there was one thing I knew that got me through, YOU," I cried, splaying my hand towards her.

"I thought there was one person in my life who doesn't care how I look, what I wear, what I do, and even though I was a freak, you were there with me."

"Don't call yourself that, stupid," Clara cried.

"Look at me, *stupid me,"* I scoffed, tears rolling down my cheeks. "I never thought why this person was being so good, so understanding. How could she fathom me so much that she even accepted my glitch, but now I know why, because it was your need, *you did it out of your necessity.*" I said the last line through clenched teeth.

Clara shook her head like it was a lie.

I hate myself right now. "Mom was right. She told me that no one in this world would understand me. They'll use me. I wasn't made for this world. I wasn't made to be loved."

Kayden stepped forward to reach out to me, he had pain spread through his face, but Nathan shrieked. "ARGH!"

We turned to Nathan, he was whimpering in pain, holding his head.

"She's near, she's coming," Clara started whimpering too. "I can feel her presence. Nathan was possessed by a shadow, that's why he can feel her too," she looked back in the mirror, which was now moving mystically, turning into a veil.

"You want to meet your mother, right?" I asked. "Let me give you what you want. Let's finish this. Then you could go your own way. Then you would have no bounds to befriend a girl like me."

I stalked towards Nathan and planted a kiss on his temple. "Sleep, Huggy-bear. I got you." I told him, and he fell on the ground with a thud. I was a healer. I could do that.

Being broken to this extent, it gave a certain amount of clarity that I knew what was happening and how to handle everything.

"You said this is my house," I mused. "Then this must be the oval office. Obviously, that's why I was not allowed in it. Apparently, you all were always in the team—*let's make a fool out of Eloise."*

Kayden winced at my words.

I started throwing all the books on the floor, trying to find *the Wandering Star*. That's what Clara wanted. I smashed down everything in my reach aggressively, unable to control my rage.

"Shhh..." Kayden held my hand, he was scared.

"Kayden, leave me," I closed my eyes, seriously hurt. "You guys can meet your mother, you should be happy about it."

"We cannot meet our mother, at least not this way," Kayden whispered. "Because *she's alive."* And with that, Clara gasped in horror. Even I felt blood drained from my face.

"No…no, that's not possible. Dad said she died giving us birth," Clara held her throat, shivering.

"Metaphorically. He didn't want us to meet her ever again after she left us. He didn't want us to remember her." He looked broken as well as angry as he talked about his mother. Disappointment and betrayal flashed his face.

Clara broke down on her knees as Kayden went to her, sharing her pain. It was a big revelation in her life. Now, she must be feeling like a fool for cracking a deal with the demon.

"It's creepy as hell. I think it's dangerous," Homer was standing near the glass cage. "Believe me, I just saw someone in there."

I strode towards it. That's when things inside the mirror started swiveling, and red lights began beaming from the edges. "I don't think it's dangerous. Instead, I think it's—"

"Beautiful?" asked a soft voice, startling me, finishing my sentence. "I knew you would come."

I froze for a second, just feeling my heart beating fast. I wasn't sure, could it be true?

I gazed inside the veil at the obscure shadow. I waited impatiently to look at her, but she slowly got cleared. I was sure it was her.

We could finally see each other and look into her electric blue eyes, just like mine. (Clara shrieked in absolute pain)

Chapter 35
The Catalyst

"MOM," I whispered, shocked to the core, rubbing my eyes, not trusting my vision. She was my mom with the same blue eyes, soft skin, and silky red hair. "Oh my-mom-oh-mom," I said, leaping towards the glass box, smashing my head on it. Fuck! It hurts.

"You are alive. You won't believe how happy I am." *She didn't die.* "I don't understand. How?" I asked turning back, looking back at my friends. Kayden had Clara moved back behind him, Homer had his eyes on me, while Nathan was lying on the ground, not moving. They seemed to be taken aback, shivering. Even Kayden seemed stunned. They all seemed to be in shock even more than I was.

"I am trapped here, Lizzy," she told me. "Tortured. They imprisoned me behind this veil, honey, please break me free. She will kill us," she said, looking behind her. "Somebody's coming, Lizzy, hurry up. Open this box and get me out." She whimpered. "I am scared, my little cherub. Please help me."

Little Cherub?

But I had no time for semantics. I stepped back, smashing my fist on it, trying to break it.

"OUCH," I screamed in pain, shaking my hand. What was I thinking?

"Eloise," Kayden called out.

"We need to break open this cage," I turned around, slamming myself into Homer, who was hovering over me.

"I need something, a stone or anything sharp," I said, pushing him. "Search for it," I ordered, hyperventilating. My mom was alive, she was fucking alive, just trapped.

My hands were shivering. "Mom, Noni—Grappy—you…are you a Shadow Walker too?" I asked.

"I am sorry, honey, now is not the time. Help me out," she was on edge. Wearing a red blouse and a Moschino skirt, torn in places. I saw a few scars on her face, but they were fresh ones.

"Mom, there are monsters in the Shadowland," I divulged. "I told you, I have never seen anyone, but now I can see them all."

"Yeah, I heard from the whispers," she answered tautly. "They never acknowledged you before because you were hidden. Your grandmother's blood in your veins made you appear unharmful to them. You were never a threat to them as it veiled the angelic blood in you."

"But what's the difference now?" I asked her. "How can I see them? How can they see me?"

"I think it's this boy," she pointed her fingers at Kayden. I spun back to look at him. His eyes went wide as if he was in shock. Not just Kayden, everyone was astonished.

"What about Kayden?" I frowned. "How is he related to any of this?"

"He is your *catalyst*, my dear," she answered me. "That's why you seem so attracted to him. That's why he is so captivated by you. He cannot leave you because he is your personal catalyst."

"You lost me," I told her. "How can he—a human—be a catalyst?" I was so confused. What does a catalyst have to do with me being a Shadow Walker? Ok, this was all so confusing.

"You offered him a part of your soul, and he accepted. You had an unbreakable bond, so he acted like a vessel and developed some qualities to help you power up without any permanent change in you. We call this is—*Androgynous bond*, or *Ardhnarishwar* or twin flames, it goes by many names, but it's *being of becoming*, you're the one who will help her put *infinite into finite*," she told Kayden. "Just by being with her, you complete her."

"What?" I was shocked. "Kayden is my mate?" Really, I mean, how? Till now, I practically hated him. Could it be true?

To my horror, she nodded. "He's your twin flame—two pieces of one soul."

"But when did I offer you my soul?" I turned to Kayden, mystified.

"The day you saved me, I think you generated some qualities in me, some powers. That's why I feel them when anything comes to you." Kayden rubbed his face, his eyes furrowed as if he was in deep thought.

Kayden has powers? My eyes went wide.

"I didn't know what I was doing. I was just trying to save you," I said, stunned. Fuck! "I created a bond unknowingly."

"This bond cannot be created, it's a gift from beyond, a magic that cannot be reversed." Mom spoke. "You were one. That's why you'll always choose each other."

"She chose me," Homer interjected, fidgeting, but Mom shot him an angry look, making him stumble back.

"Kayden, you have powers? Are you a Shadow Walker too?" I was shocked, my blood started boiling. How much was he hiding from me? "Why didn't you tell me?"

But he furrowed his brows like he didn't know the answer himself.

"He is a *being of becoming*, your catalyst," Mom continued. "He completes you, helps you see this world, helps you find yourself," there was a hard line at the corner of her mouth.

I went very, very still. Kayden makes me see shadows. He was the difference, not the ring. *He* completes me. My glitch was no longer a glitch because now I was a complete Shadow Walker but with him.

Fuck! What have I done to Kayden?

"Elmo, this is all gibberish. You chose me," Homer shook me desperately.

That's when I heard a growl from the other side of the veil. "They are coming, honey, get me out, hurry up." Mom tried to fight the veil and come to this side, but her efforts were futile.

"GIVE ME SOMETHING," I snarled back at my friends, making them flinch, but no one moved. "NOW."

I was beyond fretful as they started looking around the room for something.

Kayden held my hand, his eyes wide, dark and terrified. He shook his head. "Eloise, I don't think you should let her out."

"Get your hands off me," I was scared.

What had I done to him? We'll figure this catalyst thing out a little later. But right now, my focus was on Mom.

"This won't open without charms," Mom explained. "You need to use your powers, the stones you have." She pointed hungrily at the locket I was wearing.

"But I don't know how to use it," I told her, shifting my weight from one leg to another.

"Then, find *the Wandering Star*. It will upsurge your powers," she said, crying. "Hurry up, honey," she was scared. "It has to be inside that safe, behind that picture," she pointed at a picture of a stupid, handmade drawing of a little girl holding her mother's hand. Behind it was a small house on a hill, with the moon and stars shining over them.

"That's a painting I made when I was seven years old on your birthday," I said, walking up to it. It was my first painting.

I ran towards the safe, but Clara got behind me. "She is not your mom," she whispered in my ear. "Lizzy, it's her, I am telling, she's deluding you."

"Don't you dare talk to me again, ever." I snapped at her, making her flinch, but that didn't stop her from holding my wrist.

"No, Lizzy, please understand me. I've been in your place," Clara spun me towards her. "This is what I saw, but at that time, it was my Mom, believe me, this isn't right, come on, let's go." She tugged me, but I jerked my hand free.

"Shut up, will you," I snapped. "What's the password?" I asked loudly from my mom.

"It's your birthday, honey," she answered. I rolled my eyes.

I quickly opened the safe. "God! Anyone could rob you if they knew when my birthday is." I put the code in, and it went green.

"Stop chattering. Just open this cage," she snapped, making me pursed my lips.

"Lizzy, she's the monster." Clara was shivering.

"Is it so?" I asked, busy rummaging through the safe. I wasn't going to trust her from now on.

All the stupid stuff was kept inside, including a wooden doll. I took it out, it was handmade, and the clothes were hand-stitched.

Tiny crystals were embarked on its chest, making a pattern. It had blue hair made from wool, with no legs but a tail. It seemed like a voodoo doll.

What exactly was this old voodoo doll doing in here? I threw it out with some papers and files, and there it was at the end, inside the pouch that Leticia gave to that child or Noni, for a matter of fact. I quickly took the velvet pouch scattering the papers from it on the floor.

"I won't let you do it," Kayden said, blocking my way. "We need to get out of this place," he was being forceful. "Look at me," he snapped, his angry eyes bored into mine. "She's not your mother. She's just a shadow, all we can see is an obscure shadow."

"What's up with you guys?" I groaned. "Why are you stopping me from helping my Mom? You should be happy yours is at least alive, let me help mine now."

"There comes great responsibility with great powers, Eloise. You have to understand it," Kayden glowered towards me, towering, intimidating. I gulped down hard. These twins were an obstacle between Mom and me. "At least, give us the benefit of the doubt, we deserve that."

"You deserve nothing after letting me die that day," to my horror, it came out from my mother's mouth. "If it were up to you, I would have been dead. You just stood there and watched me get into an accident."

I whipped my head towards my Mom so fast, I felt a kink in my neck.

"What?" Something inside me just dropped, it fell hard and crashed loudly, and that thing was trust. "What is she talking about?" I looked at Kayden, my hands were trembling.

But he stumbled, his focus was on the veil. "I didn't leave you—you gesticulated me not to interfere." He looked pale, more than ever. I saw sweat beads on his forehead as he wiped them off with his hands shivering. Kayden, the strongest boy I knew, was shaking.

"I begged you to help me," Mom blamed him.

"No—no, you didn't." Kayden stepped towards her, agitated. "You said no."

"You let me die, you coward." She snarled.

"I didn't," he flinched. "I wanted to help, but you said NO," with that, he turned to me, taking my face in his hands agitatedly. "Believe me, Eloise, I wanted to help her, but she shook her head."

"You were there when she met with the accident?" I asked in horror.

"Yes, I was there." Kayden's throat bobbed. "There were three people in the car that night, and the one sitting in the back held a knife to her throat, and I wanted to stop, I was ready to hit her car, but she shook her head. Told me not to intervene, and I slowed down, taken aback. And before I could act, the driver in a red hoodie rolled out of the car, and the truck that was following the car got disbalanced, and hit the car." Guilt flashed on his face as the blood drained my body, leaving me cold. "I tried to chase the guy, but he escaped, he might have taken the same Limestone Cave route. And then, there was an explosion." He closed his eyes, agonised. "I didn't know she'd die. I didn't know what to do. I am sorry, I really wanted to help, trust me."

My whole world shattered at his words. Tears pooled into my eyes, as they sprouted anger.

"Trust you?" I asked, removing his hands from my face, too stunned by his confession. His story matched with the truck driver's. The guy was right, but there were three people. If Lea Perker jumped out, where did the person who held the knife to her throat go? And why? Were they mugging her? Why was Lea lying? Is that what Jason was up to? Kayden told Jason but not me? He knew all along, when he came to the hospital, when he came to my house. He could have told me the truth anytime but chose not to.

It didn't matter, like I was nothing to him, I was never anything to him but a game. This devil chose to play with my feelings, to break me like he promised.

So, this was his game.

My throat was on fire, my ribs ached as an unknowing pain took over me.

"You lied to me," I sobbed.

"I didn't want to. I even tried to reach out to you, but they told me to back off. They made me do so," he again reached out for me. But I raised my hand, telling him not to touch me. "I wanted to go to the cops, but they stopped me," he groaned as his raised hands brushed his hair. "Please believe me."

"Who are '*they*', telling you to back off?" I arched my eyebrow.

He didn't reply. He kept looking into my eyes, wanting me to believe him, but I couldn't handle it anymore. At last, I started to trust him with my life, but it turned out he was punishing me.

"Lizzy—" Clara reached out for me.

"Stop," I raised my hand. "No more," my voice broke.

I felt deceived. Homer was right. All Kayden was doing was using me to rescue his sister. He was the sole witness to my mother's death. Still, he didn't come forward. They all were mean, MEAN PARSONS.

"Eloise," Kayden whispered, seeming mortified.

"TELL ME WHO THEY ARE?" I screamed over the top of my lungs as tears rolled down. My cheeks were hurting, but most of all, my trust was shattered. Two people with whom I felt safe, complete, wanted, cared for, and loved were just using me, betraying me.

Suddenly I heard footfalls descending the stairs.

"*MIJA*," I heard Noni. She was standing on the last stairs, her eyes wide open, her face went pale as she saw us. Mayor, Hannah, Robin, and Jason followed her.

Chapter 36

Truths or Lies

A wave of shock ran through their faces as they looked at us. All of us, the friends I said washed up, were standing here in my house with Kayden and me.

How will Noni clean up *this* mess?

"Clara, oh my sweet baby, Clara," Mayor lunged towards her as she ran to hug her father. "DAD," she started crying as soon as she wrapped her hands around him. "Where were you, sweetheart? What happened to you?" He looked into her eyes, wiping her tears off. "No, baby, don't cry. I am here for you now, don't worry," he bent down to kiss her on the forehead, which was drenched with shadowfiend's blood, and his eyes widened in horror, in realisation.

My stomach churned.

"What the hell is happening here?" Mayor growled, sniffing the dark liquid. "Kayden? What is all this?" His eyes went past him to the veil. His hands fell off Clara's. Blood drained from his face. "Wha-what?" He pulled Clara behind his back, covering her, shielding her.

"Kayden, come here." He ordered, but he walked to stand next to me, his knuckles brushing the back of my hands. I dared not retrieve my hand because I was scared too.

"Eloise, careful," Noni extended her hand to me.

"Good grace, schemers, are here," Mom spoke before I could take Noni's hand. "C'mon, Kayden, go on, tell her, who told you not to spill that you saw my murder, who told you to stay away from cops?" she added as I turned to Kayden. His eyes were filled with remorse. "Who forced you to lie to Eloise, who made you hurt her?"

Everyone in the room went still, in shock.

"SAY IT," my mother shrieked, making me wince, reaching for Kayden's hand to hold myself in place. He took it naturally and grabbed it tight. He was cold.

Homer ran to hide behind Jason, revealing Nathan lying on the ground.

"Isn't it Nathan Royce?" asked Hannah, her eyes scrutinising him. And then she walked past us.

"Help the boy," Noni's voice went taut as she nudged at Robin. Just by a glance at Nathan, she knew what was wrong with him.

"It's not here. It's gone." Hannah rummaged through the safe behind me, but I waited for Kayden to speak.

"It's with Eloise," Homer said aloud. I tore my gaze from Kayden to eye Homer, but he hid behind Jason.

That's when everyone's eyes fell on my hand.

"Lizzy, it's just a shadow with no shape. It's darkness, taking the shape of whatever or whomever you want to see, it's *forsaken*," Noni told me, trying to take that pouch from my hand.

"Then you must be pleased to meet your mother," I jerked it back. Instead, it fell on the ground.

The pouch went loose, and a shining orb with mystical purple smoke peaked from inside. It was different and beautiful, and my eyes became accustomed to the brilliant glare.

The Wandering Star.

I sucked a deep breath before quickly picking it up and closing the pouch.

"*The cursed child.*" I exhaled, tucking the pouch inside my pocket. "You knew everything about it from the beginning and let me suffer."

"Not just you, honey. She hid the truth of my death," added my mother.

"YOU?" I gasped as I felt bile rising my throat. I turned to Kayden. "*She* asked you not to tell anyone?" He didn't answer, but nor did he deny it. I was dumbfounded.

I stumbled back, Kayden's hand caught me, but I shrugged him away. His hands fell without fighting.

"*MIJA,*" Noni strode forward to help me, her face was filled with guilt.

"Don't you dare touch me," I warned her to stay back, showing her my stern hand. I was hurt. My own *abuela* betrayed me. "You knew about Shadowland all along. You knew my mother was murdered, and still, you lied to me?"

"I can explain, *mija.* Please listen to me." She stepped forward, but I stepped back.

"You stopped Kayden from going to the cops. You stopped Bill from telling the truth about Mom's outburst." I was connecting the dots. "Was it you who tried to kill her?" I asked in horror.

"ELOISE," Mayor scowled at me. "She's your *abuela.* Julia was her daughter before she was your mother."

"Were you part of her plan too?" I asked him, tears rolling down my eyes. "That's why she is here, in the veil, trapped in her office. Did you both trap her?"

They all were taken aback. Nobody answered, why would they? Their truth was out, they had nothing to hide.

"What else would explain why you stopped Kayden from telling the truth? What else would you ground him for, take his car keys so he couldn't tell anyone what you two are up to?" I remember Kayden being sad because his dad wasn't listening to him.

Everything fits in. Why was Kayden outside my house? Why was he keeping an eye on me?

He was guilty, not because he cared.

He thought his father might be the murderer, and still, he chose to hide the truth. FUCK!

All the hope I had in my heart was now drained from my body. There was nothing left except emptiness.

My hand reached up to my heart as if stopping the ache, but it was harsh. It was getting hard to breathe.

"They all are traitors, love, come to me, open this gateway, and then we'll both leave this city and start a new life of our own," Mom spoke from behind.

"You really think I would let them away with it?" I turned to Mom sharply. "They tried to kill you. *I'll burn this whole town with you all,"* I growled at Noni, mostly. She flinched, and so did others.

"She is not Julia, *mija,* Julia is dead, and she is playing with your emotions," Noni muttered.

"Of course, you would say that because you wanted her dead," I snapped.

"She was my daughter, my only living daughter. Why would I want her dead?" Noni stepped towards me angrily. "She was born out of my womb. No mother in this world can kill her child once she holds her in her hand," Noni was growling at me. "Julia was my lifeline, and I would do anything to punish who did this to her. And I am searching for it, getting in it deep. But at the same time, I had to safeguard Kayden from not getting in it these people's hands. This is not what you children think. It's a mutiny, a move against your mother, against Hectors." She was going on, but I don't trust her anymore.

"And the car, we had to hide it away so that no one could find it was Kayden in his car. We have to protect you both from the danger of this world, you both are just kids, and we felt the disturbance in the vibes, it was much bigger than we thought, and now I realise what it was," she turned to look at Clara. "It was a void," her eyes narrowed as Clara whimpered. Mayor's hands tightened around her.

"Let's get done with this, Lizzy," Mom was getting impatient. "She's not to be trusted."

"Don't listen to her. She's manipulating you," Hannah walked forward, extending her hand for me to hold, but I kept glaring at her hand before raising my eyes to look at her face.

"You knew it too?" I asked her, and she looked at Noni and then at me. "You were teaching me about the herbs and Robin's training," I took out the Cosmic blade, not missing their knowing glances towards the weapon and back to me. "You both knew and still lied to my face."

Robin's eyes darted from Noni to Mayor as his jaw became taut.

"We never lied to you. We were teaching you everything, Lizzy, everything we could. Do you think, every girl is trained like you? No—you have gone through basic to advance to additional skill training at the age of sixteen, and we were now working on your specialised skills, *fourth-level* training, but we couldn't come clean because of your mom. She couldn't be part of this, and you…you were too young to understand."

"So, we were working on you, to shape you. Why do you think you could survive all this?" She pointed at my black tar drenched clothes—the blood of the shadowfiend, "You have been taught to be a Shadow Walker since childhood. You think it's normal for all the girls to have such strength that they kill shadow monsters on the first attempt?" I looked towards Clara. Of course not. While Clara was afraid, my whole focus was on survival.

"Not just monsters, she killed a demon too." It was Clara who spoke from behind her dad. She had a broad smile on her face, which soon faded as Mayor shot her a furious glare.

"Which demon?" Blood drained from Noni's face.

"*Thamex*," I blurted, and she sucked a deep breath, was she upset I killed a demon?

"That's why she's here. The gatekeeper is gone." Mayor glanced at Noni cocking his head towards veil, his hands balled up into fists, angry and scared.

"He was holding them in Demon's Den, so she had to," Kayden spoke, ignoring his father, holding his ground next to me with determination on his face. He had always stuck up for what was right and charmed everyone into believing him too.

"You were in Demon's Den?" Mayor turned to Clara, turning white as a ghost. "That's why we couldn't track them," he gulped down, scrutinising Clara, turning to me, his eyes filled with mixed emotions. "You went to Demon's Den to save them?"

"She impaled the Den to get them out," Kayden smirked, his chest swelled with pride as I felt his sidearm, but I didn't believe in him, not anymore.

"You killed *Thamex*, Lizzy?" Jason's eyes went wide. "You took a demon in your first attempt?" He made it sound like it was a damn big deal.

"See, you're taught to be a survivalist. You were trained to fight this, to overcome any circumstances. All the training that we have been given at the age of eighteen was given to you since you were a kid. That's how you easily took a demon with tentacles." Hannah seemed delighted by the news.

"Every Shadow Walker shows the signs when they are mature enough to understand all this, to hold the responsibility of being a Shadow Walker. They generally get chakra at the age of eighteen, but you were too young. We were waiting for you to get to the age. We were waiting for your eighteenth birthday, they start their basic training at eighteen, and here you are—seventeen, already on the fourth level out of five."

Eighteen? But I've been shifting since I was four years old.

"Yes, exactly, you were just *four*," Hannah raised her eyebrows as if we were thinking on the same wavelength. "You came as a shock to us as much as you are surprised right now. We didn't know what to do. She didn't know how to help. You were too small," Hannah pointed at Noni. "We tried our best to train you, but believe me, your powers were too hard to fathom. You were too early for your age, and your powers were primal. *You used to shift to Shadowland, whereas we all take portals, you just shift without portals.* Only *Cosmics* can do that. But you were born out of a human womb, you aren't a *Cosmic*, and still, you hold primal powers. It took us a lifetime to fathom that you weren't getting invisible but shifting to *Shadowland*." She pointed at the veil inside the glass box.

"So, Mathew created this portal for you—as you used to shift anytime, we didn't know how to help you. What blew us off was that you never saw any monsters, nor could they see you, it was so difficult for us to gather how to put things together for you, what to tell you when you couldn't even see them. You were harmless, Eloise. Even in *Shadowland*, you were innocuous by their advances. It was like you were shifting there in *Astral Plane*, where they couldn't feel you nor could you, but still, we trained you for this day."

It was too much to grasp. I was different from them, too much glitched. They needed portals. Even the Shadow Walkers in that memory travelled through a portal, they all created one, but I never needed any. And she was right. I hadn't seen any monsters before today. They couldn't attack me, but she got it wrong.

"It's not an astral plane, but being a part demonic hide me from shadows. They think I am like them, so they never attacked me." I mused what Mom had told me.

Noni looked astonished, and so did Hannah.

This is all so twisted.

"Fuck, I didn't know what you guys were up to. I was at Mansion when we got a call from headquarters that a portal had been created at Murkwood. Valerie gets notified whenever a portal is created using a moonstone ring. You see, we are all connected through this *Chakra*," he turned around and lifted his hair to show me the nape of his neck, and slowly I watched a chakra getting revealed. The sigil of Shadow Walkers was embedded on the nape of his neck, and the fucking snake was moving as if it was alive. Holy Shit!

"She told me that a portal was being created, and thank god it was at our house, so Dad covered you guys. I looked for you both. Your washroom was all trashed. I thought someone attacked," Kayden looked confused, but I bit my lips. I trashed his washroom. "But we couldn't find the portal anywhere, only shattered mirror..." he explained, but my mind was on Chakra.

I had seen in that memory that Leticia pressed that chakra when things went down. She told all the Shadow Warriors to go away as they pushed their chakra as if calling someone. Not someone but Valerie. Who was this Valerie I was middle named after?

"I can't see it," Kayden interrupted Jason.

"Because you are not a Shadow Walker, brother, only Shadow Walkers can see it," Jason turned back.

"But I have sight, I can see shadows," Kayden persisted, his fists tightly clenched.

"Because you're a Shadow Walker kin, we all get sight but only a few get chakra passed on," Jason eyes held pity which made Kayden grind his molars.

"Do I have a chakra?" My voice was barely audible. I rubbed my neck.

"Since you were four years old, no one in the history of Shadow Walkers has shown signs so early," Hannah nodded. "And your mother made it so much more challenging. All she wanted was to hide away from the world. She was obsessed with hiding you. We couldn't help it."

"Because she had no clue what I was, what you are," I growled. "But you all knew I was a Shadow Walker. You still didn't offer any help. I was crying, tormenting myself, thinking my friends were stuck in Shadowland and nobody would understand me. What was I asking for? Just a little help, just an explanation, but no, none of you thought it would be great to pass on a little knowledge about my family history, about me. Don't tell me I am young because I could have been told what was happening to me. I could have at least been guided…was it too much to ask?" I was shattered, betrayed by my own people.

"We were trying to protect you," Noni whispered.

"Now, did you?" I snapped. The vein in my neck throbs, and my hands balled into fist. "*I saved you.* I am the one who protected you from *Yamendo* by shifting back in time. I saved Clara by stopping her from handling the *Wandering Star.* I saved Kayden from that shadow monster who was sucking his soul out, and you think you can protect *me*?" I laughed with arrogance, I must look like a maniac to them, but that's what I felt like. Chills spread through the room, and I could feel everyone getting cold. "Now, tell me, Noni, who is protecting all this? Is it you or me?"

She gave me a grievous look as shock washed over her face. Everyone in the room looked at each other.

"No, this isn't possible," Noni mumbled, shaking her head, her jaw reverberating.

"Oh really, you want me to tell you about your birth, about your parents, Paloma and Miguel, how he asked for a child from *Yamendo.* How Maurice made Lara a shapeshifter for the ritual that could provide you all these powers you have, how Leticia gave her life saving you because she thought you'll be the bringer of *Hara.*" I crossed my arms over my midsection like a badass, as elders looked like they had no blood left in their bodies. They knew this story. They had been brought up listening to this, but I'd seen it with my own eyes. I knew much more details that they did.

And by their expressions, I could say they believed me. They all seemed as if the floor beneath them had turned into sand, and they'll slip any second. "So, let me ask you, are you sure you were able to protect me? Because last time I saw Leticia gave this *Wandering Star* to *me,* while you were just a baby whom she shoved down in my arms, asking *me* to protect." A smirk rose on my face, feeling invincible.

"You can travel back in time?" Jason asked, gaping at me. I could feel everyone's stares, and for a change, it didn't creep me out. Even Robin had turned white.

"I can *shift* into memories," I told him, extending my smirk. "Anyone's memories and *alter them.*" It was a threat, and they all knew it because their eyes narrowed, and my smirk turned to a grin. They were scared of me, good.

I like this feeling—being someone they were afraid of.

Noni was speechless. Her legs wobbled beneath her as Hannah held her.

"Dad, Jason, you knew about all this? And still, you didn't help Lizzy to save us?" Clara snapped. "Don't even dare give me eighteen-year-old crap because Kayden and I turned eighteen last month. You didn't tell us anything."

"It's complicated. Moreover, we couldn't even think she took humans with her to the *Shadowland.* Humans can't survive there," Mayor spoke in horror, cocking his head at me.

"I. Didn't. Take. Them." I stressed the words through my clenched teeth, on the verge of exploding, ready to tear him into ribbons.

"Of course, how could she when she couldn't even visit *Shadowland* of her own will," Robin spoke for the first time. "Her shifts are not in her control. She always gets sucked in and can never take anything with her. Clara must have taken them through the void. The disturbance you felt was a void, and it was soon gone because it closed once they all were trapped," he turned to Jason, who now looked ashamed.

"No, Clara's mind was shielded. Her blood was warded." Mayor became protective as he tried to shield Clara.

"It ruptured," Clara confessed in a small voice as she told him about what happened when Kayden drowned, blood drained from his face.

I felt a glint in Robin's eyes. Even though he betrayed me, but I still have loads of respect for him because I know him to the core. He was my mentor, he'd stand with the right.

"Why didn't you tell me?" Mayor moaned, rubbing his forehead.

"I didn't know whom to tell. You never told us anything, Dad. You even lied about Mom being dead even when she's alive," Clara gave him an appalling look as he glared at Kayden for being a tattletale, but he held his ground.

"Don't look at Kayden like that," she hissed. "Everything here is happening because I thought Mom was dead and only something supernatural could bring her back."

Jason cursed under his breath. "I told you not to lie to them," he fumed at his father, who just narrowed his eyes.

"You all chose to make a fool out of us, and don't say you were trying to protect us because it didn't go well, has it?" She eyed them angrily. "A little leap of faith would have helped us. We would have come to you for guidance instead of finding answers to our life on our own."

She left Mayor speechless. Good.

"So, now you all know my powers, I can walk back in memories. If you don't tell me, I'll find the truth on my own, so it's better for you to speak now. What happened to my mother? Who trapped her in there?" I pointed at the veil.

"Eloise, she's not your mother," Jason raised his hands in peace. "See, we Shadow Walkers have a league called *Umbra-Mae.* He is our Shadow Master, a king of all Shadow Walkers. We all are born out of him and *Livana*. After we get the chakra, we report to him and swore ourselves to the throne. To protect humankind from all the shadows and demons," his eyes darted to Noni as he added. "Those who are harmful to them, using this moonstone," he flashed his ring. "They train us, let us use the facilities and highest-level equipment, and promote our powers. But *Umbra Mae* is a bit crossed with your mother because she broke her vows and ran away from headquarters."

"We all thought Umbra-Mae infiltrated Murkwood, that they were after her accident as we felt a disturbance in the atmosphere. But I think it wasn't them. A void got created the day your mother died, which sucked you all in. We were wrong to stop you, to hide the truth about you, but we didn't know things could go down so badly. We didn't know you could suddenly start seeing monsters." His eyes fluctuated from me to his brother and then back to me.

"Moreover, it was your mother's choice to hide you from all this. It was Julia's decision not to let Kayden intervene in the accident. She knew something that we didn't. And I promise you. I'll help you find who did this to your mother but trust me, she isn't your mother." His gaze followed from the veil to Kayden, his eyes full of sorrow for his wrong decisions.

There was a fucking league of Shadow Walkers? How many are there? I remembered a few from my trance. They all went to Umbra-Mae using a portal, even J.P.P. mentioned him.

"If there was a league, why wasn't I sent to train, why was I chained to the vaults for having powers that you all had?" I asked, my voice void of all emotions.

"Because Julia wasn't in her right mind. As a punishment for running away from the headquarters, they suppressed her chakra and memories, making her schizophrenic." Noni's eyes filled with rage.

"And you couldn't have controlled her? Stopped her from torturing me?" I asked, arching my eyebrows. She's a demon. She had powers.

"I did," her eyes flashed at me.

"After she chained me—multiple times—without food and water," I growled in pain, Kayden's hand reached out to snake my waist, and I let him because right now, I wasn't feeling anything.

"I am sorry, but we couldn't tell you about Umbra-Mae. We couldn't send you there. Julia might have died, she loved you too much." Noni's eyes glistened in pain.

"And you let me suffer because she *might* have died?" I asked, scoffing. I didn't know how a person could break so many times. My Mom always told me I was a glitch, like I wasn't supposed to be even born. I was tired of being a side character which people could crush anytime according to their needs. I was tired of hiding, scared of whether they would accept or kill me. *Now, I will not. Now I will become someone they're scared of.*

"They never loved you. None of them ever felt anything about you. You're just a pawn in their game. They are part of Umbra-Mae, who tried to kill me." Mom spoke from behind as horror washed over my body.

Fuck! What the hell was happening?

"You, Robin and Hannah, are you part of this league too?" I asked in horror.

"No, we are not. We left them long ago," Robin asserted. "We didn't kill Julia."

I didn't know what to believe or not, but I couldn't find anything inside me to trust them.

One lie is enough to question all truths—I read it once, and today, it struck me.

Noni saw it through me because the next second, the pouch hovered away from my pocket. It was in the air, Noni was doing it. I pounced at it—the Orb rolled down, emitting purple light in the room.

Kayden ducked down to pick it up, but instead, Nathan roared loudly and leapt on him.

Kayden rolled over, and the Orb fell off his hand. I lunged towards it, blocking Hannah, who pounced back as I retrieved it. Jason was now locking up Nathan, who was roaring over the top. He opened a flask from his neck chain and popped a few drops of what seemed like water in Nathan's mouth, and as soon as the water touched Nathan's tongue, his eyes flashed open, followed by a whimper and then sank to the ground. It must have been the moonwater. They know how to tackle shadows so well. I felt left out—an outcast.

I was crushing the star in my hand when I felt warmth.

'*Hey, beautiful, it's been a long time,*' I heard the whispers coming out of the *Wandering Star.*

Chapter 37

Beyond the Veil

I was stupefied as the star spoke to me, feeling a surge of energy by holding it in my bare hands. Its mystical purple smoke was breathtaking.

"What are you?" I asked it. As silence fell in the room, it was just the *Wandering Star* and me.

'*Why don't you open me and check yourself,*' it purred at me like a lover.

"Open you. How?" I asked. I felt a tingling sensation in my body as it laughed, *a warm-cold laugh.*

"Eloise, no," Hannah stepped forward, but Noni stopped her. "It's speaking to her. Her eyes have gone violet." She gulped down. "Leticia gave her that *Wandering Star* for a reason."

Their words were far from my ears. Only the sensation of the Star was what I could hear.

'*You need me, accept it. You want me in your body and crave me every single night. You like the feel of me inside you.*' A shadow tentacle caressed my spine. I arched in response. '*See, you want me, and you know what I am.*'

Power! It was the only word that hit my mind. It would give me energy.

"Lizzy, you need to bring this to me," Mom's sharp words brought me out of my trance, out of my craving for *the Wandering Star*. It was like I swam back to the surface. I turned around to look at my mother, but Mayor caught me. I hid the Star inside the jacket before his hand could yank it, but now, I was in his grip.

"Don't make me do this," I told him. "Leave me alone," I struggled in his grip, he was strongly built.

"Argh!" Mom shouted as I stirred against him. "Help me, Lizzy."

I was frightened so was he. I saw her burning inside the mirror. "This portal is closing. It'll kill me, honey." She was crying in pain.

"Don't listen to her. She's in your mind," Mayor said sternly, but I ignored him. He wasn't trustworthy. "Hannah, bring poppy-root," he ordered my caretaker, who immediately nodded and sprang upstairs. *No, I know poppy-root is used to sedate, but they cannot do that. I need to save my mother.*

"Get your hands off her, dad," Kayden spoke in a low grumble. Even I felt his cold rage down my spine. He was powerful. I could feel his strength rippling through his body as shadows danced behind his hazel eyes. I remember this look from the night he found me with Colton.

"Kayden, you don't know the immensity of the situation," Mayor growled at him. "You both have already created a huge chaos."

"I don't care." He snarled coldly. It was as cold as ice as he took a step towards us. "You don't get to touch her." His eyes, filled with wrath, bore darkly into his father's eyes. I felt Mayor shrugging behind me. It was a little shrug, but he did, and perhaps that's what Noni felt as she stepped forward for me, and before she could touch me, Kayden jerked his head to glare at her, and she halted.

Just like that, Noni, the cursed child, the shadow demon, went immobile under his glare. Slowly, she bowed her head at him like he was controlling her.

Kayden tamed Noni, FUCK!

"Kayden, stop this." Jason stepped forward, his hands up in the air as if trying for peace out. "We'll not harm her, I promise you. Eloise is safe with us." His throat was bobbing. He was scared of Kayden, even knowing he wasn't a Shadow Walker. Then what was Kayden? What did I make him into?

My knees buckled under me, not by pain but by the loud shrieks blinding me. I tried to cover my ears, but Mayor didn't let me. Those screams were making me go crazy. I was whimpering. "I can't listen to her screams," I cried, pushing Mayor, but he didn't budge. "Let me go, let me save my mom. Please."

"She is not screaming," Kayden held my face, his hands warm, and his voice went soft. "She is not even your mom. She's taking up your mind too, as she did with Clara," his eyes were reflecting pain. "She is just your imagination. Look at me, Eloise," he whispered my name in desperation. I looked into his eyes. "*Trust me, everything is an illusion. Just me, just us, this is only real.*" He had said those words when *Thamex* was trying to lure me. Was Kayden right?

That's when Mayor's grip tightened, and I screamed in pain, and with that, Kayden growled at his father angrily. I felt the floor rumble beneath me.

My scream was cut short due to the quivering of the earth underneath me.

Kayden made it rumble with his powers, my mansion roared under his dominance, and it wasn't the first time he had done it. I remember when Colton called me a slut, the ground had rumbled. It was Kayden, of course, it was Kayden. He doesn't like when someone touches me, and his displeasure was clearly visible. His urge to protect me was rippling off his body.

I know what Kayden is—*He is being of becoming. He is my catalyst, my mate, my twin flame—FUCK!*

He was here just for me. I created him to be mine—I think I forgot how to breathe.

He made his father go still, but Jason pulled his brother into his arms, which may feel like an embrace, but he was trying to restrain him. I felt Mayor's grip getting lose.

I kicked Mayor in the foot, he stumbled as his grip loosened, and I rammed my elbow into his gut. He bent forward as I flipped back, jamming my foot on the back of his knees as he fell on his knees with a thud. My hands around his grey-brown hair, pulling his head back, my knife on his throat.

Everyone was taken aback, but little did they know about me. Robin had taught me enough self-defence to tackle this kind of grip.

"If anyone tries to stop me, I'll slit his throat," I warned everyone, tired of the drama. *I am not going to hide anymore. I'll be who I am.*

"Elmo!" Homer gasped. "*Mija!*" Noni fumbled. "Sweety," Hannah choked. "Lizzy," Clara heaved. Jason's eyes widened as he inhaled loudly, leaving Kayden, who was now smiling.

To my horror, Mayor chuckled. I pulled him hard through his hair, and he flinched. "Robin, you did a wonderful job with this little girl. She'd be our youngest warrior."

"Definitely," Jason whispered, a wicked smile spreading his face as he turned to Robin.

Robin's face glimmered with gratification and a hint of satisfaction, a proud moment for my mentor.

There was a second when everyone's eye flicked towards Robin, and I grasped the opportunity, pushing Mayor away, I lunged at the glass box. And before they could even realise what I had done, I was already near the glass box with the star in my hand.

"*Si ingerii au demonii lor—even angels have their demons,*" I whispered as I placed my hands on the glass, it was Leticia's motto, and it worked. The glass shattered into thousands of pieces, blasting. It was a powerful jolt of energy that made me blind, I shielded my face with my free hand from the shattered pieces of glass. I felt them piercing me, but I didn't care.

And instantly, the baroque angels and weird symbols lit up. The carvings around it started emitting red light, brightening up high, filling the room with the blinding beam.

"NO," Kayden growled as he tried to tug me down, but I climbed inside the veil to save Mom.

I looked behind, watching Kayden trying to get inside, his hand holding mine. He was halfway through the portal when I tried to jerk his hand off, to push him back, but as soon as he realised what I was about to do, he pushed me through, coming with me inside the veil.

And with that, I closed it like closing a door with both hands. I closed the portal, blocking them from coming after me, my chest heaving heavily as I turned to search around the room for Mom, but all I found was mist, ashes, and coldness. I was standing in the damp library like an idiot.

"You shouldn't have come after me. Just leave me alone, Kayden," I closed my eyes, heaving with rage. "You think you'll just hide something like that from me, and I won't say anything. I trusted you with my life, and that's what you give me in return," I sighed. "You all broke my trust, and you broke my heart as you promised." I felt a sharp pain inside my chest. "If you think I'm going to believe in this twin flames crap, then just cut a slack, I love Homer, and I've always loved him. No matter what but he never betrayed me or lied. He had always been true to me, his true self." I sucked a deep breath, "So, you should stay away from me, just get out of my life. I don't want you." It was a lie, but I was angry.

It was when I heard a faint cry. I opened my eyes to look at him. He was lying on the ground, whimpering in pain, he was wrapped in vines, and two vines were deep inside his temples, like electrocuting him.

"Kayden," I gasped, his eyes gone white, with no pupils. He looked scary. I sat beside him, trying to detach the vines, but they were strong. I cut them out with the blade and pulled them out from his head. It was like taking out a blood-drenched tampon.

"ARGH!" he screamed in pain. I whimpered with him like I felt his pain.

"I am so sorry, who did this?" I caressed him as the vines were out. He was still trembling. "Calm down. I am here for you now. Fuck, you shouldn't have come after me," I scolded him. My hands shook, pressing his temples with my palms, trying to stop blood from oozing out. I know whatever he did, he did because his father told him to do so. Though it was wrong of him to hide the truth about my mother's accident, still, he didn't deserve *this.*

I kept pressing his temples until his pupils were back, his wounds were healing, and my eyes widened at the realisation—*ok, I didn't need to kiss someone to heal. I could heal them just by my touch.* But suddenly, Kayden pushed me aside, bending on his four and retched all the dark black stuff out from his mouth. I rubbed his back while he barfed out all the darkness, hitting his chest with a fist. I kept rubbing his back, his shoulders to ease him, but he turned to me. "You couldn't have seen her without me," Kayden's eyes widened. He was terrified.

"Her?" I asked, not getting him, but he looked behind me, pale face. "Shift, now," he ordered.

"What?" I asked. *Why was he telling me to shift?*

"It's a trap, Eloise," he cried, pointing at my back.

"You, stupid girl," a voice came from behind. It was a snarl. I could hear the terror behind the angry voice. I quickly turned around, looking at Mom, her hands folded over her midsection.

I was right. She was Mom.

"Oh, you are alive. Thank God you survived," I leapt towards her, looking for some burnt spots but finding none.

I gasped as I felt a piercing pain around my stomach. To my horror, her nails dug deep inside my stomach. "*MOM,*" I wanted to say, but just air came out.

"You closed the portal, you stupid cow. How will I get out now?" She twisted her nail making me shriek, before pushing me back as I fell to the ground. Blood oozed out of my middle while she stood watching me whimpering in pain.

"You are not my mom," I huffed. It wasn't a question. It was a feeling of betrayal, feeling of being so self-absorbed stubborn pig-headed girl, feeling of not trusting my friends, feeling of not trusting my people, just trusting—my instincts, feelings, and love for my mom.

"Of course not," she then raised her hand in the air, and with it, some force was lifting me. She was telekinetic. She was moving me according to her will. I was beyond scared now, and before I could wrap my mind around what she was doing, she threw me towards the rack of books, making me scream hard. I probably broke a rib or two.

"Fuck! Who are you?" I asked, trying hard to get up and again felt her powers lifting, pushing me, dragging me along the floor. "NO," I screamed in pain.

She lifted me, making me hover mid-air.

"I am the Queen of Shadowland," she growled at me, before thrashing me aside.

Chapter 38

The Forsaken

I saw stars, the corner of my vision went blank. I blinked and blinked again, clearing my head, pushing away the piercing pain, creating a shield as I pushed myself off the ground. *Yamendo*, it was *Yamendo*, not my mother. Clara was right, everyone was right, she was the *Forsaken.*

I could see her clearly now. She was this horned lady with a long face and pale white skin, as white as ashes, her eyes were piercing scarlet, and a long line of blood was coming out of her eye like she was bleeding from her eyes. A red downward arrow was drawn on her throat with black ink wrapped with chains and extended to her shoulders. It was a weird tattoo. She was tall, skinny, with huge busts visible through the blue and red coloured deep neck off-shoulder gown. The neck of the dress went down to the navel, and her navel had a tattoo around it, where snakes circled it. Her nails were bigger than Clara's. Her shoulders had three spikes, each of which seemed like an animal's teeth. She wore a black stocking with a black garter. Her legs were visible from between the slits of her gown. She had silver metal wristbands, and her horns were scaled and golden, highlighting her long raven hair.

The shield I created was as weak as me, it vanished within a second, making her laugh, a spine-chilling noise that made me shiver to the core. Her eyes drifted from my face to my hand. I followed her gaze and saw the *Wandering Star* shining back at me.

But before I could shield it, she raised it in the air. I tried to grab it, but she was making it hover beyond my reach. "Finally, I will be free, all because of stupid girls and their blinding love towards their mothers," looking at me pitilessly, slit-pupil eyes.

I took a deep breath and tried casting a shield around the star, breaking her connection as it fell into my hands.

She growled in anger. I felt her powers like a storm wave hitting me, thrashing me back, but I hugged the star to my chest, gripping it tight.

"You have irked me for long enough. I tolerated all your stupid drama," she rolled her eyes. "I have waited centuries for this star. Now give it to me," she demanded, throwing me on the opposite wall, the star fell on the floor, but it didn't break.

I swiftly cast a shield around it. I would not let her have it. She tricked me into getting this star. But I won't let her have it until I was alive.

"Your feeble powers are no match to me, stupid child," she snorted as my shield whooshed again. I leapt towards the star, sending out a new shield, and with one hand, I tried to shoot green sparks in her direction with the help of my chatoyant, but nothing came out. I was determined and kept spinning it in my hand, but no green beam pulsing, it seemed dead.

"Oh, poor baby, not even taught to use the charms, not harnessed properly." She scoffed, sending a red spark, but I swiftly swayed my hand and built a shield, protecting myself. "Feisty! I like feisty girls, but now the game is over. You finally fell into my trap. You chose the wrong person to trust," she laughed. "Now, give it to me."

"You are quite wrong," I snapped at her. I was planning on destroying the star, but she looked at me. She somehow knew what I was thinking.

She was taken aback, her scarlet eyes narrowed over the top of the shield. "After such brutality, you think?" She narrowed her eyes. "Don't even kid yourself. Nobody can destroy this *Wandering Star*. It's a Cosmic vessel."

I looked down at myself. I was bruised now, drenched in blood, my stomach wound was healing, but I had lost a lot of blood. I closed my eyes—I needed a plan right now, urgently. I took a shaky breath, trying to focus and remain calm. *If I can't destroy the star, I've to ensure she can't have it.*

One—I could shift and take it back with me, but Kayden would be trapped here, and I didn't think she'll let him go. Even the thought of leaving him at *Yamendo's* mercy was excruciating. This wasn't even an option. *I cannot leave him.* I could never leave him. *He is mine. Just mine.*

The second option was to send the star away. I had to create a portal using the ring and send Kayden and the star away, separately.

I opened my eyes and found big scarlet eyes buried in mine, examining me, making me jump in terror. My heart stopped. I couldn't think of anything to distract her, to send this star back.

The red-roaring horned beast growled at me. "You will die." With a swift movement, she held me by my neck, smashing my head on the wall so hard that I heard something split.

My heart stopped, and my vision went black at the excruciating pain in my head. There was a ringing in my ear, and I could feel tears burning my cheeks, choking me on my last breath. I slid down on my back as she roared, sending smoke with a toxic smell throughout the room. I felt something hot dripping on my neck.

"NO," Kayden growled somewhere. I felt him whimper in pain as my eyes found him. He was already looking into mine, his face white as a ghost, as he fell to his knees, and soon, he held something from his hand, like a black cloak, and then he pulled it with a growl of pain and despair.

And to my horror—*Yamendo* stumbled back.

Kayden pulled Yamendo back with his bare hands!

I wasn't the only one who was in shock. Even she was startled. She turned to look at him, her eyes as wide as mine.

"How are you even alive? I killed you." Her voice went sharp, ignited with fury and astonishment. "*Bylze* took your soul away. How did you survive?"

I thought Kayden would look at me, but he didn't. His gaze didn't falter from her face.

"You were resurrected," she mused, her eyes widened at the realisation sending chills down my spine. *Resurrected?*

He did die that day. Clara was right, he died, and I resurrected him. My healing powers brought him back. The kiss, the CPR, it was the resurrection—*the Catalyst.*

FUCK!

"You were claimed. I didn't know you were already bonded when I tried to kill you," she laughed in amazement as she turned to look at me. "You resurrected him as your Catalyst. You gave him powers just to bring him back, couldn't let him go, could you?" she said through her clenched teeth. "Out of all the people in the world, you had to choose *him*. Always been a kibitzer." Her expression darkened. She didn't like that I resurrected Kayden, I could feel her chest heaving with rage, ready to attack.

Before I could shield myself, Kayden again pulled her back, but this time she didn't budge, roaring with laughter. "You might control my demons, but not me, not yet."

She breathed a cloud of black smoke towards him, forcing him to the wall. I heard him grunting and felt a sharp pain in my heart. He was hurt. Even though I couldn't see him, I could feel him inside my chest. Tears rolled down my cheeks, with hot blood from my skull.

I wanted to call out to him but couldn't find my voice. *'Please, please, be alright, please stay with me.'* I wanted to convey this message to him, but I was startled.

"You deserve this, all of this," she snarled between the smoke. "Wrecking my plan of conquering all the realms. I want my powers. I have waited for my powers for so long, it's time to take back what's mine." Her starved eyes were ready to drink the *Wandering Star*. She never touched it, just glared with an insatiable hunger.

"You killed my mom for this?" I panted, finding my voice in the piercing pain.

"Stupid girl, your mother wasn't a Shadow Walker. She *chose* to be mundane," *Yamendo* slithered closer. "I just took advantage of the news to allure you here, to bring me the star, to gain your trust by feeding on your friends' memories. You see, everyone who travels in *Shadowland* doesn't have a will. Their minds are my mind, their memories are my memories, *I spy on their dreams and thrive on their nightmares.*" She laughed maniacally.

"You set yourself in Clara's nightmares to lure me here?" I asked through pain, blocking the ringing sound. "You used her to get to me?

"Oh no! You were just a cherry topping on the icing," her eyes lit up. "I used Clara to get the *Wandering Star,* but you, my dear, were the new light I didn't even know about till I caught your friends. Clara's memories were so full of your shifts and that made me curious—how come a girl, a mere seventeen-year-old, visits my land without my knowledge? You came to me as a shock. Your existence was like a bolt out of the blue. That's why I kept your friends alive. I wanted to know more about you. I wanted to lure you back because that's what all good souls do, *stupid souls.* They choose others over themselves," she spits on the ground, so un-queen-like.

I was unknown to Yamendo like she was unknown to me—my glitch saved me and protected me from her all these years.

"Even you didn't know of my presence, never felt it, but look what this catalyst can do, he doesn't just provide you the sight, he puts you in the limelight," she chuckles, as my eyes flicked to Kayden, who was now lying on the floor, with multiple slits, drenched in blood. "*Being of becoming,*" she spit again.

Fresh tears rolled out of my eyes as I saw him. I wanted to call him when his gaze met mine. It felt like he was telling me. *'I'll stay with you.'*

"Fools, you all are fools, running after love and affection when power is everything. See, just a little power to a tormented human gave him so much boost," enunciating about Nathan.

'You're not the monster, you're the one these monsters fear. You'll become that, right?'

Kayden's words were ringing in my ears, filling me with confidence, it gave me a spark, and I took a deep breath.

"At least he would stay human without those powers," I tried to chuckle, but my throat hurt. "If it was up to you, he would be trapped in some dark realm, waiting pathetically for someone to bring him Star. He, too, would be begging me, falling on a so-called seventeen-year-old girl's feet, to return his powers. What a wuss!" I tried to laugh but coughed out blood.

She gave me a dark glare as if sizing me up.

"You're nothing without this *Wandering Star,*" I mocked her. "You can't even open it yourself. Only a Shadow Walker can open it. You need us to open this for you," I showed her my pitiful face. "Tsk, tsk, tsk, so weak."

She smashed my head again, I heard Kayden roar my name, but the pain was blinding me. Blood oozed out of my mouth as I coughed it out more, I knew I was going to die today, so I was just satisfying my ego by putting up a great fight.

"I am weak?" she laughed. "Maybe at one point, I was, you know, because of love, because I fell in love with that powerless Maverick, who was so busy in his voyages that he forgot I was there waiting for him. He was so busy being *Syntrell's* favorite brother that he forgot his own children were waiting for him. Maverick created this world full of light, but when he left, his light was gone. And only demons and monsters flourish in the darkness. He should have known this before taking away his light. I taught my children to stand alone and gave them all the necessary powers to survive."

"When he came back, he realised I had an empire running without him, a place where he had no value, where nobody thinks of him as a God anymore. Jealousy surmounted him, but my children are loyal. They shoved him behind bars, and I couldn't tell how much I enjoyed torturing him through the illusionary prison. He couldn't have gotten out in a million years if the bloody moon—*Livana* wouldn't have interfered. I was even entrusted with the *Shira, the Cosmic Poleblade,* to kill Maverick, but *Livana* ambushed me, created havoc, killed my children, stripped me of my powers and captured them in this *Wandering Star.*"

"So, I had to use *Shira* on her instead, killing her to the ground. Even as the fallen Cosmic, she broke the *Shira*, and I had nothing left to kill Maverick. Livana gave her life for him, and that impotent didn't even bore the responsibility of holding this star. I knew he would definitely give it to someone in the human realm. Being nomadic, he would never risk his life with this. It took me years to track down this star," she smiled.

"Can you believe my luck?" She was excited. "I didn't have to do anything except take advantage of a weak little girl." She let out a small laugh. "I planted myself in her open mind, gaining excess to her Shadow

Walker blood that had portal powers and being so emotionally weak, she accepted me, to fill her emptiness," she was talking about Clara. "And when the magical wall around the vault in her mind ruptured, I sensed it. It was weak, but it was an opportunity I couldn't miss. I used the void that got created near the cave. All I did was, use my powers to prolong it long enough to kidnap Clara through it. I planted the idea in her mind to get through the cave."

I was trying to grasp all the information. It was Clara's idea to take the shortcut.

Tears were swooping down my eyes. I couldn't keep my eyes open. The pain was blinding me. I lay on the floor, curled around the star, feeling nothing but pain in each part of my body. I couldn't make it. I knew I'd drift off soon. *But till my last breath, I'll protect the star.*

"And she brought me *you*, unharnessed, powerful, but raw," she smirked. "Only this star is trapping me in here, and now I'll get my powers with which I could conquer all the realms, and you'll be my pawn," she asked, flying to me, hovering over my motionless body. "You'll be my bitch, my voyager," she roared a laugh at my face. "We'll show these heirs of the Sun who owns this world."

"Go suck a dick, fucker." I wanted to flip my middle finger at her but had no strength left due to multiple fractures. I was drifting off. My eyes were closing, leaving me empty. I think I was dying. This is it.

I cried as she pierced my cheek with her long-pointed nail. Hot fresh blood oozed out of my cheeks, making me whimper in pain, but there was no energy left in me, not to even scream out of the pain I felt.

Argh! It wasn't even easy to die.

"Stop it, please," Kayden begged. "Take me instead of her, kill me, just leave her alone. You wanted to kill me in the first place. Kill me."

She turned to look at Kayden, and I immediately grabbed the opportunity to create a portal in the air. I raised my hand, but suddenly I felt an earthshattering pressure on my hand.

"Oh, that's what I am doing, killing two birds with one stone," she hissed, standing on my hand, crushing my bones, making my hand immovable. I gasped as I felt bones breaking. She was unbearably heavy. The pain was blinding. I couldn't see anything, just darkness. I'll faint, I'll die because of the agony.

No, you cannot die, you're strong, everyone had invested so much time in you, you're strong, you'll save Kayden, you'll save the star, you need to botch-up her plans to reign all the realms—I told myself.

You're not weak.

You're not weak.

I kept repeating.

"Open this now," she ordered. "Open this star and let me embrace myself with my powers."

"I'll kill you," I wanted to say, but just air came out as I opened my eyes. *I need to thwart Forsaken's plan. I'll not die not until I complete my job.*

"Eloise, NO," Kayden begged when my eyes fell on him. He was trying to fight darkness, the cloud of smoke and mist surrounded him, and every part of his body was bleeding, slashed. His eyes were full of pain. Tears rolled down my eyes as she was breaking him. My heart ached to see him like this. He needs to be saved. He doesn't deserve this. Just because he was guilty that he couldn't save my mother, just because I stupidly created him my catalyst, he shouldn't suffer like this. It was more than he should atone. I have to set him free. I have to send him back. I created him—*he is mine to save.*

"Stop it…stop it, please," I fidgeted. Unable to bear to see him like this. "Fine, I will open this. Just let Kayden out," I whimpered.

"I am not going without you." He was trying to keep his eyes open, his mind still working, but he was tired of fighting her. I could see he'll drift off soon.

She looked at me, then at Kayden. "So weak. Oh boy! See what love did to you,"

Kayden's expression went hard. He didn't like to be called weak, he didn't like not being strong enough to protect me, but he couldn't win here, he shouldn't have even come after me.

'I am sorry,' I wanted to tell him. I didn't want him to suffer like this. He turned to look at me and shook his head, a plea reflected on his face.

"Still asking for *his* life instead of yours?" She turned to me.

"He doesn't have anything to do with all this. You have this star and me. Just let him go," I bargained, ignoring Kayden's plea. "It's a fair deal."

"Fine, open this first," she pushed.

"No, first Kayden will leave," I argued. Suddenly, I felt confident again. *Once Kayden is out, I'll shift.*

But she smirked like she read my mind, and instead, she pierced a hole in my cheek with her nail. I shrieked with pain. She shifted her leg on my palm, breaking the ring I was wearing, and with her pressure, the moonstone shattered into crumbs, crushing my last hope of safeguarding them.

I let out a heart-wrenching scream.

"*Leave. Her. Alone.*" A soft growl from my right fell on my ears.

Chapter 39

The Wandering Star

I snapped open my eyes. Black shapes emerged from a new portal made midair. I gasped for the fresh air as *Yamendo* got distracted, her nail was out from my cheeks, and she was no longer on my hand, but I could no longer feel my hand. Warm blood was dripping like tears from my face.

I picked the star from my right hand and dragged myself away from them, away from *Yamendo*, away from six figures, which I noticed were Noni, Hannah, Robin, Mayor, Jason, and to my astonishment, a slender lady with umber hair—Dr. Dorcas. Was she a Shadow Walker too?

"Shadow Walkers to the rescue," Jason winked at me before hitting *Yamendo* with three jets of green light from his hand. Both father–son wore a band around their hands, emitting green sparks. Robin took out his twin blades in both hands and moved swiftly like a professional, and Hannah wielded a long spear. Dorcas whispered certain words in an ancient language that created a shield around Kayden and me. Words never left her mouth, she reminded me of Leticia.

They all had the moonstone ring except Noni and Hannah. They all were charging at *Yamendo* with their weapons and blocking her charges with the help of the shield they cast. Suddenly, a few *Grovetiles* slithered in, which Hannah and Robin took control of. Hannah stabbed each of them that darted in her way. I saw her move swiftly like a tigress, stabbing a beast and killing him on the spot.

"It's drenched in moonwater," Hannah shouted. "Does anyone want to taste moonwater?" She beckoned more with her hands as a smirk rose her face.

Robin's gaze turned to me, and he roared like a tiger, angry, his eyes filled with pain and guilt.

Yamendo instantly created a shield blocking their constant charges against her. "So, finally, baby, you are home," *Yamendo* crooned in Noni's direction.

Her gaze went from me to *Yamendo*. I found dread there. "I am not your baby." She snarled.

"Whether you agree to it or not, you are my daughter, a daughter I have in the human realm, a daughter instead of getting me out of this hellhole, is helping Shadow Walkers to trap me. What a waste of powers," she dismayed, shaking her head and clicking her tongue. "You were born to lead, conquer the human realm, be my heir, but such a waste of life."

"I would die before walking in your shoes," Noni snapped at her, sending a jet of red lights. *Yamendo* blocked them again.

"Whether you claim it or not, you are born to rule over them. It's your throne," *Yamendo* tried to lead her away. "These people are of no match. You are my child. Get on board, embrace your powers, and invoke what that stupid Star suppressed in you. Use your damn powers, accept what you are—acknowledge your fate."

"I'll choose what I want to be. I won't be bestowed upon your expectations," Noni's jaw tightened so was *Yamendo's*. "I am still living because I chose not to follow you, to accept the living world as it was, to accept human life over demons, be a good person, not—"

"Shut up!" *Yamendo* swung her hand, seeming bored. "Whether you chose human life or not, you will always be my daughter, a daughter I always regret," she snarled.

"I am happy you regret me because now you are going to regret it even more," and with that, Noni sent a red blast from her hand, hitting *Yamendo*, taking her off guard.

She snarled at her, but her expression smoothened within a blink. "Look at my daughter, fighting me, hitting me, using the powers *I provided her*, finally accepting who she is."

Noni grimaced. She didn't like it. She hated to use her powers. *Seriously? Such self-control, wow.*

"I am just making you taste your own medicine," she sent another jet of light, but this time *Yamendo* was ready. She swayed it away with her hand making it blast near me.

I screamed as the rack of books behind me fell on me with the blast. It fell on my legs, hurting them more, making them numb.

"Stay away from my *mija*," I heard as Noni snarled behind me. "How dare you use her for your screwed-up plans. She is just a child, they are just small girls. You should have fought me if you wanted that star, demon to demon," she was furious. "It shows how weak you are, using children, harming them. If you ever laid even a finger on our children, I promise I'll rip you apart like you killed everyone in my village." Noni threatened *Yamendo,* but she scoffed in return.

"Poor baby Alice got blamed for all the deaths, never loved by anyone, always treated as a pariah," she pouted pompously.

"Stop it," Noni hissed. "It was you, you let people believe it was for me."

"Oh! It was for you, my sweet, cursed child," *Yamendo's* scarlet eyes danced in excitement. "What a pretty name. You would have taken the whole world with this name. Still, all you had to do was suppress your powers and end up getting married to a human, a Shadow Walker," she spat. "You disgraced my name, fraternising with the enemies and had his children. And I thought you couldn't swoop any low."

"Mathew was the best thing that ever happened to me," Noni swelled with pride.

"It was the worst decision of your life. What did you get out of it, old age, housebound, permanent prison, dead daughters, a *lampoon* granddaughter who can't even see shadows? What good Shadow Walker would she become?" She grimaced.

I felt hands moving the rack above me. I looked at Jason. He was pushing the shelf, helping me out of it. "Move your leg," he said.

I tried to move my leg but couldn't. They seemed dead.

He saw me trying but failing, so he pushed me back with his big hands, rolling me on the ground.

"Hang in there, gorgeous, gather your energy and heal yourself," he whispered. My eyes were closed, and everything was hurting profoundly.

I am a healer. Yes, I am a healer.

I could hear them charging at *Yamendo.* I tried to open my eyes to look at them. Dorcas was making a pile of wet sand around *Yamendo*, whispering some spells. Robin and Hannah were doing a great job with the monsters. They were the perfect pair. Even their outfit matched, they wore brown leather pants with leather jackets, but Hannah's was a halter neck. She looked so pretty in those clothes, unlike those boring ones she wears at our place.

I couldn't believe my eyes, how professional they seemed. All six of them were battling fiercely. Dorcas's eyes opened, and she nodded at Jason, whose face twisted with glee as he raised his hand, the moonstone ring pulsed under his command as if providing him energy, and with it, all the pages that were lying on the floor rose and took the shape of sharp arrows. Soon they were covered in red sparks, and they shot towards *Yamendo.*

The piles Dorcas created launched streaks of water jets diluting *Yamendo's* shield, and I noticed the water never spilled. Jason's arrows hit her shield, piercing various parts of it, as Mayor closed his fist and let a bubble of air get into the cracks of the shield. That bubble enclosed *Yamendo,* sucking all air out of her lungs.

She thrashed and growled at them, but Jason roared with his powers, taking his sword from a sheath and swiftly slashing her shield down. He was enjoying fighting. He seemed like a man born for this, tap dancing while showing off his fighting skills. *Yamendo* burst out of the bubble, creating a shield to block its impact. A smirk rose on his animalistic face. He was fierce, deadly, and well aware of what he was doing as he raised his sword, which was now gleaming with the red beam, to charge at her, but she blocked it swiftly, thrashing him back.

Whoa! He was so good that I couldn't take my eyes off him. Did he learn all that from Umbra-Mae? Did they all train to fight there? I felt a need, a want to know all the stuff, especially how to fight like Jason. He was perfect, a fighting machine.

When she charged at him, he fell back, rolling towards Kayden, who was lying unconscious on the corner. Jason placed a hand on his brother's shoulder as he growled in anger as if telling him, *'I'll protect you, little brother.'* And soon, a shield got created around him.

Yamendo growled at Mayor, but Jason made the same slashing movement knocking her sideways. She fell over, jerking her legs, and her temper worsened. As Mayor again tried to trap her in the air-sucking bubble, Noni charged at her, targeting her feet, focusing on the wounded leg.

I knew I didn't have much time and had to act fast, but before that, I wanted to ensure the star was secure.

I am a fast healer.

I am a quick healer.

I was telling myself that with every breath I took, gathering strength in my body, but it was taking time as most of my bones were broken.

I slithered towards the wall and tried to get up. A shriek passed through my lips, my mind had gone numb in pain, but I stood up. I was huffing near the wall safe as I placed the Star inside and closed it. I looked back, but nobody was paying attention to me.

"Here goes nothing," I whispered before placing my unbroken hand on the safe, trying to make it shift. Suddenly, the Star spoke again. *'Hey beautiful, I see you're ready, I can feel you, so desperate, let me touch you, let me feel you,'* it was speaking like some filthy flirt, but I tried to block it and put pressure of my powers on it, or whatever left of it.

'That's it, that's it, show me what you got—strip in front of me.' Its smutty words made my skin crawl. *'Shut up,'* I wanted to snap, but no words came out as I put more pressure, gathering all my energy.

'I see you. I see you all, and you're exactly like I thought you would be,' it purred in my ears. *'Syntrell sends his regards, I accept you,'* and soon everything around me went silent.

It was just her and the star, with no beginning and no end, they were in the sky filled with darkness, and the only light was from the star. She was floating like she had lost all body mass, like the Star was wandering her away with him.

But soon, it came crashing onto me, the burning sensation, the fire, the light, like my bones were melting inside me. I wanted to cry out loud, but no voice came out.

And suddenly, it stopped as if an icy cold hand tracing my spine, making the pain go away, and I felt energy surging through my veins, electrifying my whole body, cold as ice, hot as fire, bright as light, dark as night.

I was aware of every vein in my body. I could feel power like magma leaching from my newly made bones. It felt like I was new and was being created from the inside out as I put the broken hand on the wall safe, which was mended.

I shivered at the thought.

No, I wanted to teleport the star. I had to protect it. So, I shoved everything into my core, filling a hole in my stomach, consuming it, and focused on teleporting the star to the human realm. Maybe it was working. My plan was working because it had stopped talking.

"Lizzy, Go, shift, take the star with you," Noni screamed. I flinched, backing up from the safe. I turned to look, but they all were busy fighting.

I quickly darted towards the mirror on the wall near the table and wrote a message. I was using Clara's idea on Clara.

IT'S IN THE SAFE.

I wrote it down with my blood which was now drying off, my body was healing, and I turned to Kayden.

Now, I need to save him. My heart was lodged in my throat, and my chest hurt like I hadn't breathed in a while.

I sneakily crawled towards Kayden. He seemed weak but conscious. He had red rims around his hazel eyes due to pain.

"Hey, baby girl," he whispered in agony but still trying to smile. I wanted to cry as I stared at his beautiful face that I had grown attached to, his lovely nose that he cringes when he sniffs, his dimples that I'd love to stick my tongue into, and his perfect jawline, to die for. He was indeed the most beautiful person I had ever met inside out. "Why didn't you shift when I asked you?" he whispered in despair. His urge to protect me was still rippling off his thrashed body.

I held his legs and started dragging him out of there, away from *Yamendo,* away from shadows.

"You stupid moron, why did you come after me when you knew she was *Yamendo*? Are you fucking crazy?" I heaved, cursing him through clenched teeth, dragging him. "Don't you realise coming after me will lead you to no good? You almost died with those Mer-skeletons, now

Yamendo," I panted. "You cannot follow me. I am the darkness. There is no winning with me, just… dread. It's just losing here."

"But I won, don't you get it?" he asked in a croaked, weak voice. He closed his eyes, breathing shakily in pain but then opened them to look at me. I halted, turning to look at him like he had lost his mind. "I won you by losing myself."

His words went down like a spark in my body, a warmth. Though he was insanely hurt, and there wasn't even a single part of his body that wasn't bleeding, he was still thinking about me instead.

"You won't be getting any medals here, Kayden. This is your life we are talking about. It's not some basketball match from which you can return to practice. It's now or never." I gasped, not believing his stupidity. "How hard is it to wrap your head around that you are just eighteen, a human, you can't save me, so stop being reckless and save yourself, get away from me."

"I will always come after you, Eloise. *I have to protect the one thing that I can't live without. That's you,"* he whispered, the Iron Man quote that had been written on his ceiling. He was dedicating it to me. A series of shocks went down my body. Was it written for me?

I froze, my breathing hitched, as my lower lip trembled, letting his words sink in. *What was he doing to me?* Tears welled in my eyes as my knees buckled before giving away, and I hit the floor.

"You're insane," I tried to snap, but tears rolled down my cheeks, cracking my voice. "You're saying all this because I dragged you into all this. I am sorry, I didn't know I was creating a bond. I didn't know I was making you—my catalyst. I didn't want to bestow my responsibilities on you. You've atoned too much as you couldn't help my mother, but you don't deserve this. You don't have to be around me because of that guilt. I am freeing you from all the responsibilities. You don't owe me anything. You don't have to be my twin flame because you're guilty. I release you." I felt a pain, a wail rising in my throat as I whispered those words. I want him so much, but he doesn't deserve this. For him, I have to let him free.

His hand held my jacket. Suddenly, he pulled me to him. I was hovering over his face, his breath low and weak, my hair falling around his face. "Didn't you hear, the bond was a gift from beyond. We are two parts of one soul. And being your Catalyst was a two-way deal," he breathed on my lips. "You offered, and *I accepted.* You didn't bestow anything upon me. I chose to fill you with my spark, I want to be your catalyst, I accepted your soul, not because of some guilt, but because I am honoured to be a part of you, to take care of you *all my life.*" He confessed, and with that, more tears rolled down my face. This was wrong. This shouldn't have happened to him, to us, and I brought my mouth to his.

Warmth spread throughout my body as we linked. It wasn't as powerful as it was in the vault, but it was equally electrifying. I cupped his face with my hand, as his hand lifted to reach out for my arm, and he grabbed my neck, pulling me towards him. The soft kiss became fervent within a blink of an eye. I could taste his blood in my mouth. Our mouths slid together, teeth, lips, tongue, everything was kicking desire, everything was burning.

I gave him everything I could, pouring the energy I stored in my core, healing him. I gave and gave. I wanted to show him how much he meant to me through that kiss, but I was startled by the scream. I craned my neck to look back, unable to leave Kayden's warmth. It was Hannah. She was injured while Robin was hovering over her like a mad animal, trying to protect her, as Dorcas held her hand, healing her, like me.

Jason and Mayor were hiding behind the racks, narrowly missing the red jets of light coming from *Yamendo.* Noni's whole body was covered in black burnt marks like she gets from pollution, or was it a lie too?

My mouth fell open as realisation hit me—she was using her powers. These burnt marks were the toll of using darkness.

Mayor groaned hard, stealing my attention from Noni's rotten body, who was now limping back, saving herself from *Yamendo's* advances. He was whimpering, holding his arm. They all were tired and needed healing.

I tried to get up. I was on my knees as I gasped, feeling a gut-wrenching pain in my back, like someone stabbed me, making me choke at the last breath I took. This is it. This was it. I could feel it now.

I fell back, arching. Everything went upside down. Kayden held me from my waist, calling my name, but his voice rang in my ears from a distance. The pain was so blinding that I couldn't hear anything. My eyes were looking into a pair of scarlet ones.

"WHAT…HAVE…YOU…DONE?" roared *Yamendo.* Her scarlet eyes went wide in horror. "IT'S MINE, GIVE. IT. BACK!" she demanded.

She took what was ours. Now it's our time to take what's hers—Leticia's words rang in my ears when she called Noni bringer of *Hara.*

My eyes fell on the wall safe lying open. And the *Wandering Star* was gone.

A bubble of laughter escaped me. I cackled at *Yamendo's* face for ruining her plan.

"*Suck it up, fucker!*"

All the eyes were on me. They looked at me horridly like I went insane, but soon, it was cut short as she stuck out her tongue, gliding like a snake towards me, impaling my chest. I screamed in blinding pain. It felt like she ripped my soul out and started sucking my energy. I choked, unable to breathe, as she sucked the life out of me.

I heard my name from everyone's lips. They were screaming and charging at *Yamendo*, but she was unstoppable while they were desperate. Noni went on her knees, pleading to *Yamendo*, but she wasn't listening. Suddenly, I saw my Cosmic blade slitting her tongue in two, making her explode in pain. A wave of enormous energy hit us as she growled, tossing us back. Everyone was thrown back.

I felt strong hands around my waist as Kayden ripped the remains out of my chest, making me scream in pain. Fresh blood oozed out of my chest. I could feel it in my mouth too.

"I don't like when anyone touches you, *luna mia*," He growled, shivering in anger. *He slit Yamendo's tongue to save me.* He was powerful, I always knew Kayden had some primal powers that's why I was always so intimidated by him. I whimpered in his arm, lying lopsided down, his hands trying to haul me up, but he was weak too. His voice was distant. He was fading, everything around me getting dark as I couldn't control my limbs. My head hit something hard. It was the wooden doll I had thrown out of the safe.

"Heal yourself, baby girl," I felt his shivering hand on my chest and a different set of hands on my back.

"Kiddie, she's losing too much blood," Jason's voice held fright as he held me, trying to stop my blood. I felt the powers of the moonstone ring he wore coursing through me, trying to heal me, but it wasn't enough.

"No-no, she's a healer, she's repairing her organs," Kayden shook his head.

Suddenly, a third set of hands reached out for me. "She's spent Kayden, she used her energy on you." Dorcas's hand was on my chest, more power coursed but still it was of no use. I was draining.

"Fuck! No. We just started, she cannot leave me now, not yet, not ever. I JUST GOT HER," he roared in pain, and the whole *Shadowland* rumbled beneath us in his agony.

I wanted to flip my middle finger at *Yamendo* and show how powerful my Kayden was. He dominated her *Shadowland,* he ripped off her tongue.

To hell with the moonchild, Kayden was my superhero.

But my superhero was crying, I wanted to reach out to him, to take his pain away, tell him that I was with him, but I choked as everything went quiet. No voice, no light, only Kayden's and Jason's strong hands. They were shaking me as if asking me to keep my eyes open. I looked at my saviors lying on the floor, broken by *Yamendo*. They knew they couldn't match her, but they still came to save us, even Jason. He was so young. Still, he fought beautifully. I wanted to tell him that he was strong and brave.

"Dorcas, heal her now," Noni screamed, tears rolling down her cheeks.

"I am trying, but I am parched," she hissed.

I wanted to look out for Noni, tell her that she raised me right, that even if she hid the truth, I still love her, and there was no need to bow in front of *Yamendo* for me. *We are Hectors, we never bend our knees.*

I wanted to thank Robin for teaching me all those moves that helped save my friends. I wanted to thank Hannah for always being warm and patient with me, but this pain was paralysing me.

I wanted to thank Dr. Dorcas for being patient with me, and teaching me how to meditate, even though I relented on alcohol.

I wanted to tell Kayden so many things. I wanted to put whatever I was feeling into words, but my body and mind had gone numb. I was sinking into the darkness with just Taylor Swift's melodious voice in my background—

"Romeo, take me somewhere we can be alone.
I'll be waiting, all there's left to do is run.
You'll be the prince, and I'll be the princess—"

'The time is coming,' someone whispered in my ears, and my eyes opened with a jolt. I looked around but couldn't see anyone.

'Get ready, take the doll,' it was a sweet voice ringing in my ears. Nothing like that of the star. It was of a woman. Suddenly, I felt my chatoyant pulsing. Leticia! She was telling me to take charge. I saw *Yamendo* building up her next attack, and I knew nobody could hold up to her this time.

Yamendo's fierce eyes were filled with rage. I knew it was coming. It would be annihilation. She's going to unleash herself on us. Soon she started shivering, transforming into a monster, a smokey figure as if darkness was leaking out of her. She was launching her shadow on me, trying to possess me.

"She's mine." Kayden growled.

Suddenly, I felt the string wrapping around us, merging me with Kayden as Jason and Dorcas fell back, everyone's eyes widened in shock, including *Yamendo's.* Warmth spread through me, it was weak, but it lurked from him. My bones felt it, a push, a spark.

'Varjo vaihtaminen'

'Varjo vaihtaminen'

'NOW,' Leticia commanded.

I rolled out from Kayden's arm, picked up the doll, turning towards *Yamendo*. She was just a second away. I could feel the terror on her fingertips when I pushed the doll out, sitting on my heels and screamed.

"*Varjo vaihtaminen*" with all my strength. The energy was harsh, a green-red-violet-golden-silver-bright beam blinded me. I shrieked in pain, and so did someone else. I heard a loud shriek of another woman, but it wasn't Leticia, but yet so familiar.

It took my full strength to hold that doll between us. I didn't have any force to hold onto more. My energy drained off. I couldn't keep it any longer.

Giving up. "SHIFT," I screamed through the pain.

And everything went black as I felt a throbbing pain in my head. It was like I was dying. I couldn't feel my heart anymore, my breathing almost stopped, maybe I didn't shift, perhaps *Yamendo* killed me instead.

All I remembered was a pair of scared scarlet eyes.

Epilogue

Death doesn't feel like anything, no discomfort, no pain, just falling. It's a state of nothingness and utter consciousness. I could feel my soul falling, migrating from one world to another.

There was no struggle or awareness of what was going on. I was slipping away. No white light, no tunnels, nothing, just darkness and falling infinitely.

"Come with me," I turned around. Kayden swung his bolt, a spear made up of entangling Cosmic blades, with three spikes, piercing a few monsters. He wore golden armor over a black tunic with golden embroidery matching his golden crown with a sun sigil, making him look like a prince. His face was still young and stubborn, his cheekbones a bit high, and he had a crooked nose.

What happened to his nose? I liked his current nose. It was so perfect. His hair was longer like Jason's but blonde, drenched in sweat. *Oh! This look suits him so much.*

"On your right," I screamed as a monster lunged at him. He backed off, and with a quick swing, he slit that monster, making me skip a beat. He was so powerful. I watched him wide-eyed, he was natural at this, like a true warrior. My eyes fell on monsters darting towards Kayden, he was outnumbered.

"I'll protect you. You need to come with me," he said, switching the bolt between his hands while sizing the monsters.

"I don't need your protection. I can do well on my own," I smirked at him.

"Don't humour me, not now. Take the portal, it'll take you to Cinderwild. Go get out of your palace, I hold these shadows," he ordered, outraged.

I looked back at the gilded door. It was open, exhibiting a myriad of stars and a mesmerising view. I could live my dreams of being in the stars. If I went out, I could achieve anything, but my heart was with Kayden, who was fighting for his life. Something had changed in me. It felt like I didn't even want to see stars without him, not anymore. So, I slammed the door shut, closing the portal.

It finally felt nice, a sense of contentment. It was more like I heard my heart.

"Argh!" I groaned. "You nasty piece of shit." Monsters lunged onto me, as I slit them with my Cosmic blade.

"What have you done?" Kayden's head whipped towards me, screaming over the top. He froze in his tracks and stared at me in disbelief.

"What did you do?" I asked. "Trying to be a King, sacrificing yourself. Who told you to do so?" I punched one monster, though he tried to eat my hand. I was swamped kicking their asses, stabbing them.

He swung the spear hurriedly, slitting two monsters down.

"Princess, you will get yourself killed," he hissed. "And that too because of me."

"Um," I frowned at being called stupid. "Technically, I am preventing it."

With that, he missed one shadow, and it leapt over him. I quickly pushed it away, leaping toward him, but one shadow hauled me up between his teeth and threw me hard to the ground.

"Motherfucker!" I screamed over the top, cursing the monster.

"I have never met a princess with such a filthy mouth," Kayden hissed through clenched teeth, stabbing monsters with his bolt, killing whatever came between us. When he reached me, his mouth was bruised and drenched in shadow's remains but still glowed like a devastatingly hot God. He extended his hand to haul me up, chest to chest. His hands burnt around my waist and wherever my body touched his.

"Still, you can't stop drooling over me," I rolled my eyes, hyper-aware of the heat in my cheeks and hardening of my nipples.

"Luna Mia." The grunt that slipped through his throat made me go weak in my knees. My core clenched as he smashed his lips on me like a starved man. The butterflies in my stomach did a wild summersault

as he explored my mouth with his warm tongue, making me moan so hard that I didn't know I could ever make that sound. He gave and gave until his spark, his love illuminated me, and then he broke the kiss. "You need to go. You can't save me."

"I will," I told him stubbornly.

And suddenly, the floor beneath me shuddered, and I fell from it into the darkness.

"LIVANA," I heard him screaming after me.

I plopped in the water, sinking in the darkness, enclosed by obscurity. I was sleeping as Ariel sleeps in the water, though I doubt Ariel ever wore a HVN cherry-red bikini that could barely hold my breasts.

It was cold out there, but a bright ray of light disturbed me.

"Get up, now." Someone commanded, hovering over me.

"Geez," I flinched. "You scared me," I was talking to the yellow-eyed monster again. It was darkness all around us, but no ashes, just mist, and it had finally found me here.

"I scared you?" she said. "You scared me," to my horror, the yellow-eyed monster was scolding me. "And what the hell are you wearing? Should a princess show off so much skin, you'll be the death of me, Eloise Valerie Hector."

"Mum?" I asked skeptically, confirming whether she was really there this time or was it another illusion. But the way she narrowed her eyes, judging my outfit, she was so mum.

"Yeah, now she asks," she rolled her eyes, groaning. "*Mija*!"

"But I thought it was you." I bit my lips, trying to stomp my feet, but it was useless as I couldn't feel them. "This means I am really dead?" I asked, checking out my surroundings, was this hell? Because this doesn't feel like Heaven, for sure. Or was it the aftermath, the one nobody knows about?

"Perhaps." She answered flatly, void of emotions at all, just like always, making me wince. "All I know was I warned you to avoid swamps."

She thinks I am dead, fuck!

How else could we be together? How else could I be talking to her? But she had spoken to me before. I wasn't dead then. I shifted to her. I had been to this dark place before when she warned me.

"*You* told me about the hidden ring inside the journal? You know about it? About J.P.P.?" I gasped. Her nostrils flared in anger, but she didn't deny it. And I didn't miss as she twisted her ring finger with her thumb.

"I tried to hide you, to keep you safe. I even let them suppress my powers and wipe my memories for you, but you never got contented," she retorted, crossing her hands around her midsection.

"Who, Mom, who wiped your memories?" I bit my lips, feeling concerned. She was a Shadow Walker, *Yamendo* said, that she *chose* to be mundane, a person without powers. She gave away all her might and memories—she gave away being a Shadow Walker.

But why?

"Umbra-Mae." She whispered. Her yellow eyes went wide like she was afraid of him.

So, Jason was telling me the truth, there is Umbra-Mae, a Shadow Walker league, and they don't go well with Mom. Before I could press on the topic, she continued. "Your dad will be very angry with both of us," she shivered in fear. "I should have hidden you better. I thought Murkwood was the safest, but now it isn't."

"But why did you hide me?" I asked her. "Wasn't it better if you had taught me everything about that place so I knew how to fight these monsters instead of falling into a trap? You could have taught me to accept my powers instead of suppressing them," I pouted.

"Accepting what, Lizzy?" she roared. "I am a Hybrid, daughter of the cursed child, *bringer of Hara*. Nobody will ever accept us. "She chastised.

"You rue being her daughter?" I gasped, as the realisation hit me hard. "It wasn't her fault that she is a demon's baby. She didn't want that. She didn't even like using her demonic powers," I was defending Noni. I knew she, even being a demon, would never hurt anyone. She was so cool and amazing, I didn't think being demon blood makes you demonic, but your action does. Noni was saving me, protecting Kayden from Umbra-Mae, she even begged *Yamendo* to spare my life, and a demonic person would have never gone down on their knees for me. She would have helped *Yamendo,* but instead, she was saving me, and she lived with Robin and Hannah, Shadow Walkers, under the same roof. Mr. Parsons and Jason were friendly with her. They all were Shadow Walkers, and they respected Noni, so how could she be a bad person?

Like my Iron Man said, *bad works make you a bad boy*, and I know Noni wasn't the villain, and neither was Leticia, they both were just misunderstood people. "She cared for you so much. And you beckoned Kayden not to interfere, so she thought Umbra-Mae killed you. That's why she was suppressing the matter, she is terrified of Umbra-Mae."

"Save Hara, our only salvation," Mom whispered, lost in her thoughts, holding her locket.

My mouth fell open listening to the same words Leticia told me too, suddenly she jerked open her yellow eyes.

"You need to be careful Lizzy, Umbra-Mae is dangerous. He's the heir of the sun, a Cosmic who can burn everyone with a snap. No one knows he's a cruel, sadist satyr hiding behind a mask of the saviour of humankind. They got rid of my chakra with the mere presence of *Bolt of Syntrell* because I tried to stop him." She shivered as if remembering how painful it was for her. "These Cosmics are very powerful. No human stands a chance against them. So, that makes Adray, the most powerful person on Earth. But he is not what he says he is," she held her throat. "Your father knows his truth," she added that line in a mere whisper, her eyes lost somewhere.

Adray!

His name felt weird on my tongue. I felt foreign shivers.

"Then I should go to him. He could train me too," my eyes flashed. A shadow master would train me to be a perfect Shadow Walker, like my ancestors, but my mother shook her head.

"No, *mija*, you can't go to him," her eyes went wide in terror like she had seen *Yamendo.*

"I am a Shadow Walker. He trained everyone. Jason was so perfect," I huffed stubbornly. "Why can't I go to him?

"Because you're *promised* to him," her eyes glimmered with sadness, guilt, and fear.

I instantly went cold, as if the blood inside my veins turned into ice. If I'd been standing on the ground, it would have slipped beneath me.

Promised? As in marriage-promised? WTF?

"But, then, why did you hide me from him?" Out of all the questions swarming my mind, only this fell out.

"Because he'll *kill you*," her eyes flashed at me as I choked on the last breath if I was taking any.

Umbra-Mae wants to kill me? Why?

Suddenly water started swiveling around me, my mom disappeared, and all I saw was a pink Yggdrasil tree's shadow in the middle of a lake, enclosed in the cave.

Kayden's POV

"What the hell, K? You were not in game tonight," Crew Rai Denali groaned as we stomped inside our Locker room, he splayed on the bench, pretending dead. He was the drama queen of the group but meant well. He was my next-door neighbour, and we'd been joined at the hip since we, Parsons, shifted here in Murkwood.

"Nothing, I just have my mind wrapped around something," I rolled my eyes, dragging my tired feet to the bench, removing my Jordans, and sighing in relief. Four hours, we were on the court for four hours, drilling our asses off, mostly due to my subpar performance as it made the Coach livid.

"You're distressed." Neil Datye mused quietly; his dusky eyes bored into mine as if reading me while he stretched his lean but muscular arms. He's the point guard, one of the best players and my best friend. Because Neil always knows. We both understand each other at different levels, I could share my deepest secrets with him without being afraid of being judged. While Crew was a bit eloquent, Datye was content.

But I couldn't tell him this because I myself didn't know what to make out of the information that bombarded me.

Since I read that journal—Shadowland, by someone called J.P.P., I didn't know what to get out of it. It was my sheer luck that Clara left it on her bed last night, and things clicked. I knew by then that it had everything to do with Eloise Hector.

Blood drained from Clara's face when I asked about the journal, even though she didn't want to share but I made her. I could be persuasive, and convincing my twin was the easiest job. Hence, she blabbered out most of the facts about Eloise's powers. Telling me about a book in Dad's office, which we both dug out and found a photograph of Alice and Mathew Hector with our grandparents.

Did Eloise know that both of our grandparents were best friends? They even had a matching watermark, the one on the backside of the journal.

I didn't know what to make out of it. So, Clara went to Grams to ask about their past, she'd always been nosey, and I hoped Grams would tell her.

I checked my phone, no calls from Clara yet. Fuck! I was getting impatient.

"Fuckers, let's have a locker room meeting," Shit-faced Liam Stubbs called out while I stared at my locked screen.

It was Eloise's pic, her wavy red hair bouncing off as she danced in the middle of the crowd. The blue dress was a little ridden up, showing off her delicate milky thighs. Her face wasn't visible in this photograph, but I still remember how full of life she was on her birthday eve. We kissed that day, not the kiss I wanted, not when she was drunk, but she was demanding, and how could I have said no to her when I wanted to give her everything, every damn thing, whatever she asked for. So, I kissed her, even knowing that she wouldn't remember it by the morning. I wanted to be her first.

I sighed before tossing my phone back in the locker, strolling towards the shower stall, not giving any heed when Liam demanded to claim another girl as he broke up with his last one. Guys grumbled as it was his 12th claim since we started playing this not-so-ridiculous game. Yeah, we basketball players were a bunch of motherfuckers, who liked to fuck, and act like we owned this school.

But my basis of the claim was different, I still remember, a year back, one day, she climbed out of her new Audi R8, all excited, wearing a mint-coloured two-piece crop top revealing the swell of her breasts and matching shorts with her white sneakers, showing off her newly formed curvaceous body. Sometimes she wears subtle clothes, pretending to be a princess, high and mighty. And sometimes, she brings out herself and wears the ones that make you weak in the knees.

My baby girl was vivid and changed colours, but that day she looked like a goddess. I wanted to go down on my knees and ask her out, but she made me nervous, and then I saw how other guys looked at her, even my teammates. My blood started to boil, so I laid my claim on her before anyone could pass lewd comments. I heard a few curses, but ignoring them, I went after her to ask her out, but suddenly she vanished in front of my eyes.

I turned on the shower, letting the water fall on my face.

My heart still gets lodged in my throat whenever I think about that moment. Was she in some trouble? Was she a witch or some superhero?

I had all sorts of questions messing with my mind, figuring out the mystery about my girl, what exactly she was. I wanted to confront her, but every time I tried, her angry electric blue eyes flashed before me. There was so much she hid in them, the fear, the sadness concealed in the depths of the ocean. I can never imagine what happens with her when she vanishes.

But she was brave, a hell load braver than I was, beautifully concealing her sorrow behind the mask of a perfect feeble princess that she wasn't. I know she was unhappy and hid it from everyone, but I didn't want that. I wanted her beyond those masks, to be herself and happy, and I knew I would make her happy one day.

"Murkwood Princess," I heard faintly, but in that instant, my hands reached out to turn off the shower, and I wasn't the only one who did that. Silence fell over the room. My fists clenched tightly, I saw red as I wrapped a towel around me before stepping out.

All eyes were on me.

"Liam, you know, she's already taken," Datye's voice was grave as he stepped forward, trying to handle the situation. But I didn't look at them, I just sauntered to my locker slowly, languidly, but each step was like a boulder.

"Then we'll all reclaim again, that's what this meeting is about." Liam turned to all. "C'mon guys, we all should get our chances, it's already been a year, and Parsons hasn't asked her out. He's not even interested in dating her," he splayed his hand at me. I still ignored him, letting him make his bed, wanting him to sleep in it permanently.

"Liam, for fuck's sake, don't invoke his darkside." Crew growled, rubbing his wrists.

"Hey," his eyes widened at Crew's pounding muscles, he plays the centre, as he was the tallest, around 6'6" and the buffiest team member. "I am not looking for some fight, but it isn't fair to her either."

"That's not how things work," Datye folded his hands over his midsection, taking a stance. "Claim a girl who's not taken and get over with it."

I was still busy wearing my clothes while everyone was waiting, their eyes stalked every action of mine. Tension in the room was palpable, but Liam continued.

"No, I want to ask Eloise Hector to the freshman's party. We have been talking in English, and she seemed fun and crazy hot—"

My hands halted.

"—her long hair, I want to wrap them around my hand and those puffy lips, I want them around my dick while kneading those huge b–"

"I raise a motion to kick Liam Stubbs out of the team," I called out furiously. My voice boomed throughout the locker room. I'd heard enough, the fury inside me was vibrating, a primal power waited to climb out. Suddenly Crew's hand was on my shoulder, but I jerked him away.

Everybody sucked a breath, their eyes popped out, including Liam's.

"That's not funny, I am the small forward—" he frowned.

"All the votes in favour of the motion?" I growled, cutting him off again.

Every head turned to me, and bobbed simultaneously, each one of them.

"Hey, hey, what you doing?" Liam turned to the team with trembling hands. "He can't do that, he's just the Captain, not the Coach."

"And the motion is passed," I tugged my bag, slamming the locker. "Liam Stubbs is no longer a member of Panthers."

"Y-you can't do that," Liam faltered, stuttering like a doe in headlights, as I approached him. All I wanted to do was tear his eyes off, cut off his tongue for speaking so lewdly about my girl. *My girl.*

"I just did," I smirked, but there was no humour behind it. I had to physically restrain myself for not hitting him, killing him to the ground.

"And if you ever talk about her, or to her, or even think about her," I took a step forward, towering over him while his Adam's apple bobbed. "I'll kill you."

He stumbled back, as blood drained off his face.

"K, relax." Crew held my shoulder again, he seemed nervous, while I wanted to go ape over Liam.

"Kayden, go!" It was Datye, who patted my shoulder, but my fists remained balled, and jaw locked. When I didn't nudge, both Crew and Datye exchanged a nervous look. "Go, we'll handle him."

Liam was mumbling sorry, but I didn't stay to listen. Instead, I stalled out, shivering with fury. Nobody was allowed to talk about her or even think about her. I couldn't bear to see her with anyone else. I couldn't even imagine someone else holding her, it felt like a kick in my gut. She is mine, just mine.

I reached the parking lot when I found the keys to my car were missing. I frowned, checking them in the bag when I heard a knock. A fragile hand knocked on my windscreen from inside.

I glared as I trailed forward, my eyes popped out as I saw a blonde in my car, in black lingerie. She crooked her manicured finger at me.

"Hey, handsome," Tatiana gave a sexy smile, rising to her knees. "I heard you were uptight, your best friend thought to give you a treat." As she flipped off the strap of her lacy bra, showing her tits.

Damn-it Crew!

"He shouldn't have," I growled, restraining myself from drooling over her petite body, all on display.

"Are you sure?" Her misty grey eyes darkened as she spread her legs for me. Fuck! I got in the car hurriedly, her hand instantly reached out, feeling my dick over my pants, her eyes flared with heat. "Lemme get you off, baby." Her lips clashed with mine. They were warm and red, she tasted like strawberry. But this taste was so wrong, her hair wasn't red, her eyes weren't blue, and she didn't smell like magnolias.

That's when her image flashed into my mind—the object of my desire.

I wanted Eloise so bad. To take her face in my hands and kiss her all through the night, feel the fullness of her breasts in my hands—how soft are they gonna be. I grunted, imagining the softness, craving to feel her body all against mine. It'll be wondrous to smell her—taste her—bite her everywhere before devouring her.

"I got to go," I held her wrist tightly, unwrapping myself from Tatiana, blocking her advances. "My family is expecting me."

I am so fucked.

I wanted to kill Eloise Hector for doing this to me, for wrapping her claws around my heart like this. She was my nightmare that I couldn't forget, even if I wanted to.

One day, she'll destroy me.

"Now?" Tatiana asked in a small voice. "But I did this for you." She pointed at her lacy lingerie while I picked up the dress that was lying on the back seat and tossed it towards her.

"Yeah! Talk later?" I straightened myself, trying to escape. "Can you fetch yourself a ride?" I asked Tatiana.

"Of course," She scoffed, jutting her chin out, dressing up before stepping out of my truck, tossing her hair at me.

She knew I didn't love her. Everyone knew that I wasn't looking for anything serious, just casual hookups, and chicks dig in. They just needed to show off that they were fucking Mayor's son, but little did they know I was a coward little prick who couldn't let go of the fact that the girl I really wanted to be with, liked someone else.

I nodded before reversing the car, ignoring Tatiana's gaping mouth.

How can someone who doesn't even want you have so much impact on you? My chest got tight at the fact that she liked someone else. I wanted to scream out loud, this pain was tearing me apart.

Grasping some fresh air, I turned my car towards the museum, avoiding going to my empty home.

Don't think about Eloise. She always breaks your heart. She has ruined you to the extent that you cannot even get into a real relationship with any girl. And the irony of my life was—she didn't even remember it was me, that it has always been me.

It's been eleven years, eight months, and fifteen days since we first met, but we were just kids. How could I even expect her to remember that moment? I should have known at that point that something was special about her because Jason locked me in that outhouse. After all, I got so much candy within a few hours while he got what we say handful, jealous, he hid the keys, and I slept inside the outhouse, waiting for Dad to find me and woke up to her screaming.

I should have figured out that she was going through something terrible, screaming about monsters and how she unlocked the door without a key. But when she smiled and hugged me, I forgot everything and gave her all my favorite candy, and in return, she spoke the sweetest words. She claimed me to be her boyfriend. I was on cloud nine and beyond, even as a kid, I fell in love with this girl at that moment, but then I never found her. I didn't even know her name. So, Jason called her my imaginary girlfriend and teased me in front of my friends and then when I finally found her, after four years, she was hanging out with Cooper, looking at him like he hung the moon for her.

I was about to kill him, to have a face-off with her, but Crew suggested that she wasn't betraying me, she just didn't remember me. Oh boy! It hurt, it went deep inside my soul and entrapped my heart with darkness, and I closed myself, building up walls around me, trying to shut her out and forget her, but every time I look at her with that Cooper, I feel like she was cheating on me, my blood started boiling, wanting to smash his head.

She never noticed me and was so hung over that sloppy guy who was just using her for her crush and never acknowledged her feelings. I hated how badly he treated her, and still, she had puppy eyes for him. So, I took matters into my hands to make that guy's life hell because that was the only way she gave me any attention. She was speaking to me, bickering with me on his behalf, but at that time, I realised I didn't want to be just her friend. I wanted to be her knight in shining armour, the guy she thinks about before going to bed and her first thought after waking up like she was mine.

I wanted to be her superhero, but she shut me out and started pushing me away.

I was outraged that she was choosing him over me. Maliciously, I started fucking other girls to get over her, to push her beyond, but I realised I was doing it to make her jealous. It was mostly a showoff. I wanted to hurt her like she was hurting me, but she never cared, and it dug deep.

I hated how feeble she acted in front of him, hiding her true nature, her true self, but I'd seen her taking care of my sister. She loves her. I remember her ruining Dean's car at night when he broke up with Clara. He had gone through my wrath as well as hers. My feisty little creature sneaks and takes care of her friends but wants to remain hidden from the world.

No-no, you cannot smile thinking about her, this must stop. It was high time, and I had to let her go. She didn't remember me, so I should forget her too. But it hurts, Fuck! I wanted to rip my heart off and throw it somewhere far away.

I waited for Clara to call me, fidgeting, but her phone was still off. Did she forget to plug in? I rolled my eyes, thinking about the journal, when a speeding white Maserati cut me, sending chills down my spine.

"Fuck you, man," I swore loudly.

But then I realised there was only one Maserati car in town, which belonged to Eloise's mother—Julia Hector.

I sped up following it, didn't know why she was in so much hurry. She was going towards Highway 59. That's when I realised it was not one but three people in the car. And it wasn't her mother who was driving but someone else.

I sped up, trying to bypass the car, when I saw some weirdo wearing a red hoodie, and Julia seemed stunned, white as a ghost. And the reason was the person behind her holding a knife to her throat. I couldn't see who was driving because of the dark, nor the person with the knife.

Fright spread through my body. I couldn't breathe, realising Julia Hector was in trouble. My jaw tightened as my instincts told me to rescue her, and I was about to hit the car when her eyes met mine, and she shook her head. She signaled me not to interfere.

I went horror-struck, not knowing what to do, and before I could do anything, a jack-knifed transport hurtled down the road. Quickly trailing off the driveway, I let out profanities, but the Maserati wasn't turning.

What the hell was that person doing?

The car was so fast that it was about to hit the museum. "Stop," I growled, getting out of my car, but suddenly, the person with a red hoodie in the driving seat rolled out.

My heart stopped.

What is he doing?

I gasped in horror, looking at the guy jumping out of the car, rolling down the street, getting out of the driveway, and leaving them behind in the vehicle.

With that, the transport truck lost control to save him.

BANG.

I flinched, scared. I froze to the ground as tears pricked my eyes.

With a loud bang, the truck hit the car. It went airborne, lodged in the museum. I couldn't believe my eyes. Eloise's mother met with an accident.

I went blank.

My eyes caught the guy, who was stumbling, but he didn't see me and just jumped off the highway towards the back of the Mile-O-City.

I sprang after him, running, looking for him, but he disappeared. And from afar, I heard a loud explosion. I fell to the ground in trepidation. I was shivering, tears rolling down. I spun my head towards the highway looking at the whole building, which was now emblazed with a roaring fire, burning two people stuck in the car.

I didn't know what to do, and subconsciously I called Alice, yeah, I had Eloise's grandmother's number on my speed dial because she treats me as one of her own.

She asked me to come to the mansion, and I did as she demanded. I had no thoughts, and the image of the car getting airborne flashed in my mind like carousel.

I was sitting on an armchair, fidgeting, my eyes travelling upstairs, looking for Eloise, but she didn't come down. It was late, around 1 am, and she must have been sleeping. Dad was already there at Eloise's mansion when I reached. Alice looked devastated. They were on calls when Hannah, Eloise's caretaker, brought me a mug of hot chocolate while her eyes were all wet. Their manager Robin, a somber man, looked utterly uneasy, as he had some stones in his hands that he was crushing.

I heard my dad saying they had just found one body, Julia's.

"What happened to the other person?" I asked, trying not to look at Alice's traumatised face.

My dad shot me a deadly look, shaking his head. I was taken aback.

I looked at him questioningly.

He swiftly walked towards me and put his hands on both arms of the chair; I flinched as he looked me directly into my eyes. My dad was a 45-year-old man who still looked young and had squared shoulders like me. He was still in his nightclothes, his amber eyes worn out, looking like a ghost.

"There was no other person," He roared at me, tears glistening in his eyes. I couldn't determine whether he was sad or angry.

"But there was. I saw them with my own eyes," I snapped at him.

"Shut up, Kayden, stop lying. There was only Julia, only her body was discovered." He told me through clenched teeth, getting a bit irritated.

"What?" I was scandalised. "No, Dad, I am not lying. Seriously they were two, and the third one jumped off the car, believe me," I tried to convince him.

"Just zip your mouth. Nobody knows you were there at the time of the accident, and nobody should," he glared at me. "Even Alice hasn't mentioned you in her report, so stay out of it."

"But Dad, it's not an accident. Somebody killed her, they were holding a knife at her throat, and she indicated me not to interfere a—" I was going out of my mind, fretting.

"Exactly", he pulled me close with my shirt collar. "When she told you to stay out, son, then stay out, respect the dead," his eyes were dark, deadly serious.

What was happening? Was he threatening me? My hands curled up into fists. I have always gotten my way as he had never tried to control me, then why today?

"Cops have to know the truth," I growled, getting off the chair, not falling for his threats, making him step back, his hands fell off my shirt.

"Kayden, I am doing all this to save your ass, so catch me on this," he hissed at my face. We both were of the same height.

"But—"

"No but, get out and go home." he roared. I was taken aback. What the hell? Why doesn't he want the truth to come out? "And hand me your keys. You won't be driving that car from now on," he barked at me.

"What?" I asked in shock. "It's my Hummer," I snarled. He had never behaved like that. He was calling me a liar and taking away my car keys. That was too much. He was trying to blow my ego. I wanted to go to Eloise, more than ever, to have her hold me.

"Not anymore," he snatched the keys from my hands. "It's in my name," it hurt me, he was trying to control me, but it was my life, my truth.

"Fine," I said, turning back. People should know the truth. I can put it on Mybook. I have twenty thousand followers, and everybody would hear what Kayden Parsons says.

"Oh boy! You won't do anything," Alice crooned to me like she read my mind, her eyes were lethal. "It's my decision, not yours. No one will ever know, especially Lizzy,"

I looked at her, horror-struck.

What? She wants me to hide the truth from Eloise, why?

"She deserves to know the truth," I yapped at her.

"She needs to stay out of this, you both have to stay out of this." She told me sharply, my spine straightened. "And believe me, this is for your own good, for her safety."

Did she threaten her own granddaughter's life? My Eloise's life?

I felt a wave of primal powers that washed through me with anger and my urge to protect Eloise. Each vein in my body started pumping wildly, pouring out power in my blood, and I exploded.

My eyes flared furiously.

"Never, ever threaten her in front of me," I grumbled, and with me, the ground rumbled. The whole Hector mansion felt what I felt inside me, groaning beneath me as if unable to hold whatever powers reside inside me.

Alice's eyes widened in shock, including others too. I gazed at my hands, dumbfounded. The wave went away with the shock, leaving goosebumps in the wake.

"Kayden!" Dad whispered as he slumped back on the couch like he couldn't believe what I just did.

Even I couldn't fathom what had just happened. Robin came to stand next to me, examining the nape of my neck, but he couldn't find whatever he was searching for because he shook his head at Hannah, who was holding her throat, too shocked to utter even a word.

I didn't know what was happening or whom to trust. All I knew was that I wanted to take her far away from these people who were hiding the truth and manipulating the facts. I want to protect my girl.

I turned my back on elders, climbing stairs as I made my steps to her room like I owned this house… like I owned her. If she was in trouble, then it had to go through me. I'll shield her.

I opened the door silently, not trying to wake her up, and the fresh scent of magnolia hit me. I shivered as her room smelled as sweet as hers. God! Her scent swoons me, makes me wanna swoop her in my arms and sniff her all day. There she was, sleeping silently on her canopy bed like a princess without any masks, just being herself. Her skin drank moonlight, leaving me breathless.

She should be worshipped.

I was jealous of her curls touching her face, envious of the fleece blanket wrapped around her.

I sighed loudly. Eloise's face poofed away my anger. It provided me with peace.

She seems like an angel sleeping quietly, far away from the reality of her life and what turn it has taken. My heart sank at the anticipation of her pain, she'd be devastated in the morning, and they wouldn't even tell her the whole truth.

I felt like I was betraying her by not telling her the truth. I wanted to tell her everything about what happened but was bound not to.

I strolled towards her. The urge to touch her was something beyond my control, even more than I wanted my next breath because being away from her felt far worse than death.

I sank to the floor, near her bed on my knees, her hand hanging off the bed. She sleeps like a dead. I carefully entwined it with mine, sending a zing of electric shivers down my body, but I didn't flinch because that's what she always does. Her touch, her aura, was so electrifying that it made me go weak in my knees. Warmth spread throughout my body, making my shoulders fall. She was silky soft and didn't flinch when I caressed her hand with my thumb.

Should I kidnap her and take her far away from these people?

No, she would hate me more. The problem wasn't that I couldn't tell her the truth but was that she would never trust me.

It was high time. I couldn't let her go just like that, I must earn her trust and make her believe in me.

I'll win her over.

Now, I wouldn't step back. I wouldn't let them hurt her even though she didn't like me, I wouldn't let her out of my sight. I didn't know what the adults' intentions were, I'd reach the truth, but I must take care of her too. She was mine whether she knew that or not. She belongs to me and now is the time to tell her.

There were so many questions in my mind that I must find answers to—Why didn't Alice want me to tell the truth? Why Dad wanted me to lay back? Were they up to something? Were they behind Julia's murder?

That thought iced my heart, thinking about Alice killing her daughter and my father helping her. I shivered, my hands still entwined with Eloise's as I carefully tucked it near her, kissing her forehead, whispering, 'You're not alone.'

I left her room and reached out for my last resort of finding the truth.

I hit my phone.

"Hello," a deep voice spoke from the other side.

Acknowledgement

'It takes a whole village to raise a child,' that's what my mother-in-law always says. Similarly, it took my whole team to bring this book into the world. A number of people stepped in to help me to get this story on track, and I'd like to take a moment to thank them:

First, as always, my husband, Prateek, who has always pushed me to write, even if workdays stretched into work nights. And my toddler, Vritik, for being my muse and the spark of my life whenever things get hectic.

I have been blessed to have such supportive parents and in-laws. I couldn't have written this book without your patience.

My sibling, Sahil, for always being my critic and telling me where I am lacking. When every other person told me to fly, you kept me grounded.

My alpha readers and friends, Tanvi, Komal, and Priyanshi, for always believing in me no matter what crazy idea I throw your way.

A big hug and thank you to my entire team of Nu-Voice and Hubhawks, without you guys, this book couldn't have seen the light of day.

Special thanks to Vishal Ved for your continuous guidance and support.

Appreciation to the team of Paper Towns and The Bookoholics for your constant directions and notions.

And finally, to my readers and bloggers, for continuing to inspire and posting reviews about my writing. You've always been there for me. You've always believed in me, even when I didn't believe in myself, and for that, I am forever grateful.